Michael Jecks gave up a career in the computer industry to concentrate on writing and the study of medieval history, especially that of Devon and Cornwall. He has been the Chairman of the Crime Writers' Association and a judge of the CWA Ian Fleming Steel Dagger. He lives with his wife, children and dogs in northern Dartmoor.

Michael can be contacted through his website:
www.michaeljecks.co.uk

Acclaim for Michael Jecks' mysteries:

'Captivating . . . If you care for a well-researched visit to medieval England, don't pass this series' *Historical Novels Review*

'Michael Jecks has a way of dipping into the past and giving it that immediacy of a present-day newspaper article . . . He writes . . . with such convincing charm that you expect to walk round a corner in Tavistock and meet some of the characters' *Oxford Times*

'Great characterisation, a detailed sense of place, and a finely honed plot make this a superb medieval historical' *Library Journal*

'Stirring intrigue and a compelling cast of characters will continue to draw accolades' *Publishers Weekly*

'A tortuous and exciting plot . . . The construction of the story and the sense of period are excellent' *Shots*

'This fascinating portrayal of medieval life and the corruption of the Church will not disappoint. With convincing characters whose treacherous acts perfectly combine with a devilishly masterful plot, Jecks transports readers back to this wicked world with ease' *Good Book Guide*

By Michael Jecks and available from Headline

The Last Templar
The Merchant's Partner
A Moorland Hanging
The Crediton Killings
The Abbot's Gibbet
The Leper's Return
Squire Throwleigh's Heir
Belladonna at Belstone
The Traitor of St Giles
The Boy-Bishop's Glovemaker
The Tournament of Blood
The Sticklepath Strangler
The Devil's Acolyte
The Mad Monk of Gidleigh
The Templar's Penance
The Outlaws of Ennor
The Tolls of Death
The Chapel of Bones
The Butcher of St Peter's
A Friar's Bloodfeud
The Death Ship of Dartmouth
The Malice of Unnatural Death
Dispensation of Death
The Templar, the Queen and Her Lover
The Prophecy of Death
The King of Thieves
No Law in the Land
The Bishop Must Die

MICHAEL JECKS

The Bishop Must Die

headline

First published in 2009 by
HEADLINE PUBLISHING GROUP

First published in paperback in 2010 by
HEADLINE PUBLISHING GROUP

1

Cataloguing in Publication Data is available from the British Library

ISBN 978 0 7553 7445 8 (B Format)
ISBN 978 0 7553 4421 5 (A Format)

Typeset in Times by Avon DataSet Ltd,
Bidford-on-Avon, Warwickshire

Printed and bound in Great Britain by
Clays Ltd, St Ives plc

Headline's policy is to use papers that are natural, renewable and
recyclable products and made from wood grown in sustainable forests.
The logging and manufacturing processes are expected to conform to the
environmental regulations of the country of origin.

HEADLINE PUBLISHING GROUP
An Hachette UK Company
338 Euston Road
London NW1 3BH

www.headline.co.uk
www.hachette.co.uk

In memory of George MacDonald Fraser,
whose writing influenced me enormously,
whose research spurred me to accuracy,
and whose war memoirs are still the very best
record of the life of a WWII British soldier.

Glossary

annuellar a chantry-priest, one who held specific masses dedicated to those who had paid for their services.

array raising a force to fight for the king was increasingly problematic, so Commissioners of Array were sent out to assess all the men in every hundred or township between the ages of sixteen and sixty. The healthy were taken to form the troopers of his host.

burned wine the medieval term for brandy.

centaine the grouping of five vintaines to form a hundred men in the king's host.

corrody a form of medieval pension, in which a wealthy patron would buy a post in a religious institution for a retired servant. The retired man would be given food and drink as well as accommodation and a little spending money.

eyre this was the term for the circuit of a king's judge as he travelled from one county to the next. Often he was called a 'Justice in Eyre'. In 1321 there was held the 'Eyre of London', an investigation into the powers and rights of the city of London with the aim of curbing them and probably taxing them to the benefit of the Crown. As Bishop Walter was the Lord High Treasurer at the time, many Londoners blamed him for the eyre, although I have seen no evidence to support this (only

	Walsingham, writing ninety years after the event, has suggested it).
familia	this was the term for a clerical household.
fosser	the gravedigger or sexton.
hobelar	a lightly armed man-at-arms on horseback (a 'hobby' thus the term 'hobbler'). Unlike a knight or squire, they were lightly armoured, and were used more as a highly mobile infantry, leaving their horses to fight on foot. During the Hundred Years War, Edward III used archers on horseback extensively, giving him the strategic mobility his campaigns needed.
host	the word 'army' did not exist in the 1300s. That is a much more recent concept. Instead, there was the feudal host, which comprised all those who owed service to their lord.
hundred	the most basic unit of administration in the realm. Its initial purpose is obscure: it may have been intended to provide a hundred warriors to the king's host, or to cover one hundred hides of land, but the most important aspect by 1326 was that each hundred had its own court.
millaine	a group of ten centaines would make a millaine in the military unit.
novel disseisin	a class of action very popular in medieval times, by which a plaintiff could bid a sheriff to gather a jury of twelve in order to hear that a plot or parcel of land had been stolen.
paindemaigne	at a time when all peasants were forced to consume vast quantities of bread to supplement their diet, only those of enormous wealth could afford the best, white bread, the *paindemaigne*.
seisin	seisin is one of the cardinal concepts of

English and therefore American law. It is the basic law of ownership, and although some have assumed its roots come from a violent act of 'seizing' someone else's property (and possession being nine-tenths of the law, that means they own it), in fact, legal historians generally reckon it implied peaceful ownership.

vintaine twenty men-at-arms gathered into a unit for the king's host.

Cast of Characters

Simon Puttock	once a bailiff on Dartmoor, now he is a farmer on his own little plot near Crediton.
Margaret (Meg)	Simon Puttock's wife.
Hugh	servant to the Puttocks.
Rob	youngster who is working for the Puttocks.
Edith	Simon and Margaret's daughter.
Peter	Edith's husband.
Henry	Edith's baby.
Perkin	Simon and Margaret's son.
Baldwin de Furnshill	Simon's closest friend, once a Templar, now a renowned investigator of suspicious death as Keeper of the King's Peace.
Jeanne	Baldwin's wife.
Baldwin	Baldwin's son.
Richalda	Baldwin's daughter.
Edgar	once Baldwin's sergeant, now his devoted servant.
Jack	a boy commissioned to join the king's host.
John Biset	an enemy of Bishop Walter II, who took a wardship from him.
Isabella Crok	widow of Peter Crok and Henry Fitzwilliam.
Roger Crok	son of Isabella.
Peter Crok	Isabella's first husband.

Henry Fitzwilliam	Isabella's second husband.
Ranulf Fitzwilliam	Henry's son by his first wife.
Richard de Folville	a rector from Teigh.
Sir Ralph la Zouche	neighbour of the Folville family.
Sir Ivo la Zouche	brother of Sir Ralph.
Roger Belers	the king's treasurer, murdered in 1326.
Ranulf Pestel	a squire in the service of Belers.
Rector Paul de Cockington	an unscrupulous parson.
James de Cockington	the sheriff of Devon.
Dean Alfred	dean of the cathedral.
Bishop Walter II	Bishop Walter Stapledon of Exeter.
Alured de Gydie	a merchant of Exeter.
Agatha de Gydie	Alured's wife, who was kidnapped and raped by Paul de Cockington.
Peter Ovedale	a commissioner of array.
John de Padington	steward to Bishop Walter.
Squire William Walle	nephew to the bishop.

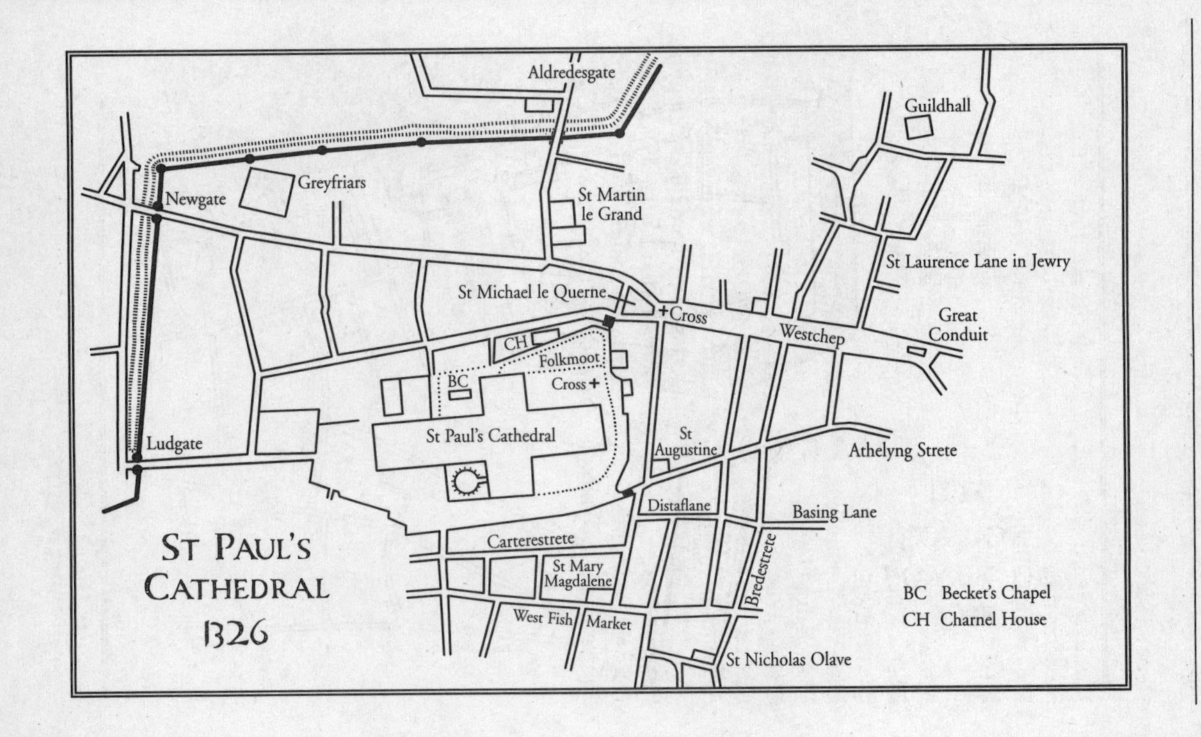
Aldredesgate
Guildhall
Greyfriars
Newgate
St Martin le Grand
St Laurence Lane in Jewry
St Michael le Querne
+Cross
Great Conduit
Westchep
CH
Folkmoot
BC
Cross +
St Paul's Cathedral
Ludgate
St Augustine
Athelyng Strete
Distaflane
Basing Lane
Carterestrete
St Mary Magdalene
Bredestrete
West Fish Market
St Nicholas Olave
BC Becket's Chapel
CH Charnel House
St Paul's Cathedral
1326

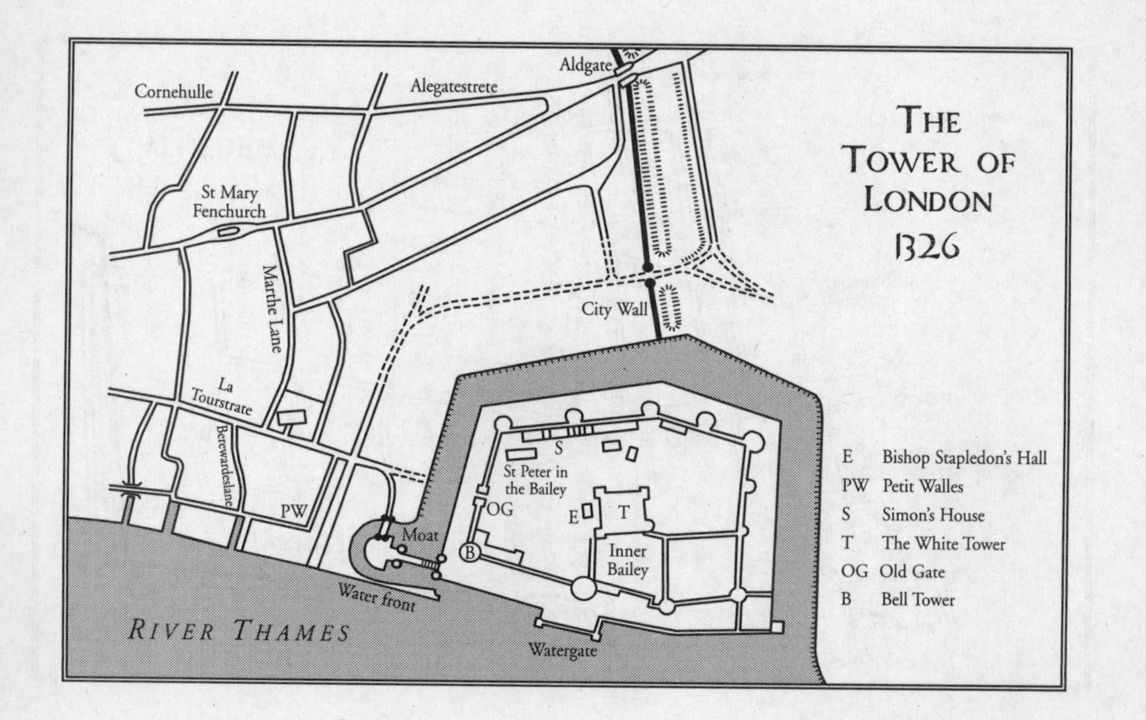
THE TOWER OF LONDON 1326
Cornehulle
Alegatestrete
Aldgate
St Mary Fenchurch
Marthe Lane
City Wall
La Tourstrate
Berewardeslane
PW
Moat
S
St Peter in the Bailey
OG
E
T
B
Inner Bailey
Water front
RIVER THAMES
Watergate
E Bishop Stapledon's Hall
PW Petit Walles
S Simon's House
T The White Tower
OG Old Gate
B Bell Tower

Chapter One

*Third Saturday following the Feast of St Michael, sixteenth year of the reign of King Edward II**

Gloucester Gaol

The stench was unbelievable.

Hundreds had gone through this place in recent months. Since the battle at Boroughbridge, the 'contrariants', who chose to dispute the king's excessive powers, had been hunted down and incarcerated – many of them here in Gloucester, and all appeared to have left their mark. The gaol reeked of sweat, piss and blood – and the little sewer outside was incapable of taking away the faeces of so many.

Men died here every day. The battle had been lost, and since then the fortunate ones had been taken out in their threes and fours, and executed on the green, where the city's folks could watch. Sometimes there was a festival atmosphere, and loud cheering and laughter heralded the latest jerking body at the end of a rope, but that was at the beginning. Now even Gloucester's people were grown weary of the sight of so many men being killed. There had been a feeling after the battle that the king's rage was natural. Not now. The dead were displayed in cages up and down the country; some, quartered, had their leathery limbs decorating the principal cities, while their blackened, skull-like heads stared out from the tops of spikes in London.

But Ranulf's father had died here today without fanfare. An

* 16 October 1322

old man, he had endured the grim misery of the gaol for nearly forty weeks, from his arrest until today. The king had not seen fit to put a stop to his suffering sooner. He was no threat, after all, so there was no urgency in hastening his end.

Sir Henry Fitzwilliam. Proud knight, good father to a motherless son, husband to a second wife, kind and generous to all servants and travellers, he did not deserve to die in this foul prison, without seeing the sun for months.

'Here he is. You want him or not?' the gaoler demanded.

Weeping, the young man lifted the filthy, light old body onto his shoulder, and walked out. In the sunshine he had a cart waiting, and he gently settled his father onto the bed, covering his foul clothing with a linen wrap. It would do until he could have his father's body washed and cleaned.

One hand protruded from the cloth, and as Ranulf tried to push it under, he saw the little leather purse.

The purse that held the symbol of Sir Henry's authority, status and power. Empty now, for the king had stolen the stamped disc months before, after his order to confiscate Sir Henry's lands last December, but still his father had retained the purse.

His father's determination to hold on to the last token of his life was the thing that made the young man break down now.

It was the last time Ranulf would weep for his father, he swore.

*First Tuesday after the Feast of the Birth of St John the Baptist, sixteenth year of the reign of King Edward II**

New Palace Yard, Westminster Palace

It was sweltering as the young knight hurried across the yard, making his way to the king's Great Hall and the offices of the Exchequer. Raucous laughter ebbed about him from the massed tents and stalls that stood so tightly packed that even the alleys between were almost impassable.

---

* 28 June 1323

He detested this place. It was the site of corruption and theft. Only dissembling politicians, conniving clerics and masters of deceit came here. Barons, lords, bishops and lawyers – all the dregs of the realm – would congregate, trying to steal for themselves whatever they could get their hands on. Well, not this time, not from John Biset. He was of age now, and he could prove it; he *would* prove it.

At the door to the Exchequer, he paused, suddenly irresolute, and glanced down at the parchment rolled tightly in his hand. It looked so mundane, just a simple legal document, but with the huge seal attached, it was so much more than that. It became, with that seal, a command. An order to obey.

The reflection was enough to make him stand taller. He would have nothing to fear after this. His persecutors would find it hard to refuse him anything now.

Above him towered the mass of the Great Hall, a fabulous construction, built originally by King William II more than two hundred years before, and still unequalled, he thought. Nearer him, at the corner, was the large, two-storeyed block that housed the Exchequer itself, and, steeling himself, he walked inside.

Immediately he was struck by the chill. The stone kept the sun at bay, and several of the clerks in here were forced to huddle within their robes when they were at work for long periods. John Biset eyed the men in the room, casting about for the bishop, but without luck. It was only when he asked a small clerk with a face so badly pocked he looked as though he had been scarred in a fire, that he was directed through the door at the rear which gave out into the Baron's Chamber, a smaller meeting room.

'Bishop Walter. I am glad to find you,' John said.

Bishop Walter II of Exeter was a tall man, somewhat stooped. He peered about him with the short-sightedness so common to those who strained their eyes late into the night with only a flickering candle to help them. 'Yes?'

John stepped forward and took the Bishop's hand, giving the ring a cursory kiss before stepping away again. 'I have it, my lord. I have confirmation.'

'Do I know you, my son?'

'I am John Biset. You may not remember me, but perhaps you recall my tenant – Sir Philip Maubank. His name will be familiar, I am sure. He's the man who died this last Whitsuntide*, leaving his grandson and heir as my ward, and placing the custody of his lands in my hands. Until you tried to take them!'

'Me?' the bishop said mildly. 'I am sure you are wrong.'

'Oh no, my lord bishop. You aided your friend Sir Hugh le Despenser when he tried to steal my manor from me.'

'Which manor was that?'

'Rockbourne in Hampshire. Sir Hugh is not content with all his other lands, now he must try to steal from me as well.'

'Oh?'

'But this proves you cannot just take my manor and walk away. Sir Hugh won't have Rockbourne, and I can prove my age.'

At the name of the manor, the bishop's eyes had grown hooded. 'How will you do that?'

'I have a statement here which proves my age.'

That was the moment when John Biset saw the quick, shrewd concentration in the bishop's eyes. 'You have a statement? Let me see it.'

'Oh no, my lord bishop. This is mine. You will see it soon enough, when I go into the court and present it.'

'The inquest is not yet held,' the bishop said.

'No. But as soon as it is, I will have my proof, and then I shall have the wardship of Maubank.'

'Perhaps,' the bishop said. But he spoke musingly, and hearing his tone, Biset thought he was merely ruminating on the vicissitudes of his life. For the bishop had sought to win the wardship for himself. Maubank was not hugely wealthy, but the amount of money which his lands would bring each year was not insignificant. And for a bishop who was attempting to fund the rebuilding

* 15 May 1323

of his cathedral, such money was not to be given up lightly.

That was all John Biset thought of the matter at first. But later that day, after the inquest held into his age, he was a little alarmed to see the clerks at the bench writing out the findings and passing them along the table until they were taken by another clerk. The latter took the papers around behind the working men at the bench, and a few minutes later, John Biset saw Sir Hugh le Despenser appear, in deep conversation with Bishop Walter.

At once a flare of alarm ran through John Biset's body. The last man he had expected to see here was Sir Hugh. Known throughout the kingdom as the most rapacious and covetous man, yet was he protected by the king, who sought always to cosset and enrich his favourite.

John Biset rose and marched to meet them, and as he arrived, he saw a man hurrying away from the chamber. 'Where is it? Where's my scroll?' he demanded.

'Being written up even as we speak,' Despenser said smoothly. 'And while we wait, I would like to discuss some matters with you.'

'There is nothing to discuss.'

'I have a wish for some land.'

'You will not have Rockbourne.'

'You say so? Perhaps you have forgotten to whom you speak?'

'I know you, my lord Despenser. You will not have my manor. And now, if that is all—'

'No, it is not all,' Despenser said. 'You will give me the manor or I shall lose the document for you.'

'You may try, but all these people saw the man take my parchment. You try to deny that the inquest has proved my age, and you will lose,' John Biset said scathingly. 'I am of age, and I own the wardship of Maubank. I will not give it away, nor the manor.'

Despenser said nothing. He set his head to one side though, and subjected John Biset to a wondering study, as though astonished that such innocence could still exist.

'Then there is nothing more to be said,' Despenser declared. 'I have held up matters as far as I may. My lord bishop, I give you a good day.'

Bishop Walter nodded, but his eyes were firmly fixed upon John as Despenser walked away. 'Godspeed, my friend.'

John Biset made as though to move away, but the bishop set his hand on John's arm, saying softly, 'You would do well to heed my friend Sir Hugh.'

'You would do well to give up trying to take my money,' John said.

The bishop left his hand resting on John's upper arm. 'Sir Hugh is not a good loser in battle. He is used to taking what he wants, and whether you agree or not, he *will* have what he wishes. If you fight him, it will end with your misery and failure. You cannot defeat him.'

'Oh aye? And when the king's court has pronounced in my favour?'

'That . . . Yes, well, I am afraid that you will find proving that more difficult.'

'When I have my—' John was assailed with a sudden doubt. He snatched his arm away, and would have dashed after the clerk with his parchment, but the bishop's calm voice stopped him.

'No. The document is gone now. And I shall make you a deal, Master Biset. If you pay me, I may allow you to have it back. I know where it is: it is safe.'

'You've stolen my proof!'

'The proof that you have come of age is perfectly safe,' Bishop Walter repeated, and now all softness was gone. In its place was a steely certainty. 'I have it, and I shall keep it until you have paid double the extent of the wardship of the Maubank boy. When you pay me, you may have your document again, and you can profit from it as you will.'

'And you want me to give my manor to Despenser too?'

'No. And I shall do you this service. If you will pay me as I ask, I shall persuade my lord Despenser to relinquish his claim on you. There! With such an offer to tempt you, how might you object?'

*Vigil of the Feast of the Assumption of Our Lady, seventeenth year of the reign of King Edward II**

Canon's Lane, Exeter

He woke with the scream bubbling in his throat, his eyes snapping wide in an instant, seeing that sword sliding in so smoothly, feeling with his mind how it snagged on the bones of the ribcage while the man stared, his eyes wide in horror, knowing that this was the end of his life. He coughed once, his lips stained crimson, a fine spray jetting over the man who twisted the blade and laughed aloud, then stepped back and yanked the sword loose again.

Master Ranulf had seen this scene so often in his dreams, he almost welcomed it. He lay silently, grateful for the freshness of the evening air, feeling the sweat slowly cooling on his flesh, thankful that he hadn't screamed out this time. It was embarrassing to wake the others with his shrill cries. They either looked upon him with expressions of sympathy, as though he had some sort of a brain fever, or with sullen incomprehension, wishing he would simply get over it, or go. They had no desire to have their evenings ruined by his nightly mare.

Looking about him, he could tell that it was the middle watches of the night, and it would be a long time before daylight lit the shutters. Yet he had to fetch something to slake his thirst. He rose and slipped his tunic over his head. Drawing his cloak about him, he padded along the chamber, and then down the ladder to the ground floor, and out to the well in the garden. There was an old copper mug by the well, and he drew a bucket to the well's side, and dunked the cup twice, draining it slowly each time, savouring the relief of liquid slipping down his throat.

Here it was never entirely silent. The cathedral was out of sight, but on a clear evening he could hear the music. At Matins, the sonorous tones of the canons and vicars singing was

* 14 August 1325

delightful to him. He would sit here and listen, staring up at the night sky. Best of all was when there were no clouds, and he could gaze in wonder at the heavens high overhead, sprinkled with stars. Someone had once told him that the stars were in fact diamonds dangling in the vast emptiness, while another man said that they were holes in a massive curtain that enveloped the world. Ranulf didn't care. To him, they were things of beauty.

Tonight there were wisps of fine silken clouds that seemed to shimmer in the air. And then he saw a marvel – a shooting star that flew across the sky and then burst into flames, roaring into magnificent life, before disappearing again.

It made his heart stop, it was so beautiful. For an age, he remained out there, staring up in awe, hoping to see another, and then mourning the loss of that one. It was a star that had fallen to the earth, he thought. Perhaps that was what happened. When a star was old, it could fall from the sky. But how did it get up there in the first place? Well, that was for God to know, and men to wonder at.

It was tempting to stay out here, in the cool night air, and avoid the eternal torment that was his service, but he could not. He must return to his little palliasse and try to sleep. For all that he hated his post here, he must keep his position, he must conceal his true feelings.

He had a task, a solemn duty, to perform: the murder he had dreamed of for so long.

Chapter Two

*Morrow of the Feast of the Assumption of Our Lady, seventeenth year of the reign of King Edward II**

Olveston, Gloucestershire

Lady Isabella Fitzwilliam wept quietly as she prayed for her poor, dear son Roger. She hoped that he was safe, but she could guess all too easily how harsh his life would have become.

Dust and ashes, that was her own life: everything she had loved and sought to defend was turned to dust and ashes. Her hopes and dreams, the children, the husbands – all would have been better, had she never lived. To be born, to live with hope, to wed a good man only to see him die; to wed again, but to have him taken from her in turn, that was too cruel. How could God, the All-seeing, the All-powerful, punish her so cruelly?

The father, her confessor, had told her that He would be eternally kind to her when she died; that her suffering in this world was to be an example to others, and that they would benefit marvellously from her bearing in this time of woe. She was a source of strength for all those who knew her. A pious woman in adversity was a wonder to all, he said.

Her confessor was lucky to be alive.

She had no wish to be an *example* to any man, woman or child. And as for her soul, what was that compared with the beauty she had created in her womb? She would willingly give it up for another year with her son – even for a message to learn

* 16 August 1325

he was safe. Her lovely boy, poor Roger.

Her early life had been so privileged, it was hard to believe that her status could have sunk so low. Poverty was a hard lord. She had loved her first husband, Peter Crok, with all the fervour and excitement that a young woman's heart could feel. A tall, fair man, with the slim, aquiline features and blue eyes that were so uncommon about here, he had set all the ladies a-twitter. However, it was she, Isabella, who had snared him. And their marriage had been entirely happy. When little Roger was born, he was the cap to their bliss.

And then all began to fall apart. Peter fell from his horse and died almost immediately. An awful tragedy, but natural. As a widow, Isabella was well provided for, and her dower was a pair of rich manors: Berwick and Olveston in Gloucestershire. She and her five-year-old son were sad to lose him, but were not destitute.

Later, marrying Henry Fitzwilliam had seemed a good idea, too. Henry was a kindly fellow, warm hearted and jolly, without the aloofness of so many other knights of his rank. He was an important man, a retainer of the powerful Maurice Berkeley, but none would guess it to see him. He was welcoming, generous and honourable. Which was why he had been killed.

It was that evil year, the year of Boroughbridge, when the king threw off all pretence of courtesy or chivalry. He had marched against the Lords Marcher in support of his lover, the foul Despenser. Sir Hugh le Despenser despoiled all, taking whatever he craved. Where he passed, all were impoverished. No man's lands, castles, treasure or even wife were safe from the intolerable greed of the Despenser.

The dispute of the Lords Marcher was with him – not with the king. They were no traitors, nor were they willing to hold up arms against the king and his standard. So when confronted with Edward's host, all the honourable men among the Marchers laid down their weapons.

Most were captured and sentenced with exceptional brutality. Even Lancaster, the king's own cousin, was beheaded. Others were thrown into irons and hanged outside their own towns and cities as visible demonstrations of the king's authority. Never again would he agree to having his power restricted or his decisions questioned. It was clear that all those who attempted to thwart him would suffer the same punishment.

Henry was captured, like so many. It was a source of some little comfort that he did not suffer the undignified death of execution like his friends: he died in Gloucester gaol before he could be attainted. But he had waited so long for his death: thirty-nine weeks. All that while in a tiny cell, without warmth or comfort. Waiting until death might come and take him. She had mourned him as a widow even while he lived.

And when he was dead, the men tried to capture her darling Roger. To this day she had no idea what had happened to him. In truth, she prayed he was safely abroad. At least Henry's own son Ranulf was alive, sent to live safely under the protection of the Church.

To lose both husband and son was unbearable. But her pain was soon to be compounded.

Because her husband had been arraigned as a traitor to the king, her manors were both taken into the king's hands. She had lost all rights to them because Sir Henry was found to have supported the rebels, even though he died before his guilt was proven. Her husband's lands, her son's and her own, were all forfeit.

Except she was told that they couldn't take her dower. These lands were of the free tenement of her first husband, so they weren't eligible to be confiscated. And Isabella had had nothing to do with the rebels, other than being wife to one and mother to another. However, when she had been discussing her affairs with her man of business, she had heard a shocking story – that the Bishop of Exeter, Walter Stapledon, had been asking about her and her manors. There were tales that Bishop Walter had grown to covet her manors, and that it was he who had told the king that she supported the Lords Marcher. It was also he who then advised that all her dower lands were forfeit, along with those of Henry Fitzwilliam.

And the bishop had taken her lands into his hands on the first Friday after the Feast of the Ascension in the sixteenth year of the king's reign*.

Her son, dear Roger, was gone. She did not know where. Both husbands were dead, and all her dower stolen, all to satisfy the insatiable greed of the bishop.

She cursed him to hell.

*Second Sunday before Candlemas, nineteenth year of the reign of King Edward II***

Near Kirby**

Sir Roger Belers knew this land, all right. He rode along like the experienced knight he was, rolling with his palfrey as the beast walked steadily along the muddy road, a strong man in his prime, hair still black apart from two wings of white at the temples, his eyes heavily lidded and inattentive. Why should a man be wary so near to his own home? This road was well used and known to be safe, for it was the main road from Melton Mowbray to Leicester, and this fellow was aware of all the efforts to keep it clear of murderers and other felons.

'Keep steady!' was the quiet whisper as the small cavalcade approached.

Richard de Folville nodded, his breath sounding loud and raw in his ears. He was a rector, of the church of Teigh in Rutland, and the thought of joining a band of outlaws had been the furthest thing from his mind. And yet here he was, crouched behind a tangle of undergrowth, gripping his sword. They were in a small stand of trees, he and his fellows. At the other side of the road, more men waited, their weapons ready, for the moment when a call would draw them out to capture this man, this *fiend*.

Belers, he was named! Sir Roger Belers of Kirby Bellers.

* 6 May 1323
** 19 January 1326
*** Kirby Bellers in Leicestershire

A name to drive fear into the heart of any man. Once a sworn ally of Earl Thomas of Lancaster, he had deserted that cause as soon as he saw how the wind was changing, and even as the earl was murdered by his cousin the king, Belers was scurrying off to curry favour. He was welcomed with open arms by the king and Despenser, and by the middle of the year, had been made a baron of the Treasury.

Avarice. The word could have been exemplified by a picture of Belers. There was no one in the whole of the shire who would regret his passing. For him, Richard Folville, this baron of the Treasury was nothing more than a thief who stole with the king's consent. No better than the foul Despenser himself.

Belers was highly favoured by the king for his change of heart before the Lords Marcher rode to defy Edward's favourite, Despenser. After the Battle of Boroughbridge, which saw the king's enemies defeated, Belers was made a commissioner of the lands of those who had stood with the Lords Marcher. And soon he began to throw his weight around, making an enemy of all those who lived in the county. He had no friends here.

There was a sudden burst of sound. Belers's palfrey had smelled something, and now it neighed, tossing its head, unnerved. Woken from his reverie, Belers glanced about him even as Richard's brother Eustace roared, *'Now!'* and leaped forward. Richard scrambled to his feet, but he was already too late. His brothers and the others were quicker – more used to ambush and fighting.

Richard thrust himself through the brambles and hollies: before him was a mass of struggling men, and the air was loud with hoarse cries and screams, swords clattering against knives, knives against cudgels, cudgels against staves. All his learning rebelled at the sight and sounds – but he was thrilled, too. He saw a short man with a steel cap fall under a flurry of blows from his brother Walter and Ralph la Zouche, blood spraying up and over the three. A man-at-arms was flying away, darting along the road like a rabbit with a hound after him, and Richard's other brother Robert sprinted off after him, pulling him down and sliding his sword into the man's kidneys, while the fellow shrieked and thrashed about.

And then it was over. Richard stood dazed, sword still clean, gazing about him wonderingly as though this was a dream. There were groans from two men near the middle of the road, and as Richard watched, he saw them despatched with a dagger-thrust to the heart, their bodies arching and twitching in their death throes. But already every man's attention was on the last man: Belers himself.

He showed no fear, only an all-encompassing rage. 'You dare to attack me? *Me*? Do you know who I am? You have killed my squire, you bastard! Yes, *you*! I'll have your cods for my dog, you arse! You pig's turd, you barrel of lard, you tun of fat!'

The man he berated turned slowly. 'You speak to me, Belers? You should hold your tongue before I have it cut out. Don't you remember me?'

He was a heavyset man in his thirties or so, a fellow with a body that looked as sturdy as a small oak, and with dark, sunburned skin to match. He was clad in a worn tunic and hosen like all the others, with a tattered cloak to keep him warm, but for all the meanness of his clothing, there was something about him that proved his position. This was a man who had held senior posts, a man of importance. It was there in his stillness, and in the intense dark brown eyes that gazed at Belers like a priest eyeing a demon.

Belers blustered now. 'Why should I? I don't bother to remember the face of every felon whose path I cross, but I will remember yours, you mother-swyving churl! I'll appreciate your looks when I see them blacken and your eyes pop as you dance for the crowds at Melton Mowbray's gibbet!'

'You threaten me – a knight with more history to his name than you? My family came here with William the Norman, and you tell me you'll see me dance?'

'You are dead, all of you!'

'Look again, Belers! Do you still not recognise me?'

'I have no idea who you are. You aren't from around here.'

'Think to the Marcher war, Belers. The family from Lubbersthorpe – remember them? The man whom you robbed of his manors and income, the mother you cast out from her home – *remember*?'

'I don't recall— '

'Lubbersthorpe. Where you took everything for yourself, and then rode away. And you had the mother's son captured and thrown into gaol. Remember?'

'That was la Zouche, wasn't it? What is it to do with you?'

'I am Sir Ralph la Zouche,' the man said, and now he drew a long dagger. 'And by my honour, I will enjoy this!'

So saying, he stepped forward towards Belers. As the baron tried to move away, hands grabbed him, and Sir Ralph reversed the blade in his hands, so that now it pointed downwards. While Belers was held firmly, Sir Ralph came to him. He studied Belers a moment, and then spat into the baron's face. The baron turned with an expression of loathing, and while his head was averted, Sir Ralph brought his knife down, thrusting past the collar bone and down into the man's breast.

Belers's body jolted like a stung stallion, and his head snapped about, until he was staring full into Sir Ralph's face, and then slowly he began to sink to the ground, while his face paled. His jaw worked as though to speak, but there was nothing more to be heard from him. His soul had fled.

'Take that piece of shit and throw it in the ditch. He pollutes the road,' Sir Ralph said, and turned on his heel.

*Monday, Feast of St Sebastian, nineteenth year of the reign of King Edward II**

West Sandford*

It was a cold, grey morning when Simon Puttock left his house. He had nothing to attend to, but he had always feared growing a paunch to rival his father's, and every day he would try to take his rounsey out for a ride to clear his head and ease his spirits.

* 20 January 1326

** West Sandford, near Crediton, Devon

A tall man of almost forty, with a calm expression on his weather-beaten face, his eyes were dark grey and steady – the eyes of a man who had suffered much and found himself strong enough to cope.

Entering the little byre, he paused in the darkness. His two cows were inside, away from the worst of the recent weather, and he slapped the rump of the nearer one, running his hand over her enormous frame, feeling the size of the calf inside. Both were strong beasts, but this had been the better milker over the years, and now that he had lost his position at Tavistock Abbey, Simon was determined to make more money from cheese and milk sales.

'She'll be fine.'

Simon turned to see his servant Hugh, a morose-looking, truculent old devil, watching him from the doorway.

'I was just patting her,' Simon said, half-defensively.

Hugh grunted disbelievingly. 'I've been looking after sheep and cows since I could first handle a sling,' he muttered, as he walked over to the two great beasts. He rested his hand on the cow's back. 'There's no need for you to come and upset them with your "patting".'

Simon smiled. In the last years, Hugh had married, had suffered the loss of his wife and the child she bore, and had returned to Simon's side. Despite his sour exterior, Simon knew that he was devoted to him and to his family.

'Have you heard from Edith?' Hugh said, without looking at Simon.

Simon felt the smile wiped from his face like a towel clearing mud. 'No.'

Exeter

The bishop was surprised to hear that there were two men to see him, but he was a believer in the old principles of courtesy and hospitality, so he nodded to his steward, John, to allow them entry.

The two were not tonsured, he saw at once. The older was a tallish fellow, with a russet tunic and tan cloak thrown back over his shoulder. He had a beard that covered his cheeks from a little below his eyes, down past his chin, over his throat and down to his tunic. His eyes were steady as they studied the bishop. His companion was much younger, a fair-haired fellow with a sparkle in his eyes, who seemed unable to grow a beard yet. He had a crossbow slung over his shoulder.

'Yes?' the bishop asked, once they had bent their knees and kissed his ring. 'You wished to see me?'

'We have been sent to speak with you,' the older man said. 'Sir Hugh le Despenser sends you his greetings.'

'I see.' Bishop Walter set his jaw. 'And?'

'There is a man who is causing my Lord Despenser some trouble, and he has asked for you to help us find him. It is a man called John Biset.'

Biset . . . Yes, the bishop knew this fellow. 'Why does he wish to find him?'

There was no answer, and he had not truly expected one. When Sir Hugh le Despenser decided to send a message to a man, it was rarely a matter of pleasantries. There would be violence.

'I know where he lives,' the bishop said slowly, 'but I am reluctant to—'

'You need not fear. All we want is the address of someone nearby who can help us,' the younger man said with a smile. He was always smiling, Bishop Walter noticed.

'I do not fear,' Bishop Walter said coolly. 'But I would not have unnecessary violence.'

'There will be none,' the older man said. 'Now give us the name of the man who can help us.'

His rudeness was almost enough to have him thrown from the bishop's room, but then Bishop Walter reconsidered. He had managed to alienate the king already, because of his failure as Edward's representative last year. That mission had been a disaster. He could not afford to upset Sir Hugh le Despenser – the second most important man in the country – as well. It was a horrible thought that he must become complicit in the attack on an innocent man, in order to maintain his own position, but he was not the first to have been forced to this. And he had done worse in the past.

'No bloodshed?'

'We don't intend to shed blood, Bishop,' the younger, smiling man said with an expression of surprise and hurt. 'We just have to leave him a message.'

Bishop Walter eyed the older man, but there was not a hint of a smile on his dark features. 'You?'

The fellow shook his head slowly.

'Very well. If you are not to cause bloodshed, I can give you my help,' the bishop said. He called to his steward. 'John, take these two to my clerk, and have them write a message to the chaplain at the church of Coombe Bisset. Tell him I ask that he helps these men and provides them with food and drink while they stay with him.'

He watched the two stride out, the younger turning and giving him a wave like an affectionate son taking his farewell before a pilgrimage. There was no unpleasantness in his manner. Bishop Walter tried to convince himself that the two strangers were not intending to cause harm.

But secretly, he felt sure that this was a vain hope. He knew Sir Hugh too well.

Chapter Three

*Feast of St Sebastian**

Exeter Cathedral

The room was warm already, with a fire roaring in the grate, throwing glorious golden light about the tapestries and illuminating the table. Made of oak, it was almost new, and the wood had not yet endured long years of smoke or stains from ink. In the gleaming firelight, it looked as though there were threads and globules of gold just beneath the surface. Another could have been tempted by the sight to take a knife and see if a little might be prised loose.

Not this man, though. He stopped at the doorway, listening intently, a shadow standing free of the candles and fire, searching with every sense for another man in the chamber. He waited with his mouth open, so that even his breath could not give him away, while his eyes flitted about the walls, chairs, stools, the rest of his body unmoving.

There was no one. Reassured, he pushed the door wide and slipped inside. It was the bishop's private chamber, but the bishop wasn't here. He had gone with his familia to the cathedral church to celebrate the Feast, and the bishop's palace was all but empty. Apart from *him*, the unseen.

In his breast he felt a shiver, beginning at his heart but then swelling and engulfing his torso, before flying away. It was a total, all-consuming desire to consummate this deed, because he

---

*20 January 1326

knew that the bishop had to die. His evil would live on perhaps, but the man's crimes were too many to be excused. And must be punished.

It would not be a swift vengeance. This was a carefully planned assassination. It would take many weeks and months. All the better for the victim to learn how to suffer, how to know true terror.

Before the familia returned, he must complete his task and escape. Glancing about once more to be certain, he hurried over the wooden floor to the table and pulled the little purse from beneath his tunic. Light and insubstantial, yet it was the heretic's death warrant. This bishop, this *Stapledon*, was the most impious, avaricious, dishonourable bishop to walk God's pure, English soil. Damn him, damn his arrogance, and his greed. They would be the destruction of him.

The little purse was placed carefully on the table. There were parchments lying nearby, and he shoved it beneath them, standing back to see the effect. It made a slight lump in the parchments, but not more than that. It was so small, after all. Yes, it would do. He stepped away from the table, going to the wall, not the middle of the floor where the boards might creak and give him away, and thence out to the doorway.

Staring back, the room was a tranquil little scene. It was the one place where the bishop was able to relax, away from the mayhem of the Close outside, away from the disputes and petty wrangles which constituted life in the cathedral.

However, the good bishop was about to discover that even his favourite chamber was not safe.

Exeter

Even from a distance the size of the city had seemed daunting. But for a man in desperate straits, this scarcely mattered.

Roger Crok pulled his cloak more tightly about him and lowered his head against the cold wind. It pulled at his clothing, and made the edges of his cloak snap and crackle, while his ungloved fingers felt as though they were growing brittle in the freezing air. He was grateful that his beard had grown so quickly, even though he now looked a scruffy remnant of his past self.

Dear God, he hoped his mother was all right! She had been so grief-stricken when the bastards had told her that she was widowed again, that it had turned Roger's heart to stone even as his mother's shattered.

Henry Fitzwilliam hadn't been that much of a catch, so far as Roger had been concerned. Roger had a simple guideline to work to, which was how a man measured against his father. Peter Crok had been handsome, powerful and clever withall. Roger's memories were so distinct: he recalled the little wrinkles at the side of Peter's eyes, the broad smiles, the great bear-hugs when his father was happy, as well as the bellow of disapproval when he was convinced his son had misbehaved. All these made his father seem almost superhuman. A magnificent man, a great warrior. It was hardly surprising that when his mother married a second time, his replacement should prove to be a sad disappointment.

But for the men who killed poor Henry to come and gloat at his widow's distress was the act of mother-swyving churls who were not good enough to clean the privy, who deserved to be punished for all eternity.

West Sandford

It took a while for Simon to calm down.

He had left the farm by the top road, then ridden up to and climbed the ridge, ducking below the trees that overshadowed the track, and down the other side. The trail turned to the right here, but he continued on down, through a gate and to the stream at the bottom.

He was still furious that Hugh could have asked about Edith, when the servant knew the terrible truth.

Simon let the rounsey drink at the stream, and then trotted up the lane on the opposite side of the ford. There was a good, broad roadway here, and he urged his beast on at a faster pace. He needed the wind in his face, the feeling of burning as the chill air froze his flesh, as though he could somehow scour the hollow space in his heart.

His wife had the same sense of loss, he knew. It was just the same as when they had lost their first little boy, Peterkin. He had been a baby still, when he fell victim to some foul malady. Over days, he wailed and whined, while Simon and Margaret did all in their power to try to aid his recovery, but their efforts were to no avail. There was nothing they could do which would alleviate the poor little boy's suffering, and at last, when he did die, Simon had a shocking reaction of relief. It was a sensation that did not last for long, but he was aware of it, and it scarred him. He had hitherto believed that he was a good father, a kind and decent man who cared deeply for his children. That sensation to him was proof that he was more selfish than he had realised.

He had been able to grow away from that memory over time. It was painful that it should return now, he thought. And with that he lashed his mount harder and galloped along at speed.

At the Morchard Bishop road he turned off, heading northwards, but there was a curious inevitability when, as though on a whim, he turned his horse's head to the south and west, following the ridge that pointed almost as straight as an arrow towards Copplestone.

Now, as he rode, he could see the lowering hills of the moors. Filthy grey-black clouds floated above them, but there was no need for threats of foul weather. The moors were already white, as though God had laid a covering of samite over Cawsand Beacon and Belstone Tor. There was a stark beauty to the scene, Simon thought, and felt his fingers loosen their grip on the reins. He allowed the rounsey to ease his pace, and sat back in his saddle as the beast jogged along.

This ride always tended to cool his overheated moods. He remembered riding here on the day he learned of the murders, when he had first met Baldwin, ten years ago, during the famine. That had been a terrible time. The only good thing had been the discovery of a new friend.

Sir Baldwin de Furnshill, his best and longest friend – and yet he too was lost to Simon.

It was shocking that Baldwin could so quickly have become almost foreign to him. In the last ten years, Simon had grown to depend utterly upon the tall, greying knight. Baldwin was dedicated to justice, to the rational explanations that always lay at the heart of any mystery; he shone as bright as a beacon in Simon's eyes. He was loyal, intelligent, and so widely travelled that Simon could only marvel at his tales of journeying from here to the Holy Land, and his accounts of the kingdoms and duchies that lay between.

But when Simon's friend had been asked to drop his sword when Edith's life was in peril, he had refused. And Simon could never forget or forgive that.

The irony was that, as soon as Simon had returned his daughter to her new family, to the man whom she loved and his parents, there had been a new demand. Her father-in-law, Charles, had told her that if she wished to remain with their son Peter, she must agree never to speak with Simon again.

Charles had been blunt and to the point. The association with Simon had put both their children at risk, and Charles was not prepared to run that risk again. He had told Edith that she must choose: her husband or her father. And she had chosen.

There was no thunderclap of ill omen to herald the event, no sudden deluge, no eclipse – but to Simon, it felt as though his world was ending. His family was all to him. His daughter had been the delight of his life, the physical embodiment of his love for his wife Meg. To accept that she had fallen in love with a man and would leave his family was hard enough; to find that she was gone from him for ever was a hideous disaster.

And to learn this just as he had discovered that he could not trust his old friend and companion, Sir Baldwin de Furnshill, the most compassionate man he had ever known, made the loss doubly painful.

Simon stopped his horse and sat staring at the moors ahead. There was an implacable permanence to those rolling hills. A steadiness that taunted him now. Once he had been a bailiff on the moors, and his life had been full and purposeful, serving the Abbot of Tavistock. That had been only a couple of years ago. And now all was lost: the abbot was dead, and with him Simon had lost his position, then his friend and his daughter.

Turning his rounsey's head, he set off back homewards again, retracing his path. He didn't look at the moors again.

It felt as though they were mocking his weakness.

Bishop's Palace, Exeter

The bishop was unamused. 'Fetch me the dean,' he snapped, as he left the cloisters and walked up the path to his palace, his robes ungainly in the cold morning breeze.

'My lord bishop?' Dean Alfred entered with an enquiring expression fitted to his face. A mild-mannered man in his late sixties, with a nature better suited to studying than vigorous effort, the bishop knew he was nevertheless still possessed of a keen intellect, which he generally concealed behind an affable manner.

'Dean, have you heard about the rector?'

The dean was experienced in the ways of the cathedral and knew that divulging too much when asked a question of this sort could result in embarrassment all round. 'The . . . ah . . . rector?' he repeated, assuming his usual air of bumbling diffidence.

The bishop peered at his dean. His poor sight was a sore irritation at times like these when he wanted to see the dean's expression more clearly.

Eyes narrowed, he growled: 'Don't try to fob me off, Alfred. We know each other too well for that. Now tell me the truth: *have you heard about the rector*?'

Seeing the look on his bishop's face, the dean decided to give up the stammering speech which he used as a device of concealment. Candour was safer when Stapledon was in this mood. 'My lord bishop, if you mean the rector of St Simon's . . .'

'Who else could I mean? Tell me, pray. I should like to know which other rector is so foul in the sight of God. *What*?'

This last was addressed to an anxious servant who had sidled up to him. 'I thought you might like a little wine, my lord bishop?'

'Put it down and get out!' While the man set the tray on the sideboard and hurriedly scuttled out again, Bishop Walter took a deep breath. 'Tell me what actually happened. So far as you can, anyway. If you can *remember* anything now,' he added snidely.

'Um, it would seem, my lord bishop, that this fellow was enamoured of a young lady in his congregation. Events took their natural course.'

'No, no, Dean! It is *not* natural for a rector to take a woman at all, let alone a married one! Was she willing?'

'I fear that the rector's lust was entirely his own. The poor lady in question was not a – ah – willing participant.'

'And he also tried to extort money from her husband?'

'Distressingly, I believe that to be the case.'

'So this fellow captured the woman, raped her, and then demanded money from her husband to have her returned. And he took the money and kept the woman. Yes?'

'I fear so.'

'What sort of man is this rector? A cretin who does not understand the foul nature of his crimes? A fool so ill educated that he cannot appreciate the correct behaviour appropriate to his cloth? He should be taken at once. I wish him here.'

'Yes. But there are difficulties.'

'Enlighten me.'

'Rector Paul is the youngest son of Sir Walter de Cockington.'

'What of it?'

'His brother is Sir James. The sheriff.'

'And?'

'It could make for tetchy relations in the city, were we to have him brought here.'

'You think we should allow him to continue in this manner?'

'No, my lord bishop. But I do think that for us to bring him here to your court may well be problematic.'

'Dean, do you condone his behaviour?'

Dean Alfred gave his bishop a long, contemplative stare. 'Not even remotely, my lord bishop. No. I personally would be more than content to throw the piece of shit to the dogs. He is foolish, arrogant to a fault, and seems to delight in shaming the Church.'

'Then why do you hesitate? Remove him from his post without delay.'

'His brother is a companion to Sir Hugh le Despenser, so I have heard,' the dean murmured.

'That I can believe,' the bishop grunted, and strode to his chair, dropping on to it heavily. 'The Despenser has friends all over the realm. Men who would take what they wish from anyone, and never pay their debts. Murderers and thieves take the protection of a lord's livery, and are secure. No man dares take the law against another who is protected by Despenser, the king's own friend!'

The bishop knew Sir Hugh le Despenser only too well. Once, Sir Hugh had been an insignificant young knight, but then, after the barons of the realm had won a dispute with the king, suddenly he was hurled into the centre of national politics. Installed in the king's household as chamberlain, he was set to monitor the king's expenditure – as a spy. Before long, he had become King Edward's most trusted friend and adviser. The bishop had grown to know him when Despenser had seemed to be working to the benefit of all. Now his true colours were on display for all to see. Except the king.

Many suggested that this was because the two were lovers. The Despenser was married to the king's own niece, Eleanor, and his father elevated to the earldom of Winchester, while he greedily took every opportunity to enrich himself at the expense of others. No one could speak to the king without first paying Sir Hugh; no suit would be presented, were Sir Hugh not rewarded. In all the realm nothing could happen, unless Sir Hugh le Despenser was in favour. He was the most powerful man, save only the king.

And any who upset him would suffer dire consequences.

'It would be dangerous to try to harm a man with such connections,' the dean said quietly.

'The man who has lost his wife – is he important?' the bishop asked after a moment.

'No. His name is Alured de Gydie. A man of no significance.'

'So he has no power to fetch his woman back?'

'None whatsoever. He is a cooper – a man of some skill, I understand – but not rich.'

'And his woman – she is still held by the rector?'

'Yes.'

The bishop drummed his hands on his table. 'The Despenser is a rich and dangerous opponent.'

'Yes, my lord.'

'So we should act swiftly. Bring the rector here. If the ransom is lost, it will go evil with that fellow! I will *not* have priests in my diocese acting in such a high-handed manner, and I do not care who his friends are. If the sheriff wishes to complain, he can come and speak with me. I shall have some choice words for him if he tries to protect a brother who is so steeped in wrongdoing that he thinks he may steal a man's wife and defile her. In Christ's name, I will *not* tolerate such behaviour! Go and fetch him to my gaol, Dean.'

'With pleasure, my lord bishop.'

'And Dean?'

'Yes?'

'Do not forget, my friend, I know Despenser very well. He is crafty and dangerous – but so am I!'

Chapter Four

Exeter

He had to visit it, just so that he could say later that he had seen the place. And now, sitting in the tavern, Roger Crok wondered why it had seemed so important to come here and try to bring home to the bishop how his offences had hurt so many. The man was incapable of human emotions. He had proved that already.

Bishop Walter II was a massively powerful man. He was second only to Despenser and the king in wealth and prestige. Somehow, walking to the cathedral and seeing it in that half-reconstructed state, had brought home to Roger Crok just how great this bishop truly was. It made his rage against the man seem pointless; someone with such authority was impregnable in his palace. The man was there trying to rebuild the great church in this city, responsible for vast sums of money, commanding hundreds of men for his own protection – he was surely far beyond Roger Crok's feeble attempts to hurt him.

Still, he must try. The bishop had been the cause of so much harm in recent years, to all in the country. It was not only Roger himself and his mother Isabella who had suffered. No, his stepfather was as much a victim as any other, even if it had not been the bishop who had seen to his death, because the bishop had maltreated Henry Fitzwilliam's widow and stolen her lands from her. That made him utterly contemptible. To rob a widow was the act of a felon, a paltry draw-latch; he was a man of no honour.

But it was more than that to Roger. Now that his mother had seen her little manors stolen from her, entirely to satisfy this intolerable bishop's greed, and at the same time Roger himself had been declared outlaw, it was not enough that the bishop should be fought in courts. He ought to have the depth of his crimes brought home to him. And that was why Roger was here, to make sure that the bishop was tormented in the same manner as his mother.

Roger called for another pot of cider and drank deeply. The drink flowed into his blood like liquid fire, and soon his fingers had recovered their feeling, his face felt hot from the great fire in the hearth in the middle of the room, and his temper became more sanguine.

The bishop might do some little good here in Exeter, but that meant nothing. It was Roger Crok's task to make him suffer, and in God's name, in God's good time, he would see Walter Stapledon endure the torments of the devil, if he could.

Bishop's Palace, Exeter

Once he was alone again, the bishop left his hall and walked to his private chapel. His chaplain was not present – he did not have need of the fellow today – and the bishop knelt alone in that quiet chamber, his eyes fixed on the crucifix.

It was the best way to think, here, abased before God. Here he could empty his mind and concentrate on the problems to hand. And remind himself who he really was.

There had been a time when he had not thought himself capable of rising in the Church. When he was younger, he had assumed that his brothers, Robert, Richard and Thomas, would be the successful ones, and he, Walter, would remain as a minor chaplain, perhaps a vicar, if he grew fortunate.

That was why, when he had been young, he had spent so much time looking at others and seeing how he might help them, even if sometimes his motives were called into question. In later years, others complained about him, especially Londoners, because they blamed him for the Eyre of five years ago, when he had been the man behind the court held to investigate all the rights and privileges of the city. However, that was not his doing. Yes, he was the figurehead, the Lord High Treasurer, when the king demanded his inquest, but it was not his choice.

There were many who loathed him. In God's name, so many! He had made enemies wherever he went, something that sometimes made him regret ever taking a leading position in the realm. But someone had to, and he was sure that at least he would be able to do some good.

Some might dispute that, no doubt. They would think that his sole aim had been to make money for himself, but they didn't realise that he took nothing. He was a frugal man, with little need for fripperies. He liked some comforts, it was true, and he had great need of his spectacles, but beyond that, he was not cocooned in gold, swaddled in silver, or laden with tin. Those who criticised were all too keen to suggest that a bishop lived in luxury all his life. Well! They should try covering a diocese like his, and getting around it in order to view all the priests and make sure that they were complying with their duties. They would soon give up any notion of luxurious living.

Yes, he had enemies, but they were for the most part irrational. London's mob was one thing, but the others who felt that he had unfairly deprived them of property or chattels had no idea what he was struggling with every day: debt. Massive, incomprehensible debt that would crush a man less determined. He had to grab all the treasure he could, just to maintain the steady flow into the cathedral's coffers and keep the building works going. For what use would his cathedral be, without the final efforts? The stonemasons wouldn't remain here without their money. The carpenters, joiners, plumbers, ropemakers and tilers, all would leave in an instant if they couldn't see their pay or their beer turning up.

That was his biggest fear. The great church had been adequate two hundred years or more ago, but it had to develop to cope with the growing population of the city. So some fifty years ago, a far-sighted bishop had taken the decision to raze and rebuild it, in sections. First to go was the Norman eastern end and, while the building works continued, the canons moved into the middle of the church. Only recently had that part of the church been completed, and now the new choir stalls and bishop's throne had been installed in the new quire, before the workmen turned their efforts to the western part of the building.

But demolishing a building was almost as expensive as purchasing the new stones, the timbers, the poles for the scaffolding – it was all hideously costly, and there was a constant need for more funds. Bishop Walter *would not* go down in history as the bishop who failed the diocese. He wanted to be known as one of the patrons of the church, and had already chosen the spot where his body would lie when he had died, a position prominently located in the quire behind the high altar. That would be suitable enough for him, the man who had increased the money given by the bishop to the church almost six-fold.

What would he be remembered for? he wondered. Perhaps for his gifts to the church. Better that he be remembered for that than for his time as Treasurer. His efforts to improve the education of so many would be a good legacy, but how many would recall that effort after his death? That was the sort of thing that the individuals would remember, not the majority. The majority, he sighed, would only remember his taking their money, and would naturally assume that he had taken it for his own purse, not seeing the new cathedral as it rose about them. But that was the way of men and there was little he could do about it.

Ach! There was no reason for him to brood. He was like an old hen, squatting here alone in his chapel. There was work to be done, and he should carry on with it.

He rose stiffly to his feet, massaging his left leg where the knee joint appeared to be growing ever more reluctant to unbend, and after making his obeisance, walked from the chapel and back into his room. His steward was not in the room, so Bishop Walter hobbled to the sideboard and poured himself a large goblet of strong red wine. Smacking his lips appreciatively, he collapsed in his comfortable little chair, and grunted with satisfaction.

It was then that he saw how the pile of documents was disordered. There was a lump in one corner, and it made him frown. Setting his goblet down, he reached across. Moving the parchments, he found himself staring at a little purse. A plain, cream-coloured purse, made of some soft skin, and with a curious dark stain that marred the outer edge. He took it up. It was extraordinarily light, and clearly held no money. Intrigued, he pulled the drawstring open and peeped inside. There was a small scrap of parchment, and he felt his eyebrows rise when he saw that there was writing on it.

He took it out and read it, then felt his scalp crawl, and the flesh of his skull tighten, as he absorbed the vile message.

*Tuesday, morrow of the Feast of St Sebastian**

Furnshill

Sir Baldwin de Furnshill stalked from his house and stood a moment, snuffing the early morning air.

It was his daily custom to walk to the pasture and practise with his sword. The idea of training, constantly improving his skills, was ingrained from his days in the Holy Land, where he had joined the *Poor Fellow Soldiers of Christ and the Temple of Solomon* – the Knights Templar.

Now approaching his middle fifties, there were few men of his age who could compare with him in speed or strength. Other, younger men might be able to dispute with him, but he was confident that his wiliness would protect him in a fight against a more powerful opponent. He had fought often enough. There were wounds all over his body, from knives, from swords, and from crossbow bolts – and he had survived all. The most obvious was the scar at his cheek, which ran down to the thin beard that followed the line of his jaw. It was peppered with grey now, but his hair was gradually fading entirely. It was only a few years ago that he had found the first white strays, and now the whole of his scalp looked like a snowed hillside. There was dark beneath, but white overlaid all.

---

* 21 January 1326

Of course, he was not remotely vain, but it was still a slight shock to realise that he was growing old. He didn't feel it.

His house was quiet still, this early, a thin smoke rising from the fire. Inside, he knew, his wife would be preparing food with their maidservant, while a second helped his children out of their beds. Edgar, his servant for so many years, would be outside with a groom, feeding and petting the horses. It was, Baldwin considered, an idyllic scene. One worth keeping, one worth protecting. And that was why he must practise. To make sure that it remained like that: safe and serene in this world of passion and blood. This world which appeared to be falling apart so quickly.

That thought was enough to give him the resolve he needed. He stood, his sword in the outside guard, his right fist punched out, the sword's blade angled upwards to protect his body, high enough so that he could peer beneath it at his imaginary opponent, and then he moved.

Feet fixed firmly at first, he swung down, chopping at his enemy's weapon, then lifting his sword to block the responding attack, swooping it low to hack at legs, thrusting hard, retreating and lifting the weapon to knock a stabbing blade to one side. He shifted his feet, all the while moving his sword incessantly, blocking, guarding, stabbing and hacking, making use of the main guards: the dexter; the sinister, with the right arm passing across his body to protect it, while his sword was angled up over his line of sight; the unicorn guard, in which he gripped the hilt before his groin, arm outstretched, so that the sword's point was at his eye level; and the hanging guard, the one he believed was the only true guard, his arm outstretched, his sword's hilt held high, while the sword's tip pointed towards the enemy, angled so that he could sweep it across to the right, chop to the left, or perform any number of manoeuvres.

Daily practice was a part of him. If the weather was too inclement, he would resort to standing in his barn, but for the most part he would come here, feeling the blood singing in his veins as he thrust and slashed. And every so often a scene would intrude upon his mind. A picture of bloody faces, of corpses lying in the rubble, of his friends writhing as they tried to hold their shattered bodies together.

Those memories had been returning more often recently. There was a terrible trepidation in him, a growing conviction that his family, his manor – even the whole shire – was threatened. The scenes in his mind were from years ago, from the last days of Acre, when that wonderful Christian city had been overrun and razed by the crazed hordes of the Mameluke King. The latter had succeeded in destroying a tower on the wall, and poured in through the breach. Baldwin himself was injured and was pulled away by the Templars, installed on one of their ships, and taken to safety as the city fell. It was gratitude at having his life saved that had made him join the Order.

That was many years ago now – thirty-five, all told. Since then, his Order had been arrested, tortured, their wealth stolen, and the Knights Templar disbanded. All because the King of France and the pope had wanted to take that money for themselves.

It was after that shameful destruction that Baldwin had come here, to the quiet West Country of England, to hide himself from the politicians and ecclesiastics who were so antagonistic to the Order he had adored.

But although he had tried to escape, there was more danger now.

Hearing steps, he turned and nodded. 'Edgar.'

'Sir Baldwin, Despot has a strain in his right front – I think it is his fetlock.'

'Again?'

Edgar said nothing. He was taller than Baldwin, and his face always held a slight grin as though he was secretly amused by a jest which others could not appreciate. Women found his suave sophistication utterly enthralling. Men were more often wary, and rightly so. As a fighter he was quite ruthless, and as swift and lethal as a thunderbolt.

'That beast is proving to be expensive. He's only just recovered from the strain.'

'He appears to be an unfortunate fellow,' Edgar agreed.

Baldwin grunted, wiping at the blade of his sword with the corner of his tunic to remove some smudges. 'Perhaps it is time he was retired. I will need a new rounsey if I cannot have faith in him.'

'I shall begin to search for a new one, then.'

'Yes – no. Find two. But it will wait until I next visit Exeter. You can join me then and look for some decent brutes.'

Edgar said nothing, but Baldwin could feel his eyes upon him. He looked up. 'Yes, Edgar?'

'Are you preparing for war?'

'We have to be ready. The king appears convinced that it may come to that.'

'You think that the queen will return with an army?'

Baldwin sighed. 'I just do not know. She is an honourable woman, I would stake my soul on that. But she has been terribly mistreated. What might she not do?'

'We should look to the defence of the house,' Edgar said.

'If it comes to war, I shall be asked to help,' Baldwin said. 'And if that does happen, I may have to leave home for some time.'

'I shall be with you.'

'I would prefer you to stay here.'

Edgar shook his head. 'When you fought before, I was always at your side, Sir Baldwin. I should be there again if you are to ride to battle.'

'I cannot ride to war knowing that Jeanne and the children are left here alone and in danger,' Baldwin said firmly. 'I am sorry, old friend. But you must remain here to protect the manor and all within it.'

'It may not come to it.'

Baldwin smiled without humour. 'The king thinks it will. From all I have heard recently, Edward is planning to defend the realm against both the queen and the French. There is a fear that there will be an invasion, possibly two.'

'But they will be seeking the king, surely?' Edgar said.

Baldwin nodded, unconvinced. 'It is possible, yes. But I have this concern: you know as well as I do, that the queen's lands were mainly here in Devon and Cornwall. Perhaps there are enough men here who have sympathy for her.'

'Sympathy for a woman who leaves her husband?'

'Don't presume to judge her,' Baldwin said. 'She has suffered enough. First her husband chose to spend his time with Despenser, then he broke up her household, arrested any Frenchmen in her service, sequestrated all her properties, confiscated all her money and income and left her with a pittance – and then even took away her children and gave them into the protection of Despenser's wife. A chivalrous man might consider that she had reason enough to wish to stay away from her husband.'

'Perhaps. However, I think there are more men in the realm who would flock to her simply because they hate the Despenser than because they admire or sympathise with her.'

'True enough!' Baldwin chuckled, but then he grew serious again. 'Yet I fear that there could be warriors marching through these fields before long, Edgar. Perhaps before spring. It has happened before.'

'So, I should find two good rounseys,' Edgar said.

Baldwin nodded and watched as the other man strode back to the house.

Baldwin had known many knights in the Order whom he could call 'friend'. There was something about a life of dedication, an existence based entirely on service to others, which had forged between the Templars an enduring bond; those who still lived were comrades who had served together in countless battles, and the obscene betrayal of their companions only strengthened it. All through those dark days, Edgar had remained at his side, and whenever there had been a risk of a fight, Baldwin had always been glad of Edgar's strong, calm presence nearby. If it were to come to it, Baldwin would feel strange riding to war without his sergeant. It would leave him with an odd sense of loneliness.

It made him think of Simon. His friend for more than a decade, Simon had been terribly offended late the previous year when Baldwin had been told to throw down his weapons by a felon. It was impossible for Baldwin to do so. If he had, matters could have ended in disaster. So he had kept a firm grip on his weapon, and the issue had been resolved. But Simon had feared for his daughter. And since that day, the two men had not spoken.

Baldwin thrust the sword back into its scabbard. It had been hard to tell Edgar he must remain. But it was harder to know that even Simon Puttock would not be at his side.

He felt truly alone.

Chapter Five

Exeter Cathedral Gaol

Paul de Cockington woke shivering.

There was a thin stream of light, which penetrated from the tiny slit of a window high overhead, and barely illuminated this side of the cell.

It was outrageous! How the bishop had the gall to bring him here, he didn't know. The man *clearly* didn't understand whom he was dealing with. He seemed to think Paul was only some feeble arse who'd submit to his will. Well, he *wasn't*. Paul de Cockington was the son of a knight and the brother to the sheriff, damn the bishop's eyes, and no de Cockington had ever accepted treatment of this kind.

He had a palliasse of linen with a rough straw filling, which was revolting. He was used to a good mattress on his beds, not a roll like this, spread out on the floor. His meal last night, if it could be so termed, was a shameful mess that he wouldn't have served his dog, and with only one blanket, he had spent much of the night huddled in a ball, trying to keep himself moderately warm. It was a *disgrace* that a man of his position should be held in such discomfort.

When the door opened, he was pleased to know that he would soon be able to express his feelings in some detail to whomsoever had placed him in this foul little pit. It must be a mistake. No bishop would treat a de Cockington in this heavy-handed manner; it was some pathetic minion who had—

'Get up!' the man rasped from the doorway, and Paul jerked his head in disbelief.

He was a short fellow, but broad. That he was strong was self-evident, but Paul knew he was only a lowly lay brother at best. 'Are you talking to *me*?'

'No – the rat. Get up!' the man said, with a grin. He apparently felt that this was the height of inventive humour.

'What is your name?' Paul asked.

'Gaoler. Now, shift yourself.'

'I asked what your name— '

The man grimaced, and entered the room. Without speaking, he took Paul's left wrist, and dragged the rector towards the door.

'Hey, leave go of my hand, you churl! Who do you think you are, eh? Get off me, you fool.'

'Who do I think I am? I'm a man from town, and friend to Alured de Gydie. You know – the man whose wife you stole and raped. The one you tried to rob! We take that sort of thing seriously down here, Rector – if you *are* a rector. You won't need a title when you're sitting in that gaol day after day, will you?'

'You turd, let me go!' Paul spat. He scrabbled with his spare hand to try to turn and get to his feet, but the gaoler had lugged him across the cell and out to the passageway before he had an opportunity. Then, springing to his feet, he tried to wrest his arm back, but the gaoler had his forearm in a grip as strong as a smith's. 'You'll pay for this!' he blustered.

'I daresay,' the gaoler said without emotion.

Paul de Cockington suddenly found that they were in the open air, and it was some surprise to note that they weren't heading to the Bishop's palace. Instead, the gaoler manhandled him past the great west door of the cathedral, and on, out to the Bickleigh Gate.

'You aren't taking me to the bishop,' he declared.

'Well noticed, Rector. With attention to detail like that, you'll go far. Perhaps as far as the *city* gaol.'

'You can sneer at me, man. When my brother the sheriff learns how you've treated me, you'll learn to regret it.'

'Go on, then. Go and find your brother,' the gaoler said, and released him. He carried on, marching east, past St Martin's, and never once looking back.

Paul looked about him uneasily. He didn't want anybody coming and discovering him. The streets were busy enough for him to be moderately safe, but there was always danger, if he were to be discovered by Gydie or one of his friends or servants. Better by far to get up to the castle.

His brother James would be able to protect him there.

Bishop's Palace, Exeter

Pulling up the collar of his tunic and drawing his cloak tighter about him, John de Padington opened the door and made his way to the bakery at the side of the cathedral. It was his usual morning task, to walk the short distance to fetch bread for his master's breakfast. Bishop Walter II was never particularly fussy about his food, especially his first meal of the day. Something plain, but filling, was all he asked. Cold meat, a little bread, some cheese and wine was enough.

Other men were much more demanding, asking for strongly flavoured dishes with sauces, and sweetmeats afterwards, but the bishop had a strong constitution even now in his six-and-sixtieth year, and John was sure that a large part of that was due to his punishing schedule of work and his tendency to avoid the richer foods, as much as it was his dislike of too much strong drink. He would generally only drink two pints of wine in a day, along with perhaps a quart of ale at lunch.

John de Padington had been steward to the bishop for more years now than he cared to remember. They had grown old together, both of them grey now, and although they had had their arguments in the past (which master and servant never found cause for dispute over the years?), John felt he knew his master as well as, or better than, anyone else did.

All the canons and priests were terrified of their powerful lord. Stapledon had been so long at the very centre of English political life, ruling the Treasury with a rod of red-hot iron, that many feared a word spoken out of turn could lead to their being taken away by officers of the King – or, worse, men under the orders of Sir Hugh le Despenser. Those taken by *his* men tended to disappear for ever.

The cemetery area was a mess, John thought, as he crossed in front of the cloisters on his way to the north tower where the bakery lay. Horses wandered about the grass, dogs bickered and snapped, and men were playing camp-ball near the west door, desultorily kicking their pig's bladder about to the risk of all who walked past. John would have remonstrated, but two of the men looked over-aggressive, and John was not one to provoke a fight when such an action could be avoided.

Children played chase amongst the hillocks of newly dug earth. One earned a roar from beneath the soil: a wheeled barrow stood near a hole in the ground, from which the fosser's head protruded, and he bellowed at the boys until they ran away. The fosser then returned to his digging, occasionally flinging a skull or other bones into a small pile ready for moving to the charnel chapel.

There was an appalling amount of rubbish here in the Close. The fish market that prevailed near the Broad Gate was not open today, but the debris from the previous market remained. The area reeked of old fish, from the piles of fish heads and guts, a sight that was not improved by the cats prowling around, all searching for a tidbit or the chance to spring upon a rat as it gorged itself.

Nor was the mess all the fault of the secular. Much was the responsibility of the cathedral itself, as the rebuilding works continued. Rubble lay about, with old timbers poking out amid the masonry. While stoneworkers chipped and hammered, there was as much noise from the carpenters with their hammers and saws, and over all, the bellowing of the master mason and his staff, all demanding greater efforts from the host of workers who scurried about at the foot of the building site like so many ants.

It was a shame, John reckoned, that the place was in such a state of chaos. He would have liked to have seen it as it was or as it would become, but just now the larch scaffolding was still all about the nave. The quire had been rebuilt already, but now the walls of the old nave had been razed and were gradually beginning to re-form. However, it would be many years before the cathedral was completed. Neither he nor Bishop Walter would ever see it finished – that would be another thirty years or more.

The bakery was popular at this time of day. Carpenters, masons, priests, servants of all types, congregated at the door, some waiting patiently in line while others fretted, especially the novices and annuellars who stood lowest in the priestly orders. John himself was able to ignore the queues and march to the front, nodding to the chief baker and taking the two pain-demaigne loaves of the highest quality that were waiting for the bishop.

William Walle was there too, and greeted John. 'Good morning, steward.'

'Not that it'll remain that way for long,' John said, nodding westwards towards darkening clouds.

'Aye, well, there's always a storm brewing somewhere,' William said easily.

The squire was a tall, gangling young man, and the steward was as fond of him as he could be. Walle was a generous-hearted fellow, kindly and polite to all in the cathedral, even though he was the bishop's nephew and need not strain himself. There were some who were born into positions of authority, John knew, who would instantly take on the mantle of arrogance and rudeness; others would treat all as equals. William fell into this second category.

'There appear to be more storms than usual this year,' John said as they returned to the palace. He did not need to explain. A grim mood lay over the entire country. The king's dispute with his wife was known to all, and a French-funded invasion was cause for terror.

'Aye, well, I believe that the summer could be good and warm, and the harvest better than we've seen for many years past,' William said. 'You know, good steward, that there is no reason to fear men. If God has decided that we need to be punished, He will allow the French to come. There is nothing we may do, except try to repel them. But no matter what happens, a good harvest will fill our bellies, and that is a thing greatly to be desired.'

'You say *this* thing is in God's hands, but *that* thing is to be desired, Master William – yet both are in His gift. Neither one more than the other.'

'True. So let us not worry about them, but instead plan for the worst and hope for the best, eh? I refuse to be alarmed while the weather is holding, and while I have my health and happiness.'

John shook his head at the sight of the squire's grin. 'I think it is proof of youthful ignorance that you mistake for optimism. There is nothing to be too cheerful about. Let us wait and see whether matters improve, whether the queen returns willingly to her husband, whether she brings their son with her, whether the French do agree that she should come home to her adopted land, and—'

'And whether the rain doth fall for all the year and our nation starve once more! Come, steward, you have been eating too much melancholy food. You need the sparkle of some fresh cider in your belly to cheer yourself.'

John chuckled. It was impossible not to like young William. He was always brimful of happiness, and although an older man might bemoan the dire circumstances in which men found themselves, yet it was good to talk to William. He had that sunny disposition that tended to drive away the grim reality of the present.

'I eat well enough,' he responded, glancing at his taller companion. 'I have all the rich, happy food I can manage. It's the benefit of being your uncle's steward. I get to finish the dishes he leaves – and he has a small appetite!'

'That is good. I would hate to think that you were suffering from hunger,' William teased.

'Aye.'

They had passed by the building works and were approaching the cloisters. As they drew near, William stopped suddenly, and said, 'Steward, you know my uncle as well as any man alive. You haven't seen him showing alarm recently, have you?'

'No. Should I have?'

William shook his head quickly, but then grimaced. 'You see, I saw him reading a note that upset him last night.'

'That's not unnatural. Your uncle has many communications from all over the diocese and the rest of the kingdom – and some are bound to be of a serious nature. He is an important man, you know that.'

'Yes – and yet he has never concealed anything from me before.'

John glanced at him with surprise. 'He wouldn't, would he, because he knows he can trust you, squire. You are of his blood, as well as having his confidence from your service to him.'

'That is true, and yet as soon as he saw me, he snatched the parchment away before I might see it, as though he was guilty or ashamed.'

'You are sure you did not mistake his action?'

'No. He deliberately hid it from me. I am certain there is something wrong. But do you keep an eye on him for me, steward, in case there is something that alarms him. I would help him if I may.'

Exeter Cathedral

There was no more galling experience than to be frightened by an unseen enemy, the bishop told himself bitterly. And he *was* frightened.

He had always known that he would be unpopular with some. Bishops were wielders of enormous power, and as such were always feared, and therefore hated. A man who had power of life and death over another did not enjoy his respect. All too often, he was the subject of loathing, because such power could seem too arbitrary to the peasant who saw a friend hanged. Bishop Walter II had tried to prevent abuses of power, but it was not always possible. And on occasion, he had been forced to use his own power – for the greater glory of the Church, not for himself.

When he was only a canon, he had been excommunicated. It was a lot of nonsense, but nonetheless embarrassing. He had heard, with another canon, of an illegal burial taking place at the Dominican Friary towards the east of the city. The cathedral jealously guarded their monopoly of all burials, because they were enormously lucrative. Those who wished for a church funeral were keen to have their souls protected with prayers, and with proximity to the high altar, and the Dominicans knew it. So they tried to have this knight buried in their priory so that they could benefit from the grave goods, the wax, the linen and rich cloths, as well as by the man's gifts to them.

Well, the cathedral had greater need of the money and goods than the Dominicans. It was ludicrous that the friars should attempt such a gross infringement of cathedral liberties. So Canon Walter, as he then was, had gone with lay brothers to chastise the friars. He had managed to get into their chapel, and there he had the lay brothers pick up the hearse, the body and all the valuable items he could find, and all would have been well, had not a belligerent group of friars come and tried to remonstrate with him. There was a scuffle, most unseemly in the House of God, and a friar was given a bloody nose before the cathedral men escaped with their booty.

They had tried to return the body for burial later, when they had held their service to justify keeping the treasure, but the friars wouldn't accept it, so Walter had told the lay brothers to leave the fellow at their gate. It remained there for some days, until the city had made pointed comments to the bishop, and Walter was ordered to collect it. In the end, it was buried in the cathedral.

The friars had blamed Walter for the assault on their priory. They almost succeeded in preventing his election to the bishopric, in their determination for revenge. Fortunately, others intervened, and he was consecrated.

All these years later, there were many more whom he had offended and who had come to hate him. But that was no reason for the foul message yesterday. How any man could seek to send such a vile note was beyond him. Well, he was determined that he would not allow it to affect him and his ministry. He had too much to see to, too much to achieve. And at the same time there was the terrible problem of the king and queen. So many issues to be resolved. He could not afford to be distracted by some anonymous threat.

Indeed, it was ridiculous.

Yet, no matter how ridiculous, the bishop could not help but glance about him, as though there was an assassin nearby waiting to slay him.

Church of the Holy Trinity, Teigh

It was a curious thing that, after participating in such a crime, he could feel so at ease with himself.

Richard de Folville stood before the altar at his little church, staring at the crucifix. It was a simple cross of wood, but with a figure that was startlingly realistic, he now realised. He hadn't seen a man dying violently before. To see Belers collapse so swiftly was oddly comforting, as though showing him that even the most evil men could be removed, and also proving that his own end need not be too terrifying. That was good, too.

The best part was the loss of fear. He had confronted his own worst horrors and come through. While struggling through the brambles, he had been anxious to get to the fight before it was over, and at the same time petrified that he might have to kill one of the men himself. The thought of blood on his hands was, before the actual killing, quite scary. But then he'd seen the dead lying about, and there was nothing to be afraid of – he realised that very quickly. God was not worried about these men. Belers was evil, and God was using the Folville brothers to punish him. It was only reasonable. The man had stolen, extorted, and thieved all his life. Just because he had been made the Treasurer, he thought he could live immune to any risks. Well, Richard and his brothers had proved to him that no man was above divine retribution.

He stared at his hands. Quite still. Perfectly calm. And his soul too felt serene, as though the blood falling on the ground was enough to remove any stain from his soul. God could not have felt that he deserved punishment, for any man who was to receive such from Him would feel the weight of that judgement. And Richard felt perfectly content. Almost gay.

The sound of tramping boots came to him then; and he tore his attention away from the altar as three men-at-arms walked in. Their leader was a tall, grizzled man with a square face and sharp hazel eyes.

'Rector? I've been sent to ask where your brothers are.'

'Why?'

'I think you know why. Sir Roger Belers is lying dead over at Kirby Bellers, and folks remember your brothers being near that place on the day. Eustace, Robert and Walter, your brothers, were all there – as were others. One was Ralph la Zouche and his brother Roger. Were you with them?'

'I do not know where they are,' Richard said. 'I have not seen them for some days. Are you saying someone witnessed the murder?'

'There are plenty saw your brothers and others on that road. And they say you might be holding some here. There are always places in churches where a man can be hidden.'

'Perhaps so – but not in here. You realise that you have no right to come in here and search?'

'We have been told to find these men.'

'Then go and seek. But you will not search in here. This is God's House.'

The older man sucked his cheek, and then his fist suddenly flew. It struck Richard high in his belly, and he fell back instantly, the breath knocked from him. Curled on the floor, he could not breathe, only gasp and struggle in agony. His stomach was a pit of torment. He was sure that he would be sick, then that he must surely die, and then, as the small pricks of light appeared before his eyes, suddenly a spasm went through his body, and he could feel the air in his lungs again. Coughing and retching, he rolled over to his knees, one hand on the floor before him, the other at his belly.

'Yes, rector, you cough it up,' the man said unsympathetically. 'And while you do, we'll look for medicine to cure you, eh? Go on, boys. Look everywhere. I'll keep the rector company and make sure he doesn't have another attack.'

Richard wiped his eyes and rocked back on his haunches, peering up at the man. 'Why do that?' he gasped thickly. 'What have I done to you?'

'Nothing to me. But your family is bad. Your brothers are murderers and thieves, and I think you are no better. I'd bet you know where they all are, don't you?'

Richard stood shakily, still rubbing his belly. 'You are a fool. No doubt if you were guilty of a homicide *you* would remain at the scene, but any man with a brain would leave the area at once. Do you really believe I'd stay here after helping to kill a man so powerful as Sir Roger Belers? No! If I'd been involved, I would have bolted immediately.'

'Like your brothers, you mean?' the man sneered.

'My brothers do not live here. You would need to ask them.'

The man gazed past him. 'Well? Find anything?'

His men returned, shaking their heads. 'Nothing in the church. No one here.'

'You see?' Richard said, emboldened. 'I said that there would be nothing here.'

Suddenly the fist struck him on the chin, and he flew backwards, tripping over a loose tile in the floor and falling headlong. Dazed, he looked up and saw the man-at-arms holding a sword to his throat.

'Look at me, little priest. My name is Ranulf Pestel – Squire Ranulf. Look on me carefully, little priest, because if I learn that there was a man in clerk's garb at the killing, I will be back, and I'll have you in irons. Then I'll have you dragged to Sir Hugh le Despenser and the king. They were friends to Belers, and they want blood for his blood. So, rector, if you had anything to do with this, you should start praying *now*!'

Chapter Six

Rougemont Castle, Exeter

The steady tramp of feet along the corridor outside was followed by a muttered series of commands, and then the door was thrown wide and Paul de Cockington found himself being studied by his older brother, the sheriff. Paul grinned and rose from his brother's chair, bowing and motioning to offer the chair.

His smile was not returned. 'You've been a complete tarse, haven't you?' James said, glowering at Paul. 'Do you realise how much trouble you've caused me? It's a miracle the bishop isn't here already. I'm half-tempted to have you taken back there again.'

'There's no need, brother,' Paul said. 'It'll all blow over. I'll pay the man back all the property he gave me, and tell him that if he keeps quiet, you won't harm him. That'll be enough.'

'You haven't been here long, have you, Cods-for-brains? This little city is Exeter, not some huge place like London, where a man could become lost among the teeming hordes. There aren't all that many people here. What, six thousand all told? You will not be able to hide. This fellow Gydie will find you if he bothers to try – and he does have some small motivation. You stole his wife and raped her, and then you kept the ransom he offered you, as well as the wench. Dear God! I hope she was worth it.'

'She was, brother – oh, she was! You don't understand what it was like! I was a celibate for so long, and then that gorgeous woman started batting her eyelids at me during services. I couldn't help but notice. No man with a heart and blood in his brains could have ignored her.'

'It's not blood in your heart or head that worries me.'

'Very funny. She had the most incredible body though,' Paul added reminiscently. 'A pair of bubbies so large, it was hard to span one with both hands. Oh, brother, you should have—'

'Spare me! No matter how you feel about her, the fact that you took her means that you will have trouble all the while you are in Exeter. You need to leave the city.'

'Oh, come on! I don't think—'

'No, you don't,' his brother said directly. 'You don't think how the bishop may react to learning you're free; you don't think how Gydie will respond to finding you here; you don't think how all this will make *me* look either, do you? No, you commit acts of pathetic theft and rape, and then leave it to me to pick up the pieces. But I am the law here, and if men learn I have shielded my brother from his punishment, I'll not be safe either. I've spent the last months trying to convince the locals that I'm trustworthy, and now you're throwing that all out of the window with last night's soil. Well, swyve a sow, brother! I won't have you ruining the best post I could have landed in the whole of Devon.'

'What do you suggest, then?'

'I shall find space for you on a boat to Gascony or France. You can go out there and try your luck for a little. I have some money you can take, and I will give you fresh clothing. When it's all calmed down, you can come back, but not until then. You understand me? You'll stay away – especially from here – until you're called back.'

'How long will that be?' Paul said, flabbergasted that his brother had decided this.

'As long as it takes.'

Tiverton Castle

The Lady Isabella was most grateful to the generous-hearted baron for allowing her to come here to this restful little castle up at the top of the hill overlooking two rivers. Without his kindness, she was not sure what she might have done when her carter's horse fell by the roadside, his foreleg snapped in a pothole.

A widow's life was never easy. The first loss of a husband had been a shock to her. A sudden, tragic death was always hard to accept, but at least her darling Peter Crok had died quickly, without apprehension, unlike Henry Fitzwilliam. He had languished for such an awful long time, in that cursed gaol, with no friends, no support or companionship. Just installed there, and left to rot for thirty-nine weeks, suffering all the torments a man may. The king would not consider a pardon; his heart forged from steel. So poor Henry waited and waited, until one day his heart simply gave out. Even then there was no honour in his treatment. His body was left in the gaol at Gloucester until his son came to collect it.

And Henry was but one of many. There were hundreds of decent, honourable men betrayed by their king as he continued his infatuation with the one knight whose every whim and fancy he would tolerate unquestioningly: Despenser. All others may be executed, bar this one. And that devil, Stapledon, was a friend of both men.

As a widow, the Lady Isabella was no threat to any man, and yet she had been persecuted by that evil bishop after her husband's death. May his name live on in infamy!

She still prayed, whenever she was at the altar, that her son was safe. Poor, darling Roger had been forced to flee so quickly when the plot to steal their lands became plain, that he had no time to speak with her and tell her where he might go. She hoped he had made his way to Ireland or France. The Irish were devoted to Sir Roger Mortimer, while the French were happy to befriend any man who was an enemy of the English king.

She heard steps, and glanced around to see the tall figure of the coroner, Sir Peregrine de Barnstaple.

'My Lady Fitzwilliam, I hope you are well?'

'I thank you, Sir Peregrine, I am as well as I could hope,' she said.

'That is good. I am pleased to hear it.'

He had a kind smile, and she felt sure that he was already fond of her. A man his age – what, some five-and-forty years? – it was a surprise that he had never married. And yet he had once formed an association, so she had heard: it was said that he had adopted two children when their mother died. Certainly he did not appear to her to be afraid of her sex.

Many men were uncaring about a woman's feelings. They some of them affected an insouciance in a woman's company, while others simply preferred the companionship of other men. Those who had been raised as knights in training were, not surprisingly, unsure how to behave with women, and could be unthinkingly brutal. There were plenty who would seek to impress a lady by taking her, as though she had no feelings, no rights, no more authority than a dog. For some, it was as though they believed that a woman would respect and adore them once she had been raped, as though that was proof of sincere adoration! When boys were sent away from home and brought up in the company of men from the age of six, many of the poor lads would never again experience womanly affection and had no idea of how to treat a lady.

Not so this fellow.

'Sir Peregrine,' she said, 'would it be impertinent for me to ask you, what do you think will happen?'

He did not do her the insult of pretending he did not understand, which she appreciated. There was little enough talk of anything else in the castle, other than the likely date of the French invasion.

'The English navy is not so feeble that it could not prevent the French from landing, yet I fear that they *will* land. The king is not as popular as the queen. Many feel sympathy for her after the way that she has been treated by her husband.'

'Yes,' Isabella said. She could understand that all too easily.

'I am sorry,' Sir Peregrine said with a slightly anxious frown. 'Of course, her husband has treated you abominably as well.'

'No. I think it is not he,' she said with perfect truth. 'I think it was Despenser and the Bishop of Exeter. Those two alone are guilty of stealing everything I possessed. They made up a case against me, and Stapledon had my lands given to him as a direct result. The king believed the bishop when he said that my husbands and my son were all traitors. But they weren't.'

'Of course not,' Sir Peregrine said.

'And last year, I thought I might recover my lands. I had a case brought against the bishop, an assize of novel disseisin.'

'Yes?' Sir Peregrine gave her a blank look. 'I have not been involved in the law.'

'You are fortunate, sir. Well, if a man or woman is disseised, or dispossessed, they can seek the king's special instruction to recover their property. It means that a jury must be summoned and the case heard before the king's justices, to answer the question on seisin or disseisin. Restoration of the property or not. After all, possession is protected by the king in our country, so if something is unjustly taken, the king himself should seek to return it.'

Sir Peregrine nodded, although there was a faintly perturbed expression in his eyes. 'I see. So, you have had your lands returned?'

'Oh, no. The bishop managed to persuade the jury that the lands, *my* lands, had been granted to him by the king for life. So it was impossible for me to have them back. And then they said that they must revert to the king when Stapledon was dead. I swear, I could have killed him there and then, were he within my reach!'

'What then?' Sir Peregrine asked. He was intrigued, listening intently.

'I was told that the case couldn't continue *rege inconsulto*, and the papers were all sent to the king himself. God bless him, King Edward placed the matter before another jury, and they agreed that my dower lands were of the free tenement of my poor dead husband, before I married Henry, my second husband. They awarded me huge damages, too – over two hundred pounds.'

Sir Peregrine nodded, but lifted an enquiring eyebrow.

'No,' she smiled bitterly. 'I don't have them. Stapledon fought back, and even now I don't know what will happen.'

'What more can you do?'

'Fight on. There is nothing else for me. My lands are all I have left. My husbands are both dead, my son is exiled – what more can a woman do?'

'So you will continue your battle in the courts?'

'I will not give up my sole means of livelihood without fighting every step,' she said determinedly.

'I can quite understand.'

She doubted that. This knight banneret was a powerful man. He had the right to call on a number of knights and command them in battle, he was a king's official in his capacity as coroner, and she knew he had the ear of powerful men like Sir Hugh de Courtenay, the baron of Devon. And yet Sir Peregrine had never had to endure the sort of fight into which she had thrown herself so wholeheartedly. He had no means of appreciating the dangerous waters on which she floated. At any time a sudden squall could overwhelm her and sink her entirely. The bishop might grow irritable and seek to have her removed. She was under no illusions about her security in this dangerous land of England. Here she was nothing more than a poor nonentity. She had no one to fight for her. If she wanted her lands back, she must *take* them back. But being a woman, she could not take them by force. Guile and the law were her tools.

'You look sad, madam,' Sir Peregrine said.

'I miss my husbands. And my son.'

'I understand,' he repeated.

This time, she rounded on him, stung by his presumption. 'You *understand*? And how do you think you can understand, when I have lost so much? You, a noble knight, full of pride and authority. I have lost two husbands and my boy . . . No, you can have no idea how I feel!'

'I never managed to marry. I was in love three times, but each time . . .' Sir Peregrine's voice grew quieter, until he was whispering. 'They died. My last love, I had hoped to marry, but she too . . . And she left me her children, whom I love. I miss them when I am away from home for too long. This feels like a very long absence. It is more than four weeks since I last spoke with them. So you see, I do understand. I have lost my loves, and now my children too.'

'Why are you here, then? Why do you not return to them, to make sure that they are all right and that you have not lost their affection?'

'I need have no concern on that. If they hold any affection for me, I am fortunate – if they do not, well, no matter. I do what I can for them in memory of their mother. It is enough.'

'Why do you not go to them?'

'Duty. And a feeling that my place is here, at Tiverton, for now. I am an experienced man. I know that the next months will be difficult, and the idea that I should hide myself away and try to avoid the great matters which are set to threaten our little realm, that would feel like cowardice. When all is said and done, deeds and honour mean everything. To behave with integrity, that is what counts. And a knight who runs off to spend more time with his family, no matter how beloved they may be, he would be a poor fellow. I cannot do that.'

He spoke quietly but with passion, and in the stillness she had to catch a sob at the sight of this decent, kind man gazing out over the valley with such sad longing.

Furnshill

Baldwin broke his fast, and afterwards he sat in his hall and listened to three disputes between villeins on his lands. None was serious, nor did they require the wisdom of Solomon to resolve, but they were the kind of little bickerings that could fester for a while and then rise up and cause real trouble.

So Baldwin listened carefully to the men as they recounted their tales of petty insults and mindless foolishness, before settling their arguments in the best manner he could, trying always to balance his justice with the need for the King's Peace to be upheld.

He could not help but wonder whether such problems would rank so highly in a few weeks. Were the country to be invaded by the queen with, as had been alleged, a French force to support her, would these same stolid peasants stand in line side-by-side, or would they turn against each other, remembering a slight given months or years before? He had the strong impression that these men of his would throw aside any ill-will, but it was hard to be sure of anything in these uncertain times.

'You have fought, haven't you?' he asked one of the older men as he dismissed the last of the claims and the rest of the petitioners filed from his hall.

Saul of Cadbury squinted up at him. He was not so old as Baldwin, but his body had been shaped by his work. He had the bent back which labour in the fields had given him, while his hands were large and powerful. Fortunately, the expression in his eyes was always amiable. Baldwin had only ever seen him angry once, and that was when a small bull had butted him into a wall. Saul had bellowed, 'Ye auld bugger!' and punched the beast so hard that it retreated, blinking. It was only later that Saul realised the bull had broken his rib.

'I've had my share. I took my billhook up to the muster when the old king wanted men for Wales.'

'What of the men now, Saul? What's the mood among the villeins?' Baldwin asked. He beckoned Edgar and passed Saul a large mazer filled with wine.

Saul was pensive a moment. 'They'll fight for you, I reckon. If a man tried to overrun our lands, they'd all fight at your side, Sir Baldwin.'

'You know the rumours.'

'We all do,' Saul said, his weather-beaten face cracking into a smile. 'The queen was a good lady, but we follow you.'

Baldwin watched him leave a few moments later with a frown of concern.

'Sir? Do you want more wine?' Edgar said.

'No, no. I've had enough,' Baldwin said. He was not so abstemious as once he had been, but he had more work to do. 'What do you think?'

'Saul is right. The people will fight for their lord, and that is you. Although I would be happier were I at your side.'

'Petronilla wouldn't, though. And nor would I. I only wish Simon was . . .'

Edgar looked at him. 'You could try to see him.'

'I don't think so. He doesn't want to speak with me.'

'Sir Baldwin, you don't know that.'

'I hurt his feelings badly. I think I was right, but that will have little impact on him. If he had forgiven me, I would have heard from him by now. The fact that we've seen nothing of Simon, Meg nor Hugh is significant. And I do not know – perhaps I couldn't forgive him if he had endangered my Richalda's life. Even if afterwards he was proved to be correct, how would I respond? Maybe it is better that we do not meet again for a while.'

'You have so many friends you can afford to lose your best?' Edgar said pointedly, and left.

Baldwin was about to call after him, but then subsided back into his chair.

He knew all about losing friends; so many had died over the years – in Acre, in skirmishes against Moslems in Spain, and then in the terror of the inquisition against the Templars. If ever a man should have grown experienced to loss, it was Baldwin.

Yet in recent times he had been more fortunate. He had been able to settle here, in the little manor in Furnshill, and marry his lovely Jeanne who had given him Richalda and little Baldwin. In his professional life he had been fortunate, too, being granted the post of Keeper of the King's Peace, and regularly serving as a Justice of Gaol Delivery too. He was busy, and he should have felt fulfilled.

But he could not. Even now, he remembered the worries that had assailed him during the night.

Pictures of death and anguish seared his mind.

Chapter Seven

*Wednesday before Candlemas**

Exeter

The bishop rose from his chair as Sir Baldwin walked into the room. 'Please, Sir Baldwin, take your ease here near the fire. It is hardly inclement for the time of year, but I confess that as I grow older, the chill sits less happily on my bones. This year seems dreadfully cold.'

Baldwin smiled and took the proffered seat. 'I admit that the fire looks most welcoming,' he said.

The bishop motioned to John de Padington, who brought a large goblet and ladled mulled cider into it, passing it to Baldwin before moving away.

Baldwin took it, blowing on the surface. 'That smells divine.'

'Then let us hope that such refreshment will be available to us in the afterlife,' the bishop said with a thin smile.

Baldwin had ridden to Exeter to meet with the sheriff, a man whom he cordially despised, and had broken his journey homewards to see his old friend the bishop, but now he looked at the older man with a measuring intensity.

'I have heard it said,' Bishop Walter said, 'that you, Sir Baldwin, can perceive a man's thoughts by studying him. Your eyes are the most feared tools of justice available in the whole of Devon, my friend. Why do you observe me so closely?'

'My lord bishop, I meant no insult to you,' Baldwin said with

---

* 29 January 1326

an easy grin. 'You look anxious though, and I wondered whether you have received ill news.'

'Ill enough. A rector of mine has misbehaved, but I have had him held in the gaol, so that should resolve *that*.'

'Would that be the brother of the sheriff? That odious little prickle, Paul de Cockington?'

'Rarely has a man had a more suitable name. You have heard of him, of his offences? Yes – well, the purblind fool can stay in my gaol for a while, until I decide what sort of punishment to exact. Although I confess that other matters seem more pressing just now.'

The bishop closed his eyes a moment, rubbing at the bridge of his nose. Then he stood and walked over to the table. Selecting a parchment, he peered down at it, then, with a mutter of frustration, picked up his spectacles and opened them out at the hinge. The two lenses separated, and he held them over his nose as he traced the words on the page. Nodding, he brought the sheet to Baldwin and gave it to him. 'Look at that.'

The knight had been taught to read and write when he was a youth, but the writing on this sheet was difficult to decipher. He held it up, so that the light from the window caught it more fully, and narrowed his eyes to read. 'From the king, then. And it's an order . . .'

'Yes. To stop all communications leaving the country. All letters which could be of use to the queen are to be sought, discovered, and their source traced.'

Baldwin frowned at the sheet. 'But how could any man search all the goods leaving Exeter? Let alone Topsham, Exmouth, Dartmouth . . . Dear heaven, does the king propose to search all the bales of wool leaving the country? All the barrels being loaded at London? There are not the men in the land to do such a job. He would need half the peasants just to search.'

'It is impossible, yes,' the bishop sighed. He rubbed his nose again. 'But the instructions are clear enough. We must have men installed in all the ports or earn the king's disfavour.'

'Are you thinking of Simon?' Baldwin said.

'Who else?' the Bishop asked rhetorically. 'This is a warning to me because I am an adviser to the king – but when the warrants are signed and arrive here in the hands of the sheriff, I will have to find the best men for the job.'

'Simon has suffered enough in the king's service. Try to leave him from this, if you can, my lord.'

Stapledon eyed him, and then nodded. 'Very well. Unless I am specifically asked about him, I will not mention him at all.'

'Thank you,' Baldwin nodded. 'This writing – it is not like those of other commissions and warrants I have seen. The writing is exceedingly poor.'

'More and more are arriving by the week. I fear that the king's clerks are strained to write out so many in so short a space of time. And when they have time, the writing is little better. Mayhap it is concern.'

Baldwin looked at him sharply. It was plain enough that the bishop meant that the men of the king's household were fearful. 'You think an invasion could come soon?'

'I have heard men say that there is a fleet off Normandy. It could sail in less than a month. I do not say that I believe it – I have no corroboration – but it shows the thinking in London. And just because there are no ships in Normandy doesn't mean that a fleet is not to be gathered.'

Baldwin felt his heart chill. This was worse than he had feared. In all the time he had known the bishop, he had never seen him so downcast. Even the last year when they had escorted the young Duke of Aquitaine, Edward, the king's heir, to visit his mother, and death threats had been issued against the bishop, even then Stapledon had remained suave and calm. Now there was a distraction to his manner, as though the threat of invasion was a constant weight on his mind.

'Is there anything I can do to help?' Baldwin asked.

'There is only one thing we can all do,' Bishop Walter said, 'and that is prepare for war. Do you return home and see to your men, sir. You may have need of armed force before long. When the array is commanded, I am sure that the king will ask Sir Hugh de Courtenay to take charge with me of this part of the country, and I will wish to delegate the task to you, so that I myself can ride to the side of the king. It is where I should be,' he added quietly.

He could not meet Baldwin's eyes.

Church of the Holy Trinity, Teigh

Richard de Folville winced as he clambered upright. Kneeling to pray was painful since that bastard's whelp had come to visit. Ranulf Pestel, he called himself. Well Richard called him Rancid Pestilence. The shit! Richard's leg was sore, his chin ached where he had been knocked down, his belly was still bruised, and his back hurt where Ranulf's men had kicked him as he lay on the ground, angry that there was no evidence of his guilt.

'Little brother, you look as though you're worn out after a long night's swyving a bishop's slattern.'

Richard nearly jumped out of his skin. Turning, he saw his brother Eustace. 'What are you doing here, you fool!' he hissed. 'Don't you realise that half the country is looking for you? The men from Kirby Bellers have been here already. They half-kicked me to death, and if they find you, what will happen then?'

'Calm yourself, little brother. You worry too much. If God wanted us to be caught, He'd have sent us to hell the day we killed Belers. That bastard deserved to die, and God Himself knows it.'

'He may do, but Ranulf Pestel doesn't.'

'Who is he?'

'A man-at-arms who served Belers. He was here two days after, and he threatened me, trying to find out where you were.'

'And you didn't tell him?'

Richard looked at his brother with exasperation. 'I didn't know,' he said, walking with a hobble to the door. Peering out, he could see Eustace's horse, a few yards away, and two more men on horseback. 'What will you do?'

'Oh, I shall keep quiet, and when it's safer I—'

'Don't you understand yet? It's not just a local squabble! Belers was a king's official – a baron of the Treasury! His men, and Despenser's, are all after us now. There is nowhere to go in the king's realm. Brother, you will be found and killed!'

'And if that happens, so be it. Richard, you are the man who is supposed to be telling me of the wonderful life to come. What is the matter with you?'

'The matter with me is that you should run away. Go abroad, perhaps. To France, or Flanders. There are many nobles who would be happy to have your sword at their side. Don't stay here and get killed. It would be shameful.'

'It would be more shameful to run and hide,' his brother growled.

'Better to live than die,' Richard said. 'Find a ship to take you over the water. You can make a new life.'

'You are most keen to dispose of me, brother,' Eustace said.

'You haven't seen these men. They have no respect for God's House; they will kill even a priest for fun.'

'They were harsh with you, then?'

'Very. Look at this.' Richard lifted the hem of his robe.

The bruises stood out lividly against his pale flesh, and suddenly Eustace's face altered. 'They did this to you? What were their names?'

'I only know the leader – Ranulf Pestel. A big man, strong and cruel. I thought that he was going to kill me when he started, but they only knocked me down and kicked me a few times. It could have been much worse.'

'I will find him. And when I do, I'll castrate the son of a whore for hurting you, little brother.'

'Eustace! No! Look, he hurt me, yes – but it was only because he was frustrated in his search for you and the others. If you kill him too, you will have the full might of the king's men on your backside. You will never be able to escape them. Just leave me and fly the country. Please.'

'You know who Pestel is, don't you?' Eustace said grimly. 'He's the king's man, all right – one of those who lives and breathes his service to his master. If he's on my path, I had best kill him before he finds me.'

'How do you know him?'

'He was in the king's household at the same time as me. This makes it all more troublesome.'

'Why?'

'If he is showing an interest, then who else is involved? It could be the king, but who else would want Belers avenged?'

His tone was thoughtful as he and Richard left the church and walked towards the rector's modest home. Richard glanced at him. 'Is there anyone? His widow? A relative?'

'Or perhaps his colleague . . .'

'Who?'

'Sir Walter Stapledon. The present Treasurer wouldn't want to think that the sort of man who could kill Belers might still be walking abroad, would he?'

'No. It cannot be him.'

'Why not?'

'The bishop is not here. He must be in Exeter, or in London. Pestel was not sent here at short notice from either city – he was here already, arrived at the church too soon after we killed Belers. No, it can't be the bishop.'

'Perhaps you're right. But I know this, little brother: the man Stapledon is a danger to all. He will steal our money and say it's fair taxation; he'll hold an Eyre and say that we don't have this or that right; he'd sell our souls if he saw profit in it.'

'That may all be true, but it makes no difference. You must go. There is nothing more for you here, Eustace.'

They had reached his house, and now Richard entered and brought his brother a skin of wine. 'Take this – but leave now. Don't delay, and don't come here again, in Christ's name! There is only death for you here. Run abroad.'

Eustace gave a lopsided grin. 'Aye, you were ever the bold one, Richard, weren't you? Maybe I will, at that. There's nothing here for a man with balls. The country's falling apart. Perhaps France would be better. My thanks for the wine.'

'Godspeed, brother,' Richard said, and stood at his door to watch the older man stride out to his horse and mount.

Then, with his companions, he waved once, wheeled, and rode off.

Richard was sad to see him go, but glad at the same time. His brother was a potential embarrassment, after all. But then, he thought he caught sight of some smoke. Peering in that direction, he saw a rising cloud of dust. And it approached at speed, before moving off around the vill and hurtling off in pursuit of Eustace.

He couldn't see the faces of the men in that posse, but the rider in front, he saw, was a large man. Like Pestel.

Exeter

It was late afternoon when Baldwin finally walked from the bishop's palace and into the bustling High Street.

He had left Edgar at the market seeking two horses, and had hopes that his servant would have had some luck, but trying to make his way there was sorely trying in this crush. He had to push past many men and women, scowling ferociously all the while, until at last, when he was close to Carfoix, he was ready to bawl at anyone who came too close, let alone shoved him. And it was here that he saw Edith, Simon's daughter.

She was an easy woman to spot, even in a crowd like this. Tall, slim, fair, she was as beautiful as her mother Meg, but with the freshness of youth about her. Many men stopped to ogle her as she passed, and Baldwin grinned to himself.

'My lady!' he called. 'Mistress Edith? It's me, Baldwin.'

There was a young man with her. Not her husband, but an ill-favoured servant with a mean look about him. He glared at Baldwin and raised his staff threateningly as though preparing for a fight.

Edith put her hand out to him. 'Sir Baldwin is a friend,' she said quickly.

Baldwin was confident that, if the youth had tried to harm him, he would soon have learned the error of his ways. 'Sorry, friend,' Baldwin said. 'I know this lady well.'

'My master said—'

'Your lady is now telling you not to be so foolish,' Baldwin said mildly.

'How do I know who you are?'

Baldwin's smile became a little fixed. 'Friend, I am the Keeper of the King's Peace. If you do not wish to find yourself in gaol, you will now be silent while your mistress and I talk. Edith, you are looking radiant.'

'Thank you, Sir Baldwin. I am very well.'

'And your husband?'

'Oh, Peter is well enough. He is recovered, although—'

'Look, I don't—' The servant stepped forward, as though to push between Baldwin and Edith.

Baldwin said nothing, but as the fellow shoved his staff ahead of him, the knight grasped it in his left hand, yanked it forward, pulling the man off balance, and gripped his throat with his right. '*Do not interrupt me again*,' he said, then pushed the man away.

The servant withdrew, rubbing at his throat, leaving the staff in Baldwin's hands.

'I am glad to hear that,' Baldwin continued. Edith's husband had recently been arrested on false charges, probably so that the sheriff could try to extort money from his father. Corruption was rife in the kingdom at present. The poor boy, who was only in his early twenties, was utterly broken by the experience. Gaol was a bad enough place for those who knew that they deserved incarceration, but for a man who was entirely innocent, the experience could be devastating, especially when the victim had no idea what his crime was, nor who was accusing him. In cases like his, where the case itself was a fiction, there was not even the certainty of hiring a pleader to fight on a man's behalf. All was dependent on the cynicism and greed of the man sitting on the judge's seat.

'At least we did manage to rescue him from that,' Baldwin said. He glanced over at her. 'How are you?'

'I . . .' She licked her lips and gave a short shake of her head. 'I am well. But would you please pass on a message from me to

Father? Just tell him that I love him very much. And Mother. And I miss them . . . I miss them very much . . .'

'Edith, are you all right?' Baldwin asked. To his horror, she began to weep quietly, the tears streaming. He put out a hand to her, but she gently removed it.

'No, sir. Please, just tell them I love them. And now I must go. I am sorry, sir.'

The servant with her was chewing at his lip, his head darting forward and back as he tried to gauge Edith's mood, anxious that he might be failing in his task of protection, but fearful of upsetting a knight wearing a sword.

Baldwin said slowly, 'Edith, if you truly do not want to confide in me, that is your prerogative and I will understand, but please believe me when I say that if there is something which is upsetting you, I can help. Let me know if you wish for my aid.'

She made no comment, but simply nodded, and then, with her head bowed, she continued on her way.

The servant was about to scurry after her when Baldwin grabbed his arm, and the man squeaked as he was drawn round to face the knight.

'You will watch over her like the most faithful hound in the world. You will not allow anyone to harm her, understand? And if you learn that someone is hurting her, you will defend her. Because if you do not,' and Baldwin leaned closer now, 'I will come to you and your worst nightmares will not prepare you for my wrath, little man!'

The fellow nodded quickly, eyes wide like a terrified child, and then set off after Edith.

'Boy!' Baldwin called. He held out the staff to him. Shamefacedly, the servant returned, snatched the staff, and made off after his mistress at a canter.

'That is a most distressed lady, or I am a Moor,' Baldwin muttered, and set off to find Edgar.

Chapter Eight

Bishop's Palace

William Walle was in the yard when he saw the cart being pulled by a wandering horse straight towards the ditch beside the Canon's Street. With a short cry for help, he sprang over the hillocks of old graves, past two quarrelling workmen, and managed to catch the animal's bridle just as it was about to step into the mingled water and effluent.

The owner started to remonstrate with him, as though William had been attempting to steal the beast, but a short discussion with one of the Close's beadles soon had the man apologising and offering a contribution for the rebuilding works. There were advantages to being the nephew of the bishop, William thought, especially here on church lands where the law of the city held no force.

'Squire William! May I speak with you?'

William smiled on hearing John de Padington. 'Of course, steward. How may I serve you?'

'Squire, it is about our conversation – when you spoke of a message, and how anxious you were for your uncle?'

William instantly recalled their discussion. 'Aha! So there *is* something – I knew it.'

'It is a commonplace that men will always leap to assumptions,' John said severely.

'You are quite right, of course. I am a typical fellow, in that I will rashly form judgements based on careful observation,' William nodded with mock sincerity.

'You're a young fellow, certainly,' John said sourly, 'And like most young fellows, you are also mostly wrong.'

'Have a care, old man! You speak to a squire.'

'Aye. And were the man any other squire, I would have many a care, sure not for long!'

William laughed aloud at that. 'All right then, if I cannot scare you with the power of my position, then you may as well tell me what you can.'

Smiling in his turn, the steward leaned nearer to prevent others from listening. 'I overheard him talking with a friend of his.'

'Sir Baldwin, was it?'

'If you're going to be so clever and guess at my tale, you may tell me what I learned.'

'No, no. It would be discourteous to an old man. You carry on. But please, be swift. At your age a man is likely to forget *so* quickly.'

'I can remember my lessons from when I was not yet ten years old, I'll have you know!'

'But I wager you have trouble recalling your lunch last Wednesday? Eh?'

'Enough of this!' John said, for he couldn't. 'Do you want to know or not?'

William made a gracious bow and grinned. 'If you please.'

'The king has written to the bishop and told him that all produce from the country must be checked to see that there are no messages hidden within from the queen, nor messages to her that could give her succour. I think that the letter you saw was that instruction from King Edward.'

'You think he would hide that from me?' William said doubtfully.

'Well, it is a secret of great importance. He would not wish it to be bruited about.'

'And you think my uncle would fear that of me?' William said mildly.

John said nothing for a moment. William was a genial man, but suggesting that he might be considered untrustworthy was exceedingly insulting. 'Squire, do you know me well? Yes. And I know you. I have known you these past ten years or more, and I have seen you grow from a young man into the squire you now are. If you ask, is there any secret I would think I must withhold from you, I will state on the Bible that there is none. Further, I know that the bishop your uncle would trust you with his life. I know these things as plainly as I know that I stand here in the Cathedral Close. But there are times in a man's life, even in your uncle's, when things begin to get on top of him. I think that the whole affair of the queen's betrayal, and the king's evident displeasure with your uncle, have left him confused and upset.'

'The king's displeasure? But the king and Uncle Walter are good companions. I have seen them.'

'No longer. Don't forget that the king agonises over his son's welfare, which he had entrusted to your uncle. Bishop Walter took the king's son to France and was instructed to bring him home again – with the queen. In the event, your uncle left France in great haste, and left both queen and son behind. Now the bishop knows that he is not favoured. He has made his oath with the king, and would honour it: he is no coward, but even the bravest man can find himself confused when events conspire to baffle his best intentions.'

'What do you mean? What does Uncle want to do?'

'I think he wishes to return to the king to advise him. But while the king is so angry with him, he cannot. Instead he remains here, receiving messages instructing him to search every bale of cloth, every barrel of tar, to make certain that there is no secret correspondence.'

'And you think he was ashamed of the instruction?'

'No. I merely think he knows not how best to ingratiate himself into the king's company. All the while he sits here restlessly, wanting to help and not knowing how to, the king can listen only to those others in his household whose motives are not so honourable. And it makes the bishop fretful and concerned for the king and for the realm.'

'I see.'

'And so, William, you and I must use our best efforts to ensure that your uncle is given every opportunity to rest from his affairs.

We must protect him from these dark moods of melancholy that must afflict him.'

'I will do all I may to try to help him, then,' William said, and gave a little grunt of relief. 'You know, for the last week or so, I have been growing more and more alarmed. In my eyes, Uncle Walter has become ever more pale and weary-looking. It is a comfort to think that it is only the strain of these additional responsibilities.'

West Sandford

Simon stood outside his house and watched as his son ran about the pasture, trying to chase the last of the hens back to their little coop. There was a great deal of whooping and waving of arms, but the little lad, only approaching four years, was blithely unaware of his failure to bring the birds in. Simon chuckled to himself as his boy hurtled over the grass, stumbling and falling over and over, giggling gleefully as he did so, quickly collecting himself and chasing after the poultry again, only to tumble again.

'He'll muss up his tunic,' came a glum voice.

'Hugh, there are times when a lad has to be able to play,' Simon said.

'I know that. Used to play myself.'

Simon looked across at his servant. Hugh wore his customary expression of deep bitterness. 'You don't look as though you remember it,' he said.

'When I was growing up at Drewsteignton, I played.'

Simon grinned to himself. Hugh had been a shepherd for much of his youth, up on the steep hills about Drewsteignton, a quiet vill in the east of Dartmoor. It was an area Simon loved. The hills rose high, and a man could see across the broad Teign Valley from the heights, a good place to live, if exhausting to cross.

But Hugh had not been fortunate in recent years. He had been graced with a lovely woman who had agreed to give herself to him as wife some years before, and he had gone to live on a little plot of land towards Iddesleigh, but she had died with her son in a house fire. Afterwards Hugh had returned to Simon's service full-time. His face wore the scars of that loss even now. Simon too knew what it was to lose a loved one. He had lost his first son, also named Peter, to a foul malady – and that memory would never leave him. There was always that awareness, that little niggling fear, that this boy too might one day be taken away.

As his sister now had been.

He felt his face harden at the thought. His lovely child. It was one thing to give up a child to her lover when she decided to become married, but quite another to have her taken away like this.

'Still, it's not as good as playing merrils in a tavern,' Hugh muttered, hitching up the hempen rope which he had bound about his waist as a belt. He hawked and spat, before lurching off in the direction of the house again.

'Come on, Perkin,' Simon called. Peter was always 'Perkin' to him now.

The little boy heard, but deliberately ignored him. He continued running about with the chickens. And then a great dog appeared. It ambled over towards him with its head on one side, and for a short moment Simon was shocked, for it was massive, and his thoughts of the last minutes made him see only the brute's size and the potential danger it posed to Perkin. But then it lowered its enormous head and shook, before trotting to Perkin and nudging him, rubbing his head all over the boy, and Simon recognised it.

When Simon looked over to the east, along the road that led here from Sandford, he saw Baldwin sitting on his horse, his arm resting on his saddle's bow, smiling a little nervously, as though fearing to be rejected.

Bishop's Palace, Exeter

The last of the accounts dealt with, Bishop Walter leaned back in his seat and motioned to the bottler as the clerks packed up their inkhorns and reeds and bowed their way from his presence.

There were times when being a prelate involved such profound disappointment that he wished he could give it up. He was sure that his father, William, had never had such doubts. He and Mabel, Walter's mother, lived quiet, unassuming lives near Cookbury, in the Hundred of Black Torrington, where they achieved much, but remained unimportant and obscure. Not for them the glories of fame, of knighthood or mercantile success. William Stapledon was comfortably off, with enough income to bring up their seven children, four sons and three daughters, without straining his resources. And he lived to see those children achieve some influence.

Richard, the next eldest in the family, was already a noted knight. He had been returned as knight of the shire in parliaments from York to Westminster, and had worked with Walter to create the magnificent Stapledon Hall at Oxford University. Robert and Thomas had both gone into the Church and had good livings from their positions, while the daughters, Douce, Joan and Mabel, were all fortunate to marry well.

Yes. William Stapledon had deserved his long life and peaceful death. Walter only wished he might have the same good fortune.

There was a knock at his door, and John de Padington, his nephew, peered around. 'Your clerks said you wanted to speak with me?'

'Yes. Can you go and see the gaoler and fetch to me the rector he is holding? It is time I spoke with the God-cursed idiot about his kidnap and rape. He should be pliant enough by now, but ask the gaoler to walk here with you.'

When the steward had gone, Walter looked down at his hands and sighed. Yes, he had done his best all through his life. No one could deny that he was one of the most hardworking diocesans Exeter had ever seen; in truth, he was notable amongst bishops throughout the realm. It was likely that no other bishop in Devon and Cornwall had managed to visit all the parishes, meet with all the priests, nuns and monks, and assess each and every one in such a large diocese.

He had not been satisfied with merely visiting, either. Only too aware of the huge benefits which had accrued to him as a result of his own education, and because he had seen too many rural priests who were more or less incapable of their duties, too old, too deaf, too steeped in wine, to be able to provide properly for the cure of the souls in their parishes, he was dedicated to improving the quality of all the men of the cloth in his diocese. For that he sedulously studied all the young boys he met in houses up and down his area. Those who showed a precocious intelligence, he would discuss with their parents, and the ones who appeared most promising, he would bring back to Exeter or Ashburton, where he had created a small school, and see them properly educated. With luck, some of them would later make their way up to Oxford, to study at the college he had founded.

In the cathedral, he would be remembered as a patron. He had provided much of the money to ensure that the works continued to the glory of God, even if he would never himself see the finished result. That was a certainty – at the present rate of progress, it could not be completed until halfway through the century at the earliest. Although Walter II was already five-and-sixty, but felt as young as a man in his fortieth year, he knew that it was too much to hope that God would allow him to remain here for another four-and-twenty years. If He did, Walter would no doubt be a drooling, feeble-minded cretin like poor Father Joshua, who could do little more than swallow now when a spoon was held to his mouth.

The bishop was enormously fond of Joshua. When Walter had first arrived here in Exeter and became a canon, it was Father Joshua who had helped introduce him to all the other canons. The rude, the hypocritical, the naive and fawning – each had been described to him beforehand, and Joshua had been a kindly and humorous influence on him from that day onward. It was Joshua who had helped Walter when the Dominicans tried to prevent him from being installed as bishop, Joshua who had assisted with the founding of the school at Ashburton, Joshua who . . . It was hard to think of any facet of his life in recent years which had *not* been aided by Joshua. The old man had been a friend and ally for longer than the bishop could remember, and the idea that he was now so befuddled and feeble was dreadful. The idea of continuing in his post without the support of the old man was appalling.

But continue he would. Bishop Walter was proud of his achievements as a bishop. And the work he had done for the king, of course.

That had all begun a long while ago now. He had been one of the many bishops who had worked to try to maintain the peace when the king first formed an unsuitable relationship, back in the early days of his reign, with that incomparable fool Piers Gaveston. The man was so acquisitive, it was a miracle that the king had a realm of any size left. Gaveston was captured and executed, and afterwards the kingdom fell into a sort of calm. Not true peace, though: it was a period of stagnation and fear, waiting for the next buffets of fate. And within a short space, they had struck.

'Bishop? My lord?'

The words cut into his thoughts and Stapledon turned quickly to the door, startled. 'John?' It was the bane of his life, this accursed feeble eyesight he had developed. At first he had merely been unable to read documents even when quite close, which was why he had invested in the spectacles – but now even objects a short distance away were nearly impossible to discern.

'Yes, it is me, my lord. I fear that there is ill news. The prisoner, the rector, has gone. And so has the gaoler.'

'What do you mean, "gone"?' the bishop asked testily.

'One of the servants said that he saw them both walking up out of the Close days ago. The gaoler hasn't been seen since, and no one seems to know where he could have gone.'

The bishop sighed heavily. 'So that is it, then. The rector was taken to his brother, I suppose, and that means he will have been sent far away. He would scarcely take the risk that I might force my way into the castle and remove him.'

'I fear so, my lord.'

'Fetch Alured de Gydie to me. And send a message to the sheriff, demanding to know the whereabouts of his brother, on his oath. I will not be lied to.'

His steward hurried away, the door slamming behind him, and the bishop returned to his contemplation of the recent past.

It was not a pleasant review.

Church of the Holy Trinity, Teigh

As soon as he had seen the clouds of dust disappearing towards the horizon, Richard de Folville had hurried back into the house. In the corner he had a large chest, and he threw it open, pulling aside the vestments and clothing within before finding the scarred leather baldric. Drawing it over his head and shoulders, gripping the sword's sheath in his left hand, he ran from the cottage.

There was a low, woven fence to mark the extent of his garden, and he took this at a gallop, leaping over it and pelting on up the road in the wake of his brother and the men from Kirby Bellers. On and on he ran, his lungs beginning to ache as he went, ducking occasional twigs, avoiding the worst of the mud and ruts, but when he had run only a little more than a mile, there was nothing more in him. His legs burned with the unaccustomed exercise, and his lungs were choked. He had to stop and bend double, facing the ground, resting his hands on his thighs.

This was madness! How could he ever have hoped to catch men on horseback. He would have to forget this and return. Perhaps there would be news later. He only prayed that it would not be news that his brother was dead.

Dear God in heaven, the thought that his beloved elder brother could be captured, or even killed, was too appalling for words!

All Richard's life, Eustace had been there to look after him. Admittedly, it was Eustace who had first beaten him, who had given him his first bloody nose, who had tripped him and sent him flying into a rock, which had cracked open Richard's head; but like so many older brothers, he saw Richard as his own private property when it came to bullying or beating. If any others tried to hurt Richard, they soon learned to regret their presumption.

Eustace was not his only brother, of course. When their father, John de Folville, Lord of Ashby-Folville, Leicestershire and of

Teigh in Rutland, died sixteen years ago, their brother John took the estates. Even now he was a Commissioner of Array for the King. There were benefits to his positions, for it was he who had given Richard this church for his living.

Of the others, Laurence, Robert, Thomas and Walter, there was little else for them to do to make their living, other than turn to serving other lords. But then they found that their estates and livelihoods were under threat. It was alleged that they were all implicated in the Lords Marcher wars against Despenser. And if a man was prepared to set his face against the Despenser, he was thought to be rebelling against the king himself. Word went out: all the de Folvilles were to be found and captured. There were only two who were safe. Richard, and John, the present Lord of Ashby Folville.

Richard muttered a swift curse, then set off again, running at a more steady pace, making this time for his brother John's manor.

Chapter Nine

West Sandford

Simon walked to the fire, waving his guest to the seat at the side where he could get warm, but he didn't sit down himself. He was filled with a strange feeling of trepidation – a premonition that this meeting would bring a crisis to his life.

It was clear that Baldwin was aware of the tension between them. Only a short while ago the two had separated with their friendship shattered. Simon had placed his trust in Baldwin, and felt that it had been flung back into his face. Baldwin had, so he believed, placed Edith's life in danger.

But he missed Baldwin's companionship.

'Simon, I—'

'It is good to see you again,' Simon interrupted. He found himself moving towards the door. 'Let me fetch some wine – I will get it. No, I'll have Hugh fetch it, the lazy bastard – about time he did something. And then some meats for you. That would be good.'

He felt as though action and movement were needed to avert disaster. If he continued talking, if he kept moving, he could block the terrible danger that he could see in Baldwin's eyes.

'Please, Simon, old friend . . . just come here and sit for a moment. I want no wine or water, only a moment's companionship. Please.'

Simon felt as though there was a rending in his belly as he tore himself away from the doorway and walked back to the fire. 'If this is about—'

'Simon, it's Edith. I saw her today in Exeter.'

'How is she?' Simon demanded urgently.

'She asked me to tell you that she loves you, Simon. And misses you. She was very sad.'

'Yes. Yes, I expect she is,' Simon mumbled, and then he found that the room seemed to shift, closer to him, and then away again, as though he was sitting upon a cart, and being pushed and then pulled. And suddenly he felt Baldwin's hand on his shoulder, gripping him firmly, helping him to a stool, and then there was a mazer filled with fragrant wine, and a hubbub of voices all around.

'Sit back, Simon. Wait until you feel better again. You nearly toppled, old friend,' Baldwin was saying, but Simon was only aware of the cool hands on his forehead, the concerned look in his wife's eyes as she peered down at him.

'Are you all right? Baldwin called me in, and you looked as though you were suffering from a fever. You feel very warm still.'

'I am fine, Meg. Really, I'm fine,' he said, and took her hand, kissing it. 'Baldwin has a message for us from Edith.'

'She looked well?' Margaret asked. She left her hand in Simon's, standing resolutely at his side.

Her face gave away none of her pain, Baldwin thought. She had always struck him as a most courtly lady, for all that she was a farmer's daughter from some obscure vill in Devon. Yet no matter what her upbringing, there was a natural elegance to her. Tall, slim, fair, with a face that was still beautiful, she fixed her eyes upon Baldwin as though challenging him.

'Margaret, Edith bade me to say that she misses you both, and that she loves you. I had only a moment with her in the street in Exeter, or I would have spoken with her longer, but she was insistent that I should tell you that.'

He glanced from one to the other. Margaret had tears in her eyes as she gripped her husband's hand and looked down at him. She wiped her face with a gesture of impatience.

'There! I knew she wouldn't be happy to be away from us.'

Simon shook his head. 'Of course she wouldn't. She is still our daughter.'

Baldwin looked away. 'Well, I have delivered my message, so I should—'

'Baldwin, you will not think of leaving us! It is late, and the roads are not so safe as once they were,' Margaret said. 'You must remain here for the night.'

'I am sure that you would prefer to be alone to think of your daughter,' he said, his eyes on Simon.

'I wouldn't hear of it,' Margaret pressed him. '*We* wouldn't, would we, Simon?'

Simon hesitated momentarily, but then shook his head. 'No, old friend. No, you must stay. Please.'

At that word, and the emotion in it, Baldwin felt reluctant to trust his own voice. He simply nodded.

'You see,' Simon went on, 'Edith's father-in-law will not permit her to have any communication with us.' He paused again, and when he continued, his voice broke. 'He won't let her speak to her own parents.'

Ashby Folville

The great manor house was close by the church, and as Richard dropped from the cart, he stood for a moment staring at the home where he had spent his childhood before being sent to the church.

It had taken him all afternoon to walk five leagues. When he had been younger, it would have been a mere idle wander, but today he felt exhausted, due to his bruised and battered body. Perhaps it was also the fact of not knowing whether his brothers were in danger or not. He couldn't tell. But he did know that someone might even now be preparing to arrest him and hold him for the justices, whenever they might deign to come, and this was enough to make his neck feel a creeping horror.

No, this was ridiculous! Setting his shoulders, he marched towards the house. The chances of anyone coming to capture him here were remote in the extreme. It was foolish to have come here at all. Five leagues – fifteen miles, thereabouts – and he was going to have to turn his face back to the east and return first thing in the morning.

The hall was a marvellous old construction, with solid oak supporting the heavy roof. A fire in the middle of the chamber was fitfully sparking, four enormous logs lying parallel on a bed of glowing ash, just as it had always been when he was a boy.

John was standing at the fireside, sipping thoughtfully from a goblet. He was silent as Richard entered and gave him greeting, but motioned towards a large pewter jug and a second goblet. As Richard picked it up, he marvelled at the weight.

'Do not think it, brother,' he heard John say.

'Think what?'

John looked up. In the dim room his eyes looked entirely black. 'Do not think to rob me as well. You can drink from my goblets, but don't try to steal one.'

'I am a man of God, brother!'

'And Roger Belers was a saint. Yes.'

Richard felt a frown pass over his face. 'What's the matter with you? I came here to let you know that—'

'You and our brothers, together with those incomparable arses the la Zouches – I assume it was Ralph and Ivo? I thought so – chose to lay in wait for the baron of the Treasury and kill him, along with all his men. Marvellous. So with one swift blow, you have set our family against the Despenser, the Treasurer, and the king. They will not rest until you and the others have all had your heads taken off.'

'Brother, Eustace was at my church today, and a posse went after him, I think.'

'And you wish me to fly to his aid? To give up all my property and position to help a brother who has turned murderer? He didn't even have the courage to stand before his enemy in fair combat, but captured the poor devil and slew him like a bullock. You were there. It's true, isn't it?'

'No, it's not true. It was a hard battle, and we happened to win. But I tell you this: Belers is better dead. He would have destroyed you as well as us. You are one of us, John. Do you really think he would steal our lives, and leave you alone? Don't be naïve!'

John studied him carefully over the top of his goblet as though seeing him for the very first time. 'You believe that? I was safe before this. Now I am considered guilty, if only by association. Which is why you and the others are not welcome here. I will not put my wife and children at risk just because of your selfishness.'

'What does that mean?'

'It means, dear brother, that if I find you again on the roadside, or if I hear any evidence which connects you to the murder of Belers, I will come and attach you myself. I will accuse you, and I will see you hang for the murder. So if you have a brain in your head, copy your brothers and fly.'

'You would really see me slain?'

'Gladly, if it would protect my wife and children,' John said. He kept to the far side of the fire, and as Richard tried to circumnavigate the large firepit, his brother moved to keep the flames between them. 'No, Richard. Come no closer. You have to flee. The others are going too. Ivo and Ralph la Zouche are already in France, I think. It is possible that they will join with the queen over there. Who knows, but that you may return with her? Perhaps there will be pardons issued when the king sees her again. But for now, you must ride. Take the grey from my stable. He is a resilient beast, and should take you to the coast without much trouble.'

'Thank you, John,' Richard said stiffly. He drained his goblet and held it up for a moment. Then, with a contemptuous grimace, he tossed it to his brother, turned and stormed out.

In the room, his brother lifted the goblet, which he had caught, and prayed, 'Godspeed, little brother. God speed your feet and bring you safe to France.'

And then he fell into his chair and wept silently for his brothers.

West Sandford

Simon and Baldwin had eaten together many times, and in many different places, but few meals had been as sombre as this one.

Margaret tried to lighten the atmosphere by bringing in wine which she had mulled, and to which she had added burned wine to warm their spirits, but even that appeared to serve little purpose. She had also gone to some lengths to ensure that the meal was good, having cooked her husband's favourite pies with the last pieces of some bacon and beef with a thick gravy, and a stew of oxtail thickened with barley, both of which he usually adored, but today even they would scarcely tease his appetite.

It was Baldwin who broached the subject again after their meal. 'Did you manage to speak with her at all after this order from Edith's father-in-law? How was the message relayed to you?'

Margaret sighed. 'A letter from her husband, and signed by her. You can hardly blame her. Poor Peter went through hell when he was arrested like that. And there was the suggestion that men were attacking him in order to get at Simon.'

'I think it was much more to do with the avarice of the new sheriff,' Baldwin said.

'Be that as it may,' Simon said, 'Charles was convinced that his son was captured and gaoled just in order to hurt me. So naturally, to protect him, he wished to ensure that all contact between Edith and me was stopped. He gave her an ultimatum. She could remain with her husband, or she could remain with her parents. One or the other – not both. That was soon after we took her home again – about the Feast of Saint Martin*. Since then, we've heard nothing from her.'

'She could hardly leave her husband. She has a duty to him,' Margaret said sorrowfully.

'Of course,' Baldwin agreed, but he felt the anger boiling in his belly. Forcing a young girl to choose between her husband and the parents she adored was cruel beyond belief. Wayward, in her youth Edith had been one of those young women who fall in love with the latest man to pass her horizon. There had been knights and squires and two peasants to his certain memory, each of whom had given Simon and Margaret varying degrees of

* 11 November

anguish. Edith's relationship with her parents had eased and matured in the last year, and to remove her from them just as they began to appreciate each other as friends rather than as parents and children, seemed especially cruel.

There was a cry from the room next door, where Simon and Margaret had their solar.

'Excuse me,' Margaret said quickly, rising. 'It is Perkin. Help yourselves to more food.'

Baldwin nodded and was about to reach for the jug of wine, when a hand reached down and grabbed it from him. He looked up into the scowling face and had to hide a smile.

' 'Tis my job tonight,' Hugh said, and poured a mazerful for him, leaning over the table to top up Simon's. 'Can't have guests filling their own cups. Might take too much.'

Baldwin gave a short chuckle. He had never been a heavy drinker, preferring to sip a little fruit juice or water. Too often when a boy had he woken with a heavy head after too much wine or ale, and he had eschewed such gluttony when he joined the Templars, from fear that it might reduce his effectiveness as a knight. 'Glad to see that you persevere in protecting your master's interests, Hugh.'

Hugh said nothing, but stood glowering, as though ready to leap to the defence of Simon's stock of wine.

'Hugh is well enough,' Simon said, taking a mouthful of wine. He kept his head down, rarely meeting Baldwin's eyes. 'And I am very grateful he came back. I need someone to keep an eye on Perkin. He's into everything.'

'As a boy should be,' Baldwin said.

'It was why I didn't want him in Dartmouth, you remember?' Simon said. 'I feared he'd jump on board a ship and disappear for the next twenty years. Just as I thought Edith . . .'

Simon grimaced as he drew to a halt.

'Have you heard from the bishop?' Baldwin asked. 'He says that the king is demanding that officials should be installed at every port to prevent messages that could aid the queen and Mortimer from being sent.'

'Oh, aye? And do they have any idea how many barrels and sacks are delivered into the holds of ships each day at each port? Or how many sailors there are who could carry a message from a man in a tavern? Or how many sympathisers there are who would be delighted to memorise a message and take that instead? Despenser must have shit in his brain if he thinks this will work,' Simon growled.

'It was the king who ordered it,' Baldwin reminded him gently.

'And we know who advises him,' his friend countered.

'There is another thing, Simon. I am very worried.'

'About what?'

Baldwin was silent as he gathered his thoughts. Then, 'Old friend, I have no secrets from you. We both know that the queen was popular down here. She had so many manors, she had the rights to mining – much of Devon and Cornwall have been her allies. And so, if she decides to land in England again, with a small force, where would be most logical? And if she were to land on our coast, who can say which path her men would take? I do know that I do not wish for my wife or children to be in that path.'

'You think it will come to that?'

Baldwin made no acknowledgement. 'When she lands, where should I take Jeanne and our children? The manor will be safe no longer, and I do not have enough men to defend it. Were I to have a strong wall, I still wouldn't have enough men. Simon, this poor kingdom of ours is falling into decay. There is little we can do to protect it, but I would do all I could. Otherwise, we shall be conquered again, and the French shall rule all England.'

They were quiet for a moment. From the other room came the sounds of Perkin wailing, Margaret's calm voice soothing him. Both drained their drinks, and Hugh refilled them.

'Perkin sometimes has these dreams,' Simon said by way of explanation. 'Edith used to go to him in the night. Half the time I didn't even hear him, she was so quick. Almost as though she could tell when he was about to cry.'

'She's a good girl,' Hugh muttered. 'Always looked after him. Even when you were gone.'

'I didn't want the job in Dartmouth,' Simon said.

'You'd have to be mazed to want to live in a place like that,' Hugh grunted.

'There are some who enjoy the bustle,' Baldwin pointed out.

'There's some as like the warmth of a fire, till they get pushed into it,' Hugh said.

'Hugh, have you ever been to Dartmouth?' Baldwin wondered.

'No. Too far for me,' he responded with an expression of distaste.

'I don't suppose you've even been to Exeter too often, have you?' Baldwin said, and then his face cleared and he sat staring at the wall over Simon's shoulder for a little while.

'What is it, Baldwin?' Simon asked.

'Edith knows Hugh, and I suppose her husband does, too. But probably her maidservant doesn't.'

Simon glanced up at Hugh, studying him with a speculative eye. 'Nope. Don't think she would. Have you met Jane, Hugh?'

'No.'

'What of her husband though?' Baldwin said.

'I know him well enough.'

'No matter,' Baldwin said, and smiled at Simon. 'I think I know how you can keep in touch with Edith, old friend.'

Chapter Ten

*Thursday before Candlemas**

Rockbourne, Hampshire

It was a beautiful, clear day. For once the fog had lifted, and as John Biset pulled a tunic over his head and marched down the stairs from his solar, tugging his sleeves straight and scratching under an armpit where a particularly dedicated flea had chewed his soft flesh into a mass of reddened lumps, he felt a curious contentment. He still had the manor, and, with good fortune, he would soon be reimbursed for the efforts he had been forced to take to recover his due inheritance.

Bishop Walter of Exeter had tried to prevent him getting his money. That old sodomite had hankered after the wardship of Philip Maubank's grandson, but even though he'd tried to withold the inquest results, John Biset had fought him all through the king's courts until he had proved his rights. And now, soon, the money would be coming back to him.

He left by the rear door, crossing the cobbled yard where his horse stood patiently waiting for him, a large black stallion with a white star on the forehead and a splash of grey on the left shoulder. This great brute was the very last of his father's old mounts, and although he had once been trained as a fighter, he was so venerable now that he showed not the slightest interest in kicking or biting, although he would sometimes have a little spark of resentment against his rider and try to buck. However, it

---

* 30 January 1326

was easy to see when he was about to do so, for both ears would go back, and John, knowing that sign, would immediately clench his thighs about the beast's chest and hold himself on.

There was something deeply satisfying in knowing that he had secured the future of the place. Sir Hugh le Despenser had wanted this manor from him. When John refused to give up the wardship that was his own inheritance, Despenser and Bishop Walter Stapledon had concealed his age. From that moment it had been a fight. Despenser wanted the manor, Stapledon wanted the wardship for himself, and in the end, the two bastards had asked for double the value of the wardship. Not in return for anything – they just demanded it without discussion.

John Biset was not the sort of man to bow to another's demands. He came from stock every bit as good as Despenser's or Stapledon's. Neither of *them* was a magnate at birth. He had no idea what sort of family Stapledon came from, but he would shrewdly guess that the proud bishop was in fact little better than a mere freeman when he was born. As for Despenser, he was the son of a knight – but that was the most that could be said for *him*.

He would not knuckle under to a pair of felons like them.

So he had fought. He acquired the best legal advice he could afford; he paid pleaders and clerks; he left no stones unturned in his search for influential men at court who could help his case, and he had petitioned the king to be reimbursed for the damages done to him. That matter should soon be decided, and when it was, he would celebrate with a feast for his friends and neighbours in the area. It would be a great day.

He set off gently, warming the brute's blood with a soft jogging pace, before thrashing it on the rump and galloping for a good three miles westwards. This area was perfect for a ride. Clear of trees for the most part, and flat, a man could see a long way. And in these unsettled times, it was necessary. There were too many felons who would seek to break a man's head and empty his purse if they could, and John Biset was not foolish enough to put his life in danger for no reason. He preferred to take no chances and to go where he was safe.

The way was empty today. He carried on past Tidpit before taking the old path north, gradually making a full circuit of the lands. Here he went more slowly, feeling the comforting rock and sway of the horse beneath him. There were more trees about here, and he had to duck every so often to avoid branches, and then he was in a shady lane, with thin hedges at either side, now that all the leaves were fallen.

It was when he was halfway along this track that he saw a man up ahead, walking towards him. Just a scruffy-looking fellow in a tan cloak with a flash of russet tunic beneath, hooded against the cold.

There was nothing ostensibly to cause alarm, but John had a heightened sense of awareness after the last few months. Despenser was known to have killed men for thwarting him, and John had no illusions about his own position now: he stood in Despenser's way. The only thing that saved him, so he felt, was the sheer panic which was exhibited by all those in the king's household because of the queen's threatened invasion. That was enough to keep them all in a state of permanent abstraction.

He caught a glimpse of something. No, two things. First there was a sparkle from over to his left, such as a piece of metal might make as it caught the low sun. And then there was the man on the roadway, who had looked up – very briefly, very swiftly – like a hunter checking the distance to his quarry.

John Biset was no coward, but neither was he a fool. The sparkle from the other side of the hedge might have been a drop of water catching the sun, but it might have been the catch on a crossbow. And he had too much respect for crossbows to want to risk it.

He reined in. The man ahead of him made no movement to show that he had registered John's reluctance and continued on his trudging way.

But that itself was wrong. A man seeing a knight on horseback would be wary in case this was one of those knights whose temper was fiery, and who might well decide to spring upon a traveller to demand tolls, or merely to sweep off his head with a sword for enjoyment. The realm had lost all law and order in the months since the queen's departure for France last year.

Then he saw it. The man had moved his arm beneath his cloak, and now had firm grip of a sword.

It was enough: he jabbed his spurs into the horse's flanks, wheeled, and galloped up the road again. As he went, he heard the low thrumming as the crossbow's quarrel shot past his ear, and then he could rein in, turn again and ride back. It took time for a man to reload his bow, and John knew how fast he could ride on this old brute.

The man was still in the road, and had swept out his blade now – a short, riding sword, and stood resolutely blocking the way. Only a professional would try that, John knew. But he was not intending to attack the fellow directly. Instead, he picked the part of the hedge which seemed thinnest, and at the last moment forced his horse through it. There was a scraping at his hosen, a crackle and hiss as the blackthorn and holly tore at his legs and the horse's breast, and then they were through. In front of him, a man suddenly found himself confronted by a furious knight on a large black destrier. He was trying to span his bow with hooks fitted to his belt, but the sudden eruption of the knight from the hedge made his foot slip from the crossbow's stirrup, and the contraption sprang upwards, the stock striking him in the breast. He gave a cry, just before John's sword stabbed into the side of his neck.

The forward momentum of his horse drew the blade swiftly along the side of his neck. It clove through the soft muscles, reached the spine, and the sharp metal snagged for an instant, and then sawed through that too. As he rode on, there was a gout of blood, and the head rolled away.

John span in his saddle and saw the other felon in the gap he had made in the hedge, and then the man was off, haring along the lane like a rabbit pursued by a hound. John trotted over to the still-twitching body by the crossbow, and stared down.

The fellow was only a youth. He had scarcely enough fluff on his chin to call it a beard, and his hands and his fingers were so clean, it looked as though he might have scraped all dirt from them with a knife. And they were not hardened like most, he saw. Any peasant would have horny hands by the age of ten, but not this.

He dropped from his mount and looked through the boy's belongings, such as they were. A small crucifix at his throat had slid from the stump and now lay in the pool of blood. At his belt was a rosary, while in his purse there were a few pennies and a small lump of bread. And also, intriguingly, a piece of parchment with some scrawled writing on it.

Without thinking, John stuffed it inside his shirt as he remounted, casting about for any sign of the other man, but his delay had given the fellow a chance to run out of sight, or at the least to conceal himself.

Swearing to himself, John Biset urged his horse on, and rode at a fast pace all the way back to his manor.

Teigh

The cottage felt cold this morning as Richard de Folville rolled from his low palliasse and clambered to his feet. His legs felt stiff after his unaccustomed wanderings the day before, and the saddle of the horse he had taken from his brother had made his arse sore.

It was ridiculous that he might be forced to leave just because of the Belers matter, but there was no doubting his brother's sincerity. The men who had sought the killers of Belers had found his brother, and now they might well come searching for him as well. And no matter what happened, John would do nothing to protect him or Eustace, or any of the other members of that gang. It was shameful.

To think that all this could have been brought upon them by the advisers to the king. Both Despenser and Stapledon would rue the day they first chose to plot against him. 'Damn you both to hell for what you've done to my family,' he said with vicious emphasis.

The horse was still outside. Taking a small leather satchel, he filled it with the last of his bread and some meats, and threw it over his shoulder. Then he stopped and gazed about him, as though this was the last time he would ever see his room again. It was perilous to try to cross the sea. Many people died on the waves each year, as he knew. But it was as dangerous for him merely to remain here in Teigh. If the men who sought him truly were from Despenser and Bishop Walter Stapledon, his life was worth little, and even if he managed to put a hundred miles between him and the church here, he would still be a hunted man.

No, he would have to ride away, head for France, and hope that he might escape the posse.

West Sandford

When he woke, Simon yawned and stretched, and Margaret smiled to see his face.

'This looks to me as though, for the first time in many months, you have truly slept well,' she said.

'No, wench. I was awake half the night,' he said, stretching again with a grunt of pleasure.

'Oho, is that true? And there was me thinking that you didn't wake me last night because you were contented for once. And asleep.'

'I couldn't sleep. You were snoring too much,' he said, and then protested as she punched and kicked at him unmercifully. 'Hoi! Stop that, woman, you'll break me!'

'Then apologise.'

'For what?'

'Saying I snore, husband. Because unless you do, I may have to beat you.'

'You can't beat me!'

'I can if you're so sleepy,' she said.

'Woman, stop that or . . .'

'Or what, darling husband?' she asked sweetly, and prodded his belly. She knew it tickled him, and expected a response, but the swiftness of his reaction surprised her.

He grabbed her wrists, and pushed, rolling himself on top of her. And then, while she smiled up at him, he slowly grinned back. She saw his gaze float over her body, and wriggled her hips a little. He lifted his torso, so she could move her legs – and then he was between them, his weight on her pelvis.

Margaret could feel the blood in her veins, and it seemed to match the beat of his heart. She could feel him so near, it was a subtle torture. She wanted to prolong it, and she wanted it to end.

Which it soon did.

'Father! Mummy!'

And Perkin ran in and jumped on his parents.

Bishop's Palace, Exeter

It was with a frown that William Walle wandered the Cathedral Close that morning.

'Squire William, I wish you a good morning,' John de Padington called as soon as he saw the younger man. 'Are you well?'

'In short, no. My uncle has all the appearance of a man in great discomfort,' William said, after a little display of hesitation.

'Squire William, I hope I am in your trust? I would hate to believe that you mistrusted even me?'

'No, my friend. I trust you entirely. And yet I cannot help but wonder whether my uncle is himself suffering from a malady, perhaps? He has been astonishingly short with me this morning. I merely enquired about the sheriff and the timing of the next sheriff's courts, and I thought that my head would be swept from my shoulders in an instant!'

John eyed him sympathetically. 'I will have to be frank: you've scratched at a bad scab. He only learned last evening that the rector, the sheriff's brother, had made an escape.' He told the surprised squire about Paul de Cockington and his many offences. 'So with your mention of the sheriff, it is a miracle he did not have you thrust in gaol in place of the man's brother.'

'Where is this brother now?'

'God alone will know that. If I were to guess, I should think he will be in Ireland or in France. Or on his way, more likely. He was never a man to overstretch himself. It would be too tiring.'

'Well, that is a relief, anyway,' William said. 'I thought it was something I myself had done to offend him.'

'I wouldn't worry yourself about that,' John said.

William parted from the steward and made his way over the Close to the palace itself, and climbed the small spiral staircase to the bishop's chamber.

This smaller room was comfortable and warm, compared with the great hall, which was a chilly, unwelcoming place unless the fire had been lit and kept well fed for more than a day. The bishop, a frugal man in his own household, begrudged the waste of so much unnecessary fuel, and when he was here, he preferred generally to spend his time up in his private chamber, with a good fire in the fireplace. William preferred it simply because the smoke left via the chimney, whereas in the great hall it relied on the wooden shingles in the roof for egress.

The bishop was still in the chapter meeting, William assumed. He would often go to discuss matters with the dean and chapter when he was here in Exeter, and William set about preparing the room for the bishop's return.

Although the fire was smouldering nicely, there was still a coolness in the air, so he brought a blanket to the chair, making the cushions soft by thumping them, and resetting them. He ensured that the wine jug was full – naturally John had seen to that already – and brought inks and parchments to the table nearby. Bishop Walter's spectacles he set close to hand, along with the bishop's constant companion – a book of the thoughts of St Thomas Aquinas. When the bishop was troubled, he knew that this book would always soothe him.

It was while he was reaching across the table for a spare group of parchments, that William saw the small leather wallet.

Pale cream in colour, it was made of a good quality goatskin, from the feel of it. Or perhaps pigskin, like a good glove. Either way, it had suffered. The leather was stained on one side, and roughened, as though it had been left to soak up filth from the road. It was not the sort of object which the bishop would usually keep. And this was on his table, as though he felt the need to keep it close at hand.

William was handling it without conscious thought. He was no breaker of confidences, nor was he by nature nosy; he merely happened upon the thing, and had a mind enquiring enough to open it without consideration.

Inside was a small piece of parchment, rolled tightly. He withdrew it, and recognised it from the other evening. This was the piece he had told John of. He opened it.

'William, why did you do that?' Bishop Walter sighed as he caught sight of his squire. 'Did you read it all?'

William turned to him, his face blanched with horror. 'Uncle, why didn't you tell me? Why didn't you tell anyone?'

Rockbourne, Hampshire

John Biset's anger kept him going until he was back in his yard dropping from his horse. It was almost as though his mind only caught up with the action when he was home. A man was dead, but he deserved his end. '*Christ! Destroy all those who would murder by the wayside, all those who rob, who thieve, who kill, those who sleep by day and walk by night!*' he prayed, and was assailed by a sudden feebleness.

It began in his knees, and moved up to his hips, his belly and his heart, making him feel as though he might sag and fall like a sack of turnips. He grabbed at a wall, and was forced to take some deep breaths, but then all was washed away by the anger that coursed through his body. That any man might dare to attack him was appalling, but to try to do it so close to his home – that was an insult as well. He only wished he had caught the other man too.

There were three of his servants in the yard, an ostler and two men from the vill who were to have been helping in his fields as a part of their annual service owed to him, and at the sight of them, he wondered whether it would be possible to capture his assailant. 'Hob, take those two men with you and go out towards

Tidpit. There is a man around there somewhere who tried to waylay me this morning.'

He gave them a rough description of the man, with some idea of where he was heading, before sending them on their way. With fortune, they might find him, and that might mean that they could learn who had sent him.

Meanwhile he had the parchment, he told himself. He would take that to the priest. Old Peter would know what it meant.

Chapter Eleven

West Sandford

The rest of the morning seemed to go well. Simon, Margaret could see, was actually relaxed in Baldwin's presence. It was marvellous, the way that he occasionally laughed, and he appeared much more at ease with her, too.

When he and Baldwin had returned from the terrible affairs over west, towards Oakhampton, just before St Martin in Winter, it had distressed her to see them. Edith brought them, and she was as alarmed to see her father in such an evil mood with his old friend, and although she and Margaret had done all they might in the evening, when Baldwin left the following morning, it was obvious that the two men were as far apart as ever. The wounds inflicted upon their relationship were as deadly as the weapons they held sheathed at their hips.

Oh, but it was good to see the two together again. She sat at the table, Simon at her side, Baldwin opposite, and while they ate, and Baldwin grumbled at his dog, Wolf, who kept resting his head on the table and gazing longingly at the food, Margaret could not help but smile to see the fondness in Baldwin's face and the returning easiness that was so evident in Simon's.

It was a little while later that Perkin joined them, sitting down and enthusiastically demanding ever more tidbits, until his trencher contained a large mound of food. As soon as he arrived, the dog plainly gave up, and padded from the room.

'Eat that, and you'll burst,' Baldwin said as Perkin filled his trencher.

'I won't burst. It's easy,' Perkin said with such enthusiasm that Simon put a hand over his mouth.

'Quiet, Perkin. No need for all that noise.'

Ignoring his father, Perkin leaned forward to Baldwin. 'You know, I've got a knight.'

Baldwin glanced at Simon, who shook his head. 'Carved. Hugh has shown himself wonderfully competent with a knife and a block of wood.'

Margaret shot him a look. Usually when her husband made that comment, he followed it up with the observation that since Hugh's head was made of wood, it was hardly surprising that he had an affinity for the stuff. But she was sure that it upset Hugh to hear it repeated so often and had taken to asking Simon not to say such things in Hugh's presence. Simon had tried to laugh it off, when she first raised it, but she had pointedly told him that if he wished to take over the management of the household, he could do so. Hugh was mostly her servant in the home, and she wouldn't have him repeatedly offended.

There was no need to say anything this time. Simon returned her look with an expression of such innocence that she wanted to laugh again.

It was hard, very hard, to be aware of such happiness while their daughter was still in Exeter and not permitted to contact them. Margaret was suddenly reminded of her daughter's face, her smile, and was struck with a feeling of indescribable loss. It was much the same as that dreadful period when she had lost her little Peterkin, her first son. That death had sent her into despair for months. She had even considered that most appalling crime of all, self-murder.

She was brought back to the present by Baldwin's quiet voice, saying, 'Margaret, I will arrange for her to contact you. Do not fear.'

'But I don't see how. Her father-in-law will be sure to notice any kind of visit. If he doesn't, then Peter will, and he is such a dutiful son that he will not lie to his own father.'

That was true. Peter was a good man, but he was very young. Young and a little naïve. If he recognised a visitor, he might well feel that it would be better for him to let his father know. 'He would recognise Hugh, after all. He came to our house often enough.'

'Of course he knows Hugh. No one who has once enjoyed the pleasure of his sunny demeanour could forget him,' Baldwin said, popping a piece of apple into his mouth with a satisfied smile.

'You can look smug if you wish, Baldwin, but I don't see how you have helped us,' Margaret said.

Baldwin's grin broadened. 'It is simple, my dear. I looked at Hugh last night, and it struck me instantly.'

He was about to continue, when there was a loud bellow from the pantry, a clattering of pans and pots – and suddenly Hugh returned, his head lowered on his shoulders, his face as black as a moorland thunderstorm.

'Master, that dog's eaten the lunch.'

Simon gazed at him blankly. 'What?'

'The knight's brute got in at the food. Lucky I've got more ready. Won't be as good, though.'

Behind him, Margaret saw the great dog sidle in through the door, still licking his lips. Approaching Hugh, he showed the whites of his eyes as he watched the servant declaiming about the damage done, before slinking to Baldwin's side and shoving his head under his master's hand. Automatically Baldwin began to stroke the dog, his hand falling down Wolf's neck.

'All I can say is, let me know when you're bringing hounds into the house again, and next time I'll stand guard.' With that, Hugh scowled at Wolf again, who winced slightly, and then stomped from the room, muttering all the while about, 'Hounds and beasts coming in and eating my best pieces of . . .'

'So,' Margaret said sweetly, 'you don't think our Hugh would be quite right for a task like this?'

Baldwin gave her one of those slow smiles of his. He could be entirely charming when he wanted to be, she thought.

'Meg, your Edith has a maidservant. And *I* have a manservant who could charm the birds from the trees if he put his mind to it. Yes, I am sure that I will be able to get a message to Edith for you.'

With those words, spoken with that utter conviction, Margaret felt that now her life was about to return to an even balance.

She looked over at Simon, and saw the raw gratitude in his face, too, and was about to express her thanks, when she saw Perkin lean over and cuddle Wolf. The sight made her smile. Until, 'Baldwin, your dog!'

And Baldwin rapped Wolf sharply on the head as the beast hurriedly bolted the mouthful of Perkin's food he had grabbed.

Rockbourne

When Hob and the men returned before the middle of the day, John Biset didn't really expect much. It had been optimistic after all, to hope to find the felon in the tan cloak. 'No success?' he demanded.

'Well, Sir John, I'm not sure.' Hob followed John into the manor and stood scratching his head a moment. 'We had an idea that the man was running west of north, from what you said, so we went up there a little ways. When we came to the stream, there was mud, and marks all over of a man running. So we wondered where he might be off to, and when I thought about it, the only place seemed to be Coombe Bissett.'

'Oh yes?'

'Yes. So we went there and asked about, and one boy said he'd seen some strangers in the chapel there. Said they'd been leaving there in the mornings and coming back at night for the last few days, but today only one ran up, and soon after ran out again, and they haven't seen him since. He was wearing the same clothes you described though.'

'Coombe Bissett, eh? He's a good man, Walter de Coombe. He wouldn't have anything to do with this. Who was this priest who harbours felons?'

'Some new lad. He's only recently got his feet under the table there. Before that he was a student still, I've heard. Quiet boy, keeps himself to himself.'

'I see. You have done well, Hob. Thank you,' said John, and gave his man a few pennies to share out for his trouble.

It was an intriguing conundrum though, and he was determined to seek the truth in the matter. He pulled his hood over his head, and marched off along the lane to the chapel, which stood a little south and east.

The chaplain here was a man a great deal older than John. Old Peter was an ancient man of nearly seventy summers, and intensely loyal to the family which had installed him here. 'Sir John,' he smiled on seeing the manor's lord as he entered the church. 'How can I serve you?'

Old Peter took the little parchment from John while he listened to the news of the attack. 'That is bad, master. Bad indeed, to be set upon by men in full daylight. They must be terrible felons. You've called the coroner to report it?'

'I have sent one of the stable-boys. What of this though?'

'Well, it's a note telling someone to go, to Coombe Bissett. It says, *Find the chaplain there and show him this note. Tell him I have ordered that you be allowed to rest in his home until you wish to leave*. And it's signed. Here. It says *Exeter*.'

'So it means the Bishop of Exeter sent those two here,' John said, outwardly calm.

'Well, Sir John, all it says is, he was offering hospitality to people. No mention of attempting to rob a man.'

'I don't think they meant to rob me,' John said. 'No, they were here to *kill* me. That's why they left the chapel early each morning, returning late. Apart from today, because I discerned their plan and thwarted it.'

Old Peter eyed him for a few moments, and then shook his head, passing the parchment back to him. 'This means nothing. The bishop may have been asked by someone else to see to lodging for them. He may have sent the men here on his own business, and they chose to steal from people on their own initiative.'

'I disagree. I think this means that Bishop Walter of Exeter intended to kill me,' John said calmly.

He left a short while later, leaving Old Peter kneeling before his little altar, praying that John was wrong. But John knew he wasn't. No, this was further proof that the bishop was prepared to use any means to remove him and win the manor.

That *bastard*! The action of Bishop Walter of Exeter was so disgraceful that it quite took his breath away. He would have his revenge on that scheming murderer, if it was the last thing he did in this life. How dare he, a man of God, behave in so feral a manner! He was a disgrace to his cloth.

And yet he was still a powerful man. Perhaps the third most powerful in the whole realm, after only the king and Despenser. His servants were dedicated to his protection, and all were armed.

No matter, John decided, as he climbed the stairs to his hall. He paused at the top, staring out over the landscape.

This was his land. He would not give it up, and if the bishop tried to remove him, he would fight for it.

If necessary, somehow he would kill the bishop himself.

Bishop's Palace, Exeter

'So you asked him?' the steward enquired.

William had lost that amiable expression for which he was so well noted. 'This was so grave a shock to me – yes, I did.'

John de Padington looked him up and down with a considering expression. 'I have been called astute in my time, and one is credited with such honours by dint of hard effort and the occasional recourse to strong wines. You look like a man who is in sore need of a potent drink to refresh your mind and your heart.'

He left the little chamber for a few minutes, and William walked to the stool beside the fire, listening to the sounds of crockery clattering. Soon the steward returned, a large jug in one hand, while in the other he carried two of his most prized possessions, a pair of green-glazed drinking horns, which he set on the floor beside him, and carefully poured from the jug.

'What is that?' William asked.

'A good wine from the bishop's own stores. He opened this a few weeks ago at a feast, and I took the remainder of the barrel. It would have soured if I'd left it,' he added defensively.

'This,' William said, sniffing appreciatively, 'would have been wasted as vinegar. Your health!'

After both had taken a large swallow, he continued.

'I held this parchment up to him, and he just shook his head, wouldn't even look at it. You know how he is. Usually he would scold me for looking at one of his documents; he would rant and roar and put the fear of God into any man whom he thought had been so presumptuous. But when I confronted him with this thing, he just looked abashed. It was as though he had been scared of it, and being shown it again redoubled his fears. He walked from me, keeping his back to me, and said nothing for a long time. I kept asking him, "Why didn't you tell me? Tell any of us?" and all he would say was, "What good would that do?" '

'So what exactly did the parchment say?' John asked. He had pulled up a small bench, and now he sat on it near the fire, opposite the squire, listening intently. 'You told me it was threatening?'

'It said *You, who think yourself above the law, you, who have destroyed so much with your avarice and abuse, your reckoning is at hand. Prepare to die.*'

'What do you think that meant?'

'Obviously that he has been guilty of offending someone. Perhaps a man he stole from?'

Both of them were quite well aware of the source of the bishop's wealth. Bishop Walter II was not a violent nor a cruel man by nature, and yet all knew that he had tied his ambition to the king, and the possibilities for enriching himself had been, and still were, legion.

'I know that the folk of London hate him,' William added. 'He was the instigator of the Grand Eyre of five years ago.'

'Many detest him for that,' John agreed shortly.

It was true. Londoners were growing more and more confident in their importance during the fourteenth year of King Edward II's reign, and it was this, as well as the dire conditions of the king's finances, which led to the Grand Eyre, the public inquisition into all rights, customs, taxes and liberties within the city. To the administrative mind, it was a means of ensuring that those monies due to the crown were actually accumulated; in the opinion of the over-taxed and burdened population of London it was an unbearable trial, designed to ensure that all those who could not prove quickly with legal documents that they were entitled to their money would be forced to give it up to the king. Bishop Walter was the Lord High Treasurer, so it was he who had instigated this investigation, and thus it was he who was most loathed out of all the king's advisers. In London he was looked upon as a thief who had stolen the bread from the mouths of all inhabitants.

'What did he say?' John asked more quietly.

'You know him.' William restlessly stretched a leg, and sat staring at the flames while he chewed his lower lip. 'He said at first that he was not going to be made fearful by some anonymous threats; that the person who wrote that message was clearly lunatic, and not someone to be feared.'

'And yet he has allowed himself to become fretful because of it,' John noted.

'Aye. He denies it, but it's the truth. We both know that. He did declare that he had no idea who on earth could have sent it.'

'Where did he find it?'

'On his table. Someone had come in and put it there.'

'Who?'

'How can we find out? It was so long ago now, and my uncle didn't bother to question anyone. He didn't want people to think he was fearful of such threats, I think. His mind appears to have been set on other things at that time. He said that he didn't readily understand the import of the message.'

'So someone has said that they will see that he gets his reckoning,' John repeated, nodding pensively to himself. 'Well, you and I will have to be most vigilant. We will have to be at his side to protect him at all times.'

'When we're out here in the city, you mean.'

John turned his gaze on William. 'No, Squire William. I mean at all times. Whoever had that message delivered here knew how to get to the bishop, and also knew how to make him feel anxious. Anyone who is familiar with this city will know where the bishop lives, and what his habits are. It is not like the days when he was Lord High Treasurer and would disappear for weeks at a time. He was more or less safe in those days, for no one would be able to tell exactly where he might be at any time. And no one would ever try to attack the bishop in the king's palace. He would suffer the most hideous death the king could devise! No, my master is in more danger here than he has been for many a long year. We must stay with him. He must never be alone.'

'He will refuse to allow us to do that,' William said gloomily.

John looked at him. 'My dear squire, when you have been a servant as long as I have, you soon learn how to achieve what you want, no matter what the wishes of the master. He will not refuse *me*!'

Chapter Twelve

Exeter Cathedral

It was disquieting in the extreme, to consider that the sheriff could have freed his brother from the bishop's gaol.

'Call him here to answer to me immediately! He cannot escape my fury with a blithe statement that he knows not where his brother is,' Bishop Walter said with cold rage after reading the sheriff's reply.

Alone again, he clenched his fists. There had been a time, when he was considerably younger, when he would not have taken such an insult without immediate retaliation.

Some while later there came a knock, and the bishop fitted a cold stern gaze to his face. 'Yes?'

'Bishop. I am so glad to see you,' the sheriff said, entering with a show of respect, bowing low, walking to the bishop's side, kneeling and kissing the episcopal ring. 'How may I serve you?'

'You can tell me where your brother is.'

'You installed him in your gaol, I had heard.' James de Cockington assumed a mildly enquiring expression.

'Which is why you saw fit to bribe my gaoler and have him released. Your brother will not escape my vengeance, you realise? I will have him hunted down and brought back here, and held until I deem his crime has been paid for. Until he has submitted to my judgement, he will remain outcast.'

'Bishop, I am not concerned with that. For now, I need to speak about other matters. The king has sent to demand that the counties all begin to plan for defence. It would appear that his wife the queen is definitely preparing to attack the realm, and as you can imagine, that will leave me with much to do. I should be glad for some advice.'

'There was a time when a fellow like you would have quaked to think of the divine retribution that would be brought upon his head for flagrantly flouting the law,' Bishop Walter said with a glower as he tried to discern the man's expression.

'Bishop, I shall be entirely candid,' the sheriff said. He hesitated, but then spoke a little more quietly. 'When I heard you had arrested my brother, I was shocked. He is not some peasant who can be held, after all. He was my father's son. And I confess, I thought that the fact that my own brother could be restrained might well damage my standing in the city. It was not just that Paul is weak and would not suffer imprisonment well, but the fact of the damage that your actions might do to me, to my office, and thus to the government of the whole shire.'

'What damage is this?' Bishop Walter scoffed.

'Simply this: the shire is no more nor less stable than the rest of the kingdom. We must have strong leadership at this time. And who will be able to give it? The king, through the system of sheriffs. We receive our orders, and we execute them. No matter what the command is, we enforce it. If the king demands that I seek out all the Frenchmen in the city, I will do so. I am his representative here in Devon. And if he desires me to raise a force to obstruct an invader's might, I must do so.'

'Of course.'

'Yes. But if I am looked upon as someone with little authority, a man who can see his own brother captured and held in a prison, a man who is associated with gaoled criminals, some of the peasants may begin to believe that I am in fact no more to be trusted than a felon myself. They may consider that my own commands, legally issued in the king's name, can be easily ignored. They may come to believe that they can ignore me, ignore the king, ignore the dire circumstances in which we find ourselves.'

'This is twaddle, sheriff! The people here need a strong hand to guide them, it is true, but that does not mean that they would look down upon you, were your brother to be held here. No, it would more likely make them look up to you as a man of honour. Instead, you have set yourself apart from them. You have made it look as though you consider the law matters nothing when it is pointing at you or your family. You have brought your shrievalty into disrepute, and it will remain a shameful mark on your reputation for all time.'

'You think it is all imagined, then? I have orders here. We must provide officers to the ports to test all goods coming into the country or leaving, to see whether there are any messages secreted amidst them. That is how serious the king considers the peril to be, which faces the realm. But you know better than him, I suppose. I would have asked you to provide some potential names for these duties. I believe a bailiff of Dartmoor once was the Keeper of the Port of Dartmouth under Abbot Champeaux? He is the sort of man we need. Well, if you can think of any others, I would be grateful.'

He stood, rudely forbearing from bowing to the bishop again, but at the door he paused.

'Bishop, I do not condone what my younger brother did to that poor woman. But I believe I did the right thing in removing him. I believe it was better for all concerned. Please, do me the honour of trusting me when I say this.'

The door closed firmly behind him, leaving the bishop feeling angry, but also anxious. He sighed and offered a short prayer for Simon's protection. 'Dear God, Sir Baldwin was right. Simon has lost so much in the last year – don't make me have to send him to the coast now!'

West Sandford

It was late in the morning by the time they had finished their discussions, and the mood of both men, Margaret could see, was greatly improved. Indeed, she could hardly have believed that such a transformation was possible, had she not seen it for herself.

The genuine affection which she saw in Baldwin's eyes was enough to convince her that their old companion had never lost his friendship for them. How the two men could have grown so estranged was astonishing to her, for she had known them always to be so close. Yet it was true that the previous year, only three short months ago, the two men had fallen out, and Simon in particular had seemed entirely unwilling to forget the cause of their dispute. And it was not to be wondered at, for she knew that her husband was so entirely devoted to their daughter that he would kill to protect her; and because he was convinced that Baldwin's actions had placed Edith's life at risk, he felt he might never trust the knight again.

But with the fact of Edith's near-gaoling by her father-in-law, and because she was prevented from contacting her parents, Simon's antipathy to Baldwin was leavened by his urgent need for a friend in this troubling time. And Baldwin's arrival with a message from Edith, as well as his proposal for maintaining a communication with her, had been enough to return Simon to his earlier state of comradeship with his old friend.

Watching Baldwin ride away at about noon, she gently linked her arm with her husband's. 'It is good to see you so happy again, my love.'

'Happy? Aye, well, it is encouraging to know that he has ideas for keeping in contact with our maid. If ever a man could wheedle his way into a wench's affections, it was Edgar. The fellow has the luck of a devil when it comes to enticing women.'

'It doesn't work for every woman he meets,' Margaret said with a chuckle.

'No, well, you already have the best man in the world,' Simon said.

'I know.'

'So now all we need do is wait to hear from him . . . and from Edith, of course.'

'I will pray that we do so soon,' Margaret said quietly.

'And I too,' Simon said, his eyes fixed on the horizon. The hills about here meant that Baldwin was already out of sight, but Simon stood staring out after him as though still watching his friend disappear from view.

'He is a good friend, Simon, isn't he?' Margaret said.

'Hmm? Baldwin? Oh, yes. The best you could hope to meet. I just pray that he will be successful.'

'And what if he is? We shall still not be able to speak with her,' Margaret said. 'Even to see her would be known to her husband and father-in-law.'

'But we may at least learn that she is well, and she can be reassured to know that we still love her,' Simon said. 'And perhaps we can arrange to see her in Exeter, away from her house.'

'Perhaps,' Margaret said. 'I am only glad that we are here again, husband.'

He grunted, but she could see that he appreciated her comments. For his own part, she knew, he missed the moors and his old job of bailiff to the Stannaries. His had been one of the most important jobs on the moors: keeping the peace between the tenants and tin-miners. Miners were all working on the king's lands, and were responsible only to him, so that they could maximise their harvest of metal, which enriched him as well. But their extensive rights meant that there were frequent clashes with other landowners in the area, so Simon was forever riding over the moors and breaking up fights, attaching men to come to his next court, or trying to discover the names of the bodies which were occasionally discovered, murdered, in the wastes.

Some years ago, the far-sighted Abbot Robert had invested one hundred pounds in the farm of tin on the moors. Thus Simon had reported to him, and some few years ago, as a reward for his hard efforts, the abbot had given him a new job: that of Keeper of his Port of Dartmouth. It should have been a wonderful promotion, and that was indeed what the abbot had intended, but for Margaret it was a dreadful disappointment. Simon had been taken away from her and installed for weeks at a time in the sea port, while it was impossible for her to follow him.

Since that kindly old man's death, Simon and Margaret's lives had grown still more unsettled. The abbacy itself had become the source of dispute and bickering.

While the monks elected Brother Roger Busse, another monk, John de Courtenay, desired the position for himself. He started a bitter legal case to demonstrate that Busse was not a fit man. The wrangling had grown fierce, with both candidates making ever more wild accusations, and in that terrible environment, Simon had found his own position grown intolerable. With both men vying for power, no one in authority was safe. They both attempted to persuade Simon to use what influence he had in support of them, while threatening him with dire consequences should he fail so to do.

In this atmosphere of distrust and deception, Simon had been persecuted by Despenser too, until he lost even his home in Lydford, and he and Margaret had been forced to return here to West Sandford.

She knew it was a sore disappointment to her husband, and she greatly regretted that – but she was content to be here now. The idea that she might be forced to cope with the loss of their daughter while her husband was sent off on business for the abbot, or while he wandered the moors in pursuit of felons or thrust himself between warring parties of miners and moorland tenants, was too awful. She wouldn't be able to manage on her own.

*Friday before Candlemas**

Langtoft, Lincolnshire

It was not a place he had ever been to before. A small town set amidst the flat lands, there was nothing here to interest him – but all around was absolute emptiness, and that was what Richard de Folville wished for now.

So he had rolled himself in a blanket under the stars, cursing his misfortune and his enemies, and praying for his safe arrival in France.

---

* 31 January 1326

If only he knew where his brothers were. Their companionship was the thing he craved. He was a fool to have sent Eustace away like that. Rather than riding off to see John and tell him, he would have been better advised to remain with his brothers and ride with them.

He wished he knew which way they had taken. Eustace had mentioned that he would go to France, which probably meant heading south. That would have been direct, but Richard was convinced that with the posse being hard on his brothers' heels, they would be best served by escaping England as quickly as possible. So this morning, after a miserable night in the open, he had lit a fire while he hunched down nearby, considering his route.

There was no choice really, he thought. He had heard that Bishop's Llyn* was near to the sea, and it was surely the second or third most important port in the country, so it was ideal. He had first thought of London, but it was that little bit further, and with the king's administration being based there, much more dangerous. Even though London was a massive city, to this renegade, it felt no better than walking into a trap.

The way to Bishop's Llyn was some fifty miles or more, and he reckoned he must have ridden at least thirty yesterday. It hadn't been easy. The going was hard, with plenty of wet, muddy roads – always a danger to a man who didn't know where the potholes were.

It was dark before he had reached this place, but he had steeled himself and continued. If someone was to stop him, he would declare that he was riding on urgent business for the Bishop of Norwich. It wouldn't persuade a posse, but it might just save him from arrest for riding about suspiciously. Any stranger making a journey at dark was a source of deepest suspicion, even a man with a tonsure.

---

* The lands here were acquired by King Henry VIII after the Dissolution, at which point the town was renamed Lynn Regis or King's Lynn. The latter name stuck.

The fire was good and heartening. There was something about the sight of flames and the warmth they gave off that soothed a man's heart. It was not the mere heat itself, he was sure, but something about the colours and sparks that dazzled the intellect.

He had some water in a pot, which he had set over the flames, and now he chewed some stale bread while he waited for the water to boil. In his pack there were some leaves which he could steep – old, dried mint from last year. He could almost taste the hot drink already, and he hunched over the fire, watching the pot avidly. So avidly that he didn't hear the horse until it was almost at his side.

'So, a priest, and all alone out here, eh?'

Chapter Thirteen

West Sandford

Simon was up and about early that morning. The idea that there could be an intervention by Baldwin had given him such a sense of hopefulness that it was hard to stay in bed. Unusually for him, he was awake before dawn, and rather than run the risk of disturbing his wife, he rose and went to his hall.

The fire was cold and dead, and he set about making it afresh. Leaving the ashes to form a base, he went and fetched a bundle of twigs from his woodstore. Each year as the men laid the hedge and trimmed old twigs, they were collected and tied into faggots like this. He had a little piece of charred cloth and wisps of birch bark which he collected together, and then began to strike a spark from a flint with the back of his knife.

As he worked, his mind wandered. The scrape, scrape, scrape was comforting in some curious way, and he found that he could consider the recent events dispassionately.

His first thoughts were of absolute gratitude to Baldwin. There was no one else who would have been able to think of a speedy solution to his problems with such apparent ease and then leave to put it in force.

Baldwin was a good friend; Simon knew that. Oh, in the deepest misery of the last month or two, when he had thought Baldwin to have betrayed him, he had been unsure, as though the one incident could have altered Baldwin's personality – or perhaps showed it in its true colours. Margaret would not believe it, and she had grown quite angry with Simon on occasion as he muttered futilely about Baldwin's bad faith, his preparedness to risk all for his own safety. And it was irrational. But a man was entitled to be irrational when it came to the safety of his own daughter.

The spark caught and there was a tiny red glimmer from the black cloth. He carefully wrapped it about some more of the thin bark scrapings, and blew gently until there was a larger glow, adding a little material, some twigs and more bark about the outside of his cylinder of tinder, still blowing, gradually moving to set it on the ashes. A flame caught, and he picked up some dry rushes from the floor, which soon flared up. More bark on top, and then he could start setting twigs about and above the heat. Soon there was the healthy crackle of fire, and he gently set the faggot over the top, hoping not to disturb the tinder.

He fetched bread and some wine, and warmed the wine by the side of the fire while he brought logs inside and stacked them nearby.

It was a ritual he had performed every day when he was smaller, but now the task of preparing and making a fire was something he did only rarely. There was a sadness in that, he reflected. A man should have certain jobs, certain duties, which defined him. Simon had been a bailiff and had carried out that function for many years. Other men were not so lucky as to have a role for that long. Many died before reaching Simon's advanced age. Not that he felt old. He was the same man inside as he had always been, and yet there was no denying that his paunch was becoming as formidable as his father's had been, and the line of his throat was not so sleek as before.

But the fact of losing first one job, and then his post as Keeper of the Port for the abbot, had left him feeling dislocated. That was only enhanced when Despenser grew to know him, and decided to attack him deliberately – first by alarming Simon himself and threatening his home, and then by attacking his family. Well, Despenser had taken the house at Lydford, and Simon sincerely hoped that it would never bring in a benefit for him. Simon had loved that house, but he would be content to set fire to it now, just to deprive Sir Hugh of any profit.

As usual, a short while before the sun rose and penetrated the window, there was a rattle of small feet, and suddenly Perkin was in the room with him. He stopped dead on seeing his father, and then a mischievous grin washed over his face, and he ran at Simon, throwing his arms about him and crying, 'Hello, Daddy!'

Simon ruffled his hair. At times like this he found it difficult to put his emotions into words. His heart seemed to swell; he knew pride, he knew surprise to think that he could have created such a marvellous little man, and he knew overwhelming love. Simple adoration, the sort of affection that could never be erased.

Margaret followed soon after, as all the servants began to surface. Hugh walked in, scowled at the hearth as though disgusted that a grown man could have produced such a meagre fire, and promptly set about building it with fresh logs, until it was roaring. Only then did he nod to himself and walk out again, all the while ignoring his master. Only Margaret merited a greeting.

There was a shout, then a cry, and soon after that, a scrabble of boots and a tousled figure appeared. 'Hugh kicked me!'

'No. He kicked your bedding. Of course, you wouldn't have been abed still, not at this time of day, would you?' Simon said with poisonous politeness.

'He meant to kick me,' Rob said sulkily.

While he lived in Dartmouth, Simon had acquired this lad. He was only thirteen or so, with a dark, ferrety face and the eyes of one who knew how to rob a man's laces while he was not looking. Probably the son of a sailor, because Simon was sure that his mother would be over-friendly to any matelot with a bulging purse, he had been raised as an urchin at Dartmouth's port, surviving on whatever he could gain for himself. He was no angel, but Simon felt some sympathy for the lad. Rob had not been granted the best opportunities, yet had managed to live without gaining the close attention of Dartmouth's authorities.

'Then you should be glad he wasn't angry,' Simon said. 'Or he would have broken something.'

'It's not fair! I'm a free man.'

'You're in my employ, boy, and you have failed yet again to

get up in time.' Simon tried to speak sternly, but knew it was pointless. 'Go and fetch more logs in, then start your chores. I can't do all your jobs for you, lad.'

Margaret was grinning as Rob shuffled his feet on his way out. 'You didn't thrash him today, then?'

'How can you thrash a lad like him? He wouldn't feel it.'

'Ah, my husband, the soul of kindness, always!'

'Meg, let's take the air before breaking our fast,' Simon suggested, wanting a private word with her. 'Come and walk with me a while.'

They strolled along the old lane, to where the land rose and they could look down over a vast swathe of territory. Turning to the south-west, Simon pointed with his chin. 'Look at that. Dartmoor.'

'And it's raining there again,' his wife responded. 'What is it, Simon?'

'The next year will be dangerous, Meg. From all I've heard, Despenser will not give up power, and the king will support him in all he does. But Despenser cannot be allowed to stay. Baldwin and I discussed it last night.'

'This is dangerous talk.'

'Meg, there's no sense hiding it. I agree with Baldwin. I think war is coming.'

Her face froze at those words. She looked away, over the peaceful countryside, at the little copses, the shaws and fields. The pastures were empty, but that only added to the atmosphere of calmness. Quietly, she said, 'You think the fighting would reach here?'

'My love, Baldwin is right: the fighting may even *start* here. The queen could choose to land in Devon; the King has not been favoured here since he confiscated her territories, has he? Whereas her popularity has grown.'

Margaret could not help but throw a glance towards their house. 'Perkin . . .'

'And you. All of us would be in danger. So I think we should consider moving away for a little while.'

'Where to?'

'We may be safer in a city.'

'But cities suffer siege. Here, we could run away.'

'True, but this little farm is no haven. What could I do if I was here with you, and I knew that the children and you had no means of escape or concealment? I would be distraught.'

'There is no need to be.' Margaret took a deep breath. 'You are right, husband. We do have to consider such matters, but I refuse to live in terror. If there is an invasion, there should be some warning. And if there is not, we shall have to pray to God to protect us. There is no more that Christians can do.'

And with that, she kissed him and made her way back to the house, refusing to discuss the matter further.

However, her confidence was sorely shaken when the messenger arrived from the bishop.

Langtoft, Lincolnshire

'I am on urgent business for the Bishop of Norwich,' Richard de Folville said, scrambling to his feet.

The man on horseback smiled, and Richard could see that he was assessing this catch. Only one day from his home, and he was already snared as tightly as a rabbit in a net!

'I am sergeant to the Kirby Bellers estates,' the man said, 'and I am hunting a felon called Richard de Folville, a bald-pated priest who looks just like you, master.'

'I don't know the man. I am Peter of Huntingdon, and I am here on the business of the Bishop of Norwich, as I said. You cannot hold me. I have the benefit of clergy, and—'

'Don't give me that ballocks, priest. We know all about your "benefit" here. There was a priest killed a man a couple of years ago – and we may have released him when the bishop demanded it, but only after he'd been found guilty. You see, up here, we think that murdering scum is murdering scum. It doesn't matter what habit you wear, nor whether you've had a good shaven pate: if you kill, you're a killer.'

'I'm no murderer! I've never killed anyone – I swear it before God.'

'Perhaps. You can tell the justice when you see him. For now though, pack your gear and come with me.'

'Right away?'

'You catch on fast.'

Folville stared down at his pot. The steam was beginning to rise from the surface, and he could almost taste the mint. 'I need my drink first. And then I'll get my horse and join you,' he said. And in his heart, he knew there was no escape for him. This man would bind him and sit him upon his horse, and he would lead Richard all the way back to Melton Mowbray, to the gaol. If he was fortunate, the bishop would send a man to rescue him, eventually, and he would be transferred from one gaol to the bishop's own. It was a grim outcome.

'There is no time for that, priest. Get your things. Now!'

'But I want to—'

The man swung himself down from his horse and trampled Richard's fire, kicking over the pot, upsetting the water, and there was a rush of noise and steam that inundated the place.

Richard stared with dismay at his fire, shaking his head in disbelief. There was the smell of soggy coals already, and the steam was rising pathetically from the embers. He let out a tiny sob, and began to bend down to pick up the pot, just in case there might be a little water left in it, and now the man kicked again, his boot striking the pot and sending it high in the air.

It was his mistake. The sergeant followed the trajectory of the pot with a smirk on his face, and didn't see the flash of steel, nor register the danger until he felt the small explosion in his breast as the sharp point punctured his lungs and continued up, shearing through the muscles of his heart.

He coughed – that was the first thing that Richard was aware of – then clutched at his throat, pulling at his hood and tunic as though they were strangling him; he jerked and thrashed, while the blood poured in a crimson gush from his lips, until he slumped to the ground. A last shiver ran through the man's body, and the corpse was not a human being, it was merely an accumulation of muscle, flesh and bones. There was not even the indication of a soul.

Richard scrambled away, wanting to scream in pure horror, wanting to escape this scene of hell, this picture of his own guilt. For this man had not died at the hands of his brother, but had been killed by him – by him personally. By the one de Folville who was a man of God.

His mind was rushing on from one horrible consideration to another, and yet Richard gradually understood that it was not the reality of what he had done that scared him; it was the thought of the punishment, were he discovered. He would be safe in heaven, after all. He had studied, and he knew perfectly well that, provided he made a fulsome apology and confessed before death, his soul would be secure.

Already, all panic was leaching away, and in its place was a rational consideration. First, he must conceal the body as best he could. Second, he must also conceal the horse, if possible, and finally he must make good his escape.

Taking his knife from the corpse, he cleaned it on the man's chemise, before rolling the body away, down to the bank of a little stream. Shoving the sergeant over and into the water, he felt sure that the body would remain unseen for some little while. Then he returned to his fire and shook his head mournfully. For the want of a hot drink he had killed that man. He wanted his mint tea more than anything he had ever desired, but he could do nothing about it. First he must ride away to Bishop's Llyn.

His belly growling and his throat parched, he tiredly repacked his few belongings, then fetched his horse. Saddling it and then tying his blanket to the saddle took but little time. The sergeant's horse had meanwhile ambled over to the stream, and now was sniffing at it with perplexity. In a moment, it had started to whinny and paw at the ground, and Richard realised his error. He should have killed the brute before. Now it was too late. He was desperate to get away, to find a ship to help him escape. The thought of catching and killing a horse now was too daunting.

With a set jaw, he mounted. Beneath him, his own horse was prancing with excitement – catching some hints of the scent of blood, he thought – and then he was off, pointing the beast eastwards, and, so he hoped, to safety.

Exeter

Roger Crok had found himself a cheap lodging at an inn near the West Gate overlooking the walls, and beyond, the river and the vills that spread out in the valley and up the hills. It was the sort of view Roger could look at all day with happiness to remind himself that he was in a safe, enclosed city.

There had been little opportunity so far, but he was determined to find his way to the bishop somehow.

He walked about the city a lot of the time; it was easy to pass unnoticed among the thronging hordes. Most days he went over to the Cathedral Close and stood watching the canons and the lay brothers at their duties. There was one old fosser who always seemed ready to chat – and Roger deliberately avoided him. He had no desire to be noticed and remembered.

The sight of the canons marching to their services was always impressive, and today, it was something that made Roger pause.

It was clear that news of some sort had reached the cathedral. Was it that he was here? That was his first thought. Someone must have guessed that the bishop was an assassin's target, because as soon as the first canons strode out from their doors to the cathedral's grassed areas, he saw the extra men.

Usually the black-gowned clerics would appear quietly, their garments flapping in the wind like the wings of ravens, and wait with more or less patience as their entire household formed behind them, and then make their way to the cathedral. Today, all was different. The canons appeared to be glaring about them with intense suspicion.

When the bishop and his own familia arrived, he knew in his heart that it must be true. They had heard he was here to kill the bishop.

And then he began to see that the looks were *not* aimed at him, nor at the others in the Close. All the suspicion was aimed at each other.

Asking around in the crowd, he learned nothing about the cause of this change, and was reluctantly left with the belief that the only man who could help him was the fosser – who at the moment was up to his waist in a new grave. As Roger cautiously made his way over to the old man, he kept his gaze fixed on the bishop's household.

The bishop himself looked terrible. His skin was almost yellow, and his head was bent – as one who was carrying an appalling burden of grief on his shoulders.

'Here, my friend – what on earth's the matter with the choir?' he enquired when he reached the fosser.

The others in the bishop's household were also affected, he could see. There was a youngish fellow, well built and with the bearing of a fighter, who stood near Stapledon, with tears falling from his face.

'Bishop's old friend has died,' the fosser said, wiping his brow with the back of a muddy hand. 'Father Joshua was a popular figure up yer. 'E was old, mind. Ancient as the old cathedral, they say. Looked 'un.'

There was much more in a similar vein, about the special service being planned, the tomb under the flags in the cathedral near the altar, the mourning that would continue for the rest of the day and through the night while the bishop held his vigil over the corpse with his most loyal servants and other friends of the dead man.

'Who is that man with the bishop now?' Roger asked, pointing.

' 'Im? 'E's the bishop's nephew, Squire Willum.'

Roger nodded, half to himself, but even as he did so, he realised that his interest had been noticed. The squire and another man were staring at him openly, just as he gazed at the bishop.

And then a singular thing happened. He saw Walter Stapledon stumble, a hand at his brow.

The bishop, the evil, dangerous man on whom he had sworn direst vengeance, was no more than a frail old man, who was weeping and distraught because of the death of a dear companion.

Roger thanked the fosser, then slowly turned and walked away, out of the Close, along the old lanes to the inn. There, he paid his last bill and gathered his belongings, making his way to the South Gate, and thence leaving the city and walking down to the coast.

He was a warrior. And the sight of the bishop in such a pathetic state had convinced Roger Crok of one thing: he was no assassin of old men.

No, he must leave England and find exile in France.

Chapter Fourteen

West Sandford

'He wants me today?' Simon said.

Margaret could see that he was restraining himself with difficulty. The messenger was a short lad, perhaps fifteen years old, and rather poorly fed by the look of him. She had tried to persuade him to eat, but the boy had refused, saying that he was in a great hurry, because the bishop had demanded that the message be given urgently.

'Yes, sir. He said that you would understand the need for urgency. The king himself has said that he wants all the ports to be watched.'

'I am no *spy*!' Simon bellowed suddenly, and brought his fist down on the table before him. 'This is sheer panic, nothing else. Well, I am damned if I will submit to panic! You can tell—'

'Simon!' Margaret said warningly. 'Hugh, take our guest to the kitchen and give him food and ale. The lad needs something, he is exhausted.' She waited until Hugh had persuaded the fellow to leave, and then turned to her husband. 'You have to do as he bids.'

'If I go to wherever he sends me, when shall I see you again?' Simon demanded, his face pale. 'If war does rear its head here, what will happen to you and Perkin if I am not near?'

'Hugh can protect us. Simon, you have already upset Despenser. You only have one ally powerful enough to defend us now, and that is the bishop. Don't upset him as well!'

'I don't intend to, but in Christ's name, Meg, how can I leave you all when war is approaching? It's tearing me apart just to think of it.'

'Then don't! We'll be safe here. I swear.'

'No. I cannot leave you,' Simon said, but now there was a speculative expression on his face.

'What are you thinking?'

'The good bishop is a politician. And a politician always seeks a compromise. Well, I shall offer him one. One that will be within his gift. Wherever he sends me, he'll have to give me space for my family. I have been pushed from here to Lydford, to Dartmouth, and forced to travel across the seas too often in the last few years. I will not leave you behind again, Meg. If he wants me, he must protect my family too.'

*Wednesday after the Feast of St Mathias**

Exeter

The wind that idled along the lane was so cold, it seemed to leave thorns of ice embedded in John Biset's face as he rattled along on the cart.

In truth, he had not thought that a place like Exeter would be so cold even in the middle of winter, and to have come all the way here to leave his little message now seemed like a fool's errand. The roads had been dangerous, threatening to spill him and his load at every downhill turn. His cart was old, the steel tyres worn smooth from a thousand leagues, and it creaked and groaned alarmingly, the ancient timbers moving against each other.

But he had wanted to leave his mark. Allowing the bishop to get away with attempting to kill him was unthinkable.

So John was here to leave his own mark in return. He would see whether the bishop liked his as much.

There were few things more irritating than threats that never materialised, the bishop thought as he rose from his throne in the cathedral and went through the last minutes of the Mass.

---

* 26 February 1326

The fact that his life was now so set about with controls was itself deeply infuriating. He had matters he needed to see to. There were the parishes to the north-west of his diocese which he had not visited in rather a long time, the nunneries which needed to be checked over to see that some of the flagrant abuses were no longer tolerated. So much to do . . .

The service was finished, and he left the cathedral by the side door opening into the cloister, where his nephew William met him.

Bishop Walter said nothing as they strode out across the little grassed area, along a narrow lane and thence into his palace, but he was tempted to speak. This constant attention was surely unnecessary. It was weeks since the note, and in the meanwhile, there had been nothing whatsoever. Only the death of poor Joshua, still sorely missed.

Reaching his chamber, he sat at his table and called for his steward. John de Padington entered in a rush, wiping his hands, and the bishop asked for mulled wine and biscuits. It was a cold day, but at least this room was always cosy.

As John came back, he brought another man with him. 'This fellow says he has a gift for you,' John announced, serving the bishop.

'What is it?' Bishop Walter asked.

The man was carrying a small barrel, such as might be used to transport a gallon of wine, but there was no stopper from which to pour. Instead, it had a tightly fitting lid.

'William, you open it, please,' he asked, reaching for his goblet of wine, which was why he missed the sight as the squire lifted the lid and gave a short cry of horror.

The barrel fell from his hands to the floor, and as the bishop turned, startled, he saw the dried and salted head tumble from within, rolling clumsily over the floor until it lay still, staring up from those hideous eyeballs as though accusing Bishop Walter himself.

*Friday after the Feast of St Mathias**

Exeter

'Yes, I swear it – and no, I did not!' the bishop declared.

To William Walle, the bishop looked almost broken. The damage inflicted by that accursed note had been almost healed, but the arrival of this grisly remnant had set Bishop Walter back even further. His eyes were bloodshot from lack of sleep, and he had developed a curious shake in his left hand, which he tried to conceal by gripping it in his right.

The coroner, a bearded bear of a man called Sir Richard de Welles, snorted as he peered into the barrel again. 'So this fellow was deposited here, although you don't know him? Yet the barrel was addressed to you personally? You see me point, Bishop. Hard to believe you don't have any connection with the deceased.'

'I have not the faintest idea who it was,' the bishop said again, shuddering.

William watched as the coroner shrugged and made to take his leave. He would investigate as best he could, he declared, but the likelihood of finding a body missing a head was more problematic than people might suspect. Most men tended to keep their skulls with them.

John the steward saw the coroner to the door, and William remained in the room with his uncle. He placed the lid on the top of the barrel again, pressing it down firmly. 'I shall deliver this to the fosser,' he said. 'There's no reason for you to keep it in here.'

'No. Thank you.'

William hesitated.

'Don't you ask me as well,' the bishop sighed. 'I am sure he is not from here. We haven't missed a man with fair hair like that, have we?'

'No one has gone missing in recent weeks,' William agreed. 'I

* 28 February 1326

was wondering though, whether it could have been a while ago that this fellow died. He has been stored in salt, after all.'

'What of it?' the bishop said.

'Salt would dry out the skin, make him look older than he really was.'

'So?'

'Perhaps this was a young man? After all, he has no beard to look at, and—'

'Christ's pain! No beard?' the bishop gasped. 'Show it to me again!'

'Why, do you think . . . ?' William said, opening the barrel and lifting the foul remnant.

'The man from Despenser,' the bishop breathed.

'It was nothing to do with me,' the bishop said, sipping his wine. 'The men arrived here. You were with me, weren't you, John?'

'Aye. Didn't like them, neither.'

'No. Well. They were sent to me by Sir Hugh le Despenser,' the bishop continued. He glanced at the lidded barrel, and averted his eyes again. 'He wanted to send them to meet John Biset.'

'Who's he?' William asked.

'A boy who owns two manors that would be useful to me. I fear I . . . There is no concealing it: I was attempting with Sir Hugh to take the manors. The matter is closed so far as I am concerned now, but Sir Hugh wanted to progress, so he sent two men here, asking that I arrange for them to visit.'

'Did you help them?'

'I did not have a great deal of choice,' the bishop said heavily. 'I dared not defy Sir Hugh – you know what he is like. I asked the two if they were set upon bloodshed, and when both denied it, I felt that they were perhaps just wishing to speak with John Biset. And that was all.'

'So you did help them?'

'I allowed them an introduction to the nearest church and the chaplain. They took it, and that was that.'

'Well, it appears that Master Biset was unimpressed, since here is one of them,' William said. 'Will you write to Despenser yourself and let the coroner know?'

The bishop stared at the barrel again. 'I am tempted to send this to Despenser and leave it to him. But if I do, he is as likely to throw the head in the Thames as see to it that the fellow has a burial.'

'Then bury it here,' John said. 'It's what you were going to do anyway. Either the other man got away and Sir Hugh le Despenser knows their mission failed, or the fellow got killed, in which case Despenser knows nothing and there is no need to tell him.'

'Perhaps you are right,' the bishop said.

William shook his head. 'What if this man Biset thinks *you* sent the men? He had the head delivered here, what if he tries to take his revenge on you?'

'I don't think he'll do that. He's made his point,' the bishop said.

William nodded, but he was unconvinced. He would have to remain doubly on guard, he thought.

*Fourth Monday before the Feast of St John and St Paul**

Exeter

It was in the middle of the morning when he knew that it was safe to go to the bishop's chamber again.

Many months had passed since the first note, and it was time to turn the screw a little. That was how it felt, he thought: as if he was actually turning a thumbscrew on the man, every little twist of news adding to the man's anguish. And this was the ideal time to do it, now that Bishop Walter's first nervousness was waning.

It was astonishing to him, how badly that first message had affected the bishop. There had been an immediate deterioration in his appearance. Last year he had been a tall, striking fellow, until he had been sent with the king's son to France, to try to maintain

* 2 June 1326

peace between the English in Guyenne and the French, but that mission had been a disaster. The queen took her son and kept him with her, the boy refusing to leave her, and all the guards bar a few who travelled with the bishop threw in their lot with the queen rather than return to England with him. To the bishop's horror, he discovered that he was a marked man. Death threats were given, and he was forced to clothe himself in pilgrim's garb and flee for his life. To hear him, it sounded as though he escaped only by the merest chance.

It had been that which had led to the plot. The sight of the man who was so detested arriving back in England like a beggar, with his clothes all disordered, his face wild and anxious, registering the terror that had driven him from France, had been a source of joy to those who hated him. Making him suffer as he had caused so many others to suffer, was massively appealing.

He slipped into the hall without being seen. It was easy enough. There was no one on the door at this time of day, and he could cross to the stairs which led up to the bishop's private chamber. These were a narrow spiral set into the wall, and as he climbed, he feared that at any moment he might hear a voice demanding to know what he was doing there. Then he would be discovered, along with his guilty secret.

The stairs were dark at the top. There was a door to block the way, but it was ajar, and he pressed a palm against the timbers as he listened, eyes wide, head turned a little towards the opening, fearing disaster while also strangely hoping for it.

It was a curious feeling, this. He wanted to continue with the plan, to see the bishop wild with fear – and yet there was this odd compulsion to have it all end as well. To get caught. Part of him wanted to confront the man, to tell him who had done all this. To stand before the bishop and denounce him for his many crimes.

The deep pounding of his heart seemed to reverberate about his belly as he pushed the door open an inch, a little more, a little more again – until he could sidle through the gap.

The table stood at the far edge of the room. He crossed to it, trying to avoid the weaker, creaking boards in the middle of the room, but one gave out a shrill noise and he froze like a rabbit awaiting the talons of his predator.

He had no time to wait; he must get it over with. In a hurry now, he darted to the table. There was a mess of papers on it, and he was about to thrust the note in amongst them, when he saw the three books sitting on a nearby shelf. He picked up the first, but shook his head. It was the *Thoughts of St Thomas Aquinas*, and he couldn't pollute that. The next book was a copy of the *Chanson de Roland*. The great epic story of the Battle of Roncevaux was one which the bishop had often extolled, and this was a book he returned to often. Without further thought, he picked up the *Chanson de Roland*, opened it and thrust the parchment inside.

Quickly and quietly, he made his way along the wall, the silent wall where no floorboards creaked or screamed, and reached the door. He drew it to behind him, and tiptoed down the stairs.

'What are you doing up there?'

And hearing the voice, he stopped dead in terror.

*Fourth Monday before the Feast of St John and St Paul**

Portchester, Hampshire

Simon Puttock walked into his house and slammed the door behind him. In the distance he could hear his son shouting and screaming, and he paused a moment, long enough to guess that Perkin was again trying his luck against grim authority, represented by Hugh. He gave a grin, and walked along the narrow passageway to the hall.

There was a good fire crackling and hissing, and he sighed with pleasure to be able to stand before it, his hands stuffed into his belt.

'I did not expect you home so soon,' Margaret said, hurrying in, wiping her hands on a towel. 'You must be tired. Would you like ale or wine?'

---

* 2 June 1326

'I think today I need a strong wine. Where is Perkin?'

'Your son has been a sore distraction to me today,' Margaret said, dropping onto a stool. 'He stole a pie before noon, and tried to blame a dog for the theft. Then he started digging with his knife at the new wall, and pulled off a foot of plaster, when he knew that the man only finished the work last week, and as soon as I chastised him for that, he stamped off sulking and snapped the heads off the roses. Simon, I worry about that boy. He is uncontrollable.'

'Meg, he's not yet four.'

'There are some who say that a boy's mind is fixed sooner than that. I would hate to think that he—'

'Meg, come here and rest a moment. You've been working too hard,' Simon said, drawing up his chair. 'Tell me what this is really all about.'

'It's nothing.'

'I know it's nothing. Now tell me what is nothing?'

'I am still worried about Edith.'

Simon sighed. 'We know that she is as well as can be expected.'

'I just want to hear from her. I worry that something could have happened.'

'Baldwin would tell us,' Simon pointed out. 'He hears from her fairly often, and lets us know when he does.'

'We're so far away though. A week's journey, and . . .'

'And there's nothing to worry about. The trouble is, Baldwin's busy. You know that.'

It was true. They had been used to receiving little messages every so often, whenever Baldwin could find a man travelling in the correct direction. He had been able to use Edgar to make contact, just as he had planned, and for some weeks news had filtered through to them regularly, but recently Baldwin had been called to help Hugh de Courtenay and the Bishop of Exeter to array the men of Devon and Cornwall ready to repel any possible attack. Baldwin had conveyed a message with a tranter to say that all was well, but that he had been sent with another man, by name of Peter Ovedale, to array the men at Launceston. Since then,

Simon had heard nothing from him. And that had been at the time of the Feast of the Discovery of the Cross – about a month ago.

There had been times when Simon himself had wondered about that delay. It was a long time to have heard nothing from Baldwin. Usually they kept in touch each fortnight even when they were both busy, but now things were changed. Simon had occasional irrational fears that Baldwin could have grown irritated with him because of their falling-out last year, and then he grew anxious that the knight could have met with an accident. There was no logical reason to think this, but the lands west of Exeter were always rather lawless compared with the rest of the kingdom, and since the queen had lost all her lands in Cornwall the previous year, the area had grown still more dangerous.

The news from all over the realm was not reassuring. It was good to be one of the first to hear it, because as a king's officer at the port, he was given a great deal of information daily: sailors from London with their bizarre language and tones telling of the expectation in the city itself, with stories of arms being stored in the Tower, along with barrels full of saltpetre and honey, ready to manufacture that marvellous black powder that so terrified horses and men alike in battle.

Reports from other places were no less chilling. There were tales of French troop movements all along the Guyennois border, and other reports spoke of men mustering in Hainault, as well as the accumulation of ships. If Simon believed half of the stories he had heard, England would be absorbed into France within a matter of weeks. Fortunately, he was aware that these reports were likely exaggerated.

Just then, there was a commotion from outside, and Simon lifted his eyes to the door as Perkin ran in, Hugh stomping along behind him, a fierce glower on his face.

'Daddy!'

'How are you, little man?'

'I am—'

'He has knocked over the dish with the supper,' Hugh said, with grim satisfaction.

Chapter Fifteen

Paris

Rector Paul de Cockington was not unhappy to be in France.

As soon as his brother had been able to guarantee a safe passage for him, Paul had taken his place in a small band of wandering merchants, men-at-arms and lawyers bound for Exmouth where they intended taking a ship to Guyenne.

The past year had seen confusion over England's control of the French possessions. There had been wrangling for a long time over the rights of the King of France to the King of England's great Duchy of Aquitaine. The bitter enmity between the French and English sprang from ancient causes; ever since the Duke of Normandy had invaded and taken the English crown for his own, the French Kings had deprecated the presumption of England's kings. The presumption was escalated by the warmonger Richard I, Cocur-de-Lion, who forced the French King to build his magnificent fortress, the Louvre, in order to protect his city against a potential attack from Richard's Norman territory.

Once Richard I was dead, the French wasted no time in confiscating all the English lands in Normandy, with such efficiency and resolve that soon nothing remained.

However, this did not affect the jewel in the English crown: Aquitaine. This vast swathe of France had been given by France to England as a dower, and its loss was resented. Especially since this present English King Edward II refused to travel to France to pay homage for the territories even though he held them as a feudal lord from his liege lord. He was King of England, perhaps, but in France he was a mere duke, and he must bend his knee to

King Charles IV and promise to serve his king, just as any man might.

The fact that King Edward II would not come served to polish the hatred that already existed until it gleamed. And so King Charles had waited until there was a pretext for war, and when it presented itself, he swiftly ordered the invasion of Aquitaine. The operation had been so well planned in advance, it took little time to overwhelm the English garrisons. In a matter of weeks, France had reclaimed the whole of the Duchy and the English were left spluttering with futile rage back in their island.

Negotiations had immediately been instigated. The Pope tried to forge an alliance between these two nations, that they might soon join and renew their assault on the Moslem hordes which had overrun the Holy Land. But he failed. It was only when Edward II's queen, King Charles IV's sister, travelled to France that the stalemate began to ease. Her son was sent to her, duly invested with the magnificent Duchy, in order that he might give homage for it in his own right. And the magnificent territories had been returned to the English.

So now, many officers, warriors and lawyers were hurrying to Aquitaine in the hope of enriching themselves – much like miners who had heard of a rich seam of ore. They flocked to the place in their hundreds. In a land which had recently seen war and devastation, there was always hope for lawyers and men trained in weapons, just as there was the hope of king's officials that they might resolve disputes and accept bribes in return. Territory only recently at war was always a source of good pickings.

Except, as Paul had learned soon after arriving, a fresh dispute had arisen. The queen declared her hatred for her husband's favourite and refused to return to England. Equally, she utterly refused to send her son home. While she wished to remain, the French king was reluctant to evict her, for he would not remove the offer of hospitality to his own sister, and thus there was a pause, while both nations stood and watched, almost as though both were holding their breath, daring the other to start the war again.

But for a cleric, such concerns were less pressing. Paul had a comfortable post in rooms near the cathedral, and he happily sauntered about in the sun. One of the clerks with whom he had travelled to Paris was a man in the pay of the Earl of Winchester, the father to Sir Hugh le Despenser, and Paul was able to help with some of his duties, for he spoke fluent French, having come from a good noble family. So for the last weeks, Paul had enjoyed his temporary exile.

There would one day be a reckoning, he was aware of that. He would have to return to England to learn what the Church intended to do with him, for there was no doubt that the Bishop of Exeter would refuse to return him to his post. Rather, he would wish to put him back in the bishopric's gaol from which he had escaped.

That was not an outcome which appealed to him. The next time he was incarcerated, it would be a great deal more difficult to escape, no matter how much his brother bribed the guards and gaolers.

Paul lounged on a wall near the cathedral, overlooking the Seine and enjoying the sights in the sun. It was a glorious day, and he was debating whether to go to the little pie shop up near the Louvre which had become to him a delightful bolt-hole, or to walk over to the tavern near the eastern gate, when he caught sight of two women strolling along the road. Both, he sighed, were worth a second look. Adorable, the shorter one. Petite, with olive skin and luscious dark hair, she was his favourite. Light and bouncy, with a pair of breasts that would be enough to suffocate the man who shoved his face between them, and a backside that would grace a small pony, she was quite delectable, especially with her cheeky grin.

The other was a little taller, stronger, and fairer. She had grey eyes that held that challenging, 'Damn you' expression he so mistrusted. Women, he found, were better when they were smaller. Then the enthusiastic could be supported, while the recalcitrant could be forced. Larger women could prove to be too much of a handful, in his experience.

'I wouldn't, if I were you.'

The voice was that of a man immediately behind him, and he turned, startled, to find himself being studied by a shortish fellow with very clear blue eyes. He was only perhaps three- or four-and-twenty, and from the look of his fit, muscular frame and slim waist, he was used to fighting. And from the look of the creases at the corners of his eyes, he was also used to laughing.

'Wouldn't what?' Paul asked.

'Try to entice those ladies.' He winked and turned to watch the women walking away along the street, and nodded shortly beyond them. 'See those two?'

Paul gave a fleeting frown. His eyesight was not very good, but he could discern something. 'Is it two men?'

'Aye, friend. And I think we should be leaving this place.'

'Why?'

'Well, those two look to me like the sort of churls who'd quite like to investigate what your bowels would look like, looped over a fence. You're English, they're French, and even though you only eyed two Frenchwomen and didn't make a move, I think they'd take you apart for the fun of destroying an Englishman.'

Oakhampton Castle, Devon

The entrance to the great castle of the de Courtenay family, guarding the main road into Cornwall from the valleys of Devon, was imposing.

Originally the castle had been a simple motte and bailey construction, Baldwin guessed as he trotted down the roadway. From here he could see the keep on its enormous mound. Many serfs would have been employed to manufacture that, because originally it had been a long ridge of rock; the first Normans had forced the local population to hack and dig at it, heaving heavy baskets of rock and soil away and tipping them on top of the mound, bringing its height up above the original ridge and making it still more imposing. No doubt much of the rock dug away would also have been used in constructing the early walls. No matter. The main fact was, by the end of it all, and thanks to the efforts of the poor townspeople, there was a huge fissure dug from the rock so that the castle keep stood isolated on a separate mound. And that was when the real building could begin.

The keep was a tall tower, square sided, and secure by virtue of the steep hill on which it stood. Below was the main hall and all the supporting buildings, enclosed within their high wall. Smoke was drifting into the air from the cooking fires and the forges, and the sound of hammering crashed into Baldwin's ears as smiths went about their business making arrowheads, knife and sword blades, chains, steel balls for maces, and armour. The full paraphernalia of offence and defence. All a man could wish for, were he to desire to kill without dying.

At the bottom, facing the road, was the long corridor of the bastion, which curved up to the main gate.

'De Courtenay has a strong fortress here,' Peter Ovedale commented.

Baldwin shot a glance at him. 'Yes. This is a good position for a man who wishes to guard the approaches to the town.'

'It is better than that. It's an excellent place from which to guard against attackers from Cornwall and thus to defend the realm,' Ovedale said.

Baldwin grimaced. 'Perhaps. Unless the attackers sweep around it and continue on their path.'

'When these mercenaries arrive, sir, they will not wish to leave a solid little post like this,' Ovedale said sententiously, then sniffed.

Baldwin grunted. The insufferable knight had been speaking like this for all the time he had known him, and he was heartily bored with it. Ovedale appeared to have decided he was competent to assess the defensive capabilities of any town or castle while they were involved in the commission of array, and had assumed responsibility for judging and reporting on them all. In his mind, it was clear that the queen with her mercenaries from France would land in Cornwall and sweep their way up this road, not stopping until they were met by the levies of Devon, at which point they would be annihilated.

'You must concede, Sir Baldwin, that such mercenaries will not appreciate the full strength of the English and Cornish peasantry until they meet them.'

'That, I believe, is quite correct,' Baldwin said quietly. He had fought at Acre, when he was a raw, untested warrior who had thought that with God on his side, he must inevitably win. He had learned early on that a warrior who was practised would be more likely to survive a battle on his feet, and he knew that most mercenaries had already been tested in battle, and to line against them the poor, foolish, or even strong and intelligent of the countryside, was to give them a perfect series of targets for their weapons.

Swords and lances, spears and axes, all would crush opposition when the latter was comprised largely of peasants who had little understanding of combat, nor of the sheer hideous ferocity of war. A few would consider themselves fighters, and they might be keen to join the fray, thinking that their ability with fists or a dagger, after a night's drinking scrumpy until fear was utterly eradicated, would have shaped them for modern warfare, but Baldwin knew otherwise. When the artillery hurled shot at them from trebuchets, or the foul, modern metal tubes belched fire and smoke, a man's heart would quail; when hordes of screaming iron-clad men hurtled towards them, all gleaming with silver steel, rattling like a thousand cauldrons filled with bolts and nails, then the peasants would find their courage leaching away like blood soaking into the soil. War was not a sport for the faint-hearted.

'Yes, we will show the queen that she cannot simply ride some small boat over here and expect a welcome with open arms! Hah!'

'Come, let us halt here and rest,' Baldwin said. Grimacing, he dismounted. Today's journey from Cornwall had been long, and he was desperate for a chair and, unusually for him, a large goblet of wine. Although, with his thirst, perhaps a quart of ale would be a better choice.

The steward met them at the gate and bellowed for ostlers.

Soon they were ensconced on a broad bench, backs against the wall, while the steward told them of the number of men in the town and about the castle. For the array here, the king could depend upon almost a hundred.

As commissioners, Baldwin and Ovedale had simple instructions. To find the strongest men in each hundred, arm them and put the more competent into armour, and then group them in their twenties, called vintaines, which were the basic unit of the king's host. The vintaines were lumped together into centaines, hundreds, and ten of these formed a millaine. Thus was the king's force composed, with each man knowing his vintaine, his centaine and millaine. Orders could be sent from the commander to the groups without difficulty, and each unit should be able to operate, in theory, to ensure success.

But not, of course, when the individual components were unready.

The steward here was a cheery-looking fellow named Sir Giles de Sens, who smiled a great deal. He had a large paunch, a round face, and the high colouring that spoke of his enjoyment of drinking and good food.

'How are matters in Cornwall?' he asked as soon as the two men had drunk enough to take the edge from their thirst.

Food was being prepared as they waited, and Baldwin's mouth watered at the smells emanating from the kitchen a short distance away. 'Not so bad as I feared,' he admitted. 'The men appear fit and ready. However, there is a great deal of loyalty to the queen there. She was popular among the miners.'

'But they will do their duty to God and their king!' Ovedale stated. 'They love their king, and will obey him.'

'Perhaps,' Baldwin said.

'You doubt their loyalty to the king?' Ovedale asked, shocked.

'I doubt no one. Nor do I trust them when they have not yet seen the size of the force that opposes them.'

'If,' Sir Giles said, 'you are correct, Sir Baldwin, pray, what do you think of their devotion to their king, or to, say, my lord Despenser?'

Baldwin shot him a look. The man looked easy and relaxed, but that was no guide. He had just asked a dangerous question, because it related directly to Sir Hugh le Despenser, and Baldwin was sure that Ovedale was a firm supporter of Sir Hugh. 'I think it is as strong as any man's in the land,' he said at last.

'Even so?' the steward said, and now he grinned, and Baldwin saw his eyes flit over towards Ovedale. So this man was fully aware of Ovedale's position then, and was testing Baldwin. His eyes were shrewder than Baldwin had first thought.

It was much later that he sought out Baldwin. Ovedale had already gone to find a suitable bed for the night, and Baldwin was enjoying the peace without him. He was staring up at the stars, admiring them as they twinkled in the clear sky, watching occasional gossamer-thin clouds drifting past in the deep, dark blueness, when he heard the steps.

'I am sorry to have asked in front of that fool, Sir Baldwin,' he said.

'Asked what?' Baldwin murmured.

'Oh, I wouldn't worry. Down here, we know where our loyalties lie. We serve Sir Hugh de Courtenay, and that makes our task all the easier.'

'I am sure that he would make it very easy,' Baldwin said tersely. 'He, like any other knight, must support the king.'

'The king, yes. Not his favourite, though. There is almost no one in the land who has any warmth of feeling towards Despenser.'

Baldwin shook his head sadly. 'Goodnight, friend.'

'No, please, Sir Baldwin. Wait a moment or two more. I have been asked to speak with you by Sir Hugh de Courtenay himself. He wishes to know whether you will support . . .'

'I have given you my answer,' Baldwin said. 'I can give no other.'

'Oh. Well, that is a shame, Sir Baldwin. There are strange things happening all over the realm, and you will soon find that taking this kind of attitude isn't very sensible.'

'Are you threatening me?'

Sir Giles smiled with an appearance of regret. 'Oh, I don't seek to threaten, Sir Baldwin. No. All I want to do is to help you to make your own choice. You cannot want to support Despenser, after all. No man would wish to see that knuckle-headed dollypoddle stay in a position of authority. He is a danger to the realm, to the king himself, because he foments trouble all the while. Do you deny this?'

'I deny nothing,' Baldwin said heavily. 'But I have given my oath.'

'There is no shame, Sir Baldwin, in serving the kingdom. You could say that you were seeing to the interests of the crown itself, in the authority itself, rather than the man.'

Baldwin turned to him. 'You seek to twist words? I am not a man of law, I am a simple rural knight, and I have no need for such dissembling. You mean to ask me to deny my oath to the king. I shall not. I like the queen, and I would do all in my power to protect her – if it was *in* my power – but I have made an oath before God, and I will not break that.'

'Then I am sad, my friend,' Sir Giles said. 'Truly sad. For I fear that all such oaths will be thrown into the pot soon, and only those who seek the good of the people of this land of ours will be honoured.'

'So be it. But I will stay true to my word.'

'You will defend those whom the king orders you to?'

'Yes.'

'So perhaps we shall one day meet on a field of battle, with you protecting Despenser, eh, Sir Baldwin?'

Baldwin said nothing. He turned his face to the stars once more, and Sir Giles waited a few moments, and then strolled away.

There was nothing more to be said. When the queen at last invaded, they would instantly become enemies.

Chapter Sixteen

Louvre, Paris

Paul de Cockington gazed about him with wonder at the sight of the soaring walls of the great fortress at the western end of the city. He had seen them often enough, of course, for no one could miss the fortress from anywhere in the city. It loomed over all, as much a symbol of dominance and control as it was of protection, but he had not come so near to its huge white walls before, and from here, they were stunning.

'Who are you?' he asked his new friend.

'My name is Roger Crok. I am a squire.'

'But not in the service of the king,' Paul said shrewdly. No man here in France was in the English king's service.

Crok's face hardened. 'I was once a loyal squire. My father was a contrary old man, and he died some years ago. When my mother remarried, she tied herself to a gentleman who was opposed to Despenser. So Despenser took his revenge and had my stepfather arrested. He died in prison. Not content with that, Despenser and Bishop Stapledon stole my mother's dower, and finally sought to capture and execute me. That is how Despenser and the bishop operate, after all. They capture men, allege treachery, and then conspire to steal their victims' lands and treasure. I preferred not to wait for that day. I took to the sea as soon as I realised my danger.'

He smiled still, but there was an edge to his voice that told Paul not to push him further. Not that he had a desire to. Paul could recognise a dangerous man when he met one. Still, he was a dangerous man himself. There was no need to be scared of a fellow like this. Not when his brother was sheriff of Exeter.

It was humiliating to be stuck here in this strange land, without friends. The clerk with whom he was lodged had no interest in him whatsoever.

'What are you doing here?' Crok asked.

It was Paul's turn to smile. 'I was accused of a crime and forced to leave the kingdom. I would prefer to return, but have been told it would be better were I to stay away for now.'

'Likely true enough,' Crok said. 'Did you do it?'

'What?'

'The crime you were accused of.'

Paul felt his face begin to redden. 'I would hardly . . .'

'So you did, then,' Crok noted. He eyed Paul speculatively, in a way that increased the latter's wariness.

'It is undoubtedly a matter of some embarrassment, which is why I'm here,' Paul said stiffly. 'But I'm not bereft of friends even now. Just because I've made one mistake means nothing. I am a friend to the Earl of Winchester, for example, and to—'

'Then I would be silent if I were you,' Crok said, and now his tone was markedly different. 'Do you have no understanding about your position here? In Christ's name, man, you are in Paris amidst all the king's enemies – his wife among them! And you boast about being friendly with Sir Hugh le Despenser's father? He would be pleased, I doubt me not, were he to learn that you were here, so that you might spy for him on the camp. You are not a spy, are you?'

The suddenness of his question threw the befuddled Paul off balance. 'Spy? Me? I wouldn't—'

'No, you don't have the look of a spy. That would imply dissembling, and you don't seem very good at that, do you? Still, I would watch your tongue when in the company of Englishmen. There are many here who would happily execute a friend of Despenser's.'

'I . . . I had not thought . . .'

'Plainly. Here, you are safe from the French. In this castle you are protected by the King of France himself. But that won't serve to help you if you tell all inside that you are a friend of the Despenser. Even the French King detests the man.'

*Third Wednesday before the Feast of St John and St Paul**

Louvre, Paris

He had thought that the blessed realm of France was one of continual sunshine and delight, but this was the second day on which Paul de Cockington had awoken to find that the skies were black with filthy clouds that were determined, apparently, to wash all evidence of the castle from the city. The rain fell in torrents, until a man standing at one side of the great courtyard at the Louvre might find it impossible to see the wall opposite. Paul had never seen such appalling weather.

In England, he had heard France spoken of as the epitome of style, culture and elegance. Well, as far as Paul was concerned, the people ate mostly peasant food, even here in the castle, and the French knights and squires he had met appeared to lack even a modicum of politeness and civility.

It was not as if he had offended anybody. After his little chat with Crok, he had been enormously careful to whom he spoke, and what he said. There was no point in taking risks. If it were not for the men he had seen with Crok that day, he would have returned to his little chamber . . . But that would mean going back to the companionship of that tedious clerk, and in fairness to the staff of the Louvre, it was probably better here than there.

Especially since there were so many Englishmen here in the castle. In some ways, it put him in mind of a massive gaol, with so many malcontents all living together. If King Edward could have simply locked the doors and set fire to the whole place, it would have saved him a great deal of time, effort and worry, for almost every soul inside was his enemy. The only significant two who were missing were Queen Isabella and the appalling Roger

* 4 June 1326

Mortimer, the man whom all knew as the greatest traitor this king had been forced to suffer. Mortimer had escaped from his captivity in the Tower of London and, so all said, was now the lover of the king's own wife. The poisonous little vixen! Paul would like to chastise her properly. Ha, that would be a wonderful experience. She was said to be the most beautiful woman in all Christendom.

Yes, but even without the two most significant enemies, the rest of the fellows cooped up in the Louvre were all dedicated to ending the oppression of his rule. If they were not dedicated to regicide, which was a peculiarly hazardous ambition, bearing in mind God's anointing of King Edward, they were all devoted to the death of his ally and adviser, Sir Hugh le Despenser.

Sir Hugh was so cunning, so able and devious, that he had contrived to steal the houses from about the ears of many men. Not alone, of course. Since arriving here in Paris, Paul had been staggered by the number of men who spoke with scorn and detestation of his own bishop. There were many who said that Walter Stapledon was just as guilty of theft and extortion as Despenser himself. All of which came as a big shock to Paul, who had assumed all believed the bishop to be as nearly saintly as was possible for a man on this earth. Stapledon had always been spoken of with regard, in his experience. All in Devon knew how hardworking and assiduous in the improvement of the diocese, how organised and effective he had been. Not that it changed Paul's opinion of the bastard! And yet here, he found himself just one among those who considered the bishop to be the least honourable clerk in Holy Orders. It was refreshing.

The weather began to clear at midday, and Paul walked outside in order that he might find a local tavern in which to spend the afternoon, but as he stepped over the threshold and found himself in the lane just south of the Louvre, he saw a group of men sitting at a table, all talking earnestly, one jabbing with a finger, while others nodded seriously.

'Here's a man who can assist us,' said Crok, glancing up as Paul approached.

'Assist? I shall, if I may,' Paul said. He took pains to ensure that he held the appearance of an honourable priest whenever he met with others, and he attempted that feat now, as he clasped his hands and bowed his head respectfully.

'We are to be honoured with the presence of a notable fellow soon,' Crok said. 'But although we and others can form his honour-guard, he will require a priest as well. Would you stand as his confessor?'

'If he be a man without evil in his soul, I would be pleased to be his confessor. But who is this man? One of you here?'

Paul looked about them smiling vaguely at each man in turn. He knew them all. There were the two brothers, one fair, one dark, both tall and with eyes that appeared too close together: Sir Ivo la Zouche of Harringworth and Sir Ralph la Zouche; the strange young man with the black Celtic hair and blue eyes called Sir John Biset; the young man with the tonsure still growing out, who called himself Sir Richard de Folville, and of course Roger Crok, the man who had saved him from the French in the street, and brought him here to rescue him. Of them all, he was sure that Crok would be the safest.

It was Ivo la Zouche who curled his lip and chuckled. 'You think it's one of us, eh? No, little priest. We have a better man for you to concentrate on. You will be the confessor to the Earl of Chester.'

'The Earl of Chester?' This was better than he had hoped. There wasn't an Earl alive who didn't have a purse filled with gold. As confessor to a man like that, he would have access to better food, a new chemise, perhaps even the odd trinket of his own . . .

'He's counting the coins already!' Crok said delightedly.

Richard de Folville was eyeing him with a look of disdain. 'He hasn't any idea who you're talking about, Sir Ivo. Tell him.'

'Don't you know who the Earl of Chester is?' Sir Ivo asked. He looked slightly shocked when Paul shook his head.

'He is the son of the king, man,' John Biset said, and gave a sour grin at the expression of sheer horror that passed over Paul's face.

Exeter Cathedral Close

The familia gathered outside the little chapel and waited for the bishop to arrive.

It was Bishop Walter's routine to have his people wait outside for him, and then they would all troop into his private chapel together for the morning's Mass. Later, he would have a quiet period of prayer with his chaplain alone, and only on feast days would he go to the cathedral itself and take his throne, the new massive wooden seat which he had helped design as a part of the rebuilding of the quire. More commonly, this most devout bishop preferred a quiet service, away from the noise of the rebuilding and the public.

To John's eye, it was too austere. He had mentioned it often enough, but Bishop Walter would not listen.

'You ought to be in full fig, and with a golden goblet and cross,' the steward grumbled.

'All that folderol is unnecessary in my own chapel. I want peace in there, so that I can concentrate. That is not too much to ask.'

'So you praise God while denigrating Him by wearing that old black robe,' John said dismissively.

The arguments would always rage from that point, with the bishop convinced that there was no point in excess in his private chapel, while John remained certain that God would expect it.

It was months now since the discovery of that message and the head's appearance. Months in which John and William Walle had stayed alert, ever watchful in case some stranger might attempt to approach the bishop and slide a dagger in under his ribs, or fire a crossbow, or poison him. The number of ways in which a man could be killed was alarming to John, once he had begun to learn a little about assassination. There was a master of the arts of defence in the city who had taken delight (and several coins) in instructing John in the more dangerous aspects of protecting a man. Of course, like most masters of defence, this fellow was more keen to ensure that his client was safe, and it was difficult for him to appreciate the difference here, bearing in mind that the man being protected was not the man paying him his money.

'Can't you bring him to me?'

'He would not be keen.'

'I've had unwilling clients before,' the man had laughed.

'Not like this one,' John said with certainty.

He and William had become pretty comfortable that their charge would be safe while both were near to hand. The main task appeared to be to prevent anyone from approaching within a few feet of the bishop. There was always the possibility of a lone archer trying his luck, of course, but there were few places in which an archer could hide without being seen; likewise, if a man attempted poison, he must get right into the bishop's palace kitchen. John had set the cooks to be wary and prevent strangers from gaining access.

In all the months since John and William had started to take precautions, nothing had so far happened. As was entirely natural, they were growing gradually less and less alert to danger. In the weeks after the first note, William and he had searched all crowds for an assassin, and William once thought he had seen one, a shifty-eyed fellow in the Close at about the time of Father Joshua's death, but there were no further developments. Even now, John found himself looking up at the sky, observing the movements of birds, idly noting that the elm tree over towards the Close would have to have the limb that pointed southwards lopped off, if it were not to fall on a man's head.

Thus it was that the bellow of shock and fear came as a sudden bolt of lightning from a clear summer's evening.

'The bishop!' he gasped, and set off at a run. Rounding the corner of the building, he saw the sight he had dreaded for so long. There, on the ground, was his master lying prostrate. 'My lord! My lord, what has happened to you?' he cried, throwing himself down at the side of the bishop.

'I tripped, you blithering idiot!' the bishop rasped. 'Help me up, both of you! Who left that plank there? The builders are not supposed to be *here*! Is there nowhere a man may find peace, even in his own grounds? This is ridiculous!'

Before long, John and William had managed to lift the bishop to his feet, where he stood, dusting off the mess from the pathway.

'You aren't cut, nor broken?' John asked solicitously.

'Do stop fussing, man! All that happened was, I missed my footing. If I could wear my spectacles more, I should be fine, but the things are too clumsy. I hate holding them up to my eyes as I walk about, it makes me fall more often. When all is said and done, I am an old man. Never needed help before, but as soon as I became fifty years old, my sight began to falter. Ach! Look at me!'

'My lord bishop, let me fetch you a little wine.'

'No. I am late enough as it is.'

So saying, the Bishop of Exeter swept up his gowns and marched purposefully onwards. John fell into step beside William. 'I am relieved that this was a mere accident.'

'Yes. He looked quite comical as he fell, though I doubt he would have been pleased to know he afforded me a degree of amusement.' William was still smiling at the memory: the bishop had taken a fair tumble, his gowns and cloak flying in all directions like the tattered remains of a crow shot by a sling.

'I begin to wonder whether the man who wrote the note simply sought to instil fear?' John mused. 'It has been such a long time since it was found. We're halfway through the year. I've never known a man threaten violence and then allow his threats to mature for so long.'

'You are right, of course. It's perfectly likely that we did overreact,' William agreed. But then he stopped and glanced at the steward. 'But what if we relaxed our guard, and that happened to be the very day in which the killer took the bishop's life? Would we ever be able to forgive ourselves?'

'No.'

They entered the chapel, bowing and genuflecting as they entered, using a little of the holy water from the conical stoup set into the wall by the door, and made their way down to the bishop, kneeling immediately behind him, their hands clasped together like a prince's paying homage.

The service, so William felt, was too slow. He had a mind that could rarely remain focused on one matter for too long, and he found it wandering as he listened to the interminable muttering of the chaplain. He was too old, and his teeth unsure, so his breath whistled as his voice rose and fell in the familiar cadences. It was a surprise that such an old fellow was retained by the bishop, for usually he sought younger fellows who would have more stamina. Not only must they be prepared to act as the bishop's private chaplain here in Exeter, but when he must travel about his diocese, the chaplain would have to ride with him; if he was called to London or York to meet the king, again, his chaplain would be at his side. William wondered if having an older man with him reminded him a little of his old friend, Father Joshua.

When the service was over, William was pleased to be able to leave the chapel and gain the open air again. He looked about him quickly, but there was no sign of danger, and he continued on his way, looking at all the places which might be useful for an assassin to hide in.

'Here we are, Uncle,' he said, as he opened the door to the bishop's private chamber.

The bishop walked in as William stood holding it wide, and crossed the wooden floor to his little seat near the fire. John had seen to it that the room was prepared. A fire crackled and hissed most reassuringly in the hearth, a jug of wine had been set near to his elbow, a silver goblet beside it. There was nothing the bishop could require that had not been provided already. Even his favourite books were placed near to hand, the *Chanson de Roland*, and *Girart of Vienne*, both beautifully illustrated works, and a book of St Thomas Aquinas.

'My life has been one of service, you know, William,' the bishop said heavily.

'You have served all well, Uncle: your king, your flock, and God.'

'You say that so glibly. I wonder whether it is true? I have done what I thought was right, but perhaps I have failed. I have sought to serve God and see to the ministry of His souls. What if that was not good enough? I have tried to serve our kingdom, tried to mediate between the king and his queen, but my efforts served no purpose. Did I bring them back together? No. Even now she sits like some great spider in France, her web woven, waiting for us to fall into her clutches. And behind her, damned Mortimer, the best general our king ever had, and well he knows it! What have I achieved?'

'You have made the Treasury efficient, you have secured education for many, you have . . .'

But the bishop was not listening. He gazed into the fire, his fingers drumming on the table top beside him. William went over and poured wine into his goblet.

Absently, the bishop took it up and drank. His fingers reached for St Thomas Aquinas and he opened the book, his eyes running down the text without seeing. William passed him his spectacles, and he took them, but then shook his head, closed the book, and reached for his copy of *Roland*. 'The *Chanson*. It always soothes me,' he murmured, and lifted the cover as his nephew walked back to the door, bowing and taking his leave.

His gasp of horror was enough to make the young squire rush back to the bishop's side.

There, inside, was a second note.

Chapter Seventeen

Louvre, Paris

There was a crunch behind him, and Ralph la Zouche immediately dropped low, span round upon his toe and snatched at his sword, sweeping it out in a slither of steel, eyes narrowed, left hand ready to block any sudden attack.

The ostler gaped, dropping his saddle and almost turning to flee at the sight of this grim, bearded Englishman. *'M'sieur, je veux . . .'*

'Put your sword up, Sir Ralph! Do you want to have the whole castle upon us?' Richard de Folville hissed.

Sir Ralph carefully inserted the point of his sword into the scabbard, then thrust it home, but stood a few moments, staring at Folville. The Folvilles had been allies of his family for years, but this one, this Richard, who had been sent to become a priest and yet who now allowed his tonsure to grow out, was not made from the same mould as them. This shit-britches would run to mummy at the first sign of trouble. If he dared to tell Sir Ralph what to do, the knight would squash him like a fly.

Beckoning the ostler, Sir Ralph pulled out a coin from his purse, flipping it into the air, and stalking away before anyone could say anything more.

Folville had not laughed. That fact had saved his life, because a shitten priest wouldn't laugh twice at Sir Ralph. No, not even a Folville could insult Sir Ralph.

He was the eldest of his brothers, and the one man most aware of the family's honour. Ever since their first arrival in England from Normandy, his family had been at the forefront of English politics. They had come with William the Bastard, and they had been at the vanguard of his host as Duke William rode hither and thither over the realm, quelling all the rebels who tried to use terrorism to evict their lawful conquerors. Those must have been hard days: sitting long hours in the saddle, then riding down the pathetic English rebels at the point of the lance. Sir Ralph wished he could have been born in those days, with the chance of fighting them. It was what he was born for: fighting.

There had been times for glory only recently, too. It wasn't only dead history. In King Edward I's reign, there had been thrilling opportunities for a man to go to Scotland or Wales. His own father had fought in both countries, making himself a small fortune in the process, when he captured two Welsh princes and ransomed them. The money from those two had bought the family two good manors, which had in some ways compensated them for the other difficulties that they had encountered with neighbours. The Belers family was always a difficult competitor, and they had always sought to influence people to the detriment of the la Zouches.

The feud had its genesis far back in the distant past. Grandfather had once said that it actually went back to the times before the invasion of the country. In France, their ancestors had maintained a running competition since the days of Roland, bickering and quarrelling over their rights to different parcels of land. When they came to England, Duke William had given all his knights tracts of land which were diversely spread over the whole country, so that no one man would have enough power in any shire to be able to gather up forces to threaten his own rule, and also so that the knights would be too busy travelling from one manor to another to be able to foment trouble. As a policy, it had worked. But in succeeding years, all the lords and barons had gradually accumulated more lands in their own favoured locations, and some had formed strong power bases.

In their territories, it had perhaps been natural that the Belers and the la Zouches should have come to view each other askance. As they soon did. But it was all the fault of the Belers family.

That much was clear. It was why the la Zouches had been forced to take such drastic action.

And why Sir Ralph was here, he told himself, watching the ostler settling the saddle on his mount's back.

That rector didn't like him. Well, that was fine by Sir Ralph. If Richard Folville's brothers had all been here, maybe Sir Ralph would have been concerned. But they weren't, so the priest should stay out of Sir Ralph's way.

The others here in the Louvre were an unknown quantity. He could utterly rely on his brother Ivo, of course. But the others: John Biset, Roger Crok, and now this new priest Paul de Cockington as well, were not the sort of men to inspire confidence in a commander.

If these were the only men who were designated to protect Duke Edward of Aquitaine, Sir Ralph would have his work cut out.

There was no denying that he felt the edginess of the others. They were all too short with each other, too prepared to snap and argue. Just as he was himself, if he were honest. All of them were too well aware of the dangers they ran in being here. But for them there was nowhere else to go. Nothing to do. They were victims of the cretinous king and his lover, Despenser.

Because they all knew that they were now considered to be traitors. They were each of them worth money to the king and Despenser . . . dead.

Bishop's Palace, Exeter

John was glad of William's presence when he heard of the second message.

'What does it say?' he demanded, while the men-at-arms ran about the palace, searching all the most likely, and several frankly impossible, places of concealment.

'Look for yourself,' William said curtly.

Taking it, John read aloud. '*The author of so much misery must pay for it all. Death, and Hell, await you.*'

'How dare he accuse my uncle of being the architect of

misery! A kinder, more thoughtful and considerate man never walked the earth,' William said heatedly.

John nodded. 'There is nothing to show how this was brought to the palace. Who would dare to enter my master's private chamber and fiddle with his books?'

'The very same man who would dare to threaten him with death and damnation.'

'How did he get into the palace?' John wondered. 'The doors should have been locked.'

'Do the familia lock all the doors when they go with the bishop to the chapel or church? I doubt it. All our careful planning has come to nought, John. We didn't think of that.'

'Why should we? It's been five months. We were both beginning to think that the danger had receded.'

'I certainly had,' William said. His face was gaunt as the full import of the afternoon's event was brought home to him. 'Someone was here, John – in his private chamber, and even knew to place the parchment into that book. The courage of the devil.'

'We shall have to find this man,' John said. 'It is someone who must know about the bishop's movements at certain times.'

'All I can think of is a man who could hate so much, but who also holds the power to enter a palace like this. It seems like more than one man, does it not?'

Neither heard the door behind them open, as William continued speaking, taking the parchment back again.

'So, it must be someone enormously powerful – and bold enough to walk in here, or prepared to pay someone else to do it.'

Bishop Walter stepped forward and took the scrap of parchment. He glanced at it, then flung it aside. 'I am one of the most powerful men in Exeter, yet I have no idea who could have done this!'

William nodded, but glanced at John as he said, 'Could you show us the first message, please? I think it would be useful for John to see it as well.'

The bishop set his jaw. 'Very well. John, it is in the large chest in my bedchamber.'

John nodded and walked from the room by the small spiral staircase set into the corner of the chamber.

'Who could want to do this to you?' William asked.

'You have asked me that before. I don't know.'

'Uncle, there is a man whom you have upset enough to make him loathe you. You could surely not have inspired such hatred without knowing it!'

'Nephew, I hold power in this cathedral and my diocese; I have held extraordinary power as the Lord High Treasurer. Men hate me for both of these roles. I have negotiated with the queen on behalf of the king, so she hates me. Others think I helped take too much of their lands or treasure for tax and they too hate me. There are many, many men who would happily see me sink into hell.'

John returned, holding the cream-coloured purse. He passed it to the bishop without a word.

'So, the first told you that the reckoning was at hand, while this second says more definitely that hell awaits you.'

'And I have no idea who could have written them.'

John was studying the purse itself. 'This stain – it is old blood. The purse has lain in a man's blood.'

The bishop reached for it and studied the brown marks. 'How can you be so sure? It looks like mud to me.'

'I am sure,' John said.

William looked at his uncle. 'Have you killed a man?'

'No. I have fought, but never slain.'

'Well, there are no guards on your doors,' William said. 'In the Cathedral Close there could have been a thousand men and women today, so it is not possible to work out who could have come to this room while we were in chapel. All we can do is wait for him to try it again.'

'And next time, with luck, we shall catch him,' John said. He looked at his master, and felt as though his heart must tear in two at the expression of dismay on the bishop's face. 'Do not fear, my lord bishop. We shall catch him.'

'You will not be hurt by this man,' William added.

'No,' the bishop said, but he did not sound convinced. A short while later, John and William were outside his room.

'Squire William, I am scared.'

'Master John, do not be. All we must do is ensure that my uncle is safe from intruders. If we can do that, and stop these ridiculous messages reaching him, he will soon be himself again.' But as William turned away, he thought sadly that the bishop looked like a frail old man, a man who had not many more months to live.

Paris

Their path took them up the roads away from Paris itself, and soon Richard Folville was glad to see that their route was taking them away from the woods, as well. There was a steady sense of anxiety in his belly whenever he was in a close-confined area.

The murder of Belers was a passing memory now. It had been necessary because the thieving scrote had tried to steal too much from the Folville family as well as the la Zouches. Belers was always happy to enrich himself at the expense of all-comers. Well, he could rob peasants as often as he wished, but if a Belers tried to grab the lands of an old established family like the Folvilles, he would have his hands cut off.

Folville had been lucky in his escape. As soon as he reached the port, he had found a man who was more than willing to stow him away on board, and within a few hours he was at sea on the fishing vessel, bucketing about in the middle of the Channel. It took a mere two days to cross (the weather had been foul), and soon Richard Folville made his way to Paris, telling the story of how his family had been impoverished as a result of the Despenser hold on power at the king's court.

There had been little surprise at his arrival. During his first day at Paris, he had himself seen a steady stream of men with similar tales, men who had lost everything because of the appalling greed of Sir Hugh le Despenser, or because of the irrational behaviour of the king.

It was curious, watching all those men. Some had been utterly broken, their spirits gone. One man in particular, he recalled, had behaved as a supplicant, weeping, his hands claws, smearing ashes and filth into his beard and hair. The sort of man, in short, whom Richard would have refused entry to his church. This was the type of vagabond who would have earned himself a sharp kick to the backside and a poke with a heavy staff to tempt him to find alternative accommodation. It was surely a credit to the patience of the French that they not only endured his whimpering, but gave him a hearing. It led to his telling some tale of his daughters being raped and murdered, while his wife was imprisoned, and he himself had been due to be executed. Not that he had been, of course. He had escaped, to come here and whine.

The astonishing thing was, all manner of men were accepted here in Paris. Rich and poor alike, for many who travelled to Paris would be poor when they arrived. The mere fact of leaving England was an assurance of poverty, for the king would confiscate all lands, all treasure, all income. Nothing was too small that it would be ignored by the king's clerks. Every item in a house or castle would be listed, down to the smallest pin, and removed.

He wished he knew where his brothers were. There was a man in the Louvre who had said that the rest of them had travelled up to Hainault, to be with the queen and her lover Mortimer, but Richard was not yet convinced. Another man had grave news: he said that Roger had been captured and was being held in gaol, but he didn't sound entirely sure. Perhaps he was wrong. It would be terrible to think that Roger was dead.

As it would to hear that any of his brothers had fallen. Richard would avenge any of them, if he might.

And he would be able to. The despatching of the man in the wastes before escaping England to come here had shown him that he was indeed a strong man, capable of killing when necessary.

All through his youth, he had looked upon his brothers as more powerful. They had been taught in arms, while he had been taken away when he had shown an especial ability with words and reading. A man able to read and write was always a valuable asset to a family, and if there was the inevitable result that the poor fellow concerned would be forced into the Church, well, that was a price worth paying. In particular because it meant that there would be a confessor for the brothers when they unfortunately behaved as men sometimes would, and killed a man. At those times, Richard had felt his nerves quail. There was something so masculine about them in the way that they stormed into the church, demanding to be heard, taking delight in telling him all about their offences as though he would be proud of their exploits. It made him jealous.

No longer. Now he knew that he was as competent as they. It was a matter of slipping a blade into a torso, that was all. And next time, perhaps, he would watch more closely. Watch the eyes, see how they dilated and contracted as his knife cut through arteries and veins, punctured the heart, stopped the brain. It would be wonderful to watch all that, to see a man actually dying before him.

He was looking forward to the next man he would kill.

Chapter Eighteen

Bishop's Palace, Exeter

The fire was dying gradually as evening drew in. Bishop Walter had dismissed his servants except for his steward, John de Padington, and now his nephew, the squire William Walle, rejoined them.

Bishop Walter had both scraps of parchment in his lap, and he peered from one to the other through his spectacles, rereading them both time after time, while his brow remained furrowed.

William broke the silence. 'Perhaps you should put them away, Uncle? There is little you can do about the matter tonight.'

'I know that,' Bishop Walter said with a sigh. William was right, but that didn't help matters. He pushed the two fragments back into the purse and drew the string tight. 'Do you think that this purse was intended to be recognisable to me? I know nothing at all about it, but it was sent with the message as though I should find it significant.'

'You are quite sure you don't know it?' William asked.

'If I had any idea where it came from, I would have said so,' Walter replied, quite gently.

The pair of them were worried, he could see. Both had the impression that whoever was responsible for sending these messages would not stop there. They would be sure to try to act out the threats. Someone was going to try to kill him.

It was *infuriating*! He clenched a fist and thumped it on his table top, sending one goblet flying, and stood, head down, staring into the fire. 'This is ridiculous. Someone sends threats like this, and my household is frozen with fear. It will not do!'

'We're worried,' William said firmly. 'First a message, then a man's head, now another message threatening your death – do you think we can afford not to take these matters seriously?'

'Bishop,' John said, 'we seek only to ensure your protection.'

'Very well. Do so, then, but do not expect me to assist you in destroying my reputation and making more of this than I need. For sooth! Someone has shown cunning and skill in sending these two messages to me, but that is all. A low cunning is not proof of intellect. The writer is nothing more than a felon who seeks to extort a response by instilling fear in me. Well, I will not submit to it. I know nothing of this purse, nothing of the messages. I do not know who has sent them, so I will not live in terror as though I am under a sentence of death. Do you both watch over me, but no more. I shall not allow this matter to change my life or rule my behaviour.'

'Perhaps we could increase your guard, my lord Walter?' John asked tentatively.

'What, have another twenty men? Thirty? That would look marvellous to the crowds, wouldn't it? A bishop living in terror of his life. And how soon before all heard of these messages and wondered whether there was much truth in the affair? They would soon speculate about the murders I had committed.'

'Uncle, no one who knows you would think you guilty of such a crime.'

Bishop Walter looked at him. 'You know I was under excommunication for some while? No? Then do not leap to conclusions, William. There is more to me than perhaps you know. And many people remember this, and would take delight in attacking me.'

'But if you will not allow us to increase your guard, what would you have us do?'

The bishop considered a moment. 'There is one thing, perhaps. Ask Sir Baldwin de Furnshill to come and advise us.'

*Third Saturday before the Feast of St Paul and St John**

Tiverton Castle, Tiverton

Sir Baldwin de Furnshill trotted into the castle and shouted to the ostler, 'Take my horse,' as he dismounted and stood a moment, tugging the gloves from his hands.

'Not a good day, then? What have you done with your companion?'

Baldwin turned to find himself confronted by the smiling face of William Walle. 'Squire William! My friend, I am very glad to see you! In truth, were I to have to spend another evening with that dull-witted slobberdegulleon, Ovedale, I would be driven to distraction. If it were not for the fact that the fool was a comrade of Sir Hugh le Despenser, he would not have any authority. As it is, though . . .'

He paused, catching sight of a slight grin on his friend's face. 'Very well, Squire William. So you take my words as the foolish maunderings of an old man, I suppose? Be that as it may, I am only a little more than double your age, and I have no more lost my faculties than have you or my good friend, your uncle.'

Immediately he saw the look that passed over William Walle's face, as the squire replied, 'Sir Baldwin, it is about him that I have come to speak with you today.'

'Why? The good bishop is well, isn't he?' Baldwin asked sharply.

'May we speak in private?'

Montreuil, Northern France

The weather was, for once, mild and dry. After the last few days, that itself was a cause for celebration, Ralph la Zouche felt as he followed their guide in through the city walls and along the narrow streets.

It was a pleasant city, this. Flowers in pots seemed to

---

* 7 June 1326

proliferate, with many bright poppies and roses. After all the rain, the roads had been washed clean, and there was the smell of fresh, damp soil rather than the normal odours of excrement and rotten foods. The buildings were all pleasing to Sir Ralph's eye, with good limewashed timber and daub, while the people seemed less surly than some peasants he had known. Yes, all in all, it was a pleasant place.

Their ride had taken some days, but if the weather had been dry, they would have been able to walk such a short distance without trouble. It was noticeable that the roads were of poor quality, and in the rain it was hard to see where the horses might place their feet in safety. However, the roads in much of England were little better. He could not blame the people here for that failing.

At the little castle, all the men dismounted, with a slight sense of anticipation. It was not every day that a group of knights were to meet a duke.

They were divested of their mounts in short order, and soon all were being led up some stairs to the great hall.

It was richly decorated, and Sir Ralph could feel the eyes of the others on all the decorations and hangings. Much gold thread had been used, and the paintings on the walls were the very finest. At various places there were silver bowls, crosses with gilt hammered over them, while on the table, drinks were set out, and all the goblets were of solid silver. It was enough to make a man's mouth water.

However, there was one more delight here for a man's eyes.

She entered a short time after them. A small, slender woman, not yet thirty, clad all in black like a widow. She stood, elegant and still, like a small statue, until they had noticed her presence, and then she slowly walked along the hall to study the men one by one.

Sir Ralph frowned a little at the sight of this woman. She appeared to glide from one to another, without speaking. Behind her came a saucy little blond piece with a roguish eye, and in the doorway stood a young man, of perhaps fourteen or fifteen years.

He at least appeared to show the respect due to a force of men like these.

'I think you must be in charge of these men,' the woman said to him.

'I suppose I might be,' he grunted. 'Your Highness.'

She had dimples in both cheeks when she smiled; it made her appear even more fetching. 'You know me?'

'I could not mistake you. Not with your son in the doorway, my queen.'

She turned and nodded to her son. He began to walk across the floor towards them. It struck Sir Ralph that the son was equal in beauty to his father, but there were differences. Both had the same courtly bearing, and both were broad shouldered, as a knight must be, but for all that, this fellow was so much younger, his brow was smooth. Where the king had scowling lines engraved deeply in his forehead from all the times his wishes had been thwarted by his subjects, this boy had a more enquiring manner. He appeared genuinely interested in other men, if Sir Ralph had to guess.

Not that it mattered. He was a duke at present, and from the way things were progressing, it was unlikely he would ever be a king. 'My lord, I hope I see you well,' Sir Ralph said respectfully.

'Sir Ralph la Zouche, I believe. I am pleased to see you,' the fellow responded. He snapped a finger, and two servants ran to the table. While one cleaned an already spotless goblet, the second poured a small measure into a cup, swilled it, sniffed it, and then took a deep swallow with a contemplative air. He nodded, and poured a larger measure into the freshly cleaned goblet, before bringing it to the duke, bowing low. As soon as Duke Edward had it, the man stepped away silently, walking backwards the whole way.

The Duke hardly seemed to notice. 'Sir Ralph. You have come here from England. Why is that?'

'There were matters. It was better that we should all evade Sir Hugh le Despenser's men.'

'You have caused him embarrassment?' Queen Isabella asked

breathlessly. She was as quick and eager as a polecat, Sir Ralph thought to himself.

He nodded. 'I and my family killed one of the Despenser's men. He was ever stealing from me and my family, and we could not tolerate it any longer.'

'Who?' the Duke asked.

'You know Belers? His favourite in the Treasury?'

'This is good news!' the queen said with delight. 'My husband must be feeling desolate. You have killed his favourite in the Treasury, while I have taken delivery of his silver.'

'Silver?' Sir Ralph repeated.

'He sent five barrels of silver to bribe the peers of France,' Duke Edward said. 'But the ship was captured by our friends. They took the barrels to the Duke of Hainault, who naturally passed it to us.'

Sir Ralph said nothing, but thought a lot. The fact that the queen and her son possessed a vast sum in silver was worth knowing. They could reward their friends – which was no doubt why they had told him. 'You asked us to come here to look after you,' he said solemnly. 'What do you wish from us?'

The duke answered. 'I have my own household, of course, but my father is growing ever more irrational, I fear. I seek more men to guard me and protect me from capture. There are tales of ships which are being provisioned to bring Englishmen to France to catch me and take me back. I would prefer not to have this happen.'

There was just a slight hint of reticence as he spoke: the proof of a boy not yet a man, who would prefer not to alienate his father.

Sir Ralph nodded. 'We have all these men – proven fighters – and they'll be as loyal to you as I am.'

'Do you think any of them could be persuaded to return to the king?' Queen Isabella asked.

'Any of us?' Sir Ralph laughed. 'I will be hanged if I return, as will my brother and the others. We are all enemies of Despenser. What, would you think we could return to England with the threat of our lives, in the hope that we might sell news to the king? No. We are all here because we have no life in England now.'

'There is a man there with a tonsure.'

'He is a priest from Exeter, I think. He's run here too.'

The queen's face hardened, and if it was possible, Sir Ralph would have said that the room grew chill.

'If he came from Exeter, I do not blame him. It must be foul – disgusting – to live in the same city as that accursed Bishop, Walter Stapledon!'

Tiverton Castle

It was not easy for Baldwin to listen to William as the squire told all his news. The idea that a man might send messages to warn the bishop that he was soon to die seemed so irrational as to be insane. However, there was the appeal of a desperate man in Squire William's eyes, and Baldwin would not desert the bishop when he needed Baldwin's help. True, in the last year or more, Stapledon had been less than deft in his dealings with Despenser, and had a few times put Baldwin and his friend into difficult situations with that most powerful magnate, but that was no reason not to help him.

'You are sure of all this?' Baldwin asked. 'What sort of messages were they?'

The squire related everything he could remember about the messages, describing the parchment, the little purse, everything. 'But the real difficulty is, the bishop has no recollection of anyone whom he could have hurt, and a man who was stabbed and wounded would surely have etched himself on Bishop Walter's memory?'

Baldwin nodded vaguely. 'Perhaps. Not all men remember those whom they have hurt in such a manner, but I agree, I think that Walter would do so, certainly. Why did you say "a man who was stabbed"?'

'The purse has a stain upon one side, which to me looked like blood. So I thought, if the bishop had once hurt a man, so that the man fell down later, and his blood marked his purse, perhaps then the fellow would harbour a grudge, and would try to—'

'No, it will not do!' Baldwin declared with certainty. 'You propose that a fellow is stabbed, so violently that his blood is permitted to leak and stain the ground all about him? If that was the case, it would be remarkable if the man lived. Yet you say he does live and seeks revenge? Hardly likely. Then you say that he had this purse. It soaked up the blood. That is possible, but again, it would mean significant effusions of the vital fluid. Finally, you say that these notes were written. My friend, if notes were written, it is not at all likely that the man who was wounded would have written them. Unless your uncle unwittingly stabbed a clerk.'

'A clerk?'

'The only profession in which writing is an essential skill. But if he had stabbed a priest or cleric, he *would* recall it.'

William was suddenly pale as a thought struck him.

'Speak your mind,' Baldwin said. 'Come – speak!'

'He mentioned to me only the other day, when he sent me here, that he was once excommunicated. Did you hear of it?'

'Yes. It was a long time ago though. I was abroad.'

'The cathedral had a dispute with the friars, the Dominicans. They were attempting to bury a corpse, against the rules of the cathedral, and my uncle and another man went to the friary with the aim of bringing the corpse back to the cathedral. They took the funerary items, the candles, the cloth, all the items you would expect.'

'And he was accused of beating a man, I recollect.'

'Certainly the party was accused of spilling blood. Perhaps this could be one of the friars? They can write, they live nearby, and they had a man who had bled profusely, if the tale is true.'

'And there were probably two other men badly beaten that same night who were nowhere near the friary. The pouch could have been taken and dropped into another pool of blood. There is nothing to say that the good bishop had anything to do with it. And if there was a fight and men were beaten, then it would have been the lay brothers, not your uncle, who did the beating. No, I don't believe that is very likely.'

'Oh, so it wasn't one of them.'

'Perhaps it was,' Baldwin said kindly. The squire appeared to be quite crestfallen. 'It would be wrong to ignore any possibility until there has been a chance of considering it in more detail. Now, what is the bishop doing about this possible threat? Let me guess – refusing to tolerate any change in his plans or routines?'

'Absolutely. He says that to do so would only prove to those in the city who mean him harm that there was substance in the story.'

'And he may be right. However, if the cost of proving your confidence in your innocence is your life, perhaps a different fee could be considered, eh? Well, you have convinced me. I shall ride back to Exeter with you. We will leave very soon, and stay overnight at my house. It will be good to return and see my wife once more,' he added.

Chapter Nineteen

Montreuil

'So, Sir Edward, I hope I can serve you well enough?' Paul de Cockington said nervously.

It was the first time in his life that he had been so close to a member of the royal family, and that knowledge was making his mouth work all on its own, as though there was no need for him to engage his heart or his brain to keep talking. Before he walked in here, he had been sure that he would soon show the lad that he was considerably wiser. How hard could it be, to control a mere boy? But there was something in this fellow's face that stopped a man from taking liberties.

'Father, I am sure you will suffice for me,' the Duke said. He wore a slight smile on his face, as though he understood Paul's effusiveness, and found it endearing. Like a man who enjoyed a puppy's tail wagging. 'I hope your duties will not be too arduous.'

'I should be delighted to help you,' Paul said. 'I would do anything to serve you, my lord.'

'Then first discover the benefits of silence, eh?' Duke Edward said. 'I have a need for some moments of peace.'

They had left the main chamber, and had reached the smaller room above it. The Duke was a little distracted, Paul could see, but he was scarcely interested in the feelings of the Duke, since his own mind was growing so disordered. All he could think of was that he was here, alone, with the heir to the English throne.

'How long will you need me?' Paul asked.

'Hmm? Oh, I don't know. My last confessor has been forced away, and my tutor and other men from my household have been given other duties. Good Sir Roger Mortimer has persuaded me that they must serve me in Aquitaine. So I have need of more. And those who are in England would be . . . a little difficult to recruit at this time.'

Paul knew that. There was the small matter of Queen Isabella's rift with her husband. Whereas before it would have been easy to hire men to serve the Duke, now no man would be allowed to leave England to come and swell the queen's small host. And any who were, would be viewed as spies sent by the king and therefore rejected by Queen Isabella. However, men who were already exiled from England and who would be glad of a promised pardon in exchange for their service, would be loyal. That was why he and the Folvilles and others had been brought here.

It was not long before there was a knock at the door. When Paul opened it, he found himself gazing into the blue eyes of the queen's lady-in-waiting. She curtseyed, grinning all the while, and he found his own attention being absorbed by her embonpoint. Noticing the direction of his look, she gave him a mockingly stern shake of the head, before motioning him aside.

Commanded by this imperious little angel, Paul moved from her path, and the lady entered the room. A few paces behind her was the queen. In a few moments, Paul found himself outside the room, staring at the closed door.

'Come, Father. I would speak with you.'

This was from a tall, strong man. He could have been well past his middle forties, from the look of him, for his face showed the passage of a number of tribulations. There was an immensity of sadness in his eyes, as well as resolution and anger. It was the anger which Paul saw most, and the sight made him pause with some anxiety, until he realised that the rage was not directed at him.

'Sir?'

'You are Paul de Cockington, eh? I don't know nor do I care what brought you here to France, fellow. But know this, you have a sacred duty here to the next king of England. Understand that, and understand that you must help me to serve him by telling me of any danger that shows itself.'

'Who are you, to tell me what to do?' Paul said haughtily.

'Further, if you are to have any possibility of returning to England and winning a pardon for whatever you have done to drive you away, you will keep me informed of all who come to meet the young duke and anything else which pertains to his safety, the security of his person, and the realm which he is to inherit.'

'I am most sorry, but if you think that I will submit to you in this, you are—'

'You will do all this, and be richly rewarded. Fail me, little priest, and you will learn that I am not an understanding opponent.'

'Perhaps you are not, but my duty will be to the duke, and no one else.'

'Priest, you will be answerable to me alone,' the man said, leaning forward. 'For I am going to invade the kingdom, and that boy in there will soon become king. And if anything happens to him and I find you implicated in it, I will personally take great pleasure in dissecting your body.'

He stared coldly into Paul's eyes for a few moments, before abruptly turning and striding out. Almost as soon as he had gone, the door reopened and the queen and her lady-in-waiting walked out without speaking to Paul.

In the chamber, the duke stood pensively staring through the window. He heard Paul's steps and turned quickly. The afternoon sun shone full upon the lad as he caught sight of Paul, and the rector was shocked into immobility at the expression in his eyes.

For the very first time, Paul appreciated that, although this was a powerful man, the son of a king, and a Duke in his own right, in the lad's eyes, he saw only terror; the terror of a boy who knew that his parents loathed each other, and for whom there could never be peace in his family again.

*Third Monday before the Feast of St Paul and St John**

Bishop's Clyst, near Exeter

Baldwin trotted up the roadway to the bishop's great house with an eye open to all dangers.

Only the last day, there had been some acts of hideous treachery committed. To hear of rape and murder was one thing, but to learn that the crimes had been committed on the Sabbath was most shocking, even to a man like Baldwin, who had witnessed so many foul crimes in his long life.

'I am sorry that your journey was increased,' William was saying again.

The poor fellow looked quite worn down, Baldwin thought, which was unlike him.

'I am sure that it is merely a matter of sense,' he said. 'The bishop has so many calls upon his time, it is not surprising that he might decide to move away from the palace for a few days. Perhaps it was only to relax a little. He is always such a hard worker.'

'Yes, you're probably right,' William said, but he retained an expression of watchful anxiety as they clattered over the drawbridge and up to the main yard.

There was good need for his concern. As Baldwin looked about him, he saw seven men-at-arms in the court, and up at the hall, he saw two more. That wasn't counting the men on the walls. This was not a peaceful residence away from the city, it was a fortified manor in preparation for war. A sudden chill settled in his breast at the thought that the long-feared war might even now be at hand. It had not occurred to him that there could have been recent news about the queen and Mortimer. But if there were to be reports of imminent attack, it was natural that the bishop would go and see to the defences of his favourite house outside of Exeter.

---

* 9 June 1326

So it was with some nervousness of his own that Baldwin dropped from his mount and made his way hurriedly from the court to the hall. Seeing John de Padington, he was reassured to recognise the stolid, unperturbable steward.

'Sir Baldwin, you are most welcome. I hope you had a good journey? I am sure the good squire will have entertained you on your way.'

'I wasn't in the mood for entertaining,' William said.

Baldwin nodded with mock severity. 'No. He sought to avoid entertainment entirely, master steward. Rather, he saw fit to distract me from all pleasant contemplation of the roads, the fields, the woods, and ensured that I was engaged all the while in discussion of serious matters.'

'I only spoke of the coming . . . oh. You jest!' William said, with a roll of his eyes.

'Friend, let's see what the bishop has to say,' Baldwin murmured, not unkindly.

'He has much to tell you,' John said. 'There's been another note.'

Montreuil

The weather was fine. That was the first thought that ran through Paul's head as he gradually awoke. He could tell it was fine because he had forgotten to draw the shutters the night before, he had been so merry, and now he found that the light was a most unwelcome distraction.

At least he had slept well. His problem had been the drink. Usually he could cope with a quantity of ale, but last night, jealous of a squire with his wench on his arm, Paul had retreated to a small, smoky den at the back of the castle's yard, near the kitchen, where he had found a small group of men playing at knucklebones for pennies a throw. The merry fellows were keen to welcome him in among their games; later, it was a still more merry bunch of men, while Paul's mood had risen to elation, only to crash to misery as his gambling flowed and then inevitably ebbed. He had drunk more than he should, especially of the strong local red wine, and when he left that party, he had been almost cleaned out of all money.

Recalling their faces now, he wondered whether he had been fleeced as many gulls in a new town would be. There was something about their looks which had struck him as perhaps a little secretive. One man with a face so bearded he looked like a gorilla, had winked to a companion as soon as Paul entered. That was odd, now he came to think of it: the men had all exchanged glances when he walked in, and the bearded man had been the one who accepted him into their game, but they had none of them asked who he was. After all, he was a stranger in their midst. But perhaps his face was already known to the garrison. He was the confessor to the young duke, after all.

With a flash, he remembered that today he was supposed to be aiding the duke with his lessons.

His predecessor as tutor had been a very widely read man, apparently, called Bury. But he had been sent to be Constable of Bordeaux, because Roger Mortimer had said that the town needed a good man at this difficult time. Now the prince seemed to feel the need for more education, almost as a defence against more work.

Rising and washing his face quickly, Paul shivered and made his way to the duke's chamber.

'Enter!'

'My lord, I hope I find you well?' Paul said as he knelt just inside the doorway.

'No one has poisoned me today. Not that I know of, anyway,' Edward replied, somewhat dully.

Paul licked his dry lips. 'I am sure no one would wish to do that, my lord.'

'Are you? Then you don't know the world in which I live, priest,' Edward said with heat. 'My mother looks upon me only as a sacrificial groom, to marry to the best family she can find. My father hates me – he thinks I have defied him and am staying here of my free will, with the man whom he detests above all others – Roger Mortimer. He blames me, because I am to be married against his will. He made me promise that I should not allow myself to accept any treaty of marriage while I was here with my mother, but she began negotiating to sell me six months ago. The only man who has no say in it is me!'

Paul was not prepared for such a declaration. His lips felt gummy, his flesh was clammy, and he had an oily churning in his belly. 'I am sure you would prefer to have some peace, my lord. Look, I'll leave you this morning. You are feeling out of sorts, and won't want lessons from a poor instructor like me. You should get some rest, and we can continue tomorrow.'

'No, stay here. In faith, you are truly my man, aren't you? You are my confessor, my own private companion?'

'I hope so, my lord. I have the duty of secrecy.'

'Then advise me. What should I do? I cannot escape this trap here. I would have to run a long way to outrun the guards set all about me. Yet I ought to return to England. I promised my father that I would do that.'

'Whether you promised or not, if you are being held against your will, it matters not. It is not your fault if you are prevented from doing your father's will.'

'You say that, but I am a duke! I was born to command. From my first weeks, I have been a royal earl in England. I have managed my household, controlled my estates – with a little help, it's true, but mostly on my own. And yet here I don't have anyone I can rely upon.'

'There are some. The men I came here with, they are all determined to serve you.'

'Oh, really? They are determined more to remain as far as possible from Sir Hugh le Despenser, I have heard. Assassins, felons – outlaws all. They do not fill me with confidence.'

'They should, my lord. They may appear to be little more than draw-latches, but they are strong, and they have little to lose. It's true that they're all enemies of the Despenser, but if they can demonstrate loyalty to you, they may be able to hope for a pardon, if you could speak to the king on their behalf.'

'You think so?' The Duke of Aquitaine closed his eyes in

despair. 'You do not know my father, nor the Despenser. The latter is vile. He considers only his own interests. I don't know how he has inveigled his way into my father's affections, but there is no doubt that he has done so with enormous skill. My father will do nothing without the approval of Despenser. He will not order his men-at-arms, he won't command the admirals, he won't rest or even take a piss, I sometimes think, without gaining the approval of that cursed knight! And if Despenser thought I was a threat to him personally, I would wager heavy odds that my life would be at threat.'

'No matter. Despenser can't live for ever. While there is the chance that you may return to England, the men here are your best guarantee of security. They will not throw away the only asset they have: your friendship.'

'You think so, seriously? You believe that they could prove to be a reliable force to protect me?'

'Yes, I think so. Look at them: what would they gain by being traitorous to you? The friendship of Despenser – who would trust to that!'

'My father,' the duke said bitterly.

Chapter Twenty

Bishop's Clyst

The bishop tried to concentrate on the latest set of accounts for the rebuilding of the cathedral, but his mind would not focus. He had never known such doubts. Even in France last year, when he learned that the queen and Mortimer were plotting his death, he had not been as confused and scared as he was now. Once upon a time, he had taken upon himself all the accounts for the Exchequer and had sorted them into rational blocks, making the taxation a simpler task and freeing the king to do more as he wished. In those days, he had possessed the most logical brain in the country, he reckoned. And now? Now he couldn't concentrate on a simple set of accounts from the cathedral fabric rolls.

It was a relief to see the knight at his door. 'Sir Baldwin, please enter – enter. It is most kind of you to come all the way out here.'

'John tells me that you have been unfortunate enough to have had another message?'

'He speaks before he ought to,' the bishop said, turning a cold eye upon his servant.

'Aye? And if I did not, what then?' John de Padington said belligerently. 'Would you willingly inform the good knight after he came to see you, or would you try to keep it hidden?'

'Enough, steward! Fetch my guest some wine and begone! You have no sense of propriety.'

'Propriety, is it?' John muttered perfectly audibly as he turned his back and walked to the buttery. 'And I suppose propriety will save a bishop's life?'

'Ignore the old fool,' Bishop Walter said. 'I am truly most glad to see you, Sir Baldwin. Tell me, how are the plans for the array proceeding?'

'Not so well, it would appear, as the plans for your death. Show me these messages, Bishop. I know that they are unpleasing, but perhaps I can learn something from them.'

'I doubt it,' Bishop Walter said. He stood and walked to a small chest placed on a table opposite the fire. Opening it, he moved some scrolls and leather wallets aside before finding the purse. 'Here it is. The notes are inside.'

Baldwin took the notes. 'Which was first, which second?'

'That one you hold there: *you who think* . . . and so on – that was first. The second was that *The author of so much* . . . and that is the latest.'

Baldwin read it. '*Your doom approaches. The city will not avail you now*. What do you think that means?'

'Simply that there is no defence in the city of Exeter, of course. What else could it mean? And it's not surprising. The city contains many who dislike me. There are men there who would willingly collaborate with an assassin. I have made enemies in the Priory of the Dominicans, I have enemies in the city itself, and there are too many easy methods of ingress to the Close and the bishop's palace. That was why I moved myself to here. I think that this should be a safer base from which to assert my freedom and independence.'

'It is well fortified,' Baldwin said. He was still studying the little scraps of parchment. 'The writer has a good hand,' he said at last. 'Each one is perfectly legible.'

'Which at least means it's less likely to be one of my parish priests,' the bishop commented sourly.

'This purse is interesting, though.'

The door from the screens passage opened and William walked in, holding it wide for John, who was carrying a large tray laden with wine, goblets, and meat as well as cheeses.

Bishop Walter nodded to the steward. 'Very good, John.'

'We want to hear what the Keeper says,' John said.

'I wish for some peace,' the bishop said firmly.

'We have to learn all we can if we're going to protect you,' William protested. 'It would be foolish for us to be turned away. What does the last message say?' he asked.

Baldwin passed the note to him, and the squire stood reading it blankly for a moment. 'What does it mean? The city wouldn't exactly rise up to defend a man, no matter who it was.'

'I agree with the bishop that it was a good idea to come here,' Baldwin said, studying the first two messages closely. His eyes were not so good as once they had been.

The bishop shook his head. 'I believe firmly that this is all nonsense, and will soon be shown to be of no consequence.'

'This purse is most curious,' Baldwin said. 'It is too small to be used as a man's purse. Good, fine leather, but so small. No man would carry something so petite. And this stain . . .'

Bishop Walter rubbed at the bridge of his nose. 'Yes, it looks like blood, I know.'

'Well, Bishop, I believe you if you say you've not killed a man,' Baldwin said with a smile.

The bishop returned it, although his own, he felt, was rather more brittle than the knight's. 'I am glad to hear you say that. I would not like to be accused of a simple murder, Sir Baldwin.'

To his annoyance, the knight appeared to pay no attention to his words.

'No. I don't think you have killed a man yourself. However, the author of these notes believes that you have. And that means he must have some reason to suspect you. Is it possible that you have a servant who has killed and that you are being held responsible? The only alternative, surely, is that you have, because of negligence or inaction, allowed someone to die. I cannot believe that.'

'Why, because you don't think me capable of incompetence or laziness?' Bishop Walter said pointedly.

Again though, Sir Baldwin did not look across at him. He remained turning the purse over and over in his hands. 'No, it is merely a matter of commonsense. If you'd allowed someone to die from either cause, you would be aware of the deaths. If it were something which you were completely unaware of, your negligence or inaction would be irrelevant. Unless it was your negligence in following up a death? But this is pointless. It is trying to weave a tapestry to form a picture when we only have one colour of thread. What we need is different colours to tell our tale. So let us consider the next scene, and see if there is more thread there.'

'I have no idea what you are talking about,' the bishop said heavily.

'Merely this, my lord Bishop. This purse – consider it carefully. It is so small, no man would use it as his purse, as I said. However, it is a useful size for certain things. I would imagine that many items would fit inside it, wouldn't you?'

Squire William leaned forward. 'What sort of thing, do you think?'

Baldwin peered at it very closely, resting his elbows on his knees. He scratched the outside, sniffed at it, studied it with his head on one side, and finally peered into the interior. He sniffed again, and then scratched at the inside, staring with a frown at his fingernail.

'Well?' the bishop said.

'Someone used this to store a seal,' Baldwin said slowly. He weighed the purse in his hand thoughtfully. 'It's very fine leather, good and soft. It would be enough to protect a man's seal, and there is a residue of red wax on the inner seam.'

'Great heaven!' the bishop breathed as he took the purse and gazed inside. 'I saw that, but didn't think anything of it. So you consider that this might have been a seal's purse. But how that can help us, I do not know.'

Baldwin was watching him closely, he noticed. 'Yes, Sir Baldwin?'

'May I be frank, Bishop? Before our companions?'

The bishop looked up at Squire William and his steward, then back at Baldwin, and he allowed a hint of steel to enter his voice. 'I have no secrets from my nephew and the man who has shown himself my most trusted servant over many years, Sir Baldwin.'

'In that case, bishop, I would ask how many manors you have acquired for yourself in recent years. This is a goodly sized purse for a large seal. That to me indicates that the seal was from a good manor. It is not a legal seal, for they are held in wooden boxes. It is not a regal seal, for they are larger. This is a middling seal for a man who was proud enough to have a leather purse made for his seal. Perhaps a rich squire, or a knight or knight banneret.'

'I have not murdered anyone.'

'That may be true. However, I am sure that there will have been occasions when you have worked with Sir Hugh le Despenser. Perhaps on some occasions he has been more . . . *energetic* in pursuing your joint ambitions than you would have been on your own.'

'I am sure that I would have learned of murder, had he committed it.'

'Do you have a list of the manors which you have acquired with his help?'

'Oh, this is foolish! There can be nothing in it!'

Baldwin stood. 'Then clearly there is no need in my remaining. I shall leave you, bishop, and return to my wife. If you change your mind, and wish for me to investigate these messages, then you will be able to find me at my house.'

He stood and bowed, and was about to stride from the room, when the bishop called him back.

'Sir Baldwin, I am sorry. Yes. I have a list of some of the manors.'

Montreuil

It was late in the afternoon by the time Paul had finished his lesson. Not that there was much he could teach the duke in any case. The young heir to the throne had been well lectured in his time by some of the best tutors in England, and the last one, to judge by the duke's fulsome praise, had been a paragon of virtue and intelligence.

Not that it was the ability and shrewdness of the duke that

caused Paul to feel so unwholesome. As he walked from the duke's hall and out into the courtyard, all he was aware of was the thundering in his head. If he had been alone, he would have thrust his fingers down his throat to make himself sick on purpose. The acid in his belly was so foul, it would have been better to try to balance his humours by ejecting as much of it as possible, and then lining his stomach with cool milk to soothe it. He was still tempted to try it even now.

The yard was almost empty, but as he stood at the stairs, he heard the duke shouting for gloves and a cloak, and a little while afterwards, he was at Paul's side.

'Good tutor, would you care to join me in a ride?'

Paul tried to smile. 'That would be most pleasant, but I am not your tutor, my son, I am your confessor. And I fear that to do my work as well as I might, I need to—'

'Father, I would be glad of your company.'

Paul tried one last refusal. 'But, Duke Edward, I am hardly the—'

'Good. So, we need a horse for you too.'

'We cannot go riding alone, surely?'

'Why not? This is France, and I feel as safe here as anywhere.'

Paul stared around wildly, hoping for inspiration. He felt foul, his mouth was rough, his belly was threatening to explode, and the last thing he wished for was a fast canter across the countryside with this wayward duke. 'What would your mother say?' was the only phrase that came to mind.

The prince looked at him with that quiet gaze that was so coldly certain. It was very much as if he could see into Paul's soul – and Paul did not like the feeling. Not that he had anything to hide. He was the son of a well-to-do knight, and brother to a sheriff. There was nothing for him to be ashamed of. But still, it was a very odd feeling to have this fellow, who was shorter than him, younger than him, less mature than him, stare at him in that peculiarly direct manner.

All right, then, he thought. If that's what you want. 'I am ready,' he said aloud. 'Let's find horses, Your Highness.'

It was as though the damn things had been laid on. In a few moments there was a great bay and a little grey, and the duke sprang up on to the bay as though he had been born to the saddle. Paul was a little less elegant, he knew, as he clambered on to the grey, but not too bad.

'Your Highness, you do realise that . . .'

But as he spoke, the boy thrashed the flanks of his beast, and without a backward glance, he was off through the gates.

Bishop's Clyst

The bishop had sent a servant for his papers, and while he waited, he stared down at his knees.

Baldwin was struck by how broken this great leader had become. He could remember the first time he had met this man – six, no eight years ago. Then Bishop Walter Stapledon had been taller, fairer of hair, altogether much more youthful in appearance, giving an immediate impression of authority, keen intellect, and honour.

Throughout the length and breadth of his diocese of Devon and Cornwall, Bishop Walter was renowned for his integrity. The barons respected him for his control of the government, especially the Treasury, for he had taken an inefficient and failing system and completely modernised it; the wealthy merchant classes appreciated his commonsense and the way that he allowed business to flourish to the benefit of all; and the poorest were solidly behind him for his enforcement of church alms, as well as for the opportunities he gave to their children for education. All were impressed with the good bishop.

But he had spent too much time in government, Baldwin thought. The bishop had been forced to compromise his principles in order to see that the realm was stable and kept secure. Bishop Walter had become too close to Despenser. The two had formed a loose, but nonetheless dangerous alliance for some years. It was in part due to that, that the queen had left the kingdom, forlorn at losing the affections of her husband as he looked ever more to Despenser for companionship. A naturally strong-willed woman, she was unwilling to accept a secondary role, for she was queen, and the daughter of a great king, Philip of France. But Despenser was jealous, and wouldn't allow even the king's wife to intrude. Her distress was sealed when her lands were sequestrated, her household broken up, all her French companions arrested and gaoled, her income confiscated, and her children taken from her, to be placed in the custody of Despenser's wife.

The final indignity, that had been. And for many women, it would have spelled a terrible end. Most would have succumbed to despair, and no doubt would have died of grief. Not this queen. She had fought back with all the skills at her disposal. Dissembling, playing the contented wife, deceiving all, until she was believed and trusted by even the Despenser himself.

She and Bishop Walter hated each other. The bishop could not understand a woman of her nature, one with an indomitable spirit and the courage to defy even a bishop. She, for her part, detested him with a ferocity that was unequalled, in Baldwin's experience. It was no surprise, for the bishop had argued with the king that she was untrustworthy when the French overran Guyenne last year. To have a French-born queen with loyal subjects who adored her in Devon and Cornwall, where she owned many manors, was to invite invasion, he argued, and his words prevailed. Thus it was that she lost her income, and in a vile twist that dishonoured both bishop and king, Bishop Walter was later to accept the income from her lands to help him organise the defence of the shires.

Their disputes had led to the queen becoming ever more fiercely opposed to the bishop, but Baldwin could see now that the bishop and she, while both growing mutually antagonistic, had exhibited vastly contrasting responses.

While the queen had seen her authority removed, brick by brick, she had demonstrated her greatness. She had used cunning and her beauty to win over all those who might be swayed, she had persuaded, cajoled and bribed, and she had come to be viewed as the poor victim, while all commented on her fortitude and her beauty, as though her looks were a proof of her innocence. And at the same time, the bishop had found himself reviled and denigrated, which had led to this: a man who appeared shrunken, wizened almost. He was only a little older than the last time Baldwin had seen him, but the contrast was notable.

Even now, waiting for the servant to return, the bishop sat with his fingers drumming on his knees. His eyes were on the fire, deep in thought.

The servant returned, and the bishop looked up with a tired smile. 'I think I should accept that I am an old man, and retire from all work for government. This life of toil is too much for a man of my age. I have the cathedral rebuilding to worry about. Why on earth should I strain myself for the government when I have so much to do? I should resign all the king's commissions.'

Baldwin smiled, but did not feel the need to say anything. The bishop was a politician to his fingernails, as Baldwin knew. He liked the bishop personally, but the man was so fully immersed in the realm's government that breaking the chains of service would be enormously difficult.

'Well, Sir Baldwin, here are the records. These are all the manors I have acquired in the last years.'

'How far do these go back?' Squire William asked.

'Five or six years, I think. My register has others – but would we need to look further back in time?'

Baldwin shook his head. 'If it were longer ago, surely the man would have done something before now.'

'What now, then?' the steward said.

Baldwin looked up from the heavy book. The bishop sat, sad and afraid, watching him, flanked by the squire and the steward. Squire William was full of determination to see his uncle protected, while the steward had a grimness about him, as though already aware that he might have to kill a man in the defence of his master.

'Now, I have to begin reading this tome with the help of any man who can tell me about each of the cases so we can begin to form an opinion about who has been sending these notes. With your leave, Bishop, I will start right away. Who was this "William atte Bow"?'

Chapter Twenty-One

*Third Wednesday before the Feast of St Paul and St John**

Montreuil

The little force was being readied as Paul de Cockington completed his lesson for the day. He was feeling smug. Never before had he been asked to tutor a boy, but he was nothing if not methodical, as he told himself, and there was little that a man with a brain could not achieve without a bit of practical effort. He would still much rather be getting to grips with the little maid who was the queen's constant companion, for she looked as though she would be worth a wrestle or two. The mere thought of stripping her and feasting his eyes upon her undoubted assets was enough to make him quiver like a hound seeing the quarry.

But it was not going to happen. Not here. The sad fact was, she was so rarely away from the queen that the opportunity would be very unlikely to present itself. And while he was proud of the speed of his assaults, he would need a little time to persuade this one. Even he wouldn't want to try to ravish a maid in the queen's service while he was in the royal lady's household.

There was another thing – the man Mortimer was always around the place. His eyes were everywhere, so it seemed. Paul couldn't even glance at a serving maid without finding that Mortimer was staring at him immediately afterwards. The fellow was desperate to know everything that was happening, as though he thought that all the men in his household, all those sitting in

---

* 11 June 1326

his hall, were plotting to kill him. Quite mad.

It was noticeable that his eyes rested more commonly on Paul than on others though, and that was a source of some fear. Paul didn't like being watched; he thought that this must be how a mouse feels while the hawk hovers overhead; unseen, unheard, but always moments away from a deadly blow.

Still, the lessons had seemed to be going well. He had managed to surprise the lad – up until yesterday, anyway.

Yesterday the boy had seemed thoroughly impressed; it was clear by the way that he had responded to his teachings. Sometimes the young duke had the temerity to question details, but Paul was always able to adopt a lofty attitude, while making up stories to prove that he was correct. That was one skill he had never lost. There were a couple of moments when the boy had tried to speak over him, as though thinking that he knew the answers to some issues, but Paul had airily waved away his protests. It would not do to have a pupil believe that he knew more than his tutor, after all.

Yes, he had been quite enjoying his teachings, spouting forth while daydreaming about the backside of the maid. Just a shame that he couldn't get to grapple with that little blonde.

The bell at the chapel tolled, and he gladly closed the book before him. Enormous, it covered the campaigns of the Greek Alexander, and the thing was tedious – and somewhat worrying, too. The boy had specifically asked for it today. Yesterday he had demonstrated an insatiable appetite for stories of the man's achievements, and it had begun to strain Paul, to come up with new facets of the warrior's character. Every time he thought that he had successfully shut down one avenue of the duke's enquiries, the little monster would come up with another. It really had been hard work. The boy seemed to delight in finding new questions. Still, Paul's inventiveness had been up to it, or so he had felt. He had told of how the man was actually not particularly brave, and that was why he had lived to such a grand old age. Alexander was, naturally, a coarse, thuggish man with the manners of a barbarian, and his appreciation of arts and the finer things in life were obviously going to extend no further than those things which he could grab and stuff in a cart to be sold.

If Paul had made it up, that was little concern at the time. No one could prove him wrong, after all. Or so he had thought, but then the duke had asked to study this book with Paul. And Paul now had a distinct feeling that he might have been trapped. This book seemed to indicate that Alexander had died rather younger than the hoary old warrior he had envisaged. If the book were to be believed, he was also rather cultured. And not an acquisitive mercenary like the modern knight Paul had imagined. It led Paul to wonder whether he had, in fact, been taken in by the lad.

'Ready for your ride?' the duke asked. He had a slight smile, and his eyes were lidded, as though he was amused by something. Or suspicious.

'Yes, of course, my lord,' Paul said, and he was aware of a nervousness as he bowed.

Bishop's Clyst

'What can you tell me about these affairs?' Baldwin asked as the bishop walked in, William Walle and John behind him.

Baldwin was sitting at the table, head resting on his fists, while he tried to make sense of the crabbed writing before him.

'Which?' the bishop asked. He crossed the floor and sat at Baldwin's side. 'Oh, the Hamo case? That was a difficult matter. The boy, his son John, was orphaned, so we thought, when his father died in the Scottish war. That damned Bruce killed so many of our men that year. May his soul rot in hell. Since Hamo atte Font was dead – or so everyone thought – we had to look after his boy. I took on his wardship, and Hamo's assets were taken.'

'It says here that Hamo's son was to be placed into the guardianship of his mother?' Baldwin said.

'Well, yes, that was suggested. But some of us felt that the matter was not so simple. Anyway, it was all resolved quickly. Hamo managed to return later, and he took up his properties in his own right.'

'I see. And you had no fights with them?'

'No. Nor did I take up a seal or try to keep his assets once he arrived home again,' the bishop said sharply.

'Very good. There are a number of other matters here though. All have been listed with this mark.'

'What mark? Oh.'

Baldwin could see the bishop's eyes move away, even as he pointed to the small 'D' at the corner of the first section. 'Bishop – what does this signify?'

'There is no secret to it. It means that it was a matter in which I involved myself with my lord Hugh le Despenser. We occasionally had need of some mutual support, I suppose, and would help people together.'

'People such as this Roger Crok?'

'People such as he, yes.'

'What happened with him?'

'He was a supporter of the king's enemies. Of the Lords Marcher. As such, his property became forfeit.'

'And that is all?' Baldwin asked.

The bishop licked his lips, then shot a look at his nephew and appeared to make a resolution. 'No. I was keen to acquire certain lands. There were two manors which his mother would have held, but since her son and her husband were both traitors, they were taken. The king settled both of her manors on me.'

'Her husband and son are dead?'

'To the best of my knowledge.'

'What of this case – John Biset?'

The bishop could feel William Walle's eyes on him as he answered. 'Oh, he was a young landowner who wanted wardship of a tenant's grandson, and I fought it. With good reason, too – the fellow was too young. Biset had hardly come of age when the wardship came up.'

'So he was of age? You said "hardly".'

'Yes, he was technically old enough. But he had to have his age proven, and couldn't.'

'Why not?'

The bishop shrugged. 'I confess, I and Sir Hugh le Despenser arranged matters so that he could not prove his age until late in June of that year, three years ago now. It meant that the wardship was automatically secured by the king. When the inquest was held, he could prove his age, but it is taking him time to win it back.'

'Why deprive the fellow of his rightful possessions?' Baldwin asked pointedly.

'I was content to be reasonable, Sir Baldwin, but he was not. I would have settled happily for the wardship, or for a manor or two. But he wouldn't agree.'

Baldwin closed the book gently, but he couldn't help the anger showing in his eyes. 'So you took from this boy his income, because he wouldn't submit to you and Despenser trying to steal his manors? I find your innocence a little hard to square with the facts of the case.'

'We did not, perhaps, cover ourselves with glory,' the bishop admitted. 'But the fellow was utterly determined. It was frustrating to have him thwart us in that manner.'

'Is he alive?'

'I believe so. Unless he has seriously annoyed the Despenser, there is no reason to think he would have expired,' the bishop said.

'Those are the cases I found which showed most promise,' Baldwin said. 'It is possible, I suppose, that Biset found your attempt to steal his manor to be so reprehensible that he sent you the notes and his old seal. Or, perhaps the seal belonged to the ward's father?'

'He was only a tenant. He may have possessed his own seal, I suppose, but I would doubt that it would have been kept in such a valuable purse.'

'The poor will often value objects that the rich consider pointless,' Baldwin said. 'The Crok family would seem to have more use for a seal though, or this man Biset. They were landowners themselves, so if one of them survived, he may carry the urge for revenge for your theft.'

'I consider that word to be most harsh,' the bishop protested.

'Then what term would you seek to use?' Baldwin demanded. 'In God's name, I declare, I have never heard such a litany of crimes confessed in all my years on the bench listening to the gaol delivery sessions! So, we have the Crok family, if any survive, and the Biset family too. I would concentrate your efforts there, Bishop.'

William nodded. 'I'll have messengers sent to learn from the local sheriffs whether the men are alive or not.'

'Any others you've forborne to record, my lord Bishop?' Baldwin asked with more than a hint of sarcasm.

'There is no one else. Occasionally there are some who will grow irritable with me,' Bishop Walter said, 'but that is natural when you are in a position of some power like me. That doesn't mean that I need to listen to all of them.'

'Such as whom?'

'Sir Baldwin,' the bishop expostulated, his hands thrown out in a gesture of openness, 'how can I count them? Be reasonable! In London alone, I was hated by the commonality. All loathed me for I was the man who instigated the Grand Eyre of five years ago. It wasn't my fault, but it was imposed on London while I had the position of Treasurer, so all blamed me. It is natural. Now, do you wish me to bring you a list of all the thousands of men who live in London? Of course not! Perhaps you would like me to compile a full audit of those who have cause to dislike my exactions in taxes in York, or in Winchester? It would leave you with many tens of thousands. That is the scale of the problem, you see. Any number could seek to assassinate me.'

'In that case, my lord bishop, I would send my messengers, and hope to learn that all the enemies are dead or gone away. For those who have fled the nation are no danger to you, while those who are dead should also be safe, unless they have children who have decided to take on the feud.'

'This is plainly someone who lives close,' William said. 'Might it be some other man who resents the cathedral for some reason, and has chosen to alarm the man who controls the canons?'

'I had wondered that,' Baldwin said, 'but I can find no matters which could give cause for a man to try to attack the bishop. Are there any cases of fighting between the city and the cathedral in recent years?'

'No, the city and we have been on most cordial terms. It is the advantage of being a Devon man through and through,' the bishop said.

'That being so, my Lord Bishop, I would urge you to be most cautious about your security and safety,' Baldwin said. 'I would suggest that you leave Devonshire for a little while, perhaps visit London, if it were not for the fact that you have told me you have alienated the whole population.'

'There are some there who still appreciate me,' the bishop smiled.

'Bishop, there are many who appreciate you, I am sure. But there is one who doesn't, and he is the one I am worried about. He has a good reason to want to kill you, I believe, and that means that I would prefer you to be far away from him. Since he knows you're here, if you could move somewhere else, that may make you safer. It all depends.'

'On what?'

'If we learn that one of these men is still alive, and could be trying to attack you in earnest, then it would be easier for all if you were to travel while your guards watched for him. And if a man tried to follow you, and he had the appearance of one of these enemies, your men would be able to guess that he is the guilty one. So send men to learn about all these fellows, and to make sure if they can, that all these suspects are dead. Because dead men don't kill.'

Montreuil

They all trotted from the town and made their way along the ridge beside the river, the curiously named *Canche*, which flowed westwards to Étaples. The duke did not want to go so far as that. Instead he took them to the old town of Berck, where they stopped at a wine shop and refreshed themselves. It had been a very easy canter from Montreuil, but the dust on the roads had clogged all of their throats, and the pints of wine they bought were very welcome, as were the thick slices of sausage and pottage fragrant with rosemary and sage. All felt considerably better afterwards.

Richard de Folville for one was glad to be away from Montreuil. Like Paul, he felt he was under surveillance. However, Mortimer was gone for now. He had ridden off earlier in the morning, apparently to meet with spies who had messages from England. He wasn't expected back for two or three days.

The idea that any man might look at Folville and think him either untrustworthy or churlish was so insulting that he was tempted to take a knife to the bastard's throat. Damn Mortimer! He was no better than Despenser! But Richard de Folville knew he had best not try any such attack. Better to be circumspect, for after all, he was a guest in this country. He could hardly kill a man here too, and run the risk of being forced to flee. Where could he go from here? Only to the outlandish wilds of the east, perhaps with the Teutonic Knights in their expansion along the coast, or down to the hot lands of the Portuguese or the Spaniards, helping protect them against the Moorish incursions. Neither was particularly attractive. Far better to return to Teigh and his church.

For now the best he could do was remain here and wait for the long-overdue invasion, at which point, if he had helped enough, he might be able to plead a pardon. Because there was no doubt in his mind that Mortimer was returning to England in force, and would soon overwhelm the country. No one wanted the king to remain. Not while he relied on Despenser. That scurrilous rat would have to be executed, and when he was gone, the king would be more pliant, more willing to look favourably on those who had protected his son while he was abroad, so long as no one mentioned Belers, and linked his death to Folville before he had a chance to explain how Belers had brought it all upon himself. Stupid, thieving bastard!

At least this ride was pleasant enough. About three and a half leagues each way, and the fresh sea air was good for a man's soul. They had a routine already, after only three days. They would ride out, find a suitable wine seller, drink and eat, and then ride along the sea shore a short way, so the prince could stare out towards England. It was as though he was showing respect to his father, trying to cross the sea even though there was no boat for him. He reminded Richard of a man he had once seen at the coast in England. He was guilty of murder or somesuch, and had claimed sanctuary for some days, before agreeing to abjure the realm, accepting voluntary exile rather than offer himself to the jury. But when he got to the sea, there were no boats, and he had walked into the water up to his groin every day in proof of his desire to leave the realm.

Hadn't helped him, of course. His body was found one morning in the midden near a tavern. Throat cut, but also one leg and both arms broken, so he'd been beaten extensively before dying. Probably his victim's family had caught up with him, or something.

'Are you ready to ride to the sea?' the confessor asked the duke, and the young fellow nodded. He had finished his wine already, and now the others all stood, draining their cups as quickly as they might, and following the heir to their king's throne, out to where the horses had been fed and watered.

The duke was first to mount, as always, and sat on his mount while he waited for the others to emulate him. All were soon ready and the cavalcade made its way through the town and out the other side to the water.

'There is England,' the duke said quietly, in Richard's hearing.

His voice was low and quiet, and desperate with longing, and Richard felt a sudden empathy for him. So young to be here, thrust from his quiet, comfortable life into the turbulent waters of great politics. A lad so young was certain to feel a certain dislocation on being hurled over the ocean at the whim of a mother whose only wish was to recover her own position and wealth, while his father longed for his return.

At least, Richard hoped that his father still doted on him. It was that which held alive his hope for a secure future with a pardon.

'Come!' the duke shouted, and spurred his beast. He whirled the horse about, and cantered away before any of the men had the chance to follow. To Richard's chagrin, he saw that Ivo la Zouche and his brother Ralph were already up and with the duke. And that was when it became confused.

There was a shout, carried on the blustery wind. Richard glanced in that direction, and saw that the priest was bellowing and pointing to the south. When he looked, Sir Richard saw a group of men on horses pounding up towards them. It was a sight to chill the marrow, and Richard quickly counted the men. Only the same number as the duke's party, with eight all told, but Richard was not fool enough to believe that it was all. He scanned the landscape and saw another party, this time riding hell-for-leather for them. So at least double their number, he thought ruefully.

The priest clapped his heels to his mount and thundered away even as Richard did the same, and Richard's mount reared, neighing with excitement. It was good to feel the thrill of battle about to commence, and Richard felt the now-familiar tingling in his spine and cods at the thought of an engagement. God alone knew who they were, but he would see to it that he took as many of them as possible before any man managed to kill him.

In front, there was a bellow, and he saw Sir Ivo drag his sword free from the scabbard, whirl it about his head, and charge. His brother was a moment or two behind him, and then he set off at the gallop as well, while the pasty-faced, smiling one, Crok, whipped out his own weapon, and suddenly shrieked like a banshee, clapped spurs to his mount and galloped as though all the demons of hell were after him, straight at the men.

Richard and the priest stayed nearer to the duke, watching. The duke twice tried to ride on too, but Richard had a firm grip on the duke's reins. He would not allow his ticket to pardon and freedom risk his life.

The first impact was a clatter of metal, with the stern clash of steel blades. Noises assailed Richard's ears. Horses neighing so highly in their excitement and rage that they sounded like women screaming. Crok's beast reared and brought a hoof down on the head of another, and his victim was felled like a rabbit shot from a sling. The rider tried to kick himself free from the stirrups, but the beast's collapse trapped his leg underneath, and the man could only stare in horror as Crok's sword thrust down, twice, and there was a short spurt of blood from the man's eye as he died.

Ivo was after the two leaders, and he crouched in his saddle, sword arm high, laughing and roaring like a drunken matelot, as he crashed into the two, his beast holding his head high, thundering into the first horse with the solid mass of horse and rider concentrated in his broad chest, slamming the other two into each other. There was a slashing blow from Ivo's arm, and a great gout of blood flew into the air, drenching Ivo in an instant. The first rider fell, the second roared defiance, and hacked at Ivo, but his blade rang as it met Ivo's, and then there was a sparkle as Ivo's blade caught the sun, whirling in a semi-circle, and the other man's head dropped forwards, held to his neck by the thinnest of slivers of flesh. Ivo's sword had ripped through bone and flesh.

The second party was with them now, and Richard looked about for a safer position, but there was no time to escape. Instead, he drew his sword, and prepared himself. He just wished he had taken more interest in the weapons-handling instruction when he had been younger.

His companion was less uncertain. With a shriek, sounding for all the world like a demented woman, the duke lifted his own sword, and pointing it at the men approaching them, he suddenly jerked his reins from Richard's hand, and was off, pounding towards the men alone.

Richard gritted his teeth and followed. At his side he saw the priest, Paul, his eyes wide in horror, clinging to his horse for dear life. He had no sword, not even a dagger that Richard could see, the fool. But he could no more turn away than fly. His horse was trained to fight, not run away, and it was charging with the others whether his rider wished it or no.

Then Richard's focus became more concentrated. There was no time for others. They must see to their own safety. A great crash knocked his horse sideways, there was a hideous crack at his thigh, and he thought it might have broken; a horse had ridden into him. No sword near his head yet. He stabbed at the horse itself, and was rewarded with a thick spray of blood. It neighed defiance, and reared, but even as it did so, its eyes rolled, and it tumbled to the ground.

A second man, this time passing beside Richard, as though to attack the duke from behind. Richard clapped spurs, and as he lurched forward, his blade slid in under the man's shoulder blade. There was a scream of hideous anguish, and the man fell, rolling over and over in his agony.

The third man was aiming at his head even as he glanced about. Instinct made him lift his sword to knock it aside, but lack of practice made his blade miss his mark and take the man's wrist and hand off. The stump shot a jet of blood, and suddenly Richard was soaked in warm stickiness, and he would have pressed home his attack, but the man leaped from his horse and grabbed for his hand as though to try to replace it.

Richard left him. The duke was his concern, and just now the young man was being pressed by another man-at-arms. Richard rode on, and knocked the man aside, seeing the duke's sword slice through the fellow's throat as he fell.

And that was it. The battle was over. All the men who had sought to attack them were dead or fleeing. And none of the duke's men were harmed, Richard saw. Ivo and his brother Ralph were trotting back, holding each other's hands, and Richard felt nothing, only a vague disquiet, as he saw Ivo's head fall to his breast, and then the man's great body slowly topple from his horse, showing a great gash in his flank that pulsed as the blood oozed.

Chapter Twenty-Two

Bishop's Clyst

When the stern-faced Keeper walked from the room, leaving the bishop sitting pale and stunned by Sir Baldwin's summary, William nodded to John to stay with his uncle, and marched quickly after the knight.

'Sir Baldwin, please. Sir Knight – a moment?'

'Yes, squire?'

William jerked a thumb over his shoulder in the direction of the bishop's chamber. 'You meant what you said in there?'

'I would not have said it else.'

'I didn't mean to insult you, Sir Baldwin. Please, do not grow angry with me. I only seek to protect my uncle.'

'You are fond of him?'

William smiled, and joined Baldwin, the two walking side-by-side out into the sunshine of the bishop's garden, then beyond to the small orchard. 'I love him greatly. He has been enormously kind to me. When I was young, it was Bishop Walter who looked after me and saw to my education. Later, when I was confused, and thought that I might seek a career in the Church like him, it was he who sat down with me and questioned my interests, my motives, and persuaded me to look hard, deep into my heart. And I found that there, although it was harder to admit it to myself when I was young, I preferred the companionship of a woman than that of many sex-starved and desperate men! I would never have made a good churchman. He was quite right. But the bishop has given me help all through my life, he has given me money, and his example has shown me the best routes to take always.'

'You speak as a man who has much to thank his uncle for.'

'I think you too have had cause to appreciate his kindness and generosity?'

The knight threw him a sharp look, which the squire found hard to fathom. It was as though Sir Baldwin was torn between anxiety and a swift anger. 'Why? What has he said to you?'

They were at the hedge that bounded the orchard now, and Squire William spoke carefully. 'Sir Baldwin, my uncle has told me only two things about you: that he has always found you entirely honourable and fair, a true seeker after justice in your dealings with felons and outlaws. That, he says, makes you a rare man among the king's law officers. He has also told me that you were once a pilgrim, and that your journeys to the Holy Land must have coloured your every thought for the long years since.'

'I see,' Baldwin said quietly. He stared out eastwards. Far away there was the ridge of the Blackdown Hills, standing grey-blue in the distance.

To William, he looked like a man rent by conflicting emotions. The scar that stretched from his eyebrow almost to his chin shone in the sunlight, and the little wrinkles at the corners of his eyes were less prominent. Instead, it was the tracks of sadness and bitterness that stood out, the deep gashes at his brow and at either side of his mouth. His was a face that had seen much anguish, and he had suffered greatly.

'Sir Baldwin, I am sorry. You are distressed. I will leave you.'

'No, Squire William. No, my friend. I was merely reflecting that when a man has given a confidence to another, it is ever his fear that his trust was misplaced. I am sorry that I have given you cause to be upset as well. I should have trusted your uncle and his discretion.'

Squire William was surprised to find his hand grasped by the knight, and then Baldwin's dark, intense eyes were turned to him, as he said, 'You are a good man. You will need courage though, in the days ahead, unless I am much mistaken.'

'What do you mean?'

'You heard us discuss the men who could wish your uncle's

death? That is all they are: the most obvious suspects. Your uncle has lived a long life, and he has made many enemies, my friend. Key among them is the queen herself. She will return to the kingdom before long, and there will be great battles fought as men protect the country from her and her invaders. Many will die, I fear.'

His eyes turned east again, and Squire William saw the haunting fear that had invaded his eyes. 'Sir Baldwin, I am sure that the king will be able to defend his realm.'

'Yes, but at what cost? There have been wars before in our poor little country, but at least they were fought by us in defence of our lands and privileges. This war is not to be so honourable, Squire. This is a battle between a husband and wife, and such battles are ever more vicious and brutal. No one will likely win. I fear for us all.'

'One or the other must win!'

Baldwin turned to him, and now the anxiety was gone, to be replaced by a shrewd calculation. 'You think so? What if the men who come over with the queen are all French and owe their allegiance solely to the French king? What if, when they have defeated our king, they refuse to honour a past arrangement, and instead decide to take the realm for the French? A man would not have to be terribly cynical to see a dreadful disaster unfolding.'

'That would not bode well, not for England, nor for my uncle.'

'You are correct there. Your uncle is detested by the French.'

'I feel it is a mutual antagonism,' Squire William said with a small grin.

'You may well be right,' Baldwin grinned back.

'But in the meantime, Sir Baldwin, would you not help us? We need to learn what we may about the men who seek the bishop's death.'

'You want me to, but I cannot. My wife is here, and I must remain with her. I could not leave her alone to face an invasion. In the last year I have travelled widely to help the king, to help your uncle, and to protect the Duke of Chester. I cannot in conscience leave my lady again. Now is the time for a man to remain at home and guard his property.'

'I understand. But there is no invasion yet. There are no ships at our ports bringing men and matériel. While the nation is still moderately peaceful, would you not help to protect your friend?'

'You cannot understand. I have a wife and children who need me.'

'Do you not think that you could spend just a little more time with us? It may be nothing, anyway. There may be no one there. These threats might be from another man altogether, for all we know.'

Baldwin held his gaze for a long while, staring silently at him. 'I will do anything I can to help the good bishop, but I have a higher loyalty. My wife, my family, are more important to me even than your uncle.'

'I understand.' William sighed and made to move away, but Baldwin's next words made him stop.

'There is one other thing,' the knight said pensively. 'These notes were all delivered to the bishop's chamber in Exeter. That would seem to show that the person who delivered them knew when the room would be empty. And more than that, no one was seen on his way to or from the place. Surely that must mean that the fellow is someone from inside your entourage – a servant, say, or an embittered priest. An annuellar maybe? There are so many inside the cathedral.'

'You are pulling my leg!' William said with a smile. 'You cannot mean that one of the bishop's own servants would do a thing like this!'

'It is as likely to be a man from within the Church as without. After all, how many men outside the Church have access to writing tools and parchment?'

*Second Thursday before the Feast of St Paul and St John**

Montreuil

It was a chastened duke who rode back with them the previous day. There had been no glory in the way that the men had beaten off the enemy. Only a stern, fixed duty.

Of course, for Paul it was very different.

The others had joked and laughed about the affair, calling it the 'Battle of the Beach', proud of the way that they had managed to protect their heir. Ralph la Zouche was the only one who betrayed his emotions, weeping over the body of his younger brother. The duke had stopped and gone to him, offering him some comfort, but Sir Ralph was beyond that. In the way he wept, Paul wondered whether he was mourning his brother, or expressing his own selfish grief at being alone. Not that Paul would be likely to mention it. Any such comment could lead to a sudden explosion of rage, and Paul had no intention of being on the receiving end of Sir Ralph's sword.

Duke Edward himself did not brag or laugh aloud. Instead he maintained a silent reserve as he rode.

It was easy to see what he was thinking, Paul reckoned. Clearly the lad, still so young, had been shocked and terrified by the battle. There were many men who would have been alarmed, Paul included, to see such a force. Well, Paul would make no bones about it. He had been scared. The mere thought of those men pounding towards him had been enough to turn his bowels to water, and if the battle had lasted a moment longer, he might have had an unfortunate and embarrassing proof of his fear to explain to the others. Still, he had survived without anyone noticing, he thought.

But for a youngster like this one, it must have been truly petrifying. He was only thirteen years old, and for him to see such

* 12 June 1326

an ambush, to know that men were prepared to assault each other in such a manner, that was surely appalling.

Later, in the castle once more, Paul had tried to go to him, to ensure that he was settled in his mind, but he received a curt rejection. The boy had his mother with him that evening, and perhaps it was better that she was there on hand to soothe the fellow. It was a woman's task, after all.

It was with that reflection that Paul waited in the chamber for the young duke to come for his lessons. It was a pleasant little room, this, with a window that peered out over the river, and Paul settled himself there, resting his back against the wall and watching the peasants at work out in the fields, a tranter or two meandering along the roadway, carts and wagons passing slowly.

The door opened, and the duke entered. The man-at-arms who had accompanied him closed the door quietly, remaining outside.

'My lord Duke, I hope you slept well?' Paul greeted him.

'I did not.'

Paul smiled benignly. 'Ah, you must not allow a little action like that of yesterday to unsettle you, my lord. No, the main thing is, you were safe.'

'You think so?'

'Of course. While you have a force such as yesterday's with you, you will be safe from robbers and outlaws.'

'You think those men were outlaws, then?'

'Yes, but there is nothing to fear from such men. You saw how poorly they fought.'

'It's true,' the duke said musingly. 'They were not a match for our men in some ways. The speed and determination of our guard was adequate to throw them into confusion.'

'Naturally.'

'But I am not concerned for outlaws; what I am worried about is the fact that I think they may have been sent for me.'

'Oh, my lord, I don't think—'

'Do you really believe that a bunch of cutpurses would be so well armoured? Do you think that they would have aimed straight for the youngest in the group – me?'

'I thought that they were all riding towards *me*! In an action like that, you see, you can be—'

'Shut up! If I want a fool to make me laugh, I can demand the services of a better trained one. Those men were sent to capture me – I hope.'

'What do you mean, you "hope"?'

'If they were not, they were sent to kill me,' the duke said, and pursed his lips.

'I think, Your Highness, you are taking this too seriously.'

'A man of my bodyguard is dead, and you suggest I am too serious?'

'No, but surely if there was such a danger to you, we would already know of it, eh?'

The duke gave him a withering look, and then took his seat on a large chair. 'Priest, you make a poor adviser. I have to understand the nature of the threat in order to be able to protect myself from it.'

'But who would want to see you harmed?' Paul protested weakly.

'Either Despenser wishes to have me captured and taken back to England, or killed. If I were to die here in France, the kingdom would blame my mother and Mortimer – and can you envisage the invasion of England succeeding if all in the country thought that? No! Despenser wishes to see me dead. Well, he will not – I will see his head on a spike first!'

'What will you do?' Paul asked.

'First, we shall move away from the sphere of my mother's influence – in order to protect her. We could go somewhere where it will be easier to remain safe. Perhaps to Paris – but the king, my uncle, is not happy to have us remain. He sees us as an embarrassment now. Or I could go to Normandy. There are plenty of safe places there for us to hide in.'

'What does your mother say?'

'Her view does not matter. This is my responsibility,' the duke said firmly.

Paul nodded, but did not speak. Uppermost in his mind was the reaction of Mortimer. He was due to return the next day.

Furnshill

There was another man in the hall when Baldwin entered. 'Sir Peregrine, I hope I see you well, sir?'

'I am very well, Sir Baldwin.'

With this man, Baldwin was perfunctory at best. He had never liked Sir Peregrine de Barnstaple. The coroner was too much the politician for his tastes and while Baldwin agreed entirely with the ambition of seeing the Despenser removed from his secure position beside the throne, he deprecated the man's enthusiasm for plotting.

To Baldwin it was a simple matter of honour: he had sworn allegiance to the king as his sovereign, and although the king could, and often did, make an appalling mess of his governance of the realm, yet he was still the man whom God had anointed with oil. He was the rightful king, and Baldwin must seek to preserve him.

'You have come here from Tiverton, Sir Peregrine? Has there been a murder?' he asked as he took his wife's hand and kissed it, saying, 'I missed you, my love.'

She rested her head on his shoulder. 'And I you,' she whispered. Then she stood away and nodded to Edgar. He strode off, returning a moment later with a mazer for Baldwin. There was already a jug at the side of Sir Peregrine, and Baldwin took it up, serving his guest first, topping up his cup, before filling his own and drinking deeply.

'No, no murder yet,' Sir Peregrine said with a smile. 'Or perhaps I should say, not recently. It is a long time since Tiverton suffered from a crime of that sort. The reason I am here is because I was on my way to Exeter, to meet with the sheriff.'

'That young fool de Cockington?'

'True, he is not so experienced as you and I, Sir Baldwin, which makes him rather a refreshing fellow to have in a position like his. The opportunities for pulling the wool over his eyes are legion. Even when he believes he has struck a hard bargain with me, I usually manage to acquire all I need.'

'That is good,' Baldwin said. He was thoughtful for a moment, and then asked, 'Do you know anything about a family called Biset? A man called John Biset?'

'I have heard of him, I think. Why?'

Baldwin shook his head. 'Something I was wondering about. Probably nothing. So, you will stay for some food? Would you accept a bed for the night?'

'I would like to, but no, I should ride on. I left only late this morning,' Sir Peregrine said, 'delayed by business. But I hope to hurry to Exeter. There is a lady there whom I would meet again.'

'A lady?' Baldwin asked, glancing at his wife with a faint smile. There was something endearing about Sir Peregrine's attempts to find himself a wife.

'Yes, the Lady Isabella, who was sadly widowed for the second time a few years ago.'

Jeanne, who was always keen for news of Sir Peregrine's romantic progress, leaned forward. 'Tell us about her – I do not know this lady.'

'She is named Isabella Fitzwilliam. Her last husband was Henry, but he was captured by the king's men and executed for treachery. Since then, she has been living in penury.'

Baldwin shook his head sadly. 'There are so many who have lost their livelihoods. It is terrible.'

'Yes. To think that an honourable lady like her . . . Well, as you say, Sir Baldwin, the last few years have seen so much injustice and cruelty, it is hard to know what to say to someone who has suffered so much.'

'But you hope to be able to comfort her?' Jeanne prompted.

'I cannot hope . . . I would like to . . . But it is impossible to even dream of such things. The poor lady has lost two husbands already. I cannot imagine that she would be keen to experience such a loss again,' Sir Peregrine said, his eyes a little downcast.

It was no more than the truth. Hard though it was to accept, Sir Peregrine was almost resigned to the fact that his life would end without a wife. He would die a bachelor.

In the past, that had been a source of extreme sadness. He had wanted to have the stability of a wife at his side, to have children whom he might teach and leave to carry on his family name. Given time, perhaps he would have seen a son of his become famous, even see him knighted in his own right. That would have been a wonder to him!

But no, it had never happened, and now, much though he desired a woman's companionship, he would have to learn to be satisfied with the friendship of others.

'You would like her for your wife?' Jeanne said definitely.

'Well, of course I would, my lady, but if I were truthful, I would have to say that my own position is scarcely sound. There are many men who are better placed than me to provide for a lady such as her.'

'What is she like?' Jeanne asked.

'Well, she is no child,' Sir Peregrine said with an embarrassed shrug. 'Oh, I do not mean that she is old, Lady Jeanne!'

'What, not as old as me?' Jeanne asked sweetly.

'You torment me now,' the knight said distractedly. 'I can say nothing without your twisting my words.'

'I shall be silent, then,' Jeanne smiled.

'She is a little shorter than you, Lady Jeanne, and a little older, I would guess. But for all that, she has a radiant smile. Her eyes are as green as a holly-leaf, and her hair is the auburn colour of a conker. And even though she has suffered so much, she smiles and laughs a great deal.'

'With you?' Jeanne said.

'She and I have laughed much.'

'Then she will welcome your suit, Sir Peregrine. A man who makes his woman laugh is a rarity. If you make her do that, you will be able to ask her to do anything. I advise you to press your suit.'

Chapter Twenty-Three

*Two Fridays before the Feast of St John and St Paul**

Montreuil

It was a very unhappy Paul de Cockington who left the chamber that morning.

The suddenness of Wednesday's attack had appalled the queen and Mortimer. The lack of warning was one aspect, but the appreciation of their danger here in France had been rammed home too. Up until the fight, they had enjoyed a fond belief that they were safe under the protection of the French king. Even the long hand of Despenser would find it hard to reach them here, so they had thought.

'I had heard all his spies here were captured,' had been Mortimer's terse comment. 'The bastard's got more, and the French will do nothing to catch them, even though they know that Despenser is their lord's enemy.'

The duke had said little as Mortimer strode up and down the little chamber, occasionally throwing suspicious looks at the men gathered about. More often than not, to Paul's disquiet, the man's eyes were on him.

Ralph la Zouche was still desperate for vengeance. 'Is there no one can tell us who planned the attack? The devils should be forced to pay for my brother's death!'

'I have asked my brother,' Queen Isabella said coldly. 'He has searched for these men and for those who instructed them to

---

* 13 June 1326

attack his nephew, but so far there is nothing. He will continue until news is forthcoming.'

'He is too slow!' la Zouche cried, in a voice that was almost a howl. 'They slew my brother! I want revenge!'

'The man responsible is in England,' Mortimer said. 'He's the one you should seek. There's no one else who would have tried such a deed.'

'My poor son,' Queen Isabella muttered, and her maid put her hand on the queen's shoulder. The queen put her own little hand over her maid's as she stared at the young duke.

Mortimer turned to him. 'Did you feel your life was in danger, my lord? It is one thing to consider that King Edward might have sought to kill your guard, and quite another to think that he could attempt your life.'

'What else would a man think?' Duke Edward demanded hotly. 'Those men were sent for me. I have no doubt about that whatever.'

'But perhaps they were not trying to kill? Perhaps they only wished to capture and take you away? Your father is desperate to have you back, I expect,' Mortimer said, with a sidelong glance at the queen.

'He would do this?' she said, eyes wide with shock. 'I had assumed this was the Despenser, but you think my husband could seek to take my son by force?'

'He'd argue you held him here by force,' Mortimer said drily.

'He knows I stay willingly,' the duke said. 'He has written to me and I have replied.'

'I know,' Mortimer said.

There was a pause on hearing that. Paul was unsurprised, because this man Mortimer would never have allowed the duke to maintain correspondence with his father – who was determined to see Mortimer dead, and who had in fact signed his death warrant – without being able to read it.

The young duke was shocked, and his mouth gaped for a moment before he caught himself and shut it again. This new proof of Mortimer's distrust of her son was enough to make the queen rise, eyes blazing with rage.

'You say you have read his letters, Sir Roger? You have opened his letters, and those addressed to him?'

'Of course. You think that we can afford to take risks? What if your husband had sought to use coercion to force your son to leave us? Could you have borne the loss of your son, lady? What if he had disappeared in the night, fled to the coast, and taken an English boat home? Your husband would have had all the money, then. He could wager anything and win. And us? We would have lost a prospective husband, we would have lost a defensive shield, and a figurehead for your army. We would have lost all. I'm not prepared to risk that.'

'You read his messages – does that mean you read mine as well?'

'I have had no need to. What would you write to your husband?'

'Whatever I may write is none of your concern!'

'Lady, everything became my concern when we first launched ourselves on this course of action.'

'My letters are my own! You have no right to open them.'

'Why? Would you return to your husband?' he sneered, his face pale.

'I may! Perhaps I would prefer to end this dreadful impasse!'

Mortimer took a step towards her, and now Paul could see the emotion in his face. It wrenched his features, as though the man was torn with desperation. 'Woman, you do that, and I swear I'll kill you myself with my dagger!' he spat, his hand on the hilt.

There was an appalled silence for a moment. All Paul could hear was the raucous drumbeat of his heart and the whistle of la Zouche's breath. There was a heightened awareness in that chamber, a sense that there might soon be an eruption of violence that would affect not only all the men in there, but all the millions in England too. Paul steadied himself, as though preparing to leap upon Mortimer, but his muscles felt as tense as a bowstring, and he found himself incapable of moving.

Instead it was the duke who spoke, 'Sir Roger, my mother meant no insult. The strain of the last few days has affected us, that is all. Kindly remove your hand from your dagger.'

All the while, he walked forward. It was not some bold action, not a challenge, but more the gait of a man sauntering to the tavern to buy his friend a jug of ale.

Mortimer eventually nodded, and turned away. 'I am sorry, my lady. This is indeed a difficult time for all of us. I think it just demonstrates that we must proceed as quickly as we may.'

'Yes,' the queen said. She sank back into her chair, blanched and discomfited after her outburst of passion. Then, even as he watched, Paul could see her face tighten, and she became the shrewd, calculating vixen he had seen before. She looked about her, smiling at Paul and her son, before catching sight of Mortimer – and suddenly she reminded Paul of a hungry snake eyeing a small creature. And then her smile became lethal.

Exeter

Sir Peregrine de Barnstaple left the castle with a light step, whistling tunelessly as he passed beneath the great gateway and strode down the cleared road to the High Street.

It was a good city, this. Rich on the trade which the ships brought each day, fed well by the numerous farms all about, and influential because of the powerful bishop who sat in the cathedral.

The streets demonstrated the city's affluence. There was abundance in all. Rich carvings on the buildings, gilt, vivid colours everywhere. The people cared little for any sumptuary code. In the days of the old king, Edward I, there had been little interest in fashions and fripperies, but under Edward II, his son, merchants aspired to magnificence no less than bishops and earls. Women wore bright garments, while men of some stature strode about with their ridiculous, tight hosen and belly-hugging overgarments. It was enough to make a man like Sir Peregrine, who was of a more serious disposition than most, feel vaguely sad. There were so many important matters for people to consider, it seemed shameful that men preferred to preen in public like so many cockerels.

Leaving the main roadway, he made for St Peter's Priory. Near this, he turned off down an alley, and soon he was at a door, upon which he knocked briskly.

'Is your mistress in?' he enquired of the servant girl, and soon he was inside.

Sir Peregrine had been to battle several times. He had killed four men in hot blood, each of them entirely justifiably, and was quietly confident in his prowess with sword and lance, and content to know that in war he did not flinch. He would hold his position as arrows rained about him, or as a fearsome lancepoint thundered towards him, gripped by a knight on a massive destrier.

So why did he feel this emptiness in his belly, and the cold sweat on his spine as he waited here to see Lady Isabella Fitzwilliam again?

It was always the same when he went to meet a lady for whom he had high regard. He would feel a similar trepidation, bordering on fear, convinced that he must surely make a fool of himself. Or that he was entirely wrong in his estimation of the lady's feelings towards him. How might a man tell what a woman wanted? They were always so unreadable. A man would be easy. If he wished to be a friend, he would smile and speak warmly; if not a friend, he would be reserved; if an enemy, he would be rude and objectionable. Sir Peregrine had experienced all of these. But a woman . . . She was a mystery not so easily solved.

'Sir Peregrine! How good of you to come and visit me again.'

'It is my pleasure, Lady Isabella. I am very glad to see you once more. I hope I find you well?'

'Very well,' the lady said, and walked to a seat, waving graciously to him to sit as well. 'I hope you are too?'

'Certainly! Never better! Hah!' Sir Peregrine felt his face freeze over as he reviewed in his mind what he had just said, and his eyes became glassy. 'I . . .'

'Perhaps you would like a little wine?' she asked kindly.

'I would be glad of some,' he admitted.

She stood and went to the sideboard herself, motioning to her maidservant to leave them, and then pouring his wine herself.

It was a revelation to him. He had not been alone with a woman for many months indeed. And it was hardly in keeping with the proprieties of polite custom for a man and woman to be together in such proximity. And then he heard the distinct sound of a jug clattering on the side of a goblet.

Peering closely, he saw that Lady Isabella stood stiffly, trying to hold the jug to the goblet with an easy nonchalance, but the show was betrayed by her nervous shaking making them rattle. She threw him an anguished look.

He stood, and in a moment had crossed the room to her. Taking the jug from her trembling hands, he set it down, and then the two of them stood staring at each other for what he thought was an age. He wanted to take her in his arms, but there was always this damned reticence that sprang from his upbringing. A man should not grasp a woman, not until he was sure he possessed her heart. Instead he sighed, and half turned away.

'It is difficult, Sir Peregrine, when you find that your feelings are the same as a maiden's, and yet you have been married. I am no child. I'm a woman, and yet the trials of such a meeting are so troublesome.'

'I know, my lady. Perhaps it would be better were I to leave you now.'

'Do you wish to?'

'In God's name, no!'

'Then please stay, Sir Peregrine.'

'You wish it?'

'More than anything. I am lonely, and I feel you are too. We could comfort each other.'

'You believe it too?' he breathed. His heart was pounding like a hammer in a forge.

'Yes, I really do.'

Montreuil

So it was agreed, then. Richard de Folville nodded as the others broke up their meeting. It was clear enough that there was no longer safety for them all here in Montreuil, especially not for the duke. They would have to move away. And as the duke himself had pointed out, it would be far better for them all to head to the west, where there were more sympathisers who could aid them, rather than travel all the way to the south to the duke's own lands.

It was the queen who had objected to his travelling to Guyenne. Although he was the Duke of Aquitaine, which incorporated the vast territories of the south, as she pointed out, 'My son has never visited the area. He has no loyal followers there, but my husband has many. There are a lot of his friends in Guyenne who are there to fight for him. If you think that it is dangerous here, because a few men from his entourage could cross the Channel, how much more dangerous would it be for him in the lands which are even now in revolt?'

It was true. The French were massing along the borders of Guyenne again, in the face of the English refusal to honour past agreements, and to allow her son to travel there at such a time would have been sheer lunacy.

'Then he will have to stay with us,' had been Mortimer's contribution. He was firm in his opinion that the only safe place for the duke was with Mortimer's own men.

Richard de Folville wondered at that. It seemed much more likely that Mortimer just didn't want the lad out of his sight. It was plain enough that he had an eye to his own protection, and that would mean keeping the king's son nearby. That way, he would continue to keep the queen on his side, he would have a greater bargaining potential with the English and French kings, and he would also be able to conclude the negotiations which all had heard of now, to have the next English king married to a suitable heiress. Mortimer and Queen Isabella both had their minds fixed on a wedding with Philippa of Hainault. She was almost nine years old, so a little young for the duke, but that was no impediment. And more to the point, her father had ships and men. Mercenaries from Hainault would be a marvellous bonus to Mortimer if he was serious about invading England again, and Richard was sure that this was the plan.

All well and good. He hoped they would take him with them,

and then he could win the usual reward of a fighter – a full pardon for his past behaviour. At which point he could return to Teigh, and resume his life.

If he wanted to. It was hard to imagine returning to that life of tedium: taking up the cure of souls, watching over the men and women of the area, holding Mass, praying until his knees were calloused, feeling the damp coldness seep into his legs and arse, and occasionally drinking a sup or two of wine – when he could afford it.

The alternative was to live life to the full. To take to the roads with his sword in his hand, and help himself to what he wanted from the world. That was more appealing.

But first he would have to have the pardon, and the assurance that these fellows would be able to win the upper hand. Bearing in mind the cretins running the country now, he had little doubt that these would find England ready to greet them with open arms, were they to try to return.

It was just as they were discussing the plans for the departure to Hainault, that a messenger had arrived from that very place. He passed a note to Mortimer, who opened it after studying the seal.

'What does it say?' the queen demanded.

'Your friend the Despenser sent those men to catch your son,' Mortimer said. He whistled through his teeth in wonder. 'Despenser has negotiated with the peers of France to have you evicted from the realm here, or to have you and Edward killed.'

Duke Edward leaped to his feet. 'I don't believe you! My father would never—'

'He would not have been told of this plot,' Mortimer said. 'Very well – that decides matters. You will both have to remain with me in my entourage. Come, we must arrange for all our belongings to be readied for departure early in the morning.'

Paul cleared his throat nervously. 'My lord duke, I think that would be a mistake.'

Mortimer rounded on him. 'Are you a strategist, Priest?'

'Hear him, Sir Roger,' the duke said. 'We discussed this yesterday. Speak, Tutor.'

'I only mean this: if there are to be more attacks with men trying to kill the queen and the duke, you would be better to have them separate. Let the queen travel to Hainault, but the duke go away from her.'

Mortimer clenched a fist. 'We've discussed this enough already.'

'We know that Normandy is loyal to his mother, and the Normans are still fond of the memory of William the Bastard. Why not ride for Normandy?'

'Your Highness, that would be foolish. Better by far to keep our forces together. Once we are in Hainault we will be safe,' Mortimer said bluntly.

'If it is truly safer, I can join you later,' the duke said. 'But for my part, I am keen to see the land of my ancestors. Normandy is almost our motherland, is it not? And I would like to visit Rouen, too. King Richard Coeur de Lion's heart is buried there, and I have a strong desire to see it.'

'What if there should be another attack on you?' Mortimer burst out. 'It is ridiculous, I will not allow it!'

'And when did you have the right to control me?' the duke said coolly. 'I was not aware that I no longer had the right to choose my own destiny.'

'You are here under my protection.'

'Sir Roger, I am here under the protection of the King of France, my uncle. And I will take my own path.'

'You should be with us so that we can take ship together,' Mortimer said, and now Richard could almost hear the man's teeth grinding.

'I will be. You ride on, and I will follow after. I will let you know where I am so you can send messengers when you need me to join you.'

'Where will you stay?' Mortimer demanded. 'Without money, you'll find lodgings hard.'

'My mother will give me an allowance, I am sure.'

'The inns of Normandy are not expensive,' Folville put in, 'and there is a good one within a few hundred feet of the abbey.

I am sure that with the usual hospitality of the Order we would be able to find good lodgings.'

And that had been that. The queen for once had been quiet – Richard thought because she was so shocked at the attack on young Edward, as well as alarmed that her son would be away from her again.

There was no argument against his words. The idea that all would remain together was wildly dangerous. They made too tempting a target: the traitor, the queen, and the son. Together they would fetch a truly royal ransom, were they to be captured.

Chapter Twenty-Four

Exeter

William Walle hurried over the grounds to the Bishop's Palace as soon as the summons arrived.

They had returned to the city only the day before. There was little point in remaining at the bishop's house when the bulk of his work was still up here, and so they had packed their belongings in the wagons and made the short journey back to town in the morning. Then, in the afternoon, the bishop had returned to his labours, while messengers were sent to seek advice on all the men whom Baldwin had suspected. Before long, with luck, the responses would arrive and the knight could be asked to come and take another look at the matter, to see whether there was anything else that might help tell who was threatening his lordship.

But now William had been called to the palace again, just as he was preparing to visit the tavern near the Broadgate. The man who fetched him said simply, 'The bishop asks that you come at once.'

He found Bishop Walter sitting in his little chair by the table in his hall, John the steward at his side, looking lugubrious. 'Another one,' he said.

'What?' William strode across the floor and took up the shred of parchment. '*You will die unmourned and alone*,' he read aloud. Glancing at his uncle, he said, 'Where was it?'

'Here, on my table,' the bishop said listlessly, pointing. 'It just lay there, like that. Face up.'

'I didn't see it myself,' John said. 'I was in here most of the afternoon, but I had to leave to supervise the arrangement of the chamber below for the ecclesiastical court next week. There's the case of de Cockington, which has to be decided. I was only gone for a short while.'

'Which means that the man who put this here is clearly someone who knows when you are here, and when you are not,' William said, remembering Baldwin's words. 'It has to be someone from within the cathedral, Bishop.'

'Come now! Who on earth would attempt such a thing!' he exclaimed. 'It is folly to think that there is a master of disguise and deviousness here in the cathedral. I will not believe it.'

'Unless you believe that the agent which deposits these things here is a devil,' John said sharply, 'then you have to agree that a man would be inordinately lucky to break in here and drop off a note without knowing when would be a good time to do so. Only a brother or a priest would have access to that information.'

'John, I understand your desire to protect me, but I still cannot think that one of the canons or a priest could have done this to me. They would know how distressing I must find it. Such evil messages!'

William shook his head, and John followed him from the room.

'He is sorely distressed,' John said. 'You saw how he looked? Like an old man.'

'Whoever is doing this to him deserves to be pilloried,' William agreed.

'Do you think I was a fool?'

'No. You have to be right. There are few enough men who would have the opportunity to enter his chamber at the best of times. To be able to walk in and be confident enough to drop a message on his table, that would be astonishing. Who do you think it might be?'

'No name instantly springs to my mind,' John said, scratching his head. 'There was no one about when I left to see to the other room. Only young Paul of Taunton – I noticed him in the corridor.'

'Would he be likely to send messages like those to the bishop?'

'No. But he could have seen someone.'

William agreed, and the two men sought the servant concerned, eventually tracking him down in the charnel chapel, where he was preparing for the next service.

'You were outside the bishop's chamber today,' John said. 'I saw you there.'

'Yes, steward. Why?'

The lad was not yet five-and-twenty, and had the astonishingly clear blue eyes and black hair of the Celt. He had been sweeping the floor clean as they entered, and now he leaned on his besom to look at them with a puzzled frown.

'Did you see someone go up to the bishop's chamber? Somebody entered while the bishop was not there, and left something. Do you know who it may have been?'

'There was a lay brother who went up. You know the man, the older one with the grey stubble who always looks as though he's about to collapse from hunger.'

'Geoffrey?' John asked, with eyes screwed up from the act of recollection.

'That's him. He used to be a squire, and now he lives here on a corrody.'

'Who is he?' William asked.

'Geoffrey of St Albans. He was a squire, and served his master well, I believe,' the clerk said, carrying on with his sweeping.

'Who was his master?'

'The Earl of Lancaster.'

William breathed out. Earl Thomas of Lancaster had attempted to curb the king's powers, and as a result had thrown the country into a short but bloody civil war. Captured by the king's men after the Battle of Boroughbridge, the earl had been stripped of his rank, drawn to his execution on an old goat, and beheaded as a traitor. It had been the start of the appalling bloodshed with which the king had sought to seal his authority on the realm.

'If he was a servant of the king's enemy,' William said, 'it is easy to imagine that he might also hate the king's advisers and friends.'

'Perhaps we should seek this man out,' John said. 'It's possible we shall not need the knight from Furnshill after all.'

Road to Paris

It was a relief to be out of that town. There was nowhere Paul would like to be less than that hideous castle. Once it had seemed a pleasant retreat, but no longer. The idea that he and the Duke of Aquitaine could be held prisoner there was frankly terrifying.

Their orders to leave had come almost as soon as they had left Mortimer. There had been some more arguing, no doubt, but now the agreement was confirmed. The young duke was to ride to Normandy with his guards, while his mother and Mortimer would go to Hainault to conclude negotiations. They had much still to arrange. The invasion of an entire realm like England was not a matter to be undertaken lightly.

The duke had bellowed at his guards to hurry as soon as the meeting was closed, and Paul was pleased for once to obey an order to be quick. He actually assisted some of the servants as they packed goods and clothing, even carrying some of the bales of clothes and helping another man with a heavy chest, taking them all out to the waiting carts.

Now they had been on the road for a half of the afternoon, from the look of the sun, and Paul was wondering where they might stay the night. 'Where shall we go, my lord?'

'Tonight? There will be an inn before long. If not, we can sleep under the stars with the weather so clement.'

'Yes, but what of the morrow? Shall we be remaining in Paris for some days?' Paul asked hopefully. There were so many more glamorous women there in the city. It was a place that offered endless opportunities to a man like him, and he would have welcomed a chance to rest there for a few days.

'No,' the duke said coldly, as though reading his mind. 'We shall turn west before Paris and ride for my ancestor's lands. I have never seen Normandy, and this will be a good opportunity to do so.'

'Oh.'

'Don't look so crestfallen, priest. It will be a delightful interlude, and safer than a place like Paris with all the intrigues that a city can afford.'

'I thought you would like to rest there a while,' Paul said lamely.

'In a place where the leading peers of the realm have been offered silver by the barrel to have me captured, and possibly murdered?' the duke said. 'Hmm. I think not.'

'But your uncle wouldn't allow it,' Paul said unthinkingly.

'Do you think he supported the attack on me three days ago? Do you suggest that he would be keen to see me murdered at Montreuil?'

'No, of course not!' Paul said hurriedly. It was not safe to speak of a king as an assassin in his own realm where any might be listening. 'But surely in Paris . . .'

'There would be plenty of opportunity for a murderer. Many men there would no doubt welcome the chance to augment their incomes. And many more would stick a dagger in my throat for the price of a barrel of wine.'

'So we will ride west to Normandy at once?'

'Yes. And there, I think, we will be safe. The hunting is said to be excellent, and the wine flows.' He cast an appraising eye towards his tutor. 'I've heard that the women there are the most magnificent in all France,' he added mildly.

'I would not care for such news,' Paul said unconvincingly.

'They tend to blondes, I've heard. All tall. And their . . .' the duke made some elaborate hand gestures about his chest. 'Enormous.'

Paul shook his head with a slight frown. 'Really, my lord duke, you should pay no attention to such matters. They are not becoming for a man of serious business, like you.'

But later, when all were preparing to sleep, all he could see in his mind's eye was a tall, blond woman with a voluptuous figure and a come-hither smile.

Exeter

It was some little while later when the coroner finally grunted that he would have to leave. He was too well known in the city, and had no desire to leave her with a reputation befouled with rumours of harlotry.

Lady Isabella Fitzwilliam rose to see him to the door, aware of a great sadness that he was leaving her. 'I do not want you to go,' she said.

'I would prefer to stay, but you know as well as I do that it wouldn't be a good idea,' Sir Peregrine said gruffly. 'But if you will permit, I shall return tomorrow.'

'I would like that a great deal,' she said, and in her belly she could feel the warmth as he smiled at her, as though his smile could emulate the sun and heat her blood.

'I shall rue the moments I am not with you,' he said simply. 'They are wasted.'

'You great fool!' she responded, and gave him a playful slap on the shoulder. 'You should enjoy *all* your moments. I shall make much of every moment you are away. Each will be precious because, in passing, they bring you nearer to me again!'

He frowned slightly, as though working through her logic, and she felt a brief irritation that he didn't understand her at once, but then she saw her error as he reached out and took her gently in his arms. And then she was unaware of the servant girl, or the room, or anything, as she felt his lips on hers. And she felt that surely she must die now. And if she did, she would be content for God to take her, because she had felt adoration once more.

He set her down, and looked into her eyes with an expression of deep intensity, saying, 'Woman, I am sorry if that offended you.'

She could scarce speak, her heart was still fluttering so wildly. 'It did not,' she said breathlessly.

'Good.' He suddenly grinned. 'I would hate to have to try to experiment again.'

'Perhaps you should?'

When he had gone, she stood at the entrance to the little hall with a hand resting on the doorframe. His visit had brought an enormous surge of energy; most of all, she felt young again. She had been sure that Sir Peregrine was a stolid, affable man who could never surprise her, and in an instant he had managed just that. It was thrilling.

But she had work to do. Before she could continue with her pleasing thoughts of the fellow, she had to get out to meet the man at the cathedral.

Exeter

They found Geoffrey of St Albans at the corner of the cloister, where he was sitting watching doves pecking at the grass.

William nodded to John, and the two approached him from behind, stepping quietly so as not to disturb him.

'They love their bread,' Geoffrey said.

He turned suddenly and threw William a grin. 'Did you think to surprise me, squire? You need to move more silently to do that. Remember, I was a warrior.' He was a curious old man. With his small bright eyes, and the way he ducked his head, he reminded William of a sad-looking bird himself.

Everyone in the cathedral knew Geoffrey well. He was an amiable fellow generally, and it was thought that he had been installed here as corrodian because he had lost his mind in a battle. The king honoured him, it was said, for his loyal service. But what if his true loyalty was still to Lancaster, the man killed by the king?

'I have heard that you were in the bishop's palace a few days ago. Do you remember that?' William said.

'You mustn't ask me about that,' Geoffrey said, and shook his head disapprovingly. 'No, not about that.'

'Why?' John asked sternly.

There was something wrong though, William could see. The man was not scared of being discovered; rather he was surprised that he should be asked. He had the look of a man who was asked whether he would consider eating a fox. It just wasn't the sort of thing a man in his chivalric position could consider.

'You were in the bishop's parlour, weren't you?' John said. 'You placed a piece of parchment in there. Who put you up to it? Was it allies of your old master, eh?'

There was a cunning look in Geoffrey's eyes now. 'You want to trick me, don't you, but you won't. You shouldn't be asking such things,' he said, and shook his head again. 'It's not right.'

'What isn't right?' William asked softly. It was tempting to grab the old git by the throat, but that wouldn't help, he knew.

'There are things a man cannot say. Not when he has been sworn to secrecy.'

'Sworn to secrecy?' John threw up his hands. 'Don't give me that ballocks, old man!'

'Master steward, please,' William said, trying to placate him, but John had already tried to grab the corrodian's clothes.

In an instant the corrodian had thrown his habit wide open and whipped out a long-bladed knife. It swept past John's face in a terrifying blur, and the appalled steward gave a startled yelp and fell on his back in his urgency to escape. 'Sweet Mary, Mother of . . .'

The knife was at his throat, and the corrodian peered down at him with a frown that was more petrifying than anything else. There was nothing resembling pity or amiableness now. Only a terrible concentration. 'You shouldn't try to attack a warrior, steward. That's not good. No, not good at all.'

He took his knife away and darted back, the weapon held low and dangerous, snarling, 'It's none of your business.'

'What isn't?' William managed.

'The guest to see the bishop. That is nothing to do with the likes of you.'

'When did you first come here, Master Geoffrey?' William asked.

His eyes were suddenly hooded, and he kept his blade in his hand as he looked from William to John, who was scrambling to his feet. 'Never you mind. You leave things alone when they're nothing to do with you, masters. Just leave things be.'

Chapter Twenty-Five

*Two Tuesdays before the Feast of St John and St Paul**

Exeter

The weather was fine and bright, but Baldwin de Furnshill felt little cheer as he walked along the castle's street down towards the High Street that day.

'Well, my love? How was it?' Jeanne asked as he strode towards her. She had been waiting outside with Edgar to guard her, strolling among the women who eyed the meats and fish on sale in the market. There was a gorgeous green material which had caught her fancy. Her husband's tunic was growing exceedingly threadbare, and this new fabric would make a suitable replacement.

'Not good,' he responded shortly. 'I am to leave here soon.'

Jeanne felt the news like a blow. 'I had hoped you would remain a little longer, my love.'

'I am sorry, Jeanne. This is not my choice,' Baldwin said. He could barely look her in the eye. 'The king has commanded it. That arrogant little puppy, Sir James de Cockington, has given me the warrant. I am to ride to Portchester and there to meet with a man called John Felton. He will be in charge, apparently, and I am to help him.'

'Help him to do what?' she asked in a small voice.

'Gather together a force to help protect the south coast. I had hoped to be released from all these trials and worries, but apparently I am still needed.'

---

* 17 June 1326

She nodded. It would not be the first time that she had seen her husband go away. 'When must you go?'

'In the next week or so. It appears that the effort of protecting our shores is likely to collapse without my own specialist expertise.'

Jeanne placed her hand in his. 'Come, husband. Let us find some food before the bile eats through your bowels!'

It was horrible that he must ride away from her again, but she would at least see that he was properly clad. She would buy the bolt of green cloth and over the next few days, make him a fresh tunic. Her man would be the best-dressed knight in Portchester. 'You will be able to see Simon again, which will be good,' she said.

'I wonder how his daughter is?' Baldwin said distantly, his eyes going about the people in the market.

'Sir Baldwin!'

The voice was known to them both, and Jeanne squeezed Baldwin's hand as he groaned.

'Sir Peregrine, how delightful to see you,' she said. 'I hope you are well?'

The coroner bowed low to her, giving Baldwin a courteous duck of the head. 'I am very well, and it is plain that you are too, my lady. Where do you go now? May I join you?'

'Of course,' Baldwin said, although Jeanne could hear the attempt to conceal his reluctance. 'You are here on business?'

'No. I am glad to say I am here to meet the Lady Isabella.'

Jeanne smiled. 'Have you asked her to wed yet?'

'My dear Lady Jeanne,' Sir Peregrine protested. 'I have hardly—'

'You make her laugh, you told me. She must reciprocate your feelings.'

'I think she has a respect for me.'

'That,' Jeanne said tartly, 'is not what I meant, as well you know.'

'Ah, well . . . Hmm. I am not convinced about affairs of the heart, my lady. I think that she may hold a certain . . . affection for me, perhaps. But more than that, I could not say.'

'Then you must ask her,' Jeanne said. 'Nay, do not laugh, you should ask her whether she would welcome your suit, because a widowed woman would be enormously grateful for the offer of the hand of a banneret like you. A notable knight, offering his hand and heart is not a thing a woman could refuse lightly.'

'Then I shall take your advice,' he said. 'Would you care to join me for some wine? We could go to the tavern near Broadgate.'

'I would dearly like to,' Baldwin said, 'but I have just been told that I must soon leave to become a Commissioner of Array at the coast.'

Sir Peregrine grimaced. 'There are to be many such commands, I fear. I myself have been ordered to travel to London to join the force sent by Lord Hugh de Courtenay to help guard the king. Apparently there is need of a great force of loyal subjects such as me.'

'You will provide all aid you may?' Baldwin said. The good Sir Peregrine had often stated his belief that the king should remove Despenser and reign on his own. He had a firm conviction that Sir Hugh Despenser was a malign influence on the king and on the realm.

'You need not fear on that,' Sir Peregrine said with a bitter smile. 'I am no regicide.'

'I hope you are successful, then. With your wooing, also,' Jeanne said as they parted. 'You will bring your lady to meet us? I should like that very much.'

Sir Peregrine bowed to her. 'I will be honoured to do so, Lady Jeanne. My lady, Sir Baldwin, Godspeed, and may He bring you safely home again when all this trouble is at last put behind us.'

Baldwin took his hand, and to Jeanne's secret surprise, rested his other hand on the knight's shoulder. 'Be careful, my friend. We have not always agreed with each other, I know, but I fear that harsh times are ahead for us. A knight who is loyal to the king will achieve all he might in terms of honour and glory.'

'I hope so, although I think there will be little enough honour or glory in the days to come,' Sir Peregrine said.

'You almost sounded as though you cared for him,' Jeanne teased as they walked on.

'I almost feel as though I do,' Baldwin said. 'It would be a shame to lose a fellow like him. He is devoted to his view of the world, and a man who has conviction is preferable to one with purely mercenary instincts.'

'I quite agree,' Jeanne said. She then took him to the stall, ignoring her husband's muttered protests that his old tunic was perfectly serviceable still, and he had a spare white linen tunic that he had hardly worn, and that there was little point in spending such a vast sum on yards of green material just at a time when he was about to leave home for weeks. She finally stilled him with a gimlet eye that would have skewered a flying duck, and negotiated a gratifying discount from the stallholder. It was as she was turning from the stall, Edgar carrying the bolt of material, that she saw a young squire hurrying towards them and recognised the bishop's nephew.

'Sir Baldwin! I am so glad to see you,' William Walle said, panting a little. 'You must come at once. We have the man who was trying to kill the bishop!'

On the road to Bayeux

'Are we to travel much further, Your Highness?' Paul managed as the horses breasted a low hill.

The duke made no comment. He sat stolidly on his horse and gazed ahead with the mien of a commander, rather than that of a boy who as yet had no need of a barber to shave him.

'Leave the duke alone, you cretin,' Ralph la Zouche snarled. 'If you were anything more than pointless weight, you'd have known that he wants to come here.'

Paul said no more. His arse was hurting from all this riding, and his inner thighs were chafed and bloody where they rubbed against the saddle-leather. It was a chastened rector who was trailing along with these others on the way to the town where the magnificent tapestry had been stored. 'I am sorry, Sir Ralph,' he said diplomatically.

The man was quite changed from the suave, elegant man whom Paul had met some weeks ago. Then he had seemed as noble as a lord, rather than an outlaw. But all pretence at gallantry and chivalry had flown since his brother's death. It was as though he had lost a limb when his brother fell, and Paul thought that a man who lost a leg or an arm could not have mourned more. Nor would he have become quite so unhinged. It was not only he who noticed this: he saw it in the eyes of Folville too. Even the duke himself had observed it, the change was so dramatic. Yet the man himself appeared either not to realise how his appearance and behaviour had slithered into the midden, or not to care. It was almost as though he saw himself as dead already.

Paul licked his lips when he saw that Sir Ralph was eyeing him closely. It was an unnerving sight, to see those bloodshot orbs fixed upon him, and not for the first time Paul felt the huge error of his ways. If only he could take back his actions with that bitch and return to England safely. But he was not likely to be safe, not while the bishop had a brain in his head. As a rector, he would be a hunted man all his days. Not even a king's pardon could save him.

A faint tickle of a thought snagged at his mind, and he gave a quick frown. No, that would be utterly ridiculous: so dangerous, indeed, he would almost certainly die for his attempt.

And yet . . . There was a glorious possibility in it, were he to play it aright. And he was, of all the rectors, chaplains, annuellars and clerks of his experience, easily the quickest witted.

Here about him there was the king's own son, with ten or eleven men-at-arms of all abilities, and all of them declared traitors. It would only take one man with a brain to let the king know where his son was, and suddenly all kinds of rewards could be forthcoming. Perhaps even a pardon.

The duke span his horse about. 'We will rest here tonight.'

Exeter

Baldwin left Jeanne in the hands of Edgar, and went after William, listening to the squire as they crossed the road, headed down to the Close, and crossed over the cemetery.

'It was very easy in the end,' William explained eagerly. 'We found the man in short order. He was a corrodian who had been sent here some little while ago by the king.'

'A knight?' Baldwin asked.

'Squire, I think. His name is Geoffrey of St Albans. Do you know of him?'

'No, it is not a name I recognise,' Baldwin said after a moment. 'What did he say?'

'He says nothing. If he won't plead, we'll have to put him to the *peine forte et dure*, and force him to make a plea. If it fails and he dies, so much the better. It'll save us the effort of a trial.'

Baldwin glanced at him. 'Have you ever seen a man put to that test? No? Then do not make light of such a horrible torture. It means putting unbearable weights on a man's chest while he lies chained to the ground.'

'I know,' William said. 'But it's only for the recalcitrant. They deserve it.'

'No one deserves it. The weights are increased steadily over days, until the victim is suffocated. He cannot breathe because the weights crush the air from his lungs. It is a slow and agonising death. Do not make jest of it.'

William caught sight of the expression in Sir Baldwin's face, and it was not the kind of look that would tolerate humour. To change the subject, he spoke of Biset.

'It is a surprise, to be honest. I had thought that the true culprit was another man entirely. Until this latest note appeared, all the evidence appeared to speak of John Biset being guilty. He could have had a seal to fit that little purse, he had reason to want revenge for the loss of his treasure, and he had reason to kill that man.'

Baldwin stopped. 'What man?'

William pulled a face. 'I should not tell you, but I doubt it matters now,' he said, and told Baldwin about the head in the barrel. 'I felt sure because of that, that it had to be Biset, but when I sent men to enquire, they learned that he had fled the country. All said he was flown to France.'

Baldwin nodded pensively, and the two men walked to the bishop's gaol. When they came to the gaoler's door, the knight was welcomed with apparent sincerity.

'My lord, please enter here, and take your ease. I remember you, sir. Oh, yes. You have been to visit me here more than any other knight in the city. How may I serve you, Sir Baldwin?'

'First, you can release the man Geoffrey of St Albans, and bring him to me. Then you could hurry to the cathedral bakery and fetch a good white loaf. I shall pay for it. And then ask for a jug of wine and four cups. Could you do all that for me?'

'Of course, Sir Baldwin. Give me but a moment,' the man said, and a short while later, Geoffrey of St Albans was in front of them.

He was not, Baldwin thought, a prepossessing sight. Where William had seen avian characteristics, Baldwin saw only the figure of a ravaged old man. All cunning and intelligence had been leached from him, and all that remained was a husk.

'Geoffrey, please be seated,' Baldwin said.

The man shook his head, and his eyes darted about, searching the ground at Baldwin's feet.

Baldwin tried again. 'Do you know what you are accused of?'

'They say I did something, but I didn't, sir. I was just told not to tell, so I didn't. Then they jumped on me and dragged me here to the prison. And I've done nothing.'

'That's what they all say,' William muttered.

'And some speak the truth,' Baldwin countered. 'Geoffrey, has anybody told you what you did?'

'I've done nothing.'

Baldwin nodded. He was about to speak, when a thought struck him. As the door opened and the gaoler returned, heavily laden, Baldwin said, 'Geoffrey, are you knight or squire?'

'Squire, sir.'

'You have fought in many battles for the king?'

'Yes, sir. I was in the last war with the Scottish – but they beat us. They slew so many of my friends . . . That Bruce, sir, he is the devil. I know it. The devil himself arrived there while we were preparing for the battle, and it was the Bruce. And then, when the battle began, there was dreadful thunder, as if the heavens were about to open up, and I looked up, but there was no cloud in the sky, not one. And then this thick, roiling smoke, and all smelling of the devil. Brimstone, that's what it was, sir, and it came upon us, and we could do little but choke. The devil came upon us, and—'

'Have you been taught your letters?' Baldwin interrupted.

'Eh?' The old man looked at him, his mind still set upon the battlefield.

'Can you read?'

'No. Why?'

Exeter

And so another stage in his life was beginning.

It was infuriating to think that he had been so close. The expression on the bishop's face was more appalled as he read each new note, and yet now the damned man was free. Even the incompetent fools who served Bishop Walter could not miss the fact that Geoffrey was too dim to be able to have composed such missives.

Still, the tale he had given the old fool had been inspired. When Geoffrey had confronted him out there in the chamber beneath the bishop's private room, he had thought his bowels would empty. The idea that he had gone through that terrifying experience up there, and was almost free and safe, only to hear that stentorian voice behind him, had frozen the blood in his veins. But then he had thought of the ingenious story – that there were threatening messages being left for the bishop, and he had personally been given the task of checking on the chamber in order to catch the man red-handed.

It had persuaded Geoffrey. More, it had been obvious that this man, who was a warrior by trade, and who detested spies and subtle strategems with every fibre of his being, would not divulge the tale to anyone unless he was convinced that they were safe. It would probably take the bishop himself to persuade Geoffrey to give the truth. No doubt they would go to that extreme.

Which was sad, because it meant that he would have to devise another means of continuing the campaign. He had to see more messages being delivered to the bishop, and then, with luck, he would at last have his chance. He would be able to draw a sword or knife and end the bishop's foul life, once and for all.

Chapter Twenty-Six

Exeter

Sir Peregrine of Barnstaple was marching towards the house which had grown to be his favourite residence in the city. Knocking, he had to wait only a very short time before he was allowed entry, and then he strode through to the little parlour and waited fretfully, taking his hat off, then resetting it on his head. He did so several times while waiting.

'Sir Peregrine, I am pleased to see you, sir.'

'And I, you. You look magnificent, lady,' he said with sincerity.

She wore a tight-fitting tunic, much in the latest fashion, with a high bodice and soft silken shawl about her shoulders, for the day was not the warmest. Hearing his tone, she arched her eyebrows slightly and smiled. 'Your compliments are always welcome, but to what do I owe this visit? You were here only yesterday.'

'Yesterday I did not have my news. I fear I am to leave the city soon,' he said brokenly. 'The king has commanded me to depart with all haste. I should have gone some days ago, but you have brought me so much joy, I could not bear to leave. However, now I have a definite order, and I may not refuse him.'

'Then of course you must go,' she said. 'Where will you travel? To his side?'

'No. The king is at the coast, helping to organise defences, I think. I am ordered to ride to London, where I am to serve in the Tower. The walls are strong, but they need men to guard them. I have to collect the knights who owe me their service, and some men-at-arms and archers, and hurry there.'

'You have been to London?'

'A few times, but it is not the sort of city I would wish to return to. Especially now I have met you.'

'It is a good city. I have been there on legal matters often enough. But you are right to say that it is not the place to stay for long. I wouldn't wish to either. I am happier with the country.'

'I regret the moments I am away from you. I would prefer to remain here at your side.'

She smiled at that. 'You are gallant and chivalrous, Sir Peregrine. But please, there is no need for so much effort. We are very comfortable in each other's company, are we not?'

'I am happy with you, my lady.'

'Well, then. Perhaps this is not so unfortunate after all. How would it be if I were to join you? I would prefer to ride with you to London than stay here alone. This city of Exeter is lovely, but without a friend, it is a poor place.'

'But of course, my lady,' he beamed. 'I would be delighted to protect you on your journey.'

'Then that is settled. I shall leave for London too. What could be more perfect?'

Much later, as Sir Peregrine considered their discussion and the decision that she would ride with him and his men, he would recall that odd expression in her eyes as she spoke, and he would realise why she had been so keen to escape the city with him; however, at the time, all he knew was the overwhelming glee that she felt an affection for him to equal his for her.

Exeter

She knew that her husband would be some while, so Lady Jeanne decided to spend as much time as possible looking round the market, to see if there was anything else she should buy, some little item that would be indispensable to a man about to set off on a long journey.

It was so tempting to demand to go with him. Simon Puttock, their friend, had gone to Portchester only a few weeks ago, and he had taken his wife with him. It was not unknown for a man to take his wife with him, even for warriors to take wives and children with them on campaign, but she knew that Baldwin was less keen than many to have women on such journeys. He was always worried that Jeanne might fall prey to thieves or killers, and while the realm was so unstable, she could not fault his reasoning. The land was falling into madness, with gangs of club-men walking the streets as boldly as the king's officers, with knights and even barons turning to outlawry to supplement their income, and hundreds of the men dispossessed of their property after the Battle at Boroughbridge trying their hands at theft just to stay alive. No, it was not a good time for a woman to travel. And at least her home was . . . defensible.

She was sad to think that they would be separated again. It had been that way all through the previous year, when Baldwin had been sent to France at different times on the king's business. She had been forced to remain at home, waiting and hoping that he would return safely. And she had been very lonely.

However, she was a woman born to a certain position in life, and she knew that tribulations of this kind were natural for the wife of a knight. He must go and serve his lord or king, and she must protect the home and their children.

She was walking with Edgar along an alley, when she saw a man's face which she recognised. It made her frown at first, because she had not seen this face in this environment. Or perhaps it was less the environment, more that the clothing or something was wrong . . . And then she saw a young woman come along, and instantly knew it to be Edith, Simon's daughter. 'Edgar – look!' she said excitedly, and darted through the crowds, not heeding her servant's hisses to stop.

'Edith!' she called, and then she had a sudden lurch in her belly as she recognised the other face. Of course – how could she have been so stupid! It was Edith's husband, Peter. Jeanne had only met him once or twice, and that briefly. Even at the wedding, she had not seen him above a minute or two. It was not possible to see much at the church itself, and afterwards Jeanne had been involved in keeping her husband's new cowman, Wat, away from the ale and wine. The fellow had drunk himself into a stupor at Baldwin and Jeanne's own wedding, and she didn't want him to act the brute at Edith's too.

The young man looked terrible. She could see how fear had etched deep lines across his forehead. His eyes were anxious too, flickering towards her and then away, as though expecting to be struck down and robbed at any moment.

'Master Peter,' she said with a gushing enthusiasm she hardly felt. 'It is so good to see you again. Do you remember me? Madam Jeanne de Furnshill, wife to Sir Baldwin, who was always such a good friend of your father-in-law. I haven't seen you since your wedding, although I know my husband did visit you, didn't he? Late last year, I think? And how are you both? My, Edith, you are looking well!'

'I apologise, madam, but we have much to do,' Peter said with a sad attempt at a smile. 'Come, Edith.'

'Edith, I hope you are well?' Jeanne said.

'I thank you, yes. I am fine, Madam Jeanne. I hope you will give my kind thoughts to your husband, and . . .' Her voice petered out before she could mention her father and mother, and instead she looked down at the ground, and Jeanne saw that there were tears in her eyes.

And it was only then that Jeanne remembered that Edith had been pregnant last October. 'Your baby?'

'He is fine, a strapping fellow, born two months ago,' Peter said, catching hold of his wife's arm. 'And now, madam, we must be gone. A good day to you, my lady.'

Jeanne nodded briefly, hardly hearing his words. Her attention was fixed upon Edith, the pale, frail-looking young woman, who turned and walked away on hearing her husband's sharp call. In her mind's eye she could see a young Edith, long legged and gawky, and the elegant, beautiful woman she had become, and somehow neither fitted with this exhausted-looking person.

Now that she was married, and had borne her own child, she struck Jeanne as being more of a child than before.

Exeter

'There is no doubt whatsoever,' Baldwin said.

Together with William Walle he had made his way here into the bishop's little chamber as soon as they had finished interviewing the corrodian.

'This man was a servant here?' Bishop Walter said.

'I can easily understand how distressing this must be for you,' Baldwin said, and it was true. To have caught the person who had been leaving those foul messages would have been extraordinarily gratifying for Bishop Walter, removing fear and anxiety and restoring him to his old confident self.

'So it wasn't him? He appeared so obvious,' the bishop said sadly.

When Baldwin had first stepped into the bishop's private room here, he had found the man transformed. He stood straighter, walked purposefully, and generally looked as though he had returned to his usual equilibrium. His world was restored.

Now, in the space of a few moments, Baldwin had destroyed it all. 'How could we have made such a simple error?' the bishop wanted to know.

'He was slightly deranged, and he reacted oddly when asked about what he saw that day.'

'Slightly deranged? He was completely insane! To draw a knife on my nephew William . . .' The bishop tutted.

'This young servant, Paul of Taunton, who was the real culprit – Geoffrey caught him, and Paul then spun him a line, which the old fellow believed.'

When Baldwin had asked William how they had come to conclude that Geoffrey was the guilty party, he heard of the servant sweeping up the charnel chapel, and immediately set off to see if he was still about. But no one had seen Paul for days. Even now, men had been sent to the city and to the sheriff to ask that he be captured if found.

'It seems clear enough that this fellow was the one responsible,' Baldwin said. 'I am sure that you will be safe now, Bishop. You were at most danger while he remained in here, in the Close, with you. Worse, he could wander in here to your palace with impunity, since he was known as a servant and lay-brother.'

'But why though? I don't know this Paul of Taunton,' the bishop muttered. He was distracted, and John poured him a little wine to soothe his spirits.

'The only thing I can suggest is, that you have a man go to Taunton to see what he may learn. Someone may remember him,' Baldwin said. 'How did he arrive here?'

The steward shrugged his shoulders. 'There are many hundreds of men in the cathedral. Especially now with the rebuilding continuing. It is impossible to keep track of all of them.'

'This man was not with the builders, John, he was in the cathedral, working as a servant in the buildings,' Baldwin reminded him.

'Yes, but there are so many. Do not forget, we have at least three and seventy clergy, and all have their own servants. The canons have entire households, and then there are the other men who work in the bakery, the kitchens, the cemetery and chapel. All told, we must have another hundred and fifty men who work in the cathedral and all about. This man Paul may have been hired by one of my servants, or he may have come from a canon's household.'

'You mean to tell me you don't know who said he could work here?' Baldwin demanded with surprise.

'If he was here, working, he would have been accepted. Who would question whether he was permitted to be here, if he was performing useful work?' John asked reasonably. 'He was just another man to help with the cleaning.'

'You do realise that if you allow just anyone to enter and remain here, working all day, then any man could walk in from the Broadgate and pretend to be a servant? What then of your lord's security?'

'Sir Baldwin, you are a man of experience and sense. Please, advise us,' the bishop murmured. 'What should we do to ensure that these threats may not be carried out?'

Baldwin frowned down at his boots. It was infuriating to be here, worrying about all this when there was so much else to take up his time. 'My lord bishop, you know full well that I would do all in my power to protect you myself. You have been a good friend to me and to Simon in the last years. I would propose that you bring in more men to guard your person here, but that will hardly do. There are too many men about Exeter for you ever to be fully safe. I think that the best and most safe route may be for you to go away, to some other part of the diocese. You could go on visitation, perhaps.'

'At this time of national peril, that hardly seems a suitable course of action,' the bishop smiled. He looked exhausted, and rubbed at the gap between his eyebrows with a thumb. 'I should be better served by joining with the king.'

'Where is he?' Baldwin demanded. The worst place, he knew, for the bishop to go would be London, where so many citizens already loathed him and would seek his murder since the Eyre which was forever associated with him.

'He is still about Dover, I think. There were some papal legates who came to see him last month,' the bishop said.

Baldwin gave a nod of relief. The bishop could go there and remain within the circle of the King's household, away from strangers, and it would be more difficult for any man to travel after him to pursue a vendetta.

'That is good,' he said after considering. 'Do you then go to the king and see whether there is aught you may do for him. He will be grateful for a friendly face at this troubling time. Meanwhile, have men search for this Paul of Taunton, if that is his real name, and have him apprehended. Are you sure you know nothing of him? You did not know a man from there who could have been his father?'

'No. No one.'

'In that case, perhaps it is an assumed name. Have you had any luck seeking the ones I found in your books?'

'Only one: the man Biset.'

'William told me. He is in France.'

'Yes. The fellow Hamo in London is dead, I've heard. So it is possible that Roger Crok was the man here.'

'You did not know him?'

'I may have seen his face, but when you have stood in front of a congregation like me, you soon tend to lose all memory for faces. There are some I can recall, but not many. Only close acquaintances.'

'It probably does not matter,' Baldwin considered. 'The fellow who was here was unlikely to be him. Those such as Biset and Crok come from positions of wealth, and they would be unlikely to demean themselves by taking up a servant's post. If they were to attempt to kill you, surely they would do so in the open, attacking you with a sword.'

'Perhaps,' the bishop said, 'but have you not heard of some of the surprising deaths in the Church recently? Poison has become a popular means of removing obstacles.' He sighed and drained his wine. 'So you would advise me to leave here and join the king. I suppose you are right, but it does give me a sense of shame to run thus.'

'It would give you more pain to feel a dagger in your breast,' Baldwin said.

'I had heard you were to go to Portchester yourself?'

'Yes. The king has asked me to go there as Commissioner of Array for him.'

'Good. Then perhaps we could travel together? That would at least comfort me a little.'

Chapter Twenty-Seven

Exeter

Edith hardly noted the journey home. Her thoughts were on her father, and his best friend.

'That woman Jeanne! She had a man with her, and I have seen him somewhere,' Peter was grumbling as he went.

'Yes, my love,' Edith said automatically.

Much of her life seemed to pass by automatically now. It was all a haze, ever since that terrible day last year when her father-in-law had told her that either she must renounce her own father and agree not to communicate with him or see him ever again, or she must accept that she was no longer welcome in her husband's home, and must leave him to go back to her parents. To have told her that, when she was only married a matter of months, when she was feeling the new life growing in her womb, was the height of cruelty. She could scarcely believe her ears, let alone understand the utter irreversibility of her decision, once taken.

Before, she might have gone home to her parents, and then there could have been a reconciliation with her husband at some time in the future, when he had remembered his deep affection for her. Her absence might have brought him back to her. It must have done! But she had left it too long, and now it was quite impossible for her to change her mind, for although she would like to return to her real home, as she now thought of it, to do so would involve leaving behind her most precious possession: her baby son Henry.

'You're quiet. Do you feel unwell again?' Peter asked.

She was able to respond with a calm enough smile, but she did indeed feel unwell. There was a queasiness in her belly that wouldn't go away. She had thought to cure it with a letting of her blood, but it only left her with a pain in her forearm and a strange lassitude.

In the past she had never known such a tiredness. It was like a woman she once saw who was ill with some affliction that made her take to her bed and by degrees, she died. Just faded away and died. And that was how Edith felt now. On some days, the feeling of complete despair, coupled with the exhaustion that came from rising in the night to see to her child, was wearing her away. It felt as though there was no life left which was her own – all was given to her husband and her child. And the loss of her parents meant that she could not even call on her mother to come and help. Her mother-in-law was a good woman, but it was not the same, relying on someone whom she did not know so well.

There was a sudden choking sensation in her throat, and she felt her eyes burning. Like a physician watching a patient, she noted her symptoms, and knew that she was on the verge of bursting into tears yet again, but with an exercise of extreme effort, she managed to keep them at bay. It would be so humiliating, to lose control here in the street. Better to blink the tears away, take a deep breath and continue on the journey home.

At least there her child was waiting for her.

'Are you sure you're all right?' her husband persisted.

She didn't reply.

*First Saturday after the Feast of Mary Magdalen**

Portchester

It had been a long and weary walk here. At last, he had been able to catch a ride with an old tranter, in exchange for help with the grooming of the man's ancient nag. The old fellow was pleased to be able to share a cup of beans and a half-gallon of ale, which the man called Paul of Taunton was equally happy to supply.

---

* 26 July 1326

Not that he could call himself that any more. There were likely to be men with serious expressions and sharpened swords who would want to speak with him about the grief he had caused the bishop. No matter. If he could, he would have them capture him – but only *after* he had actually ended the bishop's life.

But the bishop wasn't here, he had learned. His quarry had evaded him, and after he had come so far. Bishop Walter had paused here, apparently, but was already journeying farther eastward, to meet with the king. Well, so be it. The bastard would probably feel safer in a city with the king close to hand. All those guards ensuring the monarch's protection, all those men ready and waiting to repel any attacker. There must be so many now, with the new terrors of invasion. Here in Portchester, there were rumours galore about fresh troubles with France.

The king had ordered that all Frenchmen should be arrested throughout the kingdom – and now there were stories of French warriors sweeping back into Guyenne. The French king was determined to take back the whole of the Aquitaine, and there was no reason to doubt the rumours. In response, King Edward was amassing a host to defend the coast against French attack.

But Paul of Taunton had other things to concern him. First and foremost, he had to think of a new name. Perhaps he should take an easy one: his own. Ranulf was a good name. It had served many men well.

Now he would take it back for himself.

Simon Puttock woke with a feeling that all was quite well in his world. There was no urgency to his rising today, for he knew that his men were perfectly capable of pursuing the utterly pointless task of hunting for documents in amongst the bales of cloth and wool being exported, or searching diligently for secret compartments in barrels. Such pursuits were of no interest to Simon. He was looking forward to seeking out his friend Baldwin.

He had received the note yesterday, which told of the knight's arrival in the town, and he was keen to see his old companion, feeling in desperate need of a friendly face.

Baldwin was breakfasting on two boiled eggs and a thick hunk of bread when Simon arrived at his inn with Margaret.

'Simon! Margaret! I am so happy to see you both once more,' Baldwin said, his face breaking into a smile.

'It is good to see you, Sir Baldwin,' Margaret said, smiling warmly in return. 'I hope you are well. How are Jeanne and the children? Do they thrive? Clearly, Jeanne's needlework has not declined – that is a magnificent tunic.'

'Thank you, although I confess I don't know why she bothered, when my old one was perfectly comfortable,' Baldwin grumbled. Then, recollecting himself, he told Meg, 'The children are growing apace. I am astonished at how quickly Richalda is shooting up. Jeanne is fine, I thank you, and little Baldwin is the recipient of more chastisement than even his father was accustomed to, for which I am glad. I would hate to think that I could have been the worst behaved of my family! But what of you?'

'I am relegated to looking after the children at all hours,' Margaret said, casting a sly look at Simon.

'Don't listen to her,' Simon said smilingly. 'She has found all the best stalls in the market, she's an expert at haggling with the poor devils here, and she enjoys making their lives difficult beyond compare, while I am left to worry and harry the poor traders of the town.' He took a large leathern tankard of ale, and drank thankfully. 'It is hardly the easiest post, but it is made infinitely more difficult by the fact that we know we are missing things.'

'There are messages, then?'

'Oh, yes. Have no doubt of that,' Simon said. 'There are messages of all sorts flying back and forth, I am sure. But a parchment note can be rolled up into a tiny tube, wrapped in oilskins, and concealed anywhere in a ship. Where am I to search? Should I make an example of a ship, and pull it apart, nail by nail, strake by strake? And then, if I find nothing, should I broach every barrel in case there is a false bottom to it? Or perhaps I should cut open every bale of goods? Slice the tunics and chemises of the sailors and even the ship-master's hat? Pull the man's sea-chest apart, in case there is a hollowed plank? And if I fail with this first supposed spy, should I then turn to the next ship? And the one after that? It is ridiculous, like looking for a specific stem in the midst of a hayrick. It is there, and we are all fairly certain of that, but more likely it will be found in the port of London, or on a ship in Dover. Those ports have more shipping, and they happen to have access to more secrets than this place. Why, in God's good name, the king should have asked me to come here, I do not know!'

'Well, at least you and I can wander the streets companionably,' Baldwin said.

'Is there any news of our daughter?' Margaret said suddenly. 'It has been a long time since we heard from her.'

'There is news, but I do not think that it will be overly welcome, Margaret. The sad fact is, Jeanne saw Edith in Exeter,' Baldwin said. 'I was not with her at the time, but Edgar was, and Jeanne called to Edith when Edgar was in full view. Peter was with her, and recognised the beau of his maidservant, and since he is no fool, was perfectly able to make up the links in the chain that connected his maid to my servant. I am sorry. There has been no message since then.'

Margaret nodded, but her head had fallen to her breast. 'I see.'

'However, my wife had the sense to take a simple measure that I wish I had considered myself. She told the neighbour of your daughter about the problem with communicating with her, and as a result, I can tell you that your first grandchild is now almost three months old, thriving, and apparently, his bellows can be heard a full half-mile from Edith's house over the racket of the market!'

'Oh, thank you,' Margaret said, but although she smiled at Baldwin, there was a great sadness in her eyes. She so desperately wanted to see her grandchild, to pick him up and hold him. It was so distressing that she was not permitted to see him, nor even her own daughter – a torment that tore at her soul every day.

'What else have you heard?' Simon said more quietly.

Baldwin glanced about him at the other men in the chamber. 'I am here as Commissioner of Array to gather men for the defence of this part of the coast, but I came here at the insistence of Bishop Walter. He has been receiving anonymous letters,' and he outlined the matter of the mysterious parchment notes.

Simon whistled slowly. 'Poor Walter. That must have been terrifying. And these messages were all left in his private rooms?'

'Until a matter of weeks ago, yes.'

'But if the man is gone,' Margaret said, 'then the matter may well be closed.'

'Let us hope so, yes,' Baldwin said. 'But I can only think that a man who was that persistent will not give up so easily.'

*First Tuesday after the Feast of Mary Magdalen**

Portchester

As the ship gradually moved towards the coast, the men rushing up the ratlines and furling the sails, Paul could only stand clutching a rope at the front and praying. Dear God in heaven, but the journey was surely one of the very worst a man had ever been forced to endure! The water was a maddened, boiling creature, determined to destroy all those who dared to cross over it. Drowning was not the worst fate of a sailor, he decided – it was just the end to suffering.

Here, staring out at the harbour, Paul was, for the first time in several days, keen to reach the English shore.

He hadn't been so at first, knowing that as soon as he arrived, he would have to ensure that his mission was appreciated, and that he must not be passed over instantly to the bishop's men. But this port was not in Devon or Cornwall, so the bishop's writ was far less strong here. It wasn't as safe as London, true, but this was

* 29 July 1326

the first and only ship he had found, and a man as desperate as he was could not afford to pick and choose.

At least this ship was larger. When he first fled England, he had ended up on one of those cogs that sailed its way up the beach at high tide, and then waited for the sea to withdraw, so that the vessel could be unloaded at leisure in the period while they waited for the sea to return. Once empty, it was lighter, and the returning tide would easily take it back out to sea.

This was infinitely more safe and secure. It was better to sit safely on the ship, and wait until the little lighters arrived to empty her. Paul would be able to go ashore with one of them. That would be good, he thought.

And it was at that very moment that he felt the first prickle of danger – and turned to see two sailors, both wearing broad smiles, and both gripping unsheathed swords perilously close to his belly.

Portchester

Simon and Baldwin were both glad of the interruption when the man arrived and told them that there was a fellow who had been captured on a ship, and was being held in the little gaol.

This, when Baldwin saw it, was no better than a privy. Tiny, noisome, and damp, it was the kind of chamber which would enthusiastically remove the life from even the most courageous and healthy prisoner. And the man inside gave no indication that he was either.

'What have they put me in here for?' he ranted. 'I told them I had urgent news for the Keeper of the Port, but none of them listened to me! Who are you two, anyway?'

Simon leaned against the wall beside the grille that was the only aperture in the gaol's walls. 'You can talk to me. I am the Keeper here. What have you been up to? The sailors said they thought you were a spy.'

'I am no such thing! I am brother to Sir James de Cockington in Exeter. You sound like a Devon man, so you will know his name. I am no spy, I have come from France with urgent news for the king, and if you would not wish to see yourself punished, you would do well to release me, fellow.'

'You could be the sheriff's brother, it's true,' Baldwin said. 'He too is arrogant enough to think that the best way to get what he wants is to insult men who only seek to help him. What were you doing in France?'

'I was with the young Duke of Aquitaine. I have been with him for some while now, and I can help him to be captured or rescued,' Paul said slyly.

Baldwin and Simon exchanged a shocked glance.

'So, if you two know what is good for you, you will help me out of this cell and get me some food. I am starved!'

Exeter

It was so hard to get up in the mornings, Edith found. Although the baby needed feeding and changing, there was this awful lethargy that she couldn't shake off. Any value which she had put upon herself was meaningless now. She was nothing more than a milch cow for her son. A walking dairy.

Every so often she would remember a little scene from when she had been a young girl, living with her parents. Generally they were happy, those fleeting memories, of running through a sun-drenched pasture filled with flying dandelion seeds; walking with her father over the moors near home, of a candle-lit feast with her parents and Hugh looking on appreciatively . . . so many little snippets of recollection that made up her life so far. But since her marriage and child's birth: nothing.

There were times when she could easily have taken up her son and dashed his brains against the wall, and more when she could have run a dagger into her own heart. The despair she felt made her want to cry at all hours.

Nobody could understand her – she knew that. They didn't see the awful existence that was hers. She was useless – *useless* – and so stupid. Hoping to win over the heart of Peter had been a vain dream. He couldn't love her, any more than anyone could. There was a mirror in her chamber, but she had removed it so that she wouldn't have to look at her own face any more. It was become repugnant.

'Edith? Are you all right?' her husband called quietly.

He had entered so silently, she had not heard him. She stood still, as though discovered in some heinous crime, holding their son in her arms and staring at him.

'My love, you look so tragic!' he said with a catch in his voice.

'I am fine,' she said mechanically. It was the correct answer, she knew.

Chapter Twenty-Eight

Portchester

Simon eyed the man who gnawed on the lamb-shank before him. He glanced occasionally at Baldwin, but his friend sat with his eyes lidded, as though he was giving the man only half his mind, while concentrating on other matters. Of course, Simon knew that it was a show. Baldwin was capable of fierce intensity when he studied a man like this.

And the man was worth the effort.

Simon and Baldwin had been to France themselves, and Simon knew all the problems of long-distance travelling – not only the exhaustion, but the misery of a ship in poor weather, the emptiness of the belly after hours of throwing up, the natural desire for the journey to end. And late last year, he and Baldwin had been forced to fly from France in peril, so they believed, of their lives, since their friend Bishop Walter had been threatened with death while there. Now, as Baldwin had mentioned once or twice, the actual threat of death from men while they were on an official embassy from England, was probably less than they had perceived at the time. Still, Simon could all too easily remember the petrifying terror of their flight.

This fellow, so he said, had experienced the same. It was quite possible.

'Well? You will have to answer us now,' he said, his sense of urgency overwhelming him as the man reached across and lifted the jug. He seemed about to raise the whole thing to his lips, but Simon's scandalised expression made him reconsider, and he poured some into a little green-glazed pot.

'I would like to, masters. But perhaps I should wait until the king's own sheriff has arrived. This is very important information.'

Baldwin stirred, but said nothing. His head fell to his breast, and he appeared to study the table's surface near him. It was left to Simon to speak with a touch of asperity in his voice. 'I am the Keeper of this Port, and as such I have authority. If you have any news for us, I suggest you tell us quickly. You wouldn't want your information to become out of date, would you? Your value would reduce accordingly.'

'You think I care about such things?' Paul said loftily. 'I know my place, and the importance of my information, Keeper, so there is no point you trying to get what you can out of me.'

'What is that supposed to mean?' Simon demanded, and he felt the blood rush to his face as the fellow gave him a calculating look.

'Keeper, I am no fool. I know how the world works. You intend to take the news I bring and get credit for it, don't you? It won't be the first time it's happened, and it won't be the last. Well, this time I intend to gain full reward for all the risks I have taken. I'll not give it all up to the first officer who pays me one lamb shank and a cup of wine! Hah! Only a fool would do that.'

Simon sprang to his feet and would have grasped the man by the throat across the table for his insolence, but Baldwin held up a hand to stop him. 'Let me speak with him a moment, Simon,' he murmured.

Paul had shoved his stool back until it was at the wall behind him, and now he curled his lip disdainfully as he contemplated Simon. 'That's right, man. You sit down again. Your friend here doesn't need a mastiff to bate me.'

'No,' Baldwin agreed. 'I am sure I don't. Now, you told us that you were the brother of Sir James de Cockington, I believe. I know of the brother of that man. I heard about him while I was in the company of the Bishop of Exeter. But you know the bishop, don't you, rector? He is the man who seeks you here in England.'

'You cannot send me back to him! I have business with the king!'

'You will answer our questions now, fully, and in the most detailed manner possible. Afterwards, we shall consider what would be best to do with you.'

Paul licked lips which had suddenly parched. It was tempting to try to bluff his way with these two stern-faced bastards, but . . . he wasn't sure that they would fall for his stories. And if he tried to feed them a diet of invention, he was quite sure that they would be the cause of his undoing. They looked the sort of men who knew their own value; they wouldn't simply throw him to the bishop and forget him, they would make sure that any news he had was taken to the highest level possible. And he meanwhile would languish in a gaol very like the one he had just experienced. That was not to be borne.

'Very well.'

'How do you know about the duke?' Simon asked.

'I was in Paris earlier this year, and fell into his company. His last tutor was sent away, and I was taken to teach him. The queen interviewed me herself,' he added with pride.

'Did you stay in Paris, then?'

'No, of course not. There was much to see in other places, so we went to Montreuil, and would still be there, I suspect, but for an unfortunate incident.'

'What?'

'One morning we were out riding, and I saw some men coming towards us,' Paul said, embellishing shamelessly. 'It was due to my warning that the assault was beaten off, but it was clear after that, that it wasn't safe for the duke to remain so close to the coast, so near to England. He was advised,' and here his tone left no doubt as to the perspicacious adviser's identity, 'and he accepted the advice: to leave Montreuil and ride to safer places, remaining in each town only a couple of nights, not more, so that those who might seek to catch or hurt him would never be able to keep up with him.'

'What sort of guard does he have about him?' Baldwin said.

'A small number of knights and men-at-arms. There is Ralph la Zouche, Richard de Folville, some twenty or so all told now. It is not enough to protect him from a determined attack, certainly.'

'And what are they doing?' Baldwin asked.

'They guard him, of course.'

Baldwin looked at him unblinkingly. After some moments, Paul looked away, then, 'What? What is it?'

'You have insulted my companion here, the honourable Keeper of the Port. Now you seek to insult me as well. Do so, and you will learn the full meaning of pain. You are a slug who is dishonourable *and* dishonoured by your treatment of an innocent woman. Don't think to speak so freely to me again! Now: do they guard him from attack, or guard him as gaolers?'

'A little of both, perhaps. But I think that they tend to seek to serve him, not hold him against his will.'

'So they could be persuaded to come back to England with him?'

'It would cost much to bring them back! The Folvilles have been responsible for murder and robbery. You try to get them back here without a king's pardon, and you'll find your efforts wasted.'

'So you think that they would have to be assaulted and killed?'

'Oh, yes. But you can easily find him, which is the main thing.'

'But you took days to get here, I assume. So he will have moved, having taken this most sensible advice from his tutor?'

'Ah, but he is intending to be at the cathedral in Rouen for the Feast of the Nativity of Our Lady.'

'Why?' Baldwin asked. His head was set to one side as he listened intently. 'The Feast of the Nativity of Our Lady has nothing to do with Rouen; she is patron of Lourdes, and that is many miles away.'

'True. But the duke is a man most fixated with prophecies and history. Some of these ludicrous tales say that he will be a king to rival the Holy Roman Emperor himself and—' He caught sight of the expression on Baldwin's face, and reflected that this odd knight might well think that the duke was a paragon of virtue. So many people in the realm did, and deprecated any insults. 'Anyway, he has a lively fascination with all history and a desire to see the cathedral where King Richard Coeur de Lion's heart is buried. He must have loved Rouen much.'

'Why that specific date?' Simon said. 'Didn't King Richard die earlier in the year?'

'Your studies do not mislead you,' Paul said sarcastically, 'but if you had but a little more education, you would recall that, although King Richard died in April, yet was he born on a glorious day in September: on the Feast Day of Our Lady Herself. The prince wishes to visit the cathedral to see the tomb.'

Baldwin and Simon exchanged a look, then rose and made for the door. There the gaoler waited, leaning against the wall and picking his teeth with a long splinter of wood. 'All done, masters?' he said.

'For now. Don't mistreat him,' Baldwin warned.

'Aye.'

Simon shot a look back into the room before the door was closed and bolted. 'What do you think, Baldwin?'

'If it were possible for a more unpleasant little man to have wheedled his way into the companionship of the king's son, I could not imagine it. What more undeserving fellow could there be?'

'But could he be telling the truth?'

'What value could there be for him to invent such a tale? No, I think he's telling the truth well enough. And that means that we must send to the king with this news.'

'Last I heard, the king was at Dover.'

'Yes,' Baldwin said. He looked at Simon.

'I know,' Simon said. 'The last time we saw the king, he told us to take ourselves out of his sight, didn't he? How do you think he'd respond to our returning?'

Baldwin could only agree that their reception last year had been distinctly frosty. 'We had just brought news that his wife was deliberately staying in France, that she was having an adulterous affair with the king's most notable traitor, that his son was staying there with her, and that all those sent to guard his son and his wife had turned traitor too and were now in the pay of his wife and her lover. It was not the best news he could have hoped to receive!'

'True. But I do not wish to go and ask for an audience with him. That would mean speaking to Despenser – and I am not ready to have any dealings with that snake.'

'You may not need to,' Baldwin said, musing. 'The good Bishop Walter is already there. Seek him out, and explain the situation to him. I think he will himself be grateful for the news, and for the opportunity to present it to the king. Perhaps your reception will be better than you might have thought.'

*Monday before the Feast of St Laurence**

Canterbury

Their journey had been slow, and with the whining, petulant Paul in his train, Simon found it longer than it truly was.

'How do you expect me to present a decent case when you don't let me rest!' the fellow complained.

'I expect you to do the best you can,' Simon said shortly.

It had been like this much of the way from Portchester. Naturally the man was shocked when he heard it was likely that the bishop would be with the king, and his mood had slumped into melancholy. That was three days ago. Since then they had travelled along the coastal roads to Dover, only to learn that the king and his household had recently moved from there to Canterbury, where they were eating the poor prior, Henry Eastrey, out of house and home. It was a particularly hard blow for the prior, since he had already suffered several visits that year, and was still forced to house the whole of the queen's pack of hunting hounds, which she had given to him as a stern responsibility, hoping that he would look after them carefully, but

* 4 August 1326

not offering any financial assistance. Not that she could have, since the king had already confiscated all her income.

Now, at last they were entering the ancient walled city, and if anything, it appeared that Paul's resentment and nervousness were increasing. 'Can't we stop for a cup of wine? A quart of ale or cider? What's your hurry?' he nagged as they rode under St George's gateway.

Simon ignored him. He had been persuaded, much against his will, to come here to the city, but he would be damned if he was going to hang about here. He had too much to get back to, what with his wife and son waiting at Portchester, and the knowledge that the realm was clinging to peace by its fingernails.

It was some relief to know that Baldwin and the other commissioners had been successful, and that there was now a large force encamped all about Portchester, so if any French warriors sought to begin an invasion, they would find themselves seriously tested upon landing. That at least should guarantee Margaret and Perkin's safety. That – and Baldwin's sworn oath that he would not leave them alone, but would personally ride to their protection if there were an attack. Together with the sight of his own servant Hugh, grim faced and resolute as always, standing at his door with his staff in his hands, Simon was persuaded that his family would be as safe as they could be. He himself could do no better than that.

Still, he recoiled at the thought that here in Canterbury he might meet with Despenser, the man who had in the last year hounded Simon unmercifully, merely in an attempt to get at Baldwin. If he met Despenser, he must try to forget that the man had persecuted him, that he had stolen Simon's house, that he had made Margaret cry more often than any man, that he had tormented even Simon's daughter, and caused the split between Simon and Edith's in-laws to the extent that Edith could not even show them her baby son. Their own grandchild. Yes, Simon must swallow all this, must behave with perfect civility and keep his hand from his sword. Because to try to stab Despenser would inevitably lead to his own death, and to the deprivation of livelihood, home and hearth to his family. He knew that. And it helped his temper not a whit.

So as he rode up the street, he had two thoughts: first, that he must pray not to see Despenser, because he might be unable to restrain himself in the man's presence; and second, that he could hardly bear to be so close to the rapist and thief who was even now complaining yet again.

'Shut up, or I'll kick your arse!' he said and trotted ahead to avoid the whingeing.

If the fellow had a brain, he would have tried to escape on the way here. Simon and Baldwin had both realised that, which was why Simon had four men from Portchester to aid him. One was a grizzled old sergeant who had served in several wars with the king, and the other three were bright enough fellows, whom Simon had handpicked for the job of guarding their charge. Paul had never once been alone, and without at least one pair of eyes watching his every move.

The city was filled, as usual, with pilgrims. It was many years since the appalling murder of St Thomas at his altar in the church here – a hundred and fifty or more – and yet Christians poured into this wealthy little city from all over the kingdom still.

It was scarcely surprising. For a man to spill blood in a church was truly shocking. Even the felons he had captured and executed, the roughest, most hardened outlaws in the country, would draw the line at that. Steal a cross, yes; take the rings from a woman's hand, certainly; kill a priest, possibly . . . but kill a bishop at the altar of his church? *No*.

So every year, more and more people came here to seek the marvellous cures for their bodily ailments, for their misery, for redress against their persecutors. Simon drew his mouth into a moue at that thought. Perhaps he should go to pray that his own private persecutor should be persuaded to leave him alone? But what would be the point? In the last years of the effective rule of Despenser, so many must have begged God to release them from his vile exactions, and none of their prayers had been answered.

God Himself, seemingly, was struck impotent in the face of Despenser's astonishing avarice.

It was a source of great relief when Simon saw a familiar face among the teeming throng. 'William? Squire William Walle?'

The man heard his name being called, and turned to peer along the crowded roadway, and when he caught sight of Simon, his face broke into a beaming smile. 'God love you, my friend! How are you? And what are you doing here?'

Simon could almost feel the waves of horror emanating from the rector behind him as Paul tried to conceal himself behind the guards. 'Squire, I have urgent news for the king, and it may be best that I speak to the bishop to try to gain an audience.'

'Really?' William said, but a look at Simon's face made his smile fade, and he nodded. 'Come with me, then. I will take you straight to him.'

Chapter Twenty-Nine

Leatherhead, Surrey

Their passage so far had been quiet and uneventful, which was how it should have been. Sir Peregrine of Barnstaple glanced over at the lady beside him on her horse, and felt his heart glow. She was beautiful, wise, accomplished . . . He was entirely smitten with her.

'You enjoy the view, Sir Peregrine?' she asked sweetly.

'How did you know I was looking at you?' he protested. 'You were not watching me, I know.'

'My dear Sir Peregrine,' she said, turning and facing him in that strange little manner she had, her head a little lowered, her eyes studying him seriously. It was a fascinating idiosyncrasy, making him feel that she was treating him like a wayward son, but it was also enormously seductive.

'Yes?'

'You perhaps do not realise that even a widow can tell when a man is studying every facet of her dress to see where the mud lies. Or that he is searching her face for any new wrinkles.'

'My lady, you know that is not true! I have only allowed myself to view you in an entirely chaste manner, seeking to remember every aspect of your beauty so that, when I am no longer in your company, I may still be able to bring it to mind.'

'Oh, in truth, gentle charmer? I think that if you were to seek such magnificence, you would do better to have stayed last night with that delicious young wench at the inn.'

'Which?'

'You liked more than one, then?' she said, mock-chidingly.

'My lady, please do not torment me!' he groaned. 'If you

prefer, I can ride at the rear with the men in the van.'

She allowed a smile at that. 'You would be happier there?'

'No. I feel warmed by you as though you were the sun. You fill me with delight. In truth, I do not know how to describe my feelings for you. You are all kindness, all generosity, all beauty . . .'

'Enough! You must stay here, and continue to pretend to adore me with your eyes. I cannot believe you are serious, for I am a mean little creature, in truth. No, don't deny it.'

'But I do! Fervently! I have been so happy to escort you these last days, and would prefer that you wished to travel to France, or to the Holy Roman Empire, so that our time together was not to end so soon. I . . . I wish we could spend more time together, madam.'

'Oh, I am sure you would grow to dislike my pettiness, my many faults.'

'How could a man grow to dislike the stars? How could he dislike the beauty of the sun? No man could look upon you once and fail to be utterly possessed by you.'

'Really? And do I possess your heart, then?' she smiled, and in an instant the smile was blotted out, and she put her hand up. 'Nay, do not answer, I beg you.'

'I cannot hope that you may one day reciprocate my feelings?'

She looked at him again, with that serious consideration he was growing to recognise so well. 'I think that I do already, my friend. But that is one thing: to bind ourselves at this time is another. I do not wish to hurt you.'

'How can you?'

'By dying. By being taken from you. You have lost so much already. You have told me of your other women.'

That much was perfectly true. He had been so unfortunate with his loves, and he was left, at each loss, with an ever-increasing sense of his own loneliness. 'You too have known tragedy,' he sighed.

'Yes. I fear that together, you and I would be a great source of danger,' she said lightly. 'I have two dead husbands, and you have three women you have loved. What, would I die first, before we could wed, or would you expire shortly after our wedding?'

'Or would we both live, enjoying our time together, nourishing each other, and living to a happy, contented old age?'

He could hear the hope in his voice as he tried to show her how easy this would be, and for a moment, he thought he had succeeded. She turned to him again, and there was a gleam in her eyes. But then the light faded, and her face took on a sad, faraway look that he didn't understand. He wanted to speak, but the words wouldn't come, because even as he saw her expression change, and she turned away from him to face the road once more, he realised that he had lost her. She would not be his.

There was nothing more he could say. He rode on with poison in his heart.

Canterbury

The sight of Simon arriving was enough to make the bishop rise from his chair. 'Simon, you are a sight to gladden the heart of the most jaded bishop. Enter, please! Tell me all that has happened since I left Sir Baldwin in Portchester. I would have news of—' His voice was cut off as sharply as though a knife had severed his throat.

Simon had to grin. 'My lord bishop, you know this disreputable knave, I believe.'

'William – fetch a guard. I want that dishonourable churl in gaol here before he pollutes the floor of my chamber.'

Paul hurriedly fell to his knees. 'Listen, please, my lord! I have terrible news from France that must be taken to the king. Perhaps my indiscretion in Exeter was merely God making use of me as He saw fit, in His divine perfection. He took the least deserving vessel and sent me—'

'Shut up, fool! You mean to deride God Himself?'

'I think you ought to hear him,' Simon said.

'I will listen, then, until I decide he is lying. What do you mean "terrible news"? Speak out, man!'

With many a sidelong glance at Simon, Paul told his story,

finishing with the ambition of the duke to travel to Rouen. 'It should be easy to find him and capture him there.'

'You say so? You have had experience of fighting and battles, have you?'

'I only mean to—'

'Don't! Simon, what do you think?'

'If this fellow's telling the truth, it would be hazardous not to inform the king. If he lies, let the king discover it and punish this git. Better that he does than we soil our hands.'

'You think so? Even after what this evil cretin did to poor Agatha de Gydie?' The bishop stared down at Paul with an expression of intense disgust. 'You make me want to vomit, rector. Rise, and remove yourself from my sight – and William? Go with him. Do not let him near anything that he could steal, eat or drink. He is to wait on a bench in the hall until I call for him.'

He waited until they had left the chamber, and then lifted an eyebrow to Simon. 'Well, I suppose I shall have to take this unwelcome news to the king. I don't know what to make of it.'

'The clear suggestion he made was that the Despenser had paid silver to have the duke murdered,' Simon said. 'I would suggest that you leave that side of matters to the rector to bring up. You do not wish to be the man who stands between the king and Despenser.'

'True enough. Not that he has much time for affairs of any kind just now,' the bishop said.

'How do you mean, my lord?'

'He is so entangled in the webs he has woven for himself, he can find little pleasure in anything just now,' the bishop said, motioning to John to bring wine. 'He is terrified, I think, that Mortimer will arrive at our shores with an army. He is under no illusions as to his popularity in the realm, while Mortimer has the queen and the young duke with him. The mother of the heir and the heir himself, and arrayed against them are the king and Despenser.'

'The country will rally to the king,' Simon said scornfully.

'Would you, Simon?' the bishop shot out.

It was so sudden and unexpected that Simon could not respond instantly with the answer he would have intended: 'Of course!' Instead he reflected briefly, and as he opened his mouth to answer, the bishop was already smiling cynically and shaking his head.

'My son, do not lie to yourself, nor to me. You have been most shamefully treated by the Despenser, and if you were suddenly called upon in the heat of battle, would you really be able to defend the man who defends your enemy? I know what Despenser has done to you, to your family, to your daughter. So do not answer, but make sure that you behave with honour and integrity. That will be enough.'

'But I have an especial reason to hate the man.'

'So do many others, Simon. So do many others. He has treated almost all entirely shamefully, and the idea that they might soon be freed of the shackles of fear with which Despenser has bound so many of the good people of the realm, fills him with dread. As well it might. The English are an unmannerly lot. When they feel that their rulers have treated them poorly, they respond. All too often with extreme and swift brutality.'

'Does he really suffer so much?' Simon said.

'Simon, it would do your heart good to see how much he suffers,' the bishop said. He added, 'It does my own heart good to see how drawn and anxious he looks.'

Simon smiled. 'You will take the message to the king, then? Tell him about his son and the fact that he may be at Rouen?'

'I will. And then I will pray that God will give us all the judgement to decide on the proper course of action.

'I feel a sense of doom. The kingdom is on a knife's edge, and I cannot see upon which side it will fall.'

Near Lisieux, Normandy

The countryside was flat here, and Sir Richard de Folville could not help but notice how rich the lands looked. 'Much like my own homelands,' he noted.

Duke Edward heard him and glanced back with a grin. 'Makes

you wonder what on earth William the Bastard and his men were doing travelling to England when they could have enjoyed a quiet life here, eh?'

'But a quiet life would not suit them so well as a life dedicated to war,' Roger Crok joked.

John Biset agreed, but with a hint of regret in his voice. 'Just think of a life of rest and tranquillity. How tedious!'

The duke chuckled. 'He probably bethought himself that this land would be easy enough to take back, were he to lose it. And in any case, I cannot complain about his action, can I? Would I have a crown to claim when my father dies, were it not for Duke William conquering my kingdom for me? No, I do not think so. My people are too quarrelsome, and if they hadn't been conquered, God knows what might have become of the country.'

Richard nodded, but he was thinking of other matters. He had no money, and like all of the duke's bodyguards, was dependent on the youth's largesse. It occurred to Richard that it would be an easy task to knock the duke on the head and take his purse . . . Easy, but dangerous. Perhaps he could form an alliance with another man, and then kill him later to take all the profits? It was a thought. Biset seemed quite malleable. That Crok wasn't – he was too quick witted to be trusted.

While his mind meandered on along this line, he frowned quickly. 'Where is that priest?'

The duke did not turn to look at him. Not yet fourteen years old, he had the confidence of a king already. 'He has fled.'

Roger Crok was surprised. 'He was keen enough to be here with us at first, Your Highness.'

'He certainly wasn't happy when we were attacked near Montreuil, was he? Sat on his beast like a dumbstruck peasant, the poor fool. And as for his tutoring, I won't miss that at all. He has little idea of anything. It was too easy to twist him in his own tortuous reasoning. Besides, I got the impression that he was more fearful of Roger Mortimer than he was of the king. So I would not be surprised if even now he is trying to find a ship to take him home.'

'He cannot do that,' Richard de Folville said. 'If he was safe in England, he would not have been here. Only those with natural fears of Despenser or others in the king's pay would have come here, because allies of the Despenser and his comrades would not be welcome here.'

'I think he had some other secret,' the duke said. 'But whatever his reasoning, I do not wish to see his face again. He was not the most congenial company.'

Roger Crok felt a pang of anxiety at that summary. The fact that it was he who had brought the priest to their ranks made him worry that some of them might look upon Crok himself askance. He would have to be more careful, he thought, and turned to find Richard de Folville watching him from those cold, unfeeling eyes of his. They were the eyes of a killer.

Roger Crok stared calmly back at him, although inwardly he cringed. This man was truly terrifying. Roger had thought that he was a clerk of some kind who was on the run, much like Paul de Cockington, because his hair seemed to show the mark of a tonsure, but the more he saw of the man, the more he grew convinced that de Folville was a felon evading justice, and who might have shaved his head as a means of disguise, to aid his escape.

He would be wary of de Folville, he decided, because the alternative might be to wake one morning with a knife in the guts.

Canterbury

It was late when the bishop finally returned to his hall. The journey from the king's chambers in the priory was not great, but the way was filled with the masses who were here to attend as many services as possible in the great church, and he had been forced to shove and push against the press with William and John and two clerks.

At first it had been a little intimidating, but then he had grown aware of a feeling of extreme fear. It was a tightness in his breast, a hideous pounding in his ears, and he could feel, he was sure, the death that was approaching him. He did not know whether it would come at the point of a dagger, or the tip of an arrow, but he had a most definite presentiment of his approaching destruction, and the thought was enough to make him falter and almost fall. He cast about in a panic, staring wildly at the people all around, but all he received was a series of bovine looks from the pilgrims.

And then he saw the face. Only fleetingly, but *Christ's blood* it was there. Shadowy, slightly bearded, dark haired, and with blue eyes that glittered with hatred, he saw his nemesis: Paul of Taunton.

Dear God! He had nearly fainted with horror. That man should still be in Exeter, and yet here he was, ready to persecute him once more. It made his heart thunder so violently, he felt certain it must burst in an instant, but then gradually logic returned. He gazed back in the same direction, but the face was gone.

When at last they returned to the chambers in which the bishop had taken rooms, the squire looked at him anxiously. 'Are you quite well? Uncle, you look terrible.'

'I thank you for your care and attention, if not your frankness,' the bishop replied wryly. 'Some wine would be good, John! William, I saw a vision out there today. It shook me, shook me badly.'

'What?'

'The clerk – Paul. I saw him, so I thought, in the crowds.'

'What!' William had sprung towards the door, and now stood close to it, listening, as though ready to wrench it open and hurtle out to find the man.

'William, please come back here.'

'With the man who is sworn to kill you, wandering the streets just outside? He didn't get close to you?'

'No, no. He remained some distance away. It was so like him, and yet I think it must have been the light, the action of the dying sun on my eyes, or just the confusion of the mob. He couldn't really be here.'

'No, Uncle. I shouldn't think so,' the squire said, but he wore a worried frown.

'You are not to concern yourself over this, you understand me?

It is probably nothing. I was not wearing my spectacles. A face amongst all those – is it any surprise that one, two, or even a dozen, might look like my persecutor? No, it was merely my imagination,' Bishop Walter said, and drank down the first goblet of wine without pause.

'I am not sure, Uncle,' William said. He was almost at the door, and the bishop saw him glance at it.

The dear boy! William had always been one of his best-loved nephews. Perhaps because his mother had been Walter's favourite sister. Dear Mabel, so much younger than him, and she married quite late, bringing this one son into the world before she died. The young man was a reminder of his sister; he even had the vulnerability that Walter had seen in her.

'William, no. Leave it. There is no point in going down there. Do you think he could pass by so many guards on his way to hurt me without being apprehended? Of course not! So, please, just sit and be easy. There is nothing to worry about in here.'

He watched as his nephew rested his hand on the sword at his side as though to remind himself that in here, in the bishop's chamber, there was still defence enough.

'Very well,' he capitulated. 'As you say, it is safe enough in here.'

'Let us just take our ease,' Bishop Walter said tiredly. 'And then let me sit here quietly. I am not so young as once I was.'

'Do you want me to fetch Master Puttock? He should know the king's mind. And Paul de Cockington, too.'

'Yes, the rector. He is an inordinately fortunate man, isn't he?' the bishop said drily. 'To have escaped all, and now to be rewarded . . . I should have pressed the king to have him punished, but I confess, it would have been hard work, with the king looking so delighted with his news. Ach, yes. Fetch good Master Puttock. He should hear the fruits of his efforts.'

William rose and left him quietly, and the bishop leaned back in his chair with his eyes closed, thinking again about the audience with the king and the rapid advance of strategies that immediately flowed from the news. Men were ordered, plans demanded, a new view on possible risks considered, and then the conclusions were debated at length. It was one of the abiding beliefs of so many that this king was incompetent and incapable of making decisions, and yet those who said so should have seen him at moments like this; when it truly mattered, he was rational, logical and determined. If his plans sometimes went awry, and his men were not strong enough to see his commands through, that was no reflection on the king himself. It was the fault of the men he had beneath him.

Glancing about him, the bishop took stock. There was little here in Canterbury to keep him. Now that he had seen that face, his peace was destroyed. Perhaps it was time for him to return to Exeter and leave national politics altogether? He was an old man, in Christ's name! Not some youth out to make a reputation.

Seeking some peace, he rose and walked to a shelf set into the wall. Here were his favourite books, and he hesitated before taking down the *Chanson de Roland*. The memory of that cursed note had coloured his feelings about this book, but there was still a joy in reading the beautiful prose that overcame any reticence he might feel. He carried it to the table, where he set it down and opened it.

His gasp as he saw the latest note seemed to take the very breath from his lungs, and the room whirled about him, making him stagger back.

Your life will soon end. Prepare to meet thy Maker.

Chapter Thirty

Canterbury

When he was called to see the bishop, Simon had been getting to know a barrel of strong red wine from northern France. In his experience, most wines that were affordable tended to come from around Bordeaux and the Guyennois regions. This, though, was very tasty, and he was looking forward to a second jugful, when William walked into the bar and saw him.

'Master Puttock, would you be so good as to come and see the bishop?'

'He's back from the king? How did it go?'

'The king was impressed, I think, that you and my uncle managed to bring some news of his son. It is more than all the spies Despenser has had in France for the last six months have done.' William grinned. 'I think you are back in the king's favour.'

Simon grunted at that. 'So long as it doesn't mean it'll cost me money or force me to come and live in a new town yet again, I suppose that's good enough.'

'I believe the only thing he will wish from you is to return to Portchester with the rector.'

'Why with him? Can't the king keep him here? You have no idea how tedious his whining became on the way here. He was constantly complaining about the journey and the roads and the weather . . .'

'You have guards to keep him to hand? Good. If he escapes again, it would be a sore embarrassment to my uncle,' William said.

They had crossed the inner courtyard and gone through the door to the bishop's rooms. Reaching the parlour, William knocked loudly, and hearing the bishop's call, the two men entered.

'My lord bishop, are you well!' Simon exclaimed. 'You have the look of a man who has seen a ghost!'

'He saw a man in the crowds today who resembled the one who has been leaving threatening messages,' William explained. 'It gave him a shock.'

In response, the elderly man snatched up the scrap of parchment and flung it at them. 'Look on that! The damned man has been in here – in here in my private chambers – while we were with the king! Damn him!'

Simon peered at the small writing. 'Is this the same as the other messages? I heard of them from Baldwin when he came to visit me at Porchester.'

'It looks remarkably similar,' the bishop said heavily. 'Dear God, how could he have got in here? I thought this room at least would be safe for me.'

'The guards,' William said, and was instantly out through the door to see what might be learned from them.

Simon placed the parchment on the table. 'This sounds serious, my lord bishop. What on earth does he have against you?'

'I have no idea! Sir Baldwin had compiled a list of men whom he felt might have harboured a grudge against me, but how on earth could I tell which one of them might be responsible for this?'

'You say that you have seen the man here today?' Simon said.

'Yes.'

'And you are sure that his face was previously unfamiliar to you? If so, that would surely make it very surprising that he is your enemy.'

'Not necessarily,' the bishop said grimly. 'I have already explained this to Sir Baldwin. While I was Lord High Treasurer, I made many enemies.'

'I see. So this could be someone from that period of your life – someone whom you never knew, but who feels himself to have been badly treated by you. But surely, even then they would be known to you, because they would have had to present themselves in court to make any claim or defend their position against you?'

'Again, not necessarily. In the Grand Eyre of five years ago, for example, I did not attend. It was held under my name, but the justices were professionals. Besides, this fellow Paul was quite young – perhaps in his early twenties. He would have been under age at the time of the Eyre, I'd guess.'

'That young? So, for example, if he holds a grudge of some sort,' Simon became thoughtful, 'it would possibly be his father whom he sought to avenge?'

The bishop pulled a face. 'So now I have to wonder about the sons of all those who might hold a desire to punish me for any real or imagined slight? Master Puttock, you do not put me at my ease!'

'I am sorry, my lord bishop. I was thinking out aloud. I am sure that you will be safe enough, if you can only keep away from large crowds.'

'In this city?'

Simon gave a wry grin. 'Yes, that could be problematic. Perhaps if you were to return to Exeter?'

'I came all this way on the advice of our friend Sir Baldwin in order to evade the man, yet he has followed me here. I find it very hard to believe that I would be safer travelling all the way back there again,' Bishop Walter said irascibly.

'I understand.'

Just then, William returned, a furious expression on his face. He slammed the door and made an expansive gesture that took in the door, the men beyond it, and all the men-at-arms in the city. 'Those cretins would be dangerous if they had one brain between them! They were glad to allow a young stranger in because he told them that you had ordered some pilgrim badges, and he was to deliver them. They allowed him up and left him in your chamber for some little while.'

'Did they not realise that no one was to be allowed in?' Simon asked.

'Oh, they knew, yes. But the king is here in the town, and when they knew the bishop was visiting the king, they didn't bother to protect this chamber, reasoning that he was being guarded by proximity to the king. The fools did not think about a man entering the chamber here.'

In a flash, Simon and William had the same idea. One man had been up here for some while, and could have installed a dangerous device to hurt or kill the bishop. They exchanged a look, and some innate understanding of the dread word *assassin* was communicated.

But although the two searched the room assiduously, looking behind tapestries, inside the chest, behind the cupboards and even beneath the bed, there was clearly no instrument nor agent of death.

'That is a relief,' William said, 'but it still proves that it is too dangerous for you here. Exeter is no better, because the fellow managed to hide himself there before. Perhaps he has a relative or friend who lives there? The best thing to do would be to go on in the king's company. You would be safer in London, in the Tower. There are too many men-at-arms and guards there, for this Paul to ever gain access. You should be safe there.'

'I refuse to skulk,' the bishop said.

'Oh well, if you prefer to walk about as a living target for any disgruntled assassin with a bow, Uncle,' William said sweetly, 'you go ahead. You won't have to do so for long, I'm sure.'

The bishop glowered at him, but did not argue. There was no disputing his logic.

Simon looked from one to the other. 'Is that decided, then? My lord bishop, you will go on to London?'

'So it would seem. But for how long? Oh, this is ridiculous!'

'Not for too long,' William said. 'Only until we catch this fellow and put an end to these threats.'

'And meanwhile I should go to my bed,' Simon said. 'I must return to Portchester, for my wife will wonder what has happened to me, else.'

'Simon, I would be glad of your aid,' the bishop began.

'My lord, I have been away from my wife too much already in the last months. She needs my companionship, and I hers. I am sorry, but I must go home as soon as I may.'

'The country is teetering on the brink of disaster,' the bishop said. 'I know that you will wish to be with your wife, Simon, but I would greatly appreciate your help, and your strong right arm, in my entourage.'

'I have to return to my wife,' Simon stated doggedly. 'I am sorry, my lord bishop, but my family must be first. There is no one else to protect them.'

'I am sorry to hear it. But of course you're quite right,' the bishop said. He sighed and asked William to fetch John to serve wine, before addressing Simon again. 'And now to the audience with the king. He says that he would like Paul de Cockington to return to Portchester, and there to deliver messages to the Commissioners of Array, to Sir John Felton, and to the shipmasters gathered there. I shall recommend you take him back with you.'

'There were not many ships when I was there,' Simon said with a faint frown.

'You will find that altered when you return, I think. The king has ordered all the ships in the area to converge on Portchester. There will be some hundred and fifty or more, if he is right. And the Commissioners of Array will be collecting many more men. You already know the reason for the force being gathered. The king is determined to send men to find his son, to rescue him, and return him safe to England.'

*Vigil of the Feast of the Pausatio of the Blessed Virgin Mary**

Tower of London

In the grassy space near the stables, where the horses were often allowed to browse, there was an old fallen trunk that had not yet

* 14 August 1326

been cut up into logs, and here Isabella found herself on many mornings, enjoying the sun.

Lady Isabella Fitzwilliam had been so glad to reach the city, because although it had been a delightful journey with the knight, Sir Peregrine's kindness and generosity had made her feel stabs of guilt. This man did not deserve to be treated as a mere tool, a crowbar designed to pry open a gap and let her in to hurt her enemy. He deserved much better. With luck, he would find a good woman before long who would be able to give him the love he craved.

For herself, there was no love left. She had squandered her love on both husbands: squandered because neither lived long enough. They had been so young when they died that even now she was hardly ancient. Her flesh may have lost its youthful colour and softness, but for a woman of two-and-forty, she was well preserved. Even so, a man would ever look to a young filly, not a stable old nag, and she knew that she would never remarry.

But Sir Peregrine was a most attractive fellow, as well as being good and kind, loving and loyal. She could feel quite warm towards him, if she was not so set upon her course already.

Exeter

Edith set Henry on the bed while she bent to retrieve the clothes she had dropped.

There was a thump, and then a moment later, a shrill squeal of pain. Spinning around, she saw that little Henry had fallen from the bed and landed on the floor. Already, a great red wound was colouring his brow, not bloody, but a bruise beneath his precious skin. She could not move at first, her feet rooted to the boards where she stood, and then she went to him in a hideous daze, picking him up and rocking him, kissing his head, her eyes wide with horror.

She was not even a good mother. She was worthless.

*Two Tuesdays before the Feast of the Nativity of the Blessed Virgin**

Tower of London

It was fortunate that Peter had managed to provide her with a son, Isabella thought, and a son of whom she could be proud, because without Peter, her life would have been empty indeed.

Roger had been such a good boy, and now he remained loyal to his oaths, she was sure. He was so like his father. And then of course there was Henry's son, too. Although Ranulf had been more reluctant to become involved, when he saw what had happened to his father, and to Roger his half-brother, he had come to hate with a virulence and determination which equalled her own.

She wandered about the inner courtyard, idly watching the way that the clouds of smoke from all the fires in the city ambled past in a procession of fumes. It was enormously thrilling to see all this, and to know that she was living in the largest city in the kingdom. Perhaps it was the largest in Christendom?

A cloud formed before her eyes high overhead, and she gaped in wonder. It seemed to her that she was watching a ship under full sail, buffeted by the waves and the wind, thrown about. She blinked, and it was gone. In its place was a face, bearded and smiling, and for an instant she was sure that it was her dead husband Henry, who winked at her as though to say he approved of her plans.

It was enough to bring a serenity to her that eased the almost perpetual frown on her face. The idea that he approved was glorious. She would do all in her power to continue. It would have been good to confide in someone, but that was impossible. Even poor Sir Peregrine . . .

Why had she immediately thought of him? After seeing her late husband's face in the clouds, it felt almost adulterous. She

---

* 26 August 1326

had never been a traitor, not to either husband, not to her family, to her peasants, her king. She had been betrayed by the scheming bishop, and by others in her time, but she herself had remained loyal.

Her reverie was shattered by the rude blaring of trumpets, and she turned with a start, half expecting to see the king himself arrive. Picking up her skirts, she hurried over the grass to the parapet, and here she paused to look down into the entranceway.

And saw his lordship, the Bishop of Exeter, trotting in.

Bishop Walter snapped when John of Padington asked him again if he felt all right. 'Of course I do!' he snarled, and did not wait to see the impact of his black mood on his poor steward.

His temper would not be soothed until he was off this damned horse and sitting on a soft cushion before a roaring fire. The weather was pleasantly cool, the journey today had not been too stressful, yet the riding about of the last weeks had gradually worn away at him. While he had been in Exeter, then Canterbury, the death threats had been first irritating, and then terrifying. The fact that someone had been able to get into his most secret quarters had been almost enough to make him think of supernatural enemies. After all, it was only a little while ago that Sir Hugh le Despenser had been threatened by a sorcerer and necromancer, who had tried to murder him with the use of little waxen models into which lead pins were to be stuck; Sir Hugh had been forced to write to the Pope for special protection.

However, it was not the fear of demons which made him shout at his servants and insult his squire. It was the hideous pain he was suffering.

'Bishop, would you like me to see to your wine and a fire?' John de Padington asked, unperturbed by his flare of rage.

'Yes, prepare my damned room, and be swift! I see no reason why I should be forced to wait here for an age while incompetents blather at me! Are you mazed, man? *Get to it!*'

John was back in an instant. He had sent on harbingers before each stage of their journey, and the men had reached the Tower earlier in the day, commanding that the bishop's fire be ready, his wine warmed, a change of clothes which they had brought with them should be laid out ready, and that his office materials should be prepared so that he and his clerks could begin work as soon as they arrived – once he had been able to give a prayer of thanks to celebrate his safe arrival.

'Good!' the bishop muttered, wincing in agony as he swung his leg over the horse's back. His sword clanged against his thigh, and he slowly and carefully eased himself down. He felt a little unbalanced wearing his sword again, but a man had a duty to protect himself, and with the trouble flaring up all over the realm, he could not afford to leave his weapon behind. Still, its additional weight on his hip did not help.

The walk to his chamber was atrocious. He bellowed at men for infractions of rules, muttered poisonously at Squire William for not having brought him a cup of wine while he was dismounting, and tried in every manner he could to prove to all just how miserable he felt.

Messages or no messages, haemorrhoids were truly the invention of Beelzebub, he thought as he cautiously knelt at the little portable altar in his chamber.

Chapter Thirty-One

*Two Thursdays before the Feast of the Nativity of the Blessed Virgin Mary**

Portchester

Baldwin left the inn where he had taken a room and made his weary way down the cobbled street towards the place where the leaders of the force were no doubt bickering again.

Their master was a sly, weasel-like knight by the name of John Felton, who had been picked by the king himself, apparently. He had been making trouble since his arrival here in Portchester a couple of weeks ago. Less for Baldwin, it must be said, but more for the other men in the town, especially the two knights, Nicholas de Cryel and Robert de Kendale, both of whom were much more experienced in campaigning than him. However, Felton it was who had been given the king's authority, and no one was going to gainsay him, which meant that while Baldwin and the other two had successfully prepared shipping, supplies and men, the whole enterprise began to fall apart as soon as Felton started to give his own orders.

Baldwin caught himself as his boot slithered on a mossy stone. This town was quickly growing to be a place of torment for him. The days were spent in wrangling, trying to persuade one side or another to compromise in the interests of the king and of the men whom they would lead to battle, and to the glorious rescue of the king's son.

* 28 August 1326

But Felton was not the sort of man to inspire confidence. He must have two clerks with him wherever he went, because he could neither read nor write, and in Baldwin's opinion, his ability to even read a scene and make an accurate judgement was dubious at best. The man might have had the merit of a block-headed courage in the lists, but when it came to rational assessments of a battle, Baldwin would have been happier with his hound Wolf in charge. At least Wolf knew about attacking a flank to turn a sheep away from its planned route. That was more than Felton understood. To him, the only way to attack was a massive charge of chivalry. That kind of action might work well in Palestine against more lightly armoured men, but even then, in Baldwin's experience, there was a need for lightly armoured troops to attack first, to roll up the skirmishing bowmen on their own little ponies. Charging was good for the mentality of a knight – it reinforced the view of the chivalry of the nation – and led often to appalling casualties among the men-at-arms on the opposing side.

But this was to be a short, aggressive chevauchée across unfamiliar country. There had been some reports from sailors who knew the coast, but there was no one who could provide accurate descriptions of the lands about Rouen. To launch an attack under these conditions made Baldwin enormously anxious.

Nodding to some men gathered at a corner, he continued down to the office. It was lodged in an inn near the seafront, and he must push past two chatting guards to reach the door. There was no salute, no challenge, none of the serious martial structure that he was used to from his days as a Knight Templar, and that too worried him.

In the *Poor Fellow Soldiers of Christ and the Temple of Solomon*, he had been the lowest of knights, but even then he had recognised the need for warriors to fight in unison, to know when to charge together, when to wheel, when to withdraw, when to press home an attack – and all depended upon discipline and training. The men here had neither. Most had been gathered straight from their fields by bailiffs and stewards who had little understanding themselves, or, more likely, were accepting the poor devils in return for payment from the intended victims, or taking them in response to a grudge against the men. There was one, Jack, whom Baldwin suspected had been gathered up with the rest purely because the boy's mother had refused to accede to an official's demands that she should service him. The lad was only fourteen or so, from the look of him.

Yes, the lack of discipline worried him. As did the inexperience of many of the men gathering here in the port. They were collected in dribs and drabs, four, or five, or six at a time. In the absence of enough housing for so many, most were resorting to sleeping in the streets. Already there had been some deaths because of fights in taverns and alehouses, boredom and strong drink weaving their usual magic amongst men with too many weapons near to hand.

The chamber he entered was a long, low room with wooden panels at the walls to try to keep the worst of the breezes away. A glorious fire roared in the hearth, as it had every day since Felton had first arrived, and in the bright light from it, Baldwin could see the men gathered about the table in the middle of the room. Clerks sat scribbling, while messengers hurried hither and thither, and an atmosphere of restrained impatience was lying about the room like a miasma.

Baldwin walked to the table. 'Sir John, Sir Nicholas, Sir Robert,' he said to each of the men, and the last two nodded and greeted him. Sir John Felton apparently felt that there was no need for him to welcome Baldwin, but instead continued to issue orders.

It was, as usual, a perplexing day, and Baldwin was glad when he was able to leave the room. It was the middle of the afternoon now, and he walked slowly down to the little building where Simon had his office.

Here, all was cheery and as unlike the military chamber as it could be. In Simon's opinion, it was crucial that all his men believed that they were important – not only important to Simon, but to the work which they did – and the success of his approach was all too plain. The clerks and officers hurried about, but not in the same frenetic, illogical manner which was so evident around Sir John Felton. Here, men moved with a sensible coherence. There was the impression of an effective machine which was producing worthwhile results.

'Baldwin, enter, please!' Simon called. 'Look at this! It makes my heart heavy to see that we're collecting so much useful evidence of spying.'

He held out two thick parchments. They were cheap scrolls, badly cured and containing such poor writing that they were all but illegible. Baldwin had to hold them up to the candle to read the scrawl.

'It is a message from a woman to her son in France?' he guessed.

'Unless it is an enormously clever cipher which we cannot break – yes. It's Madame de Villefort, who was until quite recently a decent widow who lived over at Fareham. But now that the new orders have been issued, she has been taken into custody and can no longer commit this heinous crime of communicating with her son,' Simon said, and tossed the scrolls back onto the growing pile on his table. 'Baldwin, this job is cruel, it is pointless, and it is a waste of time. I could be at home, seeing to the harvest, instead of this. I would be as much use to the king as sitting here.'

'More. You would be helping to produce food.'

'I didn't say I would actually help gather the harvest,' Simon chuckled, but then his face grew serious. 'Let's walk, old friend. I need your advice.'

They went out and turned east, from where they could gaze out over the massed ranks of cogs waiting in the harbour. There was that curious atmosphere, which Baldwin had never quite grown to like, but which to him was the very essence of a port anywhere in the world: a mixture of the sound of thrumming hempen ropes in the wind, the squeak and rattle of rusty metal, and creaking of sodden timbers, while all about there was the smell of the sea, that sharp tang that caught in the nostrils, and the odours of tar and resin.

Behind them in the town, the common noise was the roar and hiss of the bellows, the rattle and clang of hammers on steel; here, the noises were all muted as though in respect to the waves themselves.

'Is Paul bearing his position with grace?' Simon asked.

'No,' Baldwin said. 'He is deeply unhappy to be told that he will return with the men, but so be it. He does not have to enjoy his tasks, merely obey them. What of you?'

'I am well enough. This job is ludicrous though. I cannot check every barrel, and now, with the ships preparing for the assault, there is no shipping from here anyway. There are no barrels or bales being loaded up: all that kind of work has moved from here, so my tasks are utterly irrelevant.'

'That scroll could have contained a cipher,' Baldwin pointed out mildly.

'There is as much chance of that as me having a tattoo of the shipping on my arse,' Simon said. 'And I am not doing that just to help some French invasion.'

'You would find it a painful experience,' Baldwin laughed.

'I have received news from William Walle though,' Simon said, reaching into the purse at his belt.

Baldwin took the note and opened it. Then: 'Oh no! Another message?'

'The bishop has been in London for some weeks now. He left Canterbury a while after me. A week ago, so this says. Now he has received another message threatening his death.'

'He has many men to guard him there,' Baldwin said.

'Yes, but I feel that this is a dangerous time for him. Don't you?'

Baldwin took a breath and nodded. 'I think it is a dangerous time for all of us, Simon. I wish I could go to him and try to find this fellow. He is causing the bishop a considerable amount of concern, isn't he?'

'Bishop Walter has asked me to join him – to go to London with him.'

'What will you say?'

Simon pursed his lips and stared at all the ships. Hundreds of great cogs, all swaying to the movement of the waves. It reminded him of the journeys he had made by ship, and at the memory, his belly rose. Swallowing, he turned away. 'I cannot go over there with the men. What do I know of fighting, other than hitting a man on the head with a fist? Swordplay and wielding lances or bills are not for me.'

'I agree. Oh, you are a good swordsman, Simon, do not misunderstand me – but this will be a dangerous expedition, and I would not advise you to join the venture. Nay, rather you should take Margaret and Perkin back home, and wait there to see what happens.'

'It is one thing to say that I should do so, but I would feel guilty, Baldwin,' Simon said quietly.

'Guilty? In God's name, why?' Baldwin asked.

'Here are all these men, preparing to cross the sea and do their part to try to rescue the duke from his mother and Mortimer, and all I can do is skulk about here, or scurry off homewards like some whipped cur. What sort of man would that make me?'

'A sensible father and husband, Simon. There is no glory in battle. Believe me, I used to think that there was, but I have seen enough blood and carnage to know better.'

'But I could go to London. Meg has never seen London. She thought *this* place was impressive.'

Baldwin stopped and deliberately took in the scruffy little town, noting the cottages with the daub falling from the wattles, the thin, leaking thatched roofs, the air of dilapidation and neglect. 'Bless her.'

'Yes, well, I think so too. But if I take them to London, I could see them safely installed in the city, and serve my old friend the bishop – because, Baldwin, he *has* been a good friend to me for many years.'

'I know, Simon. I have to say, it would be my own inclination to hurry back to Exeter, rather than towards London. If there is to be an invasion, it is likely to aim for London.'

'But all reports say the French will land in Cornwall and make their way from there, which would mean Margaret and me being in the path of the French host.'

Baldwin nodded. He was thinking of his own dear wife. 'But even if that were the case, you could ride away from them in Devon. You know the woods where you would be safe, you know how to survive on Dartmoor. You could take Margaret and Perkin there.'

'Perhaps. But there is little enough to eat on Dartmoor, Baldwin. I don't know. I feel torn. I would like to return home, but I really feel that the bishop needs my help. *Our* help.'

Baldwin gave a faint grin. 'If I had any choice, I would already be back at Furnshill. It is the place where my heart longs to be. But I have a duty to be here and do all I may to protect the men I have ordered gathered up here.'

'That is the thing,' Simon said quietly. 'I feel a sense of duty too, and it involves the bishop.'

*Tuesday before the Feast of the Nativity of the Blessed Virgin Mary**

English Channel

'I'm going to be sick!' Paul de Cockington wailed.

'Then put your head over the thwarts!' Baldwin bellowed, resisting the urge to kick his backside as Paul leaned forward and vomited noisily over the side.

Baldwin had not expected to be here. He was not scared of battle – he had served in many, and was too experienced to feel that bone-shattering terror that the young must know at their first actions – but he had only one desire, when his efforts to raise a host for the king's forces were done, and that was to return home, to make sure that his home was protected, that his wife was safe. It was heart-rending to be leaving the coast of England behind and heading for France and war. He knew that Jeanne would

* 2 September 1326

understand, because she was a mature woman and had been married to another knight before him, but that did not remove the strain from him. It hurt him like an infidelity, as though he was guilty of adultery again.

'I don't want to be here!'

Baldwin gazed longingly at the man's buttocks, and his foot itched to kick. With luck, were he to plant a firm enough boot in Paul's backside, the fellow might even fly into the sea. It was probably the most beneficial outcome possible, because Baldwin did not believe that their force could reach the duke. No, if he had to guess, the duke would leave Rouen within moments of the news of an invading force reaching his ears. The men who protected him had no desire to be captured and brought to England, because King Edward II would want revenge for their keeping his son from him. If one or two were to bring his son to the army and deliver him up, they might be able to anticipate rewards including pardons for any crimes they had committed, but such benefits lasted only a short time. The king was too unreliable. His favourites today tomorrow became his most despised enemies. Look at Roger Mortimer: once the king's most honoured and trusted general, and now the man whose death warrant the king had signed.

No, if Baldwin were to wager, he would bet that the men guarding the duke would pack up and hasten away, hoping that the King of France would meet the English and defeat them.

'Sir Baldwin, those men said we'll all die.'

This was young Jack. Baldwin would hazard a guess that the lad's mother was regretting her stout defence of her honour now.

'Don't you worry, Jack. You won't be killed today.'

'Were they right, though? Will we die when we land?'

'Boy, it is in God's hands,' Baldwin said, placing his palm on the lad's head and ruffling his greasy hair gently. 'When we land, with God's grace, we may find no one to welcome us, and we may complete our mission without difficulty.'

The boy nodded, as though satisfied with his reassurance, and went away to cower, shivering, in among the ropes at the edge of the deck.

Baldwin turned back to his view of the sea ahead. At least there were no French forces before them, he thought. They might even be able to land without the risk of French warships ripping into them. If there was one type of war he hated more than any other, it was seaborne fighting. The ever-present risk of falling into the sea and drowning was the final straw.

There were over four thousand sailors in this Navy. All told, some one hundred and fifty ships were strung out in loose formation, carrying over sixteen hundred warriors, with victuals and horses as well as their fighting equipment. Sixteen hundred was a massive force to race down to Rouen, but there would have to be enough to maintain the bridgehead, while small parties would be needed to protect bridges and other vital points. Baldwin was content that there was no need for more men, but the idea of landing so many inexperienced fighters was causing him alarm again.

To distract himself, he found himself wondering again about the identity of Bishop Walter's persecutor. Simon had packed his own belongings three days ago, and with luck would already be in the bishop's home or at the Tower. Either way, Baldwin only prayed that Margaret and Perkin would be safe. He hated the city of London, for to his mind it was the centre of all the vileness in the realm. It was where Despenser's power was strongest.

Who was this man who sought to terrify the bishop, who threatened him, flaunting his ability to pass through all the bishop's guards at any opportunity, and who was apparently dedicated to killing him? Baldwin had no idea, but he was sure that there must be some obvious clues, if only they could be recognised. This was a murder in the planning. There should surely be as many clues of who was responsible for the planning as there would be after a murder had been committed.

But Baldwin could not concentrate on the bishop's troubles. He opened his heart and prayed – for himself, for the bishop, for

Simon – but most of all, he prayed for Jeanne and his children, and begged God to protect them from any invading forces that might arrive.

Chapter Thirty-Three

London

Margaret Puttock's mouth fell wide with awe as she saw the bridge ahead. It was so bright, so beautiful, so . . . so *huge*!

It had not been difficult for her to persuade Simon to take them with him to London. It would not have been safe to leave her behind in Portchester. There had been too many cases reported to the town's officers of rapes, and three murders of women in the town. The idea of leaving her and their son was anathema to Simon. He had to bring them too.

They rode onward, Perkin riding behind with Hugh and Rob on a cart, while Simon and Margaret trotted along on their horses, but as they approached the great entranceway, Simon fell back and rode alongside the cart, pointing out the details of the flags and the statues which sat in recesses at either side of the main gatehouse.

'However did they build it?' Margaret gasped at last. 'It must be a thousand yards long, Simon. It looks as though it floats over the water!'

Her husband smiled. 'It isn't that much bigger than the bridge over the Exe,' he said.

'Maybe not, but the Exe Bridge only has one chapel on it. Look at this!'

It was astonishing that they had managed to cram so many houses and shops on the thing. The bridge itself was very broad, but the buildings meant that there was little space for a single wagon to pass under the arches from one end to the other. It was massive, and splendid, and Margaret felt her head swim as she peered up and about.

There were several defensive points: the Stone Gate at the southern end of the bridge, then the Draw-Bridge Gate a distance further on, while the size of the chapel of St Thomas was daunting in its own right.

The view of all the buildings was so extraordinary that she quite missed the sight of the Tower of London until they were already over the bridge, and she could peer along the line of the river towards the king's castle.

This was different, though. Fortress to protect the city, it was, but it was also to be defended from the city, and was the king's leading prison for traitors and his other enemies. There was something about it that made her shiver. 'That is where we're going?' she asked.

'It's where the bishop is, yes,' Simon said. He was easy enough in his saddle as they rode along past St Magnus the Martyr, then St Botolph, and then by Billingesgate, and as they went, the immensity of the king's castle began to dawn on her. It was not merely a building or two hidden behind a wall like Oakhampton or Exeter, this was an immense area of land that was entirely enclosed. When she asked, Simon told her that it consisted of almost twenty acres. The great white keep inside was visible from all about the city, looming threateningly over the walls. Margaret could discern nothing that was kindly or protective about it. It was there to control the people of the city.

'I don't like it,' she said quietly.

Simon glanced up, then across at her, grinning. 'This? The tower's just a building, Meg. Nothing scary about it.'

She nodded, but the impression of violence would not leave her. There was something about the high walls that seemed to scream to her, as though they were formed of the tortured souls of all those who had been incarcerated within.

The day was warm, but she shivered uncontrollably as they passed under the gatehouse.

*Thursday before the Feast of the Nativity of the Blessed Virgin Mary**

Near Honfleur, Normandy

The ships were safe, and the majority of the men had managed to let themselves down the ropes and ladders to the sea. For Baldwin, the scenes were reminiscent of so many from his youth. Ships towering overhead, rocking on their keels, while sailors scurried about, hauling on the ropes that made the screaming, angry horses rise high into the sky, only to be lowered gently to the ground where waiting ostlers could calm them. Massive bales of weaponry were deposited nearby, with squires and heralds running to rescue them from the water before they could get a soaking, and cooks and carters swearing as loud as any of the matelots when they discovered the damage done already to their meagre stocks by the ever-present rats in the holds, or more commonly by 'thieving bastard sailors' as Baldwin heard more than once.

Here the beach was good and sandy, and so far, only one disaster had occurred. A large cog with over a hundred men aboard and many good horses had struck something under the water, and sank almost instantly. The screams of the men was enough to send a stab of horror into every heart. Worse, Baldwin felt, was the terror of the horses, chained to their cradles deep in the ship as the water rose. They had no escape, no comprehension of what was happening, only a sudden realisation of their death. At least a man might grab a barrel or spar and float to another ship.

A hundred and fifty ships. It was a mighty force, and with sixteen hundred men, it was large enough to be effective, if only they could get moving.

'I am cold!' Paul de Cockington said. He was huddled nearby, arms wrapped about himself, shivering in his sodden robe.

'You should get up and walk about,' Baldwin said unsympathetically.

---

* 4 September 1326

'And *you* should be more polite to a man who is crucial to your mission,' Paul retorted. 'If you're so clumsy with my well-being, you may just find yourself responsible for my death, and then you'll regret your harshness when you return to England.'

'I seriously doubt it,' Baldwin said.

'You need me! How else will you be able to talk to the duke and make sure he comes with you? I am your most important man in this whole force, and you forget that at your peril.'

Baldwin turned on him. 'You have moaned, complained and whined all the way from Portchester, cretin! Now you think you are vital to our success? I regret to tell you that you are wrong. I know the duke personally – I was his guard when he came over here last year, and I know his mind probably better than you. You are here in order to gain yourself a pardon for your appalling crimes in Exeter, so it would be better that you put your mind to how best to survive this journey, rather than making me, your protector, wish to throw you into the sea to drown.'

'You wouldn't do that,' Paul said uncertainly.

Baldwin looked away. No, he wouldn't. But just now he had enough fears of his own to contend with rather than listening to the petty bleating of this rector.

The worst thing was, the amount of time it was taking to get the ships emptied. From his own experience, he knew that the best way to launch a raid like this was to get men and horses onto the beach as quickly as possible, and then maintain a strong ring of defence while the rest of the cargo was brought down. But there had been no plan to arrange this. Instead the ships were mingled in an untidy muddle. Some landing first had carried only horses, while the majority of the men were still on board. Baldwin's own horse had been delivered to him, but many of the other knights were still unmounted, and would remain so for a long while. There were plenty of archers here on the beach – but their arrows were stored on a different ship. Baldwin was worried that at any moment a force could arrive from Honfleur that would smash through them and repel the rest of the ships.

As if in answer to his black thoughts, there was a sudden

scream, and then shouting, from up on the dunes further inland. Baldwin turned to see a quartet of men in armour charging six men at a picket. There was nothing the poor devils could do to protect themselves: the great destriers charged, the men with their lances couched, and in short order three of the English were spitted, arms and legs waving in mid-air while the lances rose up, their points smothered in gore, the momentum of the charge carrying the screaming English up high, and over, to be deposited in crumpled heaps behind the chargers.

Baldwin winced. This was a sign of the dangers inherent in landing likc this. Hc could feel his scalp crawl as the Frenchmen wheeled. Two rode back to finish off the pickets, while two sat idly watching the disembarkation, chatting with their visors open as they took in the scene. After deliberation, they wheeled about and trotted away, rejoining their companions. There were no English left alive at that picket.

There was no sign of Felton, no sign of the other commanders. Baldwin looked down at Paul de Cockington. 'Perhaps you should not joke about dying, rector. It is perfectly likely that you will be proved correct.'

Tower of London

'Get the wine. You expect our master to serve himself?' Hugh snarled, and cuffed Rob around the ear.

Simon smiled to see how Hugh had taken to training Rob. It appeared to serve little purpose so far, because Rob had shown Hugh scant respect, but Simon hoped that the lazy, good-for-nothing boy would one day turn into a half-decent servant. In order to do so, he would need regular beatings, if his behaviour so far was any gauge.

They were in a small parlour in a house set into the inner wall of the fortress. It was pleasant enough, and there was plenty of firewood for the cool evenings, but Meg was deeply unhappy, he could see, and that worried him.

It was strange how women would fall into these moods. She was generally a calm wife, amiable and efficient, and sensible in the way that she dealt with things. For her to suddenly become like this, as though there was something in the Tower here that she should fear, was very odd. In any case, she would have to grow accustomed to the place, because now that they had arrived, they could hardly desert the bishop.

Not that it would be easy to track down the felon who had deposited all these messages.

The latest was the most curt. *You must die!* had been scrawled on a scrap and sealed with some wax. It had not been delivered straight to the bishop's books or onto his table, but had got to him by more mundane methods. A guard had been accosted by a man dressed in a thick fustian robe, his head hooded, who had paid him half a penny to give the little roll to the bishop. There was no explanation, and the guard had not expected one. But he delivered the note, only to be thrown against the wall by an enraged William Walle, who demanded to know where it had come from. He had wanted to have the guard gaoled as a suspect, but the bishop himself had dissuaded him. The idea that the fellow might be allied to the writer was ridiculous. He was a Londoner, who had been based at the Tower for years. He had not been in Exeter or Canterbury. And in any case, the bishop pointed out reasonably, the guilty man had been seen by him in Canterbury. They knew what he looked like.

When Simon reached the bishop's chambers, which were on the second floor in the tower itself, he found William and John outside, talking in low voices.

'Squire, steward, how is he this morning?' Simon asked.

'He appears well enough,' William said, 'but he is not easy in his mind. I would almost say that he has surrendered himself to fate. He looks like a man who has decided he is to die.'

Simon glanced at John, who merely nodded. 'Well, I'd best speak with him.'

He knocked and walked inside as soon as the bishop responded.

It was the room of an invalid. Bishop Walter was wrapped warmly in a thick robe with fur at the collar and cuffs, and to

Simon it made him look as though he was swamped. His face was pale and drawn, and there was a feverish look in his eyes. Yet his smile of welcome was as genuine as ever. 'Ah, Simon. I am glad to see you.'

'I have been here two days, and still can make no sense of this business,' Simon said.

'I don't expect you can, my old friend. Much though I wish it were not true, I fear that no one can protect me. This evil appears to follow me, no matter where I go. I am beginning to think there is something supernatural in it, for I cannot see how a man might enter my private chambers to deposit these messages without some form of help. Perhaps my actions in the last years have brought this divine judgment upon me.'

'Bishop, you have been a strong man who has done all he might to serve the Crown and the Church. God is not displeased with you. This is being done by a man who has a grudge,' Simon said.

'You think so?' the bishop said gently.

'No – I know so. There is no one who has served God with more devotion. You are under threat from a man, that is all. And a man is not infallible. He may be dangerous, in truth, but he is vulnerable, too. All we need do is find him and capture him.'

'That is all?' The bishop smiled.

'Yes. But for that I do need to have help. William Walle knew him, did he not?'

'Yes. He and John would be able to recognise him.'

'Good, that will help me. I spent all yesterday trying to consider the best means of drawing him out, but I have to conclude that the best approach will be to let him come here.'

'Use me as bait, then?'

'Yes. And either I will be with you, or William will. I want you to have a man at your side at all times.'

'What of my other guards?'

'I will be asking that your guard be doubled as well. And I will need William to view all those who come to guard you so that we can ensure that the man is not among them.'

'Very well,' the bishop said. He glanced pensively out through the window. 'Have you heard the people in the city when they talk about me?'

'You must not listen to the mob,' Simon said firmly.

'But I have to. It is impossible to miss their jibes and insults,' the bishop said. He spoke as a man who was exhausted, shaking his head and looking down into his lap. 'It is not one man, you see, Simon. The whole of the city seems to hate me. I can feel it like poison seeping through the walls here: the whole population of London wishes me dead. If I could, I would wish I had never come here.'

'To London?'

'Yes. I believe I will die here. This killer, this Paul of Taunton, will kill me here. I am sure of it.'

Near Honfleur

Sir John Felton had excelled himself. As soon as the first ships had delivered their cargoes, he began to wonder whether to continue with the mission. Dithering, he demanded guarantees that the whole force might be deposited safely, else he must recall them and re-embark. It was only the determined arguing of Sir Nicholas de Cryel and Sir Robert de Kendale that made him agree to continue, and even then the two stood near as though to threaten him should he change his mind again.

Baldwin waited, fretting, while the ships lay idle, convinced that at any time he would see a force arrive to repel their little attack. Paul de Cockington, after witnessing the slaughter on the dunes, had grown mercifully silent, and Baldwin had managed to find the young lad, Jack, safe and sound. If he could, he would have brought the officer who had selected Jack, in preference to the boy himself. As it was, he had found him a pony so that he could remain at Baldwin's side.

By noon, it was clear that it would take the rest of the day and much of the next, to disgorge their men and matériel.

'Let me take men ahead,' Baldwin pleaded to Felton. 'I can provide a mobile defence in case the French come to attack again.'

Felton demurred. 'We need all the men we can at the bridgehead. What would you manage on your own? There is safety in numbers.'

Baldwin had caught a sympathetic look from Sir Nicholas, then he left them in disgust. Felton was going to turn the whole venture into a disaster, and many men could be killed as a result.

He was striding away, kicking at the sand in his fury, thinking of Jeanne and of how she might hear of his death, when he heard his name called. He stopped to find Sir Nicholas hurrying to catch up with him.

'Sir Baldwin, I would have a word with you.'

'Yes?'

'Could you ride on along the river, and see if you can reach Rouen? I will arrange for a separate covering force here while you do that. We need intelligence about the town and where the duke is before we can decide how best to catch him.'

'It is a matter of catching, you think?'

'What do *you* think? If the duke wanted to leave France, he could do so. I do not believe him to be held against his will. He's obeying his mother, damn the French whore! No, we'll have to take him by force, I think.'

'What of Felton?'

Sir Nicholas frowned. 'Leave him to me.'

'But he will deprecate my efforts,' Baldwin said.

'Sir John Felton is a retainer to Sir Hugh le Despenser. And I don't think Sir Hugh is particularly bothered about the duke's safety.'

Baldwin nodded. 'I will see to it that the duke is safe, Sir Nicholas. If I can reach him and bring him back, I will do so.'

'Good.'

Thus it was that Sir Baldwin de Furnshill set off that afternoon with a force of thirty men-at-arms, one boy mounted on a pony, and a rector, to find the heir to the crown of England.

Chapter Thirty-Three

Tower of London

When he heard someone calling him, Simon was at first surprised then confused. It was the voice of a man he knew all too well, but this was not his natural environment.

'Simon! It is inordinately good to see you. And Sir Baldwin with you?'

'Sir Peregrine! In God's name, I hadn't expected to find you here,' Simon said.

'Ah, but like a rotten apple I have a habit of appearing when you least expect me. You select the apple, you clean it, you open your mouth and sink your teeth inside, and as you chew, you see the half of the worm in the rotten hole in the middle, eh? That's how you look on me!'

'Not at all, Sir Peregrine,' Simon chuckled. 'It is always good to see you. And I hope I find you well this fine day?'

'I am better than well. I am in the peak of fitness, and I feel delighted to be here in the city again.'

'You do?' Simon was surprised. 'I thought you detested this place, calling it a cesspit and midden. You used to say that London was a reflection of the people who ruled, and you usually had a word or two to put in about Sir Hugh le Despenser.'

'Yes, but I have had a most fortunate experience since then. I have discovered a lady . . .'

'And this poor, misfortunate lady is the focus of your adoration?'

'I am afraid so.'

'She surely cannot like you?'

'Ah, well, on occasion she does. When we journeyed here, my

friend, she appeared to lose some affection for me, but when we arrived, I insisted that she come to the Tower as my guest, and gradually I have felt her warm to me. I hope . . . Perhaps given time, I may, um . . .'

Simon smiled and patted his shoulder. 'In that case, Sir Peregrine, may I buy you a pint of wine? If you are as fortunate as you clearly think, I can only wish you all the good luck in the world. The love of a good woman is a marvellous thing.'

'I think I am lucky. She has been struck with misfortune herself. She has been widowed twice, while I have lost my own loves, as you know. Perhaps we shall find comfort with each other.'

'I most certainly hope so,' Simon said, as he led the way to the bar. 'And what other news do you have?'

'Little that is good,' Sir Peregrine sighed. He waved to the bottler and ordered wine for them both, then continued, 'There are plenty of tales of a fleet forming across the Channel. Over a hundred ships, they say, and a great force of men to fill them.'

'Will the queen travel with them? Mortimer surely will be aboard to lead the attack, but will she?' Simon wondered.

'Mortimer is a strong man. He wouldn't leave behind his best bargaining counter. No, he will have her with him, as a figurehead and quencher of opposition. Few would dare to raise a hand against the mother of the next king. Nor the wife of the present one,' he added as an afterthought. 'Queen Isabella covers all those who may ally themselves with the king. She protects Mortimer from all.'

'What of the people when she lands, though? I have been Keeper of the Port, both at Dartmouth and at Portchester, so I know how many men a ship will carry. Even a hundred and fifty ships would only give them some one and a half thousand men, tightly packed. That cannot be enough to roll over the opposition.'

'You may be surprised at the opposition,' Sir Peregrine said sagely. 'You know how hated Despenser is in the country. How many will seriously raise a hand to defend him?'

'I suppose that's true,' Simon said doubtfully. It was an unpleasant thought, that only a tiny number would bother to try to defend the king, and yet he would not himself. Not because he had a lack of respect for his king, but because he had an overriding detestation for the Despenser. 'Is there any news from the south coast?'

'South? No news of any attacks, so far as I know,' Sir Peregrine said. 'It all appears to be concentrating about Hainault.'

'So, anyway,' Simon said. 'Tell me about your woman . . . ?'

*Friday before the Feast of the Nativity of the Blessed Virgin Mary**

London

Simon had managed to find the extra men he felt were needed, and had viewed them all with William's help. He had insisted upon questioning all of them at length, before telling them why they were needed. The process had taken much of the previous afternoon and evening. By the time he returned to his own chamber, Margaret, Perkin and Rob were already asleep, and he had sat up in front of his fire with a large cup of wine which Hugh had brought for him.

'How's the brat?' Simon had asked, nodding towards Rob.

'Argumentative little prickle,' was the gloomy response. 'He'll not make a servant while he's got a hole in his arse.'

'The only time I have seen him obey anyone was when Sir Richard de Welles met him.'

Hugh grunted. He was quiet a moment, then, 'I think the devil himself would obey if Sir Richard stood over him.'

'True enough,' Simon had chuckled.

The memory of Hugh's glum expression made him grin again now, as he walked about the yard outside the bishop's rooms. There was little enough to make him grin else. The men were all

* 5 September 1326

in their allotted places, and the bishop was safe indoors, but in the name of Christ, all it meant was that Simon was the gaoler of the bishop.

At lunchtime, he decided that he would have to get outside the castle to stretch his legs. He had a fancy for some fish, and thought he might surprise Margaret with it, so he arranged for William to take over for a little while, and walked out.

At different times in the last year he had come to London with Baldwin. It was big, rumbustious, garish, in a way that was thrilling and worrying at the same time. He had always felt moderately safe, but not today. He had only walked a few paces before he felt the mood of the city. He should have noticed it when he arrived with Meg, but somehow he hadn't – probably because they had travelled so far that day, and his thoughts were totally focused on reaching a warm fire and a bowl of food.

But here, on the streets, he couldn't miss it.

The lanes and roadways were thronging with people. It was the sort of city where a man could become lost in an instant. Men, women, horses, dogs – the press was so thick, Simon often had to shoulder his way through. Tranters and sellers of all types bellowed their wares, and Simon was almost knocked to the ground by a horse which came from behind him as he gaped at a collection of pies in one shopfront. As it was, the thing scraped an iron-shod hoof down the side of his leg, and he had to bite back a curse as he fell. Still, it could have been much worse.

'Arrogant arsehole!' one man roared, and bent to help Simon. 'Master? Are you all right? It's the pig-swyvers like that one who cause all the trouble here in the city. How can decent fellows live when morons like that ride about like fools and threaten to break your leg for you?'

Simon thanked him and stood. All around, there were others who had seen the incident, and Simon saw a man hawk and spit in the direction of the man on the horse, while a woman clenched her fist and shrieked imprecations after him. Simon glanced about him and was shocked by the angry mood of the crowd.

It was the same wherever he went. The whole city appeared to be on edge. Many blamed the king for all their woes, while more still spoke of Despenser. As for Bishop Walter, he was disparaged loudly and with venom. One man, who was quickly hushed, roared that the sooner the king's friends were dead, the happier the realm would be. There were many who harboured that sentiment, Simon included.

He hurried to the market at Billingesgate, bought some good white fish, then set off back to the Tower, listening intently to the conversations on all sides. His concern grew at every step.

This was a city preparing to overthrow its king.

Near Rouen, Normandy

Following a poor night's rest, Baldwin had his riders ready a little after dawn. For the most part they were young fellows with no experience of war. Three were squires, who had at least trained, but the rest were peasants who happened to be able to ride. So be it.

'Come, Jack,' he said to the boy, and helped him to his pony. 'Now, don't forget, if there is to be a fight, you must hold back with the packhorses. Don't try to join us – you'll be trampled in an instant. Better that you stay back with our goods so that we can know our food is safe.'

He had insisted on bringing supplies with them. It was conventional for a force like his to live from the land on a chevauchée, but Baldwin knew it would turn the locals against them, were they to rob a farm. Better by far to slip through unnoticed, ride quickly down to Rouen, take the duke if possible, and hurry back.

It was good country down here, too. The little farms looked prosperous, their fields good and green. The harvest was in, and Baldwin often saw the families about their work in the fields, looking after their animals or working on buildings, preparing them for winter. One little boy waved happily from his pasture where he was supposed to be watching a small flock of sheep. It was a perfect pastoral picture.

They were following the river. A poor track wound about the

northern bank, and although it was occasionally muddy and foul, it was better than trying to cut their way through the pastures and hedges that lay beyond. Baldwin urged them all to ever greater efforts, trying to preserve the strength of their mounts, but maintaining a steady pace as far as was possible.

He had guessed that their route would be at least fifty miles, but with the bends in the river, he was sure that they were going much further. Still, when they reached the late afternoon, off in the distance they could see a great yellowish haze, and he knew that this was their first view of the city.

Baldwin called Paul de Cockington forward.

'That, I think, is Rouen. We need to get to it tomorrow and find the duke. Tell me, what sort of lodging does he usually seek?'

'A lowly inn – so long as the food is good and they have plenty of wine,' Paul said sulkily. 'Why, did you expect him to lie in a brothel?'

Baldwin spoke kindly. 'If I hear you speak to me in such a manner again, rector, I will break your head and leave you here in the roadway as a message to all arrogant fools who think they can bandy words with a knight. Do you understand me?' And he smiled with a sweetness that was almost angelic.

The rector gulped, and it was clear that he found Baldwin's smile more terrifying than his earlier bellows. 'Yes.'

'Good. Then tell me: what sort of inn has he gone to in the past? Expensive, large – those with, as you point out, women? Does he go to the centre of the town or prefer the quieter outskirts? Does he invariably stay within the city walls, does he visit priories, or does he have no set tastes?'

'I do not know . . . But hold! There was mention of an inn near the cathedral itself. Sir Richard de Folville spoke of it. It was very close, only a few buildings to the west, I think he said.'

'Then we may hope to be fortunate,' Baldwin said. He sighed. 'Right, we will encamp here, and tomorrow I shall ride into the town with you, Paul. So we should all try to rest as best we may. The coming day will be one of danger for all of us.'

London

Simon had returned with his prize of good fish and asked Hugh to cook it for them all. It was quite delicious when Hugh presented it with a salad of mixed leaves and some good quality bread with which to soak up the juices.

For Simon, however, the evening had lost all lustre. His experiences in the street had heightened his sense of danger, and in the afternoon, when he wandered about the yard outside the bishop's hall, he spent much of his time looking about him as though expecting at any moment to see the populace clambering over the walls of the Tower to steal the crown and jewels, and slaughter all who lived inside.

If a fortress was supposedly impregnable to attack, it was also liable to be besieged – and in such situations, women and children were commonly evicted. Simon had heard all too many stories from Baldwin of sieges in which the weaker members of the community had been turfed out, only to find themselves blocked by the surrounding armies. Usually their fate was that of starvation, stuck between the warring sides.

Well, his Meg and Perkin wouldn't suffer that, he decided. No, in preference he would have them both taken to the river and given passage on a boat of some sort. They wouldn't have to travel far before they were outside the city, and thence could make their way to some place of safety . . . he hoped. It would be terrible to release them from the Tower only to learn later that they had been caught, or murdered, or . . .

The possibilities were endless. Meg was still a good-looking woman, and could be ravished in a moment, while Perkin was just an unwanted mouth to feed. He would be killed, thrown in the river. Both gone. It was unbearable.

It was growing dark by now, and he was still musing grimly on the dangers that surrounded them when William Walle came out from the hall.

'Have you heard the talk in the streets?' Simon asked.

'The mob? Ach, they are always belly-aching about something,' William said dismissively. 'There is no man in this city who isn't convinced that he knows better how to rule the nation than the king and his advisers.'

'There is a lot of discontent,' Simon said. 'You only have to walk in the streets for a little while to tell that.'

William shrugged. 'Yes, but what can people do? There is a king on the throne, and what he wishes is the law. That's all there is to it.'

'What of the stories of the queen returning with an army?'

William scoffed at that. 'The queen? How would she control a host of men? And could she buy enough to come here? I doubt it, because all her wealth has been sequestrated by the king. Her brother won't aid her, because it was the queen who showed the world that he was being cuckolded. His first wife still resides in gaol, a constant reminder to him of his dear sister's interference. No, Simon, I don't think you need worry about that. Besides, if she did try to invade, she would have to cope with the full might of the king's response. And how many men would wish to go to war to serve a woman, when they knew that their own king, God's anointed man, was against her? Not many. No, if she were foolish enough to try it, she would find that raising a force is one thing, but then persuading men to fight for a cause which all can see is doomed, is quite a different matter.'

Simon nodded. 'I see.'

'There's nothing to worry about here.'

That conversation had been an age ago. Sleepless, Simon had sat thinking in his chamber for so long that he could hear the guards wandering down to the buttery for a warming ale before returning to their duties.

Feeling restless, Simon rose and walked outside. It was a clear night, with the stars showing like a sprinkle of diamond-dust on a dark silken sheet. Quite beautiful. And although the moon was not full, it was bright enough to show him all the court after a few moments to acclimatise his eyes.

He walked to the door that led up to the bishop's chambers and tested it. With relief he found it would not yield when he pushed, and he returned to his own chamber feeling reassured.

But even as he pulled off his clothes and settled into the bed beside Margaret, he could not get to sleep. No matter what William said, Simon was convinced that the threat of invasion was real, and the risk of an uprising here in the capital, equally real. England felt like a tinder box. And Simon thought he could hear the flint being struck all about him.

Chapter Thirty-Four

*Saturday before the Feast of the Nativity of the Blessed Virgin Mary**

Near Rouen

Baldwin had the men roused and ready and mounted before the sun had fully shown herself. He was not going to be found napping if he could help it. He was hoping that such a small force would excite little comment. They had ridden fast enough, with luck, to avoid news of the English invasion having reached this far. There were no warning beacons lit on the higher hills that he had seen, such as would have been fired over in England if the French had attacked. No, with luck they would be able to reach the city, enter it, and make their way to the duke without being challenged.

Of the squires who were with his force, there was one whom he trusted more than the others. This man, who was called Ranulf Pestel, was plainly a good, strong fighter. Baldwin would take him into the city, along with Jack and Paul, while the others would remain hidden outside. There was no point in taking too many men. Better that the rest should stay concealed, and if Baldwin and Paul could persuade the duke to join them, all well and good.

Their journey was not eased by the antics of Paul, who wavered between bravado and cowering terror at the ordeal ahead. 'Why didn't you leave me with the others?' he tried one last time as they approached the gate to the city.

---

* 6 September 1326

'You are needed, rector. But if I hear any more whinings, you will return to England without a pardon, and I will personally deliver you to the Bishop of Exeter for him to do with you as he will,' Baldwin said. 'Now, shut up – because I do not wish for this boy to be made into a coward like you.'

'You have no idea how hard this is—' Paul began, but before Baldwin could reach over and grab him, he saw a sudden movement from Ranulf. He had a small switch in his hand, and Paul gave a yelp. He put a hand to his ear, and it came away with blood on it. 'You cut me, you bastard!' he cried in a voice that was a mongrel sound, mingling rage and panic.

'I'll use steel next time. Now *shut up*,' was the laconic reply.

Baldwin smiled to himself. He disliked having to use punishments, but then again he had a very low opinion of Paul de Cockington, and if a whip over his head could make him less of a threat to their mission, he was content.

The city of Rouen was one of those happy places in which the citizens had little fear of guests. Indeed, they seemed to welcome them, and Baldwin reflected that with the Feast of the Blessed Virgin Mary only two days away, the inhabitants were well used to the sight of pilgrims and other visitors. It was ideal for their purposes.

'Where is this inn?' he asked Paul.

'How should I know?' The man shrugged. 'All I heard was, it was close to the abbey.'

'Then we must try each one in turn,' Baldwin said, and led the way along the narrow streets towards the great church that lay at the centre of the town.

It took them much of the morning to learn precisely nothing. There was no sign of the duke, and Paul swore that there was no one he recognised anywhere from the duke's entourage.

'What about this one?' Baldwin demanded as the four stood just inside the doorway of a little inn.

'There must be other rooms in this place,' Ranulf said. 'Wait, Sir Baldwin, and I'll see if I can find them somewhere else.'

'Very well. We shall wait here.'

* * *

Richard de Folville had been glad to arrive here in Rouen because the constant wanderings were beginning to wear him down. Travel was all very well, but he was used to the comfort of a good bed, and the fact that they must all keep riding to remain safe struck him as nonsensical. There was little chance that they would be the target of an attack now, surely.

Here in the city, he felt the strain of the last months beginning to slough away. They had been here for three days of peace and relaxation, and while he had not managed to liberate any additional money from the duke, he thought that he might be able to before long. The boy had let slip that he was running low on funds, and it was possible that he might need to go to a bank. His mother had funds which had been advanced, and the duke was sure that he would soon be able to acquire some.

Life was so easy for a fellow like him. Born the son of a king, he would never know hardship or the struggle that most people had to endure. It made Richard intensely, furiously jealous. He wanted a little of that good fortune. If it wasn't for Despenser advancing his own friends over the heads of those more deserving, like the Folvilles, Richard would still be in his little church at Teigh, with his brother still ensuring that his annual stipend was good, praying and keeping the peasants happy. That was where he ought to be now, and it was only the likes of Despenser who had forced him out of his own country. The king, Despenser, the Bishop of Exeter – they were all cut from the same cloth. They took, and could declare it legal purely because they had power.

Well, Richard would tolerate it no longer. He and his family deserved better. They would take what they wanted.

Perhaps he was better served to remain with the duke. The boy did at least look after them all well. He was no penny-pincher, that was true.

Richard de Folville had been out to the privy at the end of the little garden, and he straightened his hosen and chemise as he strolled back. Pulling his hat onto his head – a broad-brimmed felt hat which he had bought on the first day here in Rouen as a defence against the hot sun – he suddenly saw a man peering out from a ground-floor window.

It made his blood freeze like ice. Curious sensation. Here he was, a man who had killed before, and yet his overriding sense was of fear at the sight of this man, this symbol of power and terror.

He swaggered onwards, without looking again at the man. What was his name? *Pestel*, that was it. Squire Ranulf, he had said, and he had mentioned that he was a loyal servant of Belers. That must be why he was here: he had somehow learned that Richard had been involved in the murder of his master, and wanted revenge. He'd said as much. If he heard that there was a cleric involved . . . But Richard wasn't dressed as a rector now. He was a well-dressed Frenchman.

With that thought, he had a plan.

It was gloomy in the hall where Baldwin and the others waited, so as he left it and walked into the garden, Squire Ranulf was blinded for a moment. It was enough for him to see that there was only a single man there, wandering about idly among the herbs and flowers.

He spotted a long, low building though, and thought it would be an ideal hiding-place for the duke. Stepping forward, he peeped in through a window.

It was dark inside there too, but then he gradually began to make out voices – and one, he felt sure, was English. These were no Frenchmen, he could tell.

He drew back, a grin on his face. It had to be the duke and his entourage. Sir Baldwin would be able to come and persuade the fellow to return with them, he was sure. And then a man punched him in the back, and he gave a cry of surprise. Turning, he saw a man – the Frenchman – behind him, a knife in his hand. And suddenly Ranulf knew that he had been stabbed. It was not fatal though – he was sure of that. He grabbed for his own knife, but before he could draw it, the man was on him again. This time, the fellow took Ranulf's hand and gripped it, while the knife was thrust under his armpit, a solid blow that Ranulf felt through the whole of his breast.

There was a flowing sensation, and a weakness in his arms. He could only feel a great bruise at his side, no pain, and he was sure that he had been lucky, that the blow had missed all his organs, and he still made to yank his own knife free, but his assailant had his hand grasped too firmly, and try as he might, he couldn't release it.

'French git,' he gasped.

'Me – French? Oho, squire, if you can't remember a face, you shouldn't make such rash threats. I am Richard de Folville. You said you'd come back and hunt me, didn't you? I think I beat you to it!'

Ranulf stared. The name of Folville was known to him well enough. They were outlaws, murderers . . . but he couldn't hold on to his thoughts. There was a strange exhaustion washing over him, and he could no longer support his own weight. He had to drop to one knee. Ranulf slipped down, and then he toppled to his side, and he continued to stare at Folville fixedly as the life ebbed out of him.

A man's eyes would hold the last sight he saw, so Folville had heard. He didn't want some clever official peering into Ranulf Pestel's eyes and seeing himself gazing back. No. So he took his knife and made sure that no one would be able to read anything in Ranulf's eyes ever again.

Ralph la Zouche heard the scuffle outside, and by the time the door was opened, his sword was already out, but then he saw it was the Folville man dragging a body into the chamber. He stood, panting.

'My lord duke, this man was in there asking about you. I think there are friends of his nearby. We have to escape.'

The duke gaped from Folville to the body. 'Who is he?'

'A retainer of one of Despenser's men. I have killed him. I knew him before – his name was Squire Ranulf Pestel.'

The duke looked at Ralph. 'Have *you* heard of him?'

'The name is familiar, yes. He was one of Belers men, I think. If Richard de Folville has killed him, he has done us a service,' Ralph said, 'but you should have brought him in here alive so we all could have questioned him.' He turned to the duke. 'My lord, I think Richard is right – there will be others. I recommend that we mount and leave immediately.'

'But I wanted to see the grave of King Richard on the Holy Mother's Feast Day,' the duke objected.

'You can return another time. For now, I advise that we should ride straight to Hainault.'

'Very well,' the young man sighed. 'Have the horses prepared. We shall ride as soon as they are ready.'

Baldwin was becoming concerned at the length of time Ranulf was taking. 'If he doesn't hurry, we'll not have time to look into any other inns,' he muttered. He waited a little longer, and then gave a swift curse. 'Paul, you stay here with Jack, and I shall go to see if I can find him. We cannot stand here all day.'

So saying, he walked out of the small hall and into the garden. At that moment, the sound of shouting and commands reached his ears, coming from an outbuilding.

Quickly crossing the yard, he reached the door to the building, and pushed it wide.

'Another!'

He heard the shout and instantly threw himself sideways in case an arrow came hurtling towards him. There was none, but he could hear booted feet approaching, and then a sword appeared. Baldwin grasped the wrist and wrenched. The man let go of his sword as his arm was jerked towards Baldwin, across his body, and Baldwin picked it up in a flash. A second man came out, and now Baldwin knew he must have come to the correct place.

'Hold!' he shouted. 'I am come to speak with the duke!'

The second fellow was a swarthy man-at-arms with black hair and bright blue eyes. He had his sword held like a professional, his left hand at his groin, ready to pat away Baldwin's. His sword was held low, the blade angled up from his hand, protecting most of his body. Baldwin was sure that he would be competent, but it was not the best defence; he held his own in the *true Guardant*, with his fist above his head, the blade dropping down and towards his enemy.

His main concern right now was the first man, who had massaged his wrist, and now looked ready to grab a stone and brain Baldwin. He would have to be held and prevented. This second man was—

A sparkle of the sun on steel and the blade leaped forward. Baldwin blocked it with his own, continuing to stab downwards at the man's thigh, but he saw the danger and stepped back. Instantly Baldwin was a step nearer, his blade darting right in a feint, then left towards the man's breast. The blue eyes narrowed as he slammed his fist across, then reversed his blade and slashed at Baldwin's throat. Baldwin ducked, knocked his opponent's sword up and away, and launched himself forwards and up, his blade coming to rest upon his Adam's apple. 'Yield!' he snarled.

'Stop! I order you as you are an Englishman!'

Baldwin kept his sword at the man's throat, holding his gaze. 'Drop the sword, friend.'

'Hurt me, and you'll answer to the Duke of Chester.'

'*You* will answer to no one if you don't drop your sword!'

There was a brief narrowing of his eyes again, as though he was assessing the true risk, and then his sword clattered on the ground.

Baldwin took it up and stepped away, glancing around to make sure that the first man through the door was not right behind him to hit him, and then turned to the duke and offered the two swords to him, bowing and kneeling. 'Your Highness, I am sorry for this unseemly fracas.'

'So, good Sir Baldwin! And how do I find you here? You aren't with the men sent to kill me, are you?'

'If I were, I would die fighting in your defence, my lord,' Baldwin said, looking up and meeting the duke's eyes. 'I am here to try to persuade you to return to England, to your father, who dotes on you and misses you. He instructed me to tell you that your offences to him will be forgotten.'

'My offences, eh?'

'He said that you swore you would only pay homage to the French king and return immediately. Instead you have remained here for nigh a year.'

'Yes, well, it was difficult.'

'The life of a king's son is always difficult.'

'There are men who would see me dead.'

'Who?' Baldwin demanded.

About him now there were seven men, with the duke before him. His opponent with the blue eyes bowed, saying, 'I found one of them out here only a short while ago. A man called Ranulf Pestel. He was a devoted follower of Despenser, and said he was here to kill the duke. I know him because he was the servant of the foul Belers. Do you know him?'

Baldwin looked at him. 'I am Sir Baldwin de Furnshill, friend. And you are?'

'I am Richard de Folville.'

'Then, Master Richard, I know Squire Pestel, but I knew nothing of his loyalty to Despenser. If I had heard that he was loyal to that man and not the king, I would not have brought him with me. My lord, you know me. I guarded you all the way from the coast to Paris last year. I am no thief or liar. Nor murderer.'

'I know that. I do trust you, Sir Baldwin. I am grateful that you came here. But I think I will stay with this honour guard.'

'My lord, there is a force on its way here to find you and guard you. Sixteen hundred men under Sir John Felton. Will you not come with me so that we can protect you?'

'Sweet Jesus!' Folville said. 'John Felton? My lord duke, we must leave immediately. Felton is another of Despenser's retainers.'

'Is this true, Sir Baldwin?' the duke asked.

'In all honesty, my lord, I do not know,' Baldwin admitted. 'But I can vouch for the men in the host. I was a Commissioner of Array for them, and they were picked for their strength and merit, not their allegiance to Despenser.'

'No. I will not return with you. I trust you, Sir Baldwin, but two of my men here knew Pestel and say that he was devoted to Despenser. Now I learn that your leader is Despenser's as well. Am I to trust you and your companions, when you did not know the provence of Pestel? No. I must remain here.'

Baldwin tried to plead, but the duke ignored him. He handed the swords to their owners, Folville taking his with a sly leer at Baldwin, as though considering running him through, but then he slammed it back into his scabbard, turned and left.

The second man weighed his sword in his hand as the other men left the yard. Another stood behind him, thumbs in his belt, watching Baldwin with caution.

'Sir,' Baldwin said. 'I do not know your name.'

'John Biset,' said the man at the wall.

'I have heard of you, Master Biset. I am a friend of the Bishop of Exeter.'

Both men eyed him warily on hearing that.

'He thought you were trying to kill him.'

'Hardly unreasonable. He sent two men to murder me, after all. I had to send him a token.'

'Why are you here?'

'In March I heard that Despenser or the bishop had sent more men to find me and kill me. Would you have stayed?'

Baldwin shook his head with a little grin. 'What of you, sir?' he said to the nearer.

'I? I am Sir Roger Crok.'

Baldwin recalled the name, but it was a moment or two before he placed it. 'You are? Then I am glad.'

Roger Crok eyed him with an amused air. 'Really? You are easily pleased, Sir Baldwin.'

'It is a long story. How did you two come to ride together?'

'There are many Englishmen with grudges against Sir Hugh le Despenser who are living in France. And we tend to keep together. Is it surprising?'

Baldwin chuckled. 'No. Sir Roger, guard him well. The duke is a good, honourable young man. We cannot afford to lose him.'

'I will try!' Crok grinned.

He bowed to Baldwin, slipped his sword in the scabbard and strode back into the hall. Biset backed away and into the darkness. A few moments later, Baldwin heard the loud thundering of hoofs on the roadway outside. They clattered away, up towards the cathedral, and then turned north and east. Away from Baldwin and his men; away from Felton and his.

Chapter Thirty-Five

*Sunday, Vigil of the Feast of the Blessed Virgin Mary**

Near Honfleur

The smell was familiar to Baldwin from miles away. It was the stench of burning wood, burning wool, burning thatch. Over the roadway ahead, it rose like a column from hell. Yellowish, grey and repellent, it befouled the sky and the earth beneath.

Jack was anxious at the sight. 'What is that?'

'It isn't proof that the French have attacked, not yet,' Baldwin said. He was calculating furiously. 'If the French had been told as soon as they saw us land, that was three days ago. It would have taken a fast rider at least a day to reach help with multiple changes of horse. From there, a day to scour the land for volunteers, and a day or two to ride back. No, better make it three minimum. Probably no possibility of a force to throw us into the sea before tomorrow at the earliest.'

'I'm glad you're so sure,' Paul said sourly. 'Personally, I wouldn't have too much faith in your judgement, not after the last days. You sent Ranulf into that den of thieves and felons and got him killed, and now you're guessing when the French could mobilise? I think they're likely already there, and cutting us off from the others. We'll never escape. We should have stayed with the duke, rather than come all the way back here.'

'Shut up, fool!' Baldwin snapped. 'You argue from pessimism. I am arguing from knowledge. I may not know exactly how many

---

* 7 September 1326

men the French may be able to gather from about here, but it is quite certain that there are not enough peasants to put into the field against so many warriors and sailors.'

He spoke sharply from the anxiety that tore at him. They had been forced to ride pell-mell from the inn where the duke had stayed, leaving Ranulf behind under some old horse blankets, and Baldwin hoped only to escape immediate capture. As soon as he returned to the men waiting outside the city, he was moderately comfortable that they would be safe from arrest for murder, but now there was the mad ride back from Rouen to reunite with the others.

His mood was not helped by the reflection that the duke may have been quite right to suspect the leader of the expedition. Who was Sir John Felton, after all? Baldwin had never met him, nor heard of him before. There were not so many knights in England that one would not have heard of another. In total there were only some two thousand all told, so the idea that a man should be unknown suggested that he might only recently have been elevated to the knighthood. And if it was true that he was an ally of Despenser, that put the whole mission into a completely different light.

But they would soon learn the truth. For now, Baldwin could only feel his anger beginning to rise, along with a deepening sense of alarm. So far, they had not found any people on the roadway, and that in itself was ominous. Usually he would expect the local peasants to pack all they could, and make off into the woods to escape the men riding hither and thither. If there were none, it could mean that all had escaped, or more likely that they were dead.

His worst fears were soon realised.

Jack saw them first. A small group lying in the ditch beside the road, a man and woman, and children. There was a baby with her head crushed, as though knocked against a tree, while the woman had plainly been raped. The men had not bothered to cover her body afterwards. Nearby the man lay slumped with blood black and thick running from his throat.

'Ride on, Jack,' Baldwin said urgently, but the boy sat still, gaping at the sight. Baldwin had to take his arm, and bring him back to the present. 'Ride on, boy. There's nothing we can do for them,' he said, and the party rode on again. Baldwin could hear one of his men weeping, and another two were forced to dismount and run to the hedge to throw up.

Baldwin himself had seen similar hideous scenes when he was much younger, when he had fought in the last days at Acre, and the sight of the dead had not held any horror for him since. However, they were apt to instil a boiling rage in him. To think that Englishmen could do such things was appalling. He had expected it of the Moors in the Holy Land, because that was a religious crusade against the heathens. Except he had soon learned that the religious beliefs of the Moors were not so different from those of the Christians who were invading. And he had also learned that the Christians could be more barbaric than the Moors. Yes, he had seen such horrors before, and all too often they were committed by the English.

The land about here was showing the violence of war. As they approached the coast, all the little farms and hamlets which he had scarcely noticed in the peace of three days ago, were burning or burned. The smoke rose, and there was a fine snowy shower at one point as the ash from one farm began to fall about them. Baldwin rode on in silence now, thinking of different times, thinking of the men he had known, the villages they had attacked and burned. And he could not help but compare these little vills with his own manor. How swiftly would his home at Furnshill go up in flames! How quickly would it be destroyed, with his wife and children inside!

It was not a thought to be borne. And it tore at him as he rode. In his mind's eye he could see Furnshill with the flames roaring from the roof and windows, hear the screams of the animals, see his wife's body, perhaps, lying in a ditch, just as that poor woman had been.

They did not see Felton when they approached the shore. A couple of drunk sailors were roaring and singing in the roadway, arms about each other's shoulders, and as Baldwin rode nearer, one of them fumbled for his heavy sword, but seemed incapable of drawing it, which led to gales of laughter from the pair of them. A gust of wind brought the stench of death to Baldwin's nostrils, and he saw some bodies dangling from a tree's branch in the next field. Three young peasants. All male.

These people had been happy three days ago. He had ridden past them in their fields, and they were merely contented farmers who had brought in their harvests. And now, because of a foolish escapade trying to bring home the king's son, they had all been killed. He looked down at Jack, who was still staring stupidly at the swinging bodies, and wondered what had happened to the little lad who had been watching his sheep when they rode to Rouen.

The reflection spurred his anger, and he rode through the two laughing sailors to the beach itself, searching for someone in control.

It was fortunate that the first man he met was a grim-faced Nicholas de Cryel. Before Baldwin could speak, Sir Nicholas hurried to him. 'Thank God you have returned safely, Sir Baldwin. Matters here are going from bad to worse. Felton is a fool – he should never have been given command. He's set the sailors and men loose to pillage and kill everything. What the hell he's up to, is anybody's guess, but so far as I'm concerned, I am heartily sick of the whole affair. I believe we have one more day of safety, and then the French will fall on us like wolves. After all the wilful violence done to the local folk, they will be within their rights to slaughter us out of hand.'

'Where is Felton?'

'On his ship,' Sir Nicholas said, jerking a thumb over his shoulder. 'Drunk, I daresay. He spends most of his days with a bottle near to hand now.'

'Then we shall give the order to re-embark. The duke refused to come with us, so our cause here is lost,' Baldwin said.

'So all this was for nothing,' Sir Nicholas said, gazing about him with his lip curled. 'If I had the authority, I would get

Felton out here now and string him up from the highest tree in the area.'

The weather began to change later in the afternoon, and the lengthy process of getting all the men and horses back on board was made more hazardous by heavy rain. The decking grew slippery, and the sailors brought buckets of sand to hurl over the timbers to make it safe underfoot. With sailors hauling on their ropes, some ships were slowly drawn further away from the shore while others approached. It was no easy task, for the ships which were nearest the shore had to take care not to overload themselves, in case they remained beached as the tide came in. Those which were out to sea must run in, and stay in the shallows while men clambered up the ladders and ropes, and the horses were led into the waters, complaining bitterly. One lashing out in fright managed to hit a man's skull, and it burst open like a bladder filled with water. Baldwin saw the fellow's eyes roll up into his head, and he slid under the water without a word, the only sign to show that he had been there, the crimson flower of blood that bloomed under the water.

It was madness. The sailors were all disgruntled and most more than half-drunk. The warriors were all angry at being called back when they were sure that there were more easy pickings to be had. Most had managed to steal a barrel or two of cider or ale, while some had found a store of coin, so Baldwin had heard. When he asked about it, there were only two men who had the cache, and he wondered if there had been more, but these two had killed the others. It was more than possible. Law and order had collapsed here by the sea.

Then the French arrived.

The first warning was a shriek so high and appalling it could have come from a soul in torment. Baldwin was at the side of the ship supervising his mount as it was lifted high in a sling, ready to be installed in the hold with the other horses. Turning, he saw the glitter of swords and lances, and realised their danger. ' 'Ware! Knights!' he cried, and began to run back up the shore to the further pickets. Jack began to run with him, but he curtly ordered the boy back to the ships. This was no place for a lad of his age.

With his sword drawn, he stood in the shallows, pointing to the different ships. He bellowed for Sir Nicholas to arrange bowmen at the front castles of the cogs, and prayed that they weren't so drunk that they would kill him and the last of the men. Then he crossed himself quickly, uttered a short prayer, and waited, his sword gripped in both hands.

The first shock of the French was witheringly powerful. Their horses pounded on down the slope, their lances couched, and in an instant forty men were stabbed with the heavy ash poles. The man right next to Baldwin suddenly gave a hiccup and gurgle as the lance punctured his jack just above his belly, and he was thrust back, hacking with all his might at the timber skewering him, his eyes wide with terror, like a horse in a fire. Baldwin would have helped him, but already another man-at-arms was riding towards him, and he saw the lance aiming for his face. He crouched low, spun and beat at the lance with his sword, knocking it past his shoulder, and continued the spin, his sword now whirling with him, to slash into the horse's shoulder. There was a spray of blood, and then a jarring shock in his arm as the blade caught the animal's shoulderbone and stuck. Baldwin had to release his bright, peacock-blue sword before his arm was snatched away, and saw the horse rearing in agony, the blade projecting, while a long flap of skin waved, splattering blood in all directions.

The horse rose, legs flailing, and then crashed down, his rider beneath him. Baldwin could not approach the beast, for in its terror and pain it was thrashing about like a wild thing, but he needed a weapon. The man beside him was dead, floating in the waves, the lance badly damaged, and Baldwin fell to the water beside him, fumbling for his sword. The fellow must have dropped it here . . . Yes! He stood, in time to see the French first line wheel and ride away, ready to re-form.

There was a mass of bodies in the water. Baldwin glanced

down, and saw three men in front of him, bobbing gently in a sea of blood. It made his head spin, and he gripped his sword with the resolution of desperation. 'Hold the line, men! Hold up! Hold up!' he bellowed. And then the French came again, rattling and ringing with the weight of their armour, the horses magnificent in their bright caparisons, the men stern and determined inside their steel shells. It made Baldwin feel undressed without his armour, but it was all packed. All he might do was pray that he was that little bit faster on his feet without it.

The man riding towards him was young, his face was unmarked by wrinkles, his eyes clear and bright like a child's – but he wielded his lance like a man many years older. Its tip lowered as Baldwin crouched, and then it was thrusting towards him like a crossbow bolt. Baldwin saw how the man aimed it, and he waited until the last moment, and then threw himself to the side of the horse, aiming his sword at the beast's fetlock as it came closer. There was a jarring in his arms, and then an explosion of blood that burst about him like a fountain, and he was dying, drowning in other men's blood, salt and revolting in his mouth and nose, and he tried to reach up to the sky to free himself from this hideous bath, but his hands touched only sand, and then a face, and he tried to jerk himself from it, and found he was free, in the open air again.

Wiping the water and blood from his face, he looked about him, gasping and coughing. His opponent was nearby, on his feet, fighting with two Englishmen, and Baldwin tried to walk to them, but his knees wouldn't support his weight, and suddenly a crashing thud smote his head, and he fell back, arms outspread, and felt the black evil water filling his nose again, and saw with eyes that stung, that the sea was over his face, and that he was falling down, deeper and deeper into the waters. Falling all the way down to hell.

*Wednesday after the Feast of the Nativity of the Blessed Virgin Mary**

Tower of London

There was a hushed expectancy in the city from the first week of September, which was noticeable even to Hugh and Rob. They were both very quiet and watchful, Simon noted.

Margaret was struck with it too, and a few times Simon caught her looking at the pair of them from the corner of her eye. It was a great shame, because he had wanted her to relax and enjoy her time here in London.

Margaret had been a farmer's daughter when Simon met her, and he had hoped that she would find her stay here in the capital to be interesting. There was certainly much that was new for her, and much that would astonish, but to his sorrow, she wanted nothing to do with the city. 'There is something about this place,' she said, looking about her at the Tower itself. 'I feel so uncomfortable here. I hate it.'

'It's only a castle, Meg,' he said, trying to comfort her. 'It's a citadel to protect London.'

'No, Simon. It's here to scare London. It's here to threaten. Can't you feel it?' She shivered. 'It's like a monster in the middle of the city,' she said. 'And nothing good can come of us being here.'

'For so long as the bishop is safe because we watch over him, that is itself good,' Simon said.

'How long must we remain? Until we capture this man? What if he is not here, Simon?' she asked with quiet desperation.

'I have to remain for as long as it may take,' he told her.

It was while they were walking hand-in-hand, neither speaking, that they heard the voices outside, obviously spreading some important news. Simon felt his heart lurch, convinced that there was some kind of attack forming. He told Margaret to hurry

* 10 September 1326

to their children, and command Hugh to take up his staff, and then ran as fast as he could to the main gate.

'Ah, Simon. I thought you would be along shortly,' Sir Peregrine said.

'I heard the noise,' Simon said.

'Yes, curious, eh? It was the folks out there repeating the news they'd just heard. Something about a fleet.'

Simon swore. 'The invasion fleet?'

'I don't know,' Sir Peregrine said. He bellowed down to the men at the gate itself. 'What news?'

'The fleet has been sorely harmed,' the keeper called up.

Simon and Sir Peregrine glanced at each other. Neither had any cause to wish the rule of King Edward II and his most precious friend, Despenser, might continue, and yet as Englishmen, they were not keen to see the realm overrun with foreign mercenaries. Simon was aware of a curious sense of mingled anti-climax and relief. 'So that is that, then,' he said.

'So it seems,' Sir Peregrine nodded. They were about to walk away, when some stray words came to the coroner's ear. 'What was that?' he demanded, turning his head, the better to listen.

There was a man outside on the drawbridge. He had some messages which he had given to the porter, and now he was shouting and shrugging his shoulders, while others on the bridge itself were gesticulating and shouting too.

'What is it, Porter?' Sir Peregrine bellowed again.

'The ships, sir. They weren't the French ships,' the porter called up to him, his face suddenly drained. 'They were ours.'

English Channel

Baldwin came to with a feeling of filthiness all about his body. It was as though he had been thrown into a midden filled with sewerage, and as he felt the light on his face and began to swim up from unconsciousness, he knew that he must cleanse himself. He was struggling to do so when he felt himself restrained.

To his surprise, he felt as weak as a newborn foal. His arms and legs were so feeble, he could not even think of fighting off his attacker, and it was shame that made him suddenly give a sob as he realised he was entirely at the mercy of whoever was here. And then he jerked his eyes open as he remembered the last moments as he fell under the bloody froth that was the seashore. He was in hell!

The first thing his eyes perceived was not a demon, but the boy called Jack, who stood over him with an anxious expression on his face. 'Sir Baldwin? Are you all right, sir? I have some wine, if you'd like it.'

Baldwin took a gasp of air, and looked about him. He was in a wooden cot on the deck of a cog. About him were other men, some with hideous wounds, and there was a sobbing and a moaning all over the vessel. With slow care he lifted his hands to view. There was no blood left. Someone had washed his hands and body.

'Aye. Couldn't leave you looking like that, could we?' Paul said from beyond Jack.

Baldwin said nothing. He was quite sure that if Paul had seen the opportunity, he would have strangled Baldwin while he was asleep.

'What happened?' he asked hoarsely.

Paul answered. 'You were knocked down, and this young fool leaped off the side of the ship to pull you from the water. It half killed him, poor twit, but he dragged you to where there was a grappling hook hanging from a rope, and he managed to persuade two sailors to haul you aboard. You're lucky. If you'd stayed down there, you'd have been mangled along with the rest.'

'Ach!' Baldwin felt waves of nausea wash through his entire body, and grimaced. 'Did we lose many?'

'Too many to count. The French just pounded straight into the line, and with the sea behind us, what could we do? I reckon we lost over a hundred. And then their navy came across us this morning. We've lost three more ships. We only just made it away ourselves, with the help of some pretty effective arrow-work from the men on the castles.'

He had recovered his jauntiness, Baldwin saw. It did not make his company more desirable. 'Where are we now?'

'We'll be back to the Downs this morning. Then we can leave this old bucket of rotten wood and worms, and get back to solid ground again. And I for one will not regret it if I never see a ship again.'

He stood and peered down at Baldwin. 'See you later, Sir Knight!'

Jack remained. 'You'll be all right, Sir Baldwin. You just had a knock on the head. A destrier rode past you, and I think his hoof whacked you on the skull. You fell like a log!'

'And I owe you my life, Jack. I think that is a debt which will be hard to repay,' Baldwin said.

'I couldn't leave you there. Paul helped nearly as much. He threatened the two sailors to get you lifted up to the ship.'

'He did?' Baldwin said with surprise. He would not have expected that. A spasm jerked his torso, and he felt the bile in his throat, searing him.

'Sir, drink this,' Jack said, holding up a cup of wine. While the ship rocked, Baldwin tried to drink, but much of the wine dribbled down his beard.

'Thank you, Jack,' he said, and closed his eyes.

He was asleep in an instant.

Chapter Thirty-Six

Tower of London

The chamber in the building where Lady Isabella Fitzwilliam was installed was pleasant and airy, but she would have preferred to be back home at her old manor. Not that it was possible, with that thief Bishop Walter having stolen it. He was a man so sunk in infamy, the devil himself would have rejected him.

To learn as soon as she arrived in London that Sir Peregrine would not allow her to stay outside in the city, but instead insisted for her protection that she take a room here in the fortress had at first been delightful – but then she realised the danger. She was determined to put in place the last stage of her plan, but to do so, she must have the help of her son.

The damned bishop's presence had itself been a shock. She had had no warning that he might be coming here, and now he was installed only a short distance from her own chamber. The possibility of repaying her debt herself at any moment was now within her grasp, and yet the risk inherent in that was high. Were she to kill the bishop in full view of anyone else, she must inevitably be killed in her turn. A terrifying thought.

Still, were she to kill the man, it would mean that her boys would not do so. And she loved them both more than she loved herself. How could she not! To the one she had given life, and to the other she had given herself. They were both hers, and she was theirs.

Even now she found it hard to believe that it had been so simple a task, to install a man in the bishop's palace and to distribute messages of death.

It was always the idea that he should suffer for a long period.

At first when she had been considering the means of making his life so miserable that he would almost welcome death, she had thought that she would simply string it all out until he was entirely depressed and half-mad with fear. But it was her son who had persuaded her that there was no logic to treating him in such a manner. If he was to deliver her notes, he wanted to know that there was a set term for them. As he pointed out, she only had to think of the words, while he had to not only run the risk of delivering them, but must also plan to kill the man as well. And he must somehow prevent himself from smiting his father's murderer every day.

He was so strong, so clever. She missed him so much. He had been going to come here to London, she was sure, but she had seen and heard nothing from him.

The whole idea had been his. He had such a fertile brain! Isabella wanted originally to just slash at the bishop's throat when the chance offered itself, but it was he who had come up with the idea of making the bishop suffer for the same period as poor Henry had. Henry Fitzwilliam had been arrested and forced to languish in that hideous dungeon for thirty-nine weeks. They didn't tell her exactly when he died. To think of it! So long a time, and all the while not knowing whether he might be released to freedom and prosperity once more, or led out to be hanged before a mob of baying churls. Poor, darling Henry, to have lain in that tiny, noisome, wet chamber all that time. It had been winter when he finally expired. She thought it was the cold which had done it, but it was hard to be sure. There were so many natural causes of death in gaol: the cold, starvation, fever, thirst – all could be listed as 'natural death' in the coroner's court.

How long now? She had sent the first note at the beginning of the year, but it had reached the bishop on the second Monday before Candlemass. That meant it was already thirty-four weeks since the first note had arrived. She only had another five weeks to worry about. And then, ideally on the Wednesday, the anniversary of the delivery of the first note, she could kill him. Thus would poor Henry be avenged.

Henry would be proud of her, to see how she had planned this and managed to get matters to the stage where she could soon end the rule of the bishop. She only prayed that she would be able to strike the blow. Five weeks. It was not a very long time. She had only that long in order to plan his murder. And it would have to be a perfect murder. She did not want to die in the process of avenging her poor husbands.

It would be hard. She would have to try to penetrate his chamber while he was there more or less undefended. He had guards at all hours though, so that would be problematic. She might be able to poison him, but that was too hit-or-miss. Better to do it with a knife, as she had originally planned. But how? In the chamber would be best, but not while he was praying or at some other form of religious duty.

That was her greatest fear, that she could be consigning herself to hell for all time by killing a bishop, but the crimes of which he and other clerics were guilty were so clear and undeniable that the offence she might give would surely be lessened. His theft of her dower must itself be powerful in mitigation – if there were such a thing as mitigation in the eyes of God.

There had only ever been one other bishop murdered, of course. Saint Thomas Becket. He was one of those rare beings, a truly pious man, slain by the king of the time. His killers were punished, but in this case, removing a man who was so hated and feared throughout the realm, she must be looked upon with more favour.

She was considering this when she caught sight of Sir Peregrine and the man Simon Puttock. They were deep in conversation, and did not appear to notice her. It was good that she could approach them, listening intently.

Puttock was speaking: 'In the meantime, we have to maintain the guards on the bishop's chamber.'

'Yes. For all it's worth.'

'Sir Peregrine, don't you think we can protect him?'

'I doubt whether the rogue who sent those notes has the faintest intention of fulfilling the prediction. Look, the man started sending the notes back in January, from what John tells me. They've been coming sporadically ever since. There were some in Exeter, and the churl who delivered them was discovered and disappeared. Then he tried his luck again at Canterbury. But to do it again here, in London? How could anyone think to press through the guards here at the Tower to kill him?'

'In Exeter it was a task made easy by the laxity of the guards involved. And the bishop himself, I suppose.'

'Because neither thought to question the stranger in their midst. All assumed that because he was there, he should have been there.'

Simon nodded. 'He could try the same strategy here.'

'He could – but only if he wants to end up with more holes in him than a target on the archery field. Besides, I think the aim of the notes was clear.'

'You do? And what was it, then?'

'To scare the man. It was revenge for some misdeed, or perhaps the plot of a twisted mind. There are some who consider that torture is an entertainment.'

'True enough. So what should we do?'

'Maintain the guard, hope to catch this vile creature, and pray that he's already gone away. Give it a matter of three or four weeks, and I'd think the danger would be past.'

'To be replaced by the dangers we spoke of earlier.' Simon's tone was heavy.

'Aye. Right enough. Invasion and war.'

'If your lady were here and unprotected, she would have a terrible time.'

'I would lay down my life for her, to protect her!'

Simon chuckled. 'If you feel like that about the Lady Isabella, you should tell her.'

'I could not tolerate her rejection.'

'Sir Peregrine, think of it from her side. She will be fearful of invasion, just as all people are. But for her, she has no champion to defend her or her lands. In circumstances like these, you ought to strike while you may. Unless, of course, you are uncertain as to your feelings . . .'

'I have no doubt about my feelings for her – and I believe she feels similarly towards me. She does not look on me with contempt, I think.'

'Then tell her. You aren't children, either of you. You ought to ask her what she feels, and if she could tolerate your company, perhaps a marriage would be possible.'

'Aye, perhaps,' the knight said doubtfully.

Isabella moved into shadows before they could see her listening. There was a little smile pulling at her mouth, and an unaccustomed warmth in her lower belly, a kind of tingling anticipation, and as soon as she noted it for herself, she sternly rebuked herself. She had known for quite some time that the good Sir Peregrine was fond of her. There was nothing new in this, nothing at all. And it couldn't change anything. How could it, when her whole life's course was set already? No. It mattered not at all. And yet there was a thrill in her blood that no amount of reason could dispel.

Exeter

Peter watched her covertly from the table as his wife stood up, hesitated, and then moved slowly over the floor.

If he'd had to guess, he'd have said she was at least thirty. She looked ancient, the way she moved. Nothing seemed to stir her from this torpor.

At first he'd listened to his father, when the old man said that a woman was like a dog or a walnut tree – all needed to be birched every so often. But his father didn't believe it himself – Peter knew that. The old twit wouldn't dream of lifting a hand to Peter's mother. And nor Peter would hurt Edith.

It would be like kicking a baby, the state she was in. She didn't need a slap to waken her; she needed something else, but Peter wasn't sure what.

That day, he decided, he would take her into the city. See if something at the market could tempt her out of her black humour.

They walked out just before the usual time for dinner, and went around the stalls, but there was nothing which took her fancy. In desperation, he took her to the haberdashers' counters, hoping to tease her appreciation of pretty things, but even that failed. She walked with her head bent to the ground, her gaze fixed to the paths.

'Edith?'

Peter heard the woman's voice and recognised it immediately. This was the friend of Edith's father, the woman married to Sir Baldwin.

He stiffened his back, and turned to look at her. She was a striking woman, with red-gold hair under her coif, and wore a heavy green tunic with a bodice that bore astonishingly detailed embroidery, but most of all she wore a sad, anxious expression as she looked at Edith.

Peter's father had told him to avoid his father-in-law and his friends, because consorting with them could put his life at risk again. The best route was to tell this woman to go away and leave them alone. It would be best if he was rude to her. She should see that Edith did not want to talk to her. His wife was flinching and averting her head even now, as though she expected him to beat her for even looking at the woman.

He opened his mouth to tell her to go away, and a sob burst from him. 'Lady, please, if you can help her, please, as you love God, please . . .'

*Friday after the Feast of the Blessed Virgin Mary**

Billingesgate

An unpleasant fog had rolled along the Thames that morning, and this was enough to make the men unloading the boats curse as they struggled to manhandle their heavy wicker baskets full of fish along the narrow gangplanks.

---

* 12 September 1326

It was hard work, and the men here would not tolerate a slacker, so he must heft the basket for the man in front, then bend while the man behind lifted his basket to him. There was a leather strap that went over his forehead, while the basket lay on his back, and when it was in place, he joined the line with the other men, emptied his load in the market, then went straight back to the boats.

The first few days, his hands had been rubbed raw. His back ached, his head was sore, his neck a mass of knotted muscles. How others managed a life so harsh, he could not know. As a lay brother in the cathedral, his hands had been almost as protected as before, when he had been a rector at St Alban's. There, all he need do was occasionally sweep the floor, and keep his tools in place. His plots in the fields had been serviced by others who felt such work was beneath the man who was guarding their souls, and his hands had never roughened.

Not so here. Now his hands were growing steadily stronger, his back was bent with labour, but there was muscle in it. He felt more virile, more powerful than ever before. This was the last period before he would destroy that evil tyrant, Bishop Walter II.

His father, Henry Fitzwilliam, had been such a kindly soul. Even though his mother had died giving birth to him, yet his father had always been kind to him, and even when he chose to take a career in the Church, his father had not argued, but supported him. The fact that it meant there would be no heir, no continuing dynasty, had not altered his affection for his only son.

When the woman appeared, and he realised that his father was seriously considering marriage again, it had struck him like a poleaxe. As a young man of fourteen, he had considered the idea to be an insult to his mother. But then, when Lady Isabella had shown her courage and loyalty after his father's arrest, his attitude had changed. He realised why his father had decided to marry her. She deserved his respect and love, and the respect and love of her stepson, too.

Ranulf Fitzwilliam was a man who had built his life on faith and loyalty. At first it was to his dear father, then to his Church, but more recently, he had put the notion that the Church was entirely good to one side since he had seen for himself how power could be abused. Now, he put his faith and loyalty in his stepmother.

At the end of the day, he pulled off the leather cap with the long tail that protected his back, and walked with the others to the little alehouse at the river's side, where all would invest some pennies in a quart or two of ale, and there they would swap jokes, mutter against the bailiff who demanded ever faster work, or just sit and talk as the pain of the day gradually receded. Not him, though. No, he just stood at the riverside and stared along the muddy banks towards the Tower that loomed up above all the small shops and houses between. That was where, so he had heard, the bishop was living. The latter hadn't gone to his huge house out towards the Palace of Westminster on Thorney Island, but instead was hiding here in the king's own fortress. It showed how brave he was feeling.

No matter. He would destroy the man. He would kill Bishop Walter II after thirty-nine weeks from the first note being delivered, just as Bishop Walter had ensured his father's death after thirty-nine weeks in gaol. Now all he had to do was plan how.

Furnshill, Devon

Jeanne felt her heart lift at the sight of Edith that morning. It was as though the girl had been renewed. The ravages of the last weeks were still evident on her face, but her eyes were brighter, and Jeanne hoped that she was over the worst. The colour was returned to her face, and already her skin seemed less thin and old.

'Did you sleep well?' Jeanne asked.

'Do you need to ask?'

Jeanne felt her spirits rise. Her own wetnurse, Edgar's wife, had taken to little Henry as soon as they arrived here, and had enthusiastically fussed about the child like a mother hen. Almost as soon as the baby was taken from her, young Edith had fallen asleep, and she had slept from just before suppertime straight through to lunchtime today.

When she had seen Edith in Exeter, it was clear that the girl's strength was used up, and her mental resources were fading quickly, rent with the emotion of being forced to cleave to her husband's family and ignore her own, just at the time she needed her mother most. Divorcing her from her own mother and father just as she had a child to cope with was the cruellest act Jeanne had heard of. She could imagine how Edith had felt though, for her first marriage had become an oddly loveless affair, and she had been incredibly depressed until her first husband had died. Then, finding Baldwin and a fresh love, she had learned to be happy again.

Well, it was not too late for Edith to do the same.

'Edith, would you like to come and walk with me?'

'Yes. In a little while. Not yet.'

She sat with her hands in her lap, looking so much the child still that Jeanne marvelled that she could be married. 'You have much to consider.'

'I do not know that I shall ever see my husband again,' she said with sadness.

'I am sure you will.'

'You don't know his father. He can be very harsh. You see, he blames my father for the way Peter was arrested last year.'

'He shall have to realise that it was not your fault, nor Simon's. Simon was being persecuted, and Despenser sought to hurt him through you and Peter.'

'Knowing the cause will not make my father-in-law any more sympathetic. He wishes to guard his son from the same thing happening again. As do I.'

'You should not worry about such things, Edith. You are here to recover. Your husband agreed that you could come here with your child to recuperate. He didn't say you were to be evicted from his house, did he?'

'No, but—'

'There is no "but". You are here to be fed and allowed to sleep, and that is all. Now, are you ready for a walk?'

'Yes, I suppose so. I just wish Peter were here.'

'I am sure he will come soon enough,' Jeanne said.

Chapter Thirty-Seven

*Thursday before the Feast Day of the Archangel Michael**

Tower of London

There were not many people about when Simon walked in the castle's yard that morning. It was a cold morning, a real harbinger of the winter to come, he thought, and he glanced about him wistfully at the idea of the frost on the moors back in Devon. It was a time of great beauty on Dartmoor, when the weather began to change. He was never unaware of the magnificence of the scenery when he was out on the top of a tor, with the wind blowing in his face, a thin layer of ice crunching underfoot.

Here there was none of that. The whole of the city seemed to remain warmer, and there was little frost even on an evening like last night, when the sky was perfectly clear. It was unsettling, abnormal. If only he could return to Devon.

He had walked round the yard six times by his count when the gates were finally opened and the first folk began to enter with their loads. This was the thing about the fortress which Simon found most astonishing. There were so many people living within the walls that there was a neverending line of men and carts, bringing ale for the guards, wine for the wealthier guests, bread, meats, vegetables, eggs, milk – all the various foodstuffs so necessary to a man. And now, with the threat of invasion and siege, there were ever more provisions being brought here. As the fellows walked in, some carrying large baskets in their hands, while stevedores trudged along with their own baskets on their

---

* 25 September 1326

backs, none of them showed any interest in the castle or the people inside it. Why should they? They were mere mules, human transporters who were more convenient and cheaper than their four-legged counterparts.

There was one man who appeared to be gazing about him with rather more interest than all the others, He was dark haired, and had a slightly different look about him. Simon was wondering about him when he heard a sudden shout from the gate.

'Baldwin! Old friend, how are you?' he greeted him as he hurried down the slope towards the gate.

'I have been better,' Baldwin sighed. He had a young boy with him, who stared about him at the magnificent buildings with mouth agape. Baldwin touched a finger to his brow. 'For this once, you may offer me a cup of wine, and I will not decline in favour of water or juice.'

'Come with me!' Simon exclaimed, and in a few minutes they were in Simon's chamber, with Margaret sitting before them, and Hugh bustling about, swearing and cajoling Rob to, 'Get off your arse and fetch some wine for the knight and ale for the lad, you prickle!' while Baldwin's companion squatted silently on the floor.

'So, Baldwin,' Margaret said, when he was at last nursing a cup. 'Tell us what you have been doing. It is weeks since we last saw you.'

Baldwin said heavily, 'We have been through a hard time, Meg. My young friend here saved my life, may God bless him!'

'What happened?' Margaret pressed him.

Baldwin told them of his journey to France, their adventures there, and then his near-drowning at Honfleur. 'It was this fellow who had me dragged from the water,' he said, patting Jack's head. 'After that, we sailed back to England, and when we arrived we were told to make our way to Yarmouth, for the French were expected at any time. So on we went, and in that first night, a sudden squall hit us, and we lost fifteen of our ships! Five hundred men drowned. A terrible night. I am only glad that I slept through most of it. I was insensible for the whole journey, and for two more nights on board the ship. Since then I have been forced to rest often. Luckily, my head appears to be mending, and at last

I can ride and walk without too much strain.'

'Is there any sign of the queen?' Margaret asked, her voice hushed.

'There is no sign of anything,' Baldwin said with a sigh. 'I would almost prefer that she arrived with a vast force behind her, than this intolerable waiting. It is hard to be sitting here, unsure what the morning may bring.'

'Well, I am glad at least that you are back safe,' Simon said.

'I am at least back,' Baldwin said with a grin. 'But without a weapon. My sword was lost on the beach. Tomorrow, I must find a good armourer.'

'We can walk there together,' Simon said. 'Perhaps you would like to find a place to rest for now, though? You look exhausted.'

'I know, and yet it's still early. But I had to come here at the first opportunity to make sure that you and Bishop Walter were safe still – and Margaret too, of course,' he added with a smile.

'We are fine, Baldwin. Why did you not come last night?' Margaret asked.

'Oh, we arrived so late, I could not hurry to the Tower's gate, so instead we found a lodging near the Aldersgate. It was adequate, but I confess that the snoring of the other guests in my room was somewhat distracting, which is why I woke so early. Being without a sword is a disadvantage when one wishes to assault a snorer. In preference I packed and came here at first light.'

'Well, you are most welcome,' Margaret said. 'In fact, why don't you stretch out on one of our benches and take a little more rest now?'

Baldwin yawned and rubbed his head again. 'If you do not mind, Meg, I would be glad to accept your offer. What with lack of sleep and this damnable head of mine still aching like a lance-thrust, a rest would be very welcome.'

He had seen the man standing like a bailiff, thumbs hooked into his belt, a suspicious eye passing over all the men walking in with their loads, and it was a relief when he saw the man bellow at a friend and hurry away to see him.

The fort was huge. He hadn't quite expected it to open up in front of him in the way that it did. The entrance was at a lower level, so that those gaining access from the gate must run the gauntlet of a sunken road, while defenders could rain weapons and blows down on them from above. It left him feeling endangered, but then he saw how the path turned, and he climbed some stairs up to a wide grassed plain. Here he paused while he took in his surroundings before following the man in front to the undercrofts. There were, a series of them, and their loads of fish were for the special kitchen, he was told. He was directed with his companion down a small alley between two houses, and at the far end he found himself staring at a kitchen. A cook, when summoned, looked at the fish dispassionately, before nodding, and showing the two where to set their loads. Once divested of them, the two waited patiently, hoping for a sup of ale to quench their thirst, but the cook had already decided that he had better things to do, and had retreated to a stool from which he could watch and supervise the others.

Still thirsty, the two made their way out and retraced their steps – and it was there, almost at the cobbled way that led to the gate, that he saw her. His stepmother. And he scowled to see that she was walking and chatting flirtatiously to a tall knight. His blood boiled.

She was betraying his father, her husband.

And *him*.

Tower of London

Simon would always thereafter remember this day in two parts. The first was the joy of seeing Baldwin again, and knowing that his old friend was safe – a fact which seemed to herald better times. A little of Simon's fear and concern was eased at the sound of the knight's gentle snoring from his hall. But the second was when the dread news was finally brought to London.

Leaving Baldwin asleep on the bench, he went outside to check on the guards about Bishop Stapledon. There was trouble among some few of them, who were arguing about remaining in the Tower so long. The doom-mongers among the garrison were working their hardest to make sure that their fears were shared. Simon had recently had two of them arrested when they threatened to leave the Tower without permission. Their fate could be decided when the Keeper of the Tower chose to see them. From what Simon had seen of the two, he would probably be happy to leave them to stew for a while.

Simon heard shouting and swearing from the Wakefield Tower, and hurried towards the source of the noise with a frown. He was beginning to feel like a servant of the king in his duties here, rather than a dutiful official of the Bishop of Exeter, and he reached the Tower ready to curse any fool who was making a noise for no reason. He opened his mouth to bellow, and then snapped it shut quickly and copied all the others who thronged the street as he saw the flag, and dropped to his knee.

Clad all in armour, the king rode past on a huge black destrier that pranced rather than trotted, his heralds behind him, while Despenser rode a horse's length behind them, a fixed glower on his face. King Edward looked like a man who had the full weight of the realm on his shoulders. It was an astonishing sight, because although Simon had met with him a number of times, and had seen him at royal events when he was clothed in his full regalia, he had never seen the king looking so grim before. He rode stiffly, like a man in a daze, and his features were blank; he wore the expression of a man who, Simon thought, was terrified to let his feelings show.

Like the king, Despenser wore his armour, but his expression seemed to be wavering between rage and terror. Simon could remember the last time he had seen Despenser, and then he had noticed that the knight's fingernails were bitten so far that two were bleeding. Now the man looked close to collapse, as though he knew that all those years of inveigling his way into the king's trust and affection, all those years of deceit and plotting . . . all could shortly be thrown away. It was written in his pale, lined face. The man had aged ten years or more since their last meeting.

Simon could not regret it. He had a detestation for the man.

Despenser had personally damaged him, doing all in his power to weaken Simon's family, to harm his wife, his daughter, and Simon himself. To see him scared and fearful felt like a kind of justice.

Next to him, William Walle hawked and spat as he joined the rest of the crowd in rising after the royal entourage had passed by. 'Well, that confirms it.'

'What?' Simon asked.

'The king has come here from Westminster. He must be feeling the anxiety of the city, I think. The place is alive with rumours,' William said. 'And I don't know about you, my friend, but I am sickened by this constant waiting. I'd prefer to have a real, honest-to-God invasion rather than this. Endless preparation makes me mazed.'

Simon smiled at his words, but thought nothing of them. It was an hour later that he heard that a messenger had come from Suffolk.

Queen Isabella had landed with her mercenaries.

Furnshill

Edith had put on some flesh in the last week, Jeanne noted approvingly. She looked a great deal better for it, and now the haunted expression had left her too. The bruises under her eyes, the unhealthful pallor of her features, had been replaced with a fresh, maidenly rosiness that suited her like bloom on an apple.

Jeanne was very pleased with her efforts, but it was on this day that all appeared to take a turn for the worse.

The rider could be heard a half-mile away in the still afternoon air, and Edith heard it at the same time as Jeanne. These were not usual times, and Jeanne had a knight's appreciation of dangers, so she called Edgar, who went with a staff and stood at the doorway, while Jeanne herself took up a dagger. There were too many tales of women raped in their houses, their husbands murdered, and the houses fired when the outlaws had made their play. Jeanne and Edgar were competent to protect themselves from most gangs.

'One rider,' Edgar reported.

Jeanne went to the door and peered out. It was Peter, Edith's husband. When he had dismounted, she went to greet him. 'You are most welcome. Please come inside with me. Can I serve you some wine or ale?'

'Lady Jeanne, how is my wife?'

She sought to put his mind at ease at once. 'She is much recovered. Her sadness and weakness is much reduced. But come! You will see her for yourself.'

Edith shot to her feet as soon as Peter walked in, but Jeanne was sorry to see that the two did not rush into each other's arms, but stood at a distance like warring armies standing off.

'Edith, I am pleased to see you are looking so well,' Peter began.

'And I you.'

'I have been very worried.'

'You can see, I am much better.'

'My father sends you his very best wishes, too, and bade me to ask when you will return to us with his grandson.'

Jeanne shot a look at the boy. His father's 'grandson'? This was Peter's own boy they were discussing!

Edith looked away. 'I will come as soon as you wish it, of course. I am yours to order.'

'I don't want you until you're quite ready,' he said, and there was a wretchedness to him that told Jeanne much. He didn't want to be putting his wife through any more torment. He was too much in the shadow of his father, and it made him feel pathetic to live his life between his father and his wife.

'I don't think Edith can travel anywhere yet,' Jeanne said firmly. 'But Peter, you should come here as often as you wish. It would do you good to spend time with your son.'

'I should like to do that,' he said.

*Monday, the Feast of St Michael**

Tower of London

The Tower became a different place when the king was in residence. In the last weeks it had conveyed a peaceful, almost village-like aspect which was only occasionally disturbed by the arrival of fresh supplies. Now it had been transformed into a martial camp. Fighting men were everywhere, striding urgently, shouting and responding, practising with weapons, and there was the occasional whiff of brimstone as a small yellow cloud wafted past, the smell of the foul black powder which was being manufactured in preparation for the expected attack.

It was a scene of lunatic busyness, and it made William Walle and Simon pull their hair out in desperation. With all these strangers about the Tower, it was impossible to see who should and who should not be about. No doubt most were entirely justified in being there, but Simon and William felt quite ragged at the end of each day. They were fortunate that they were able to enlist the aid of a much-recovered Baldwin, and Sir Peregrine was available to them as soon as the rest of the garrison arrived, although his mind was plainly on other matters, to judge from his dreamy expression.

From what Simon could deduce from the gossip he salvaged from John de Padington, who appeared to have a useful informant who was a servant to the king's steward, matters had turned foul.

The force which Queen Isabella had brought with her was tiny – only some one and a half thousand men, which the king had initially derided, saying he would trample them all. Despenser did not laugh though. John's source said he probably had better spies than the king. Sir Peregrine reckoned that Sir Hugh realised that if such a small force could land with impunity, it showed that there was no one who wanted to oppose them. The invaders were more popular than the king.

---

* 29 September 1326

Although Edward had commanded that all his host should go to meet the queen and Mortimer, it proved immensely difficult to make this happen. Two days ago he had issued writs for men of arms and hobelars to march to defend the realm, but they failed to materialise. And it soon became apparent that those who did march towards the queen, did so in order to join with her forces. There was no opposition to her gentle meanderings over England.

Only yesterday, Simon had heard that fresh writs had been issued giving free pardons to all prisoners, criminals, outlaws and exiles, who would join Edward to protect the realm. And while the king put a price of a thousand pounds on Sir Roger Mortimer's head, the queen retaliated by offering twice that for Despenser's.

What Simon found most worrying was the mood of the city itself. When he went out, leaving Meg with Sir Peregrine, and taking Hugh and Rob with him, and walked among the people to escape the awful sense of enclosure that the Tower's walls were starting to give him – as though he was already under siege within it – the demeanour of the Londoners was startling. Gone was any apparent respect for their king. In its place was a loud rebellion. Men and women would come to the gates and swear and curse, shaking their fists when they saw the anxious faces of the garrison peering over the walls. He even saw a street scavenger pick up a handful of horse dung and fling it at a guard near the entrance. What was most shocking was that the man didn't retaliate, shout, or try to chase the scavenger, but instead scuttled back into the protection of the gateway itself.

'Bailiff, I'll be glad to be out of here,' Hugh said with a grimness that was unusual even for him. 'This city is grown too fiery for my taste.'

'I think we're safe enough,' Simon said, but he was less convinced than he sounded.

'What if a man like him sees us leave the fort and decides to attack us?' Hugh grunted. 'Wouldn't stand a chance in 'mong this lot.'

'If the worst came to the worst, at least the Tower has stocks to last for months,' Simon said.

It was true. The Tower could last for a long time under siege. That must have been the king's plan, Simon realised now. He wished he had known it at the time, because he would have been a lot happier to be out of London and hurrying back homewards if the stories were all correct and war was approaching.

They returned to the fortress when a thin drizzle started to fall; now, if anything, the mood amongst the populace had turned uglier, and Simon was growing alarmed.

'I don't know how we can get inside there,' he said to Hugh, who nodded morosely.

There was too much shouting and cursing for anyone to think of barging past to the gates. One or two people had been prising up stones from the roadway and were hurling them at the gates, and the men at the walls now all wore steel caps and helmets with vizors. In this mood, a mob could all too easily turn against any foreigners, and Simon and Hugh, with their Devon accents, would likely be pulled to pieces. That was the reason why Simon pulled back from the street into a doorway, wondering if there was another way up into the Tower.

Climbing the wall was clearly impossible. The whole area was surrounded by a moat, and even if the three could swim across without being brained by the mob's missiles, they would have to climb the steep ramps that led to the walls. And the walls were tall, and manned by guards with crossbows and bows. Either way, they didn't stand a chance.

The solution was given to him a moment or two later. There was a hiss from the crowd, and Simon could feel their attention moving away from the gateway itself and being diverted to the river. Craning his neck, Simon saw a great barge with rows of oars moving gently in unison, a flag fluttering at the prow.

'What's happening?' Hugh demanded.

'The garrison,' Simon said dully, 'would seem to think that it's too dangerous to use the main gates.'

Chapter Thirty-Eight

Tower of London

Margaret Puttock was feeling anxious. She had been chatting to Sir Peregrine when a sergeant had hurried past and muttered something to the coroner, who had quickly stifled a curse, murmured a polite apology and left at a trot, bellowing for men to follow him.

The rest of the time had passed in a blur as panicked men ran by, weapons clattering and clanking. There was a large number of archers, and they all ran to the entranceway, to the walls overlooking the drawbridge and down south to the river's walls. It looked to Margaret as though they were seeking to defend the areas where an attack could be launched. But then she heard the tramp of marching boots, and walked to the walls herself, Perkin at her side.

It was there that she found herself staring down into the royal barge as the king and Sir Hugh le Despenser clambered aboard, servants and guards with them. In the floor of the boat was a series of barrels, and she wondered about them for a moment, but then her attention returned to the people all about, especially as she heard Sir Peregrine bellowing again. Then he turned and seemed to catch sight of her, and his face broke into a smile of such happiness that at first Meg thought, with horror, that he might have fallen in love with her. But then she realised that he was looking at Lady Isabella Fitzwilliam, who waved to him, before stepping over to join Margaret.

The two women had exchanged a few words in the last days, and had nodded to each other from a distance, but they were living in different quarters, and Margaret was not keen to wander about the castle grounds while there were so many men in the garrison, so she had not made the effort to seek out Isabella. However, just now any companionship was welcome.

'Where is the king going?' she asked.

'He isn't going anywhere,' Isabella said. 'No, he's sending money to pay men to fight for him. They say he's ordered Sir Robert Waterville to gather fifty thousand men to repel the invaders.'

'I thought he had men there already?' Margaret said with some confusion. 'There was talk of a huge number of men – that he was sending them to the coast to stop Mortimer and the queen before they could form a hold on the land.'

'Is that what you heard?' Lady Isabella asked. 'What of your husband?'

'I don't think he knows more than that himself,' Margaret protested. 'Why? What is happening?'

'Sir Peregrine has told me what they have been discussing,' Lady Isabella said. 'He thinks that the king's reign could be about to end. There has been no fighting whatever since Queen Isabella landed. She arrived with only some thousand men, they say. The king's navy did nothing to harry them on their way, and when they landed, no one challenged them. The king's captain and arrayer for Essex, Norfolk and all about there, made no effort to halt the queen, and Sir Peregrine thinks he has gone to her side, and taken his men with him. And he believes that many others will do the same. There are few who will stand by the king.'

'Surely there must be enough men who will do their duty and obey their monarch?' Margaret wondered.

'Where? All the most loyal have been dispossessed by the king or robbed by Despenser,' Isabella said harshly. She was staring down at the men by the little landing-stage, and Margaret saw that her eyes were fixed upon Bishop Walter.

Without fanfare, the barge moved slowly away from the fort. There was a drum on board, and the oarsmen began to row to its beat, the great vessel starting its voyage up the river.

'Where will he go?' Margaret asked.

'To Westminster, I think. There he'll give orders for the country, and collect such of his household as are still loyal.'

'He looks broken,' Margaret said.

'He knows his rule in the country is over,' Lady Isabella said. 'He will come back tonight, I suppose, since this is the strongest fortress in his realm. But it will be clear to him that his reign is over. This is the end.'

Outside the Tower of London

Simon, Rob and Hugh watched the barge as it slowly passed by, and Simon was taken by the sudden change in the crowd's behaviour.

Where before there had been shouting, abuse, waved fists and occasional weapons displayed as men roared their defiance at a king no longer honoured, now there was a funereal silence.

The king and Sir Hugh le Despenser could be seen standing on the barge, amid the wonderful crimson cushions scattered on the benches. Neither sat, but both stared back at the crowds on the shore with a sort of desperation in their faces. Simon actually thought, looking at them, that they both thought they were at real risk of attack from the mob on the shore.

Certainly that was in the mind of some in the crowd, Simon reckoned. But there was an appreciation that if the king were to lose his crown, then their sovereign and protector was gone. And most people knew that when the ruler left, there was no rule. This felt like a city which was about to fall to lunacy and danger for all involved.

Simon had seen enough. 'Come with me,' he said tersely, and set off to the gate, but as he did so, he saw that the way was still blocked. The gates were closed, with no guards risking their lives by standing beyond them, and even as he watched, he saw a stone lobbed towards the gates. It struck with a dull, echoing thud that seemed to reverberate around inside the Middle Tower, but even that didn't seem to rouse the crowd from its torpor. However, the sight of a bailiff walking up to the gate and tapping to ask to be allowed inside, might be enough to do just that, and Simon wanted no part of it.

'Can't get in there,' Hugh summarised succinctly.

'Wonderful! Then how do we get into the castle, if we cannot go in by the gate?' Simon said curtly, still thinking.

'Like the king,' his servant grunted.

'What is that supposed to mean?'

'River's there, isn't it?'

Simon glared, and then turned about. 'Then we'll go to Billingesgate and see whether we can get a ride,' he said, furious with himself that he hadn't seen the obvious way in.

'Master, what's going to happen now?' Hugh asked as they trudged along the lane.

'I don't know, Hugh. The people here seem more than happy to let the city fall apart. I haven't seen much in the way of bailiffs or sheriff's men to stop the mob taking over.'

'It's a long ride home,' Hugh commented.

'I don't think it's a good time to attempt it, either,' Simon said. 'Not with the king trying to raise an army west of the city, and the queen's forces about to arrive.'

'You think they are coming here?'

'I don't reckon the king would have been running quite so quickly unless he was sure of it,' Simon said. 'If Edward reckoned he could protect the city, he'd have remained here. He provisioned the Tower against a siege for the full garrison – and that means weeks of food. He must have felt that the risk was there for him to be bottled up inside, and that no one would come to protect him.'

Hugh pulled a face. He looked up at the sky, checking the weather as a good shepherd always would, then glanced around at the street. 'Best get on, then,' he said. 'Rob, move yourself, boy!'

'You're always ordering me about,' the boy complained.

'You'll get a kick up your backside if you start that again,' Hugh said imperturbably.

Simon smiled through his concern. It was good to know that,

no matter what else happened, these two would carry on bickering.

It was worrying that the king had fled though. There was nothing in his appearance that spoke of a man making a short journey, only to return with a new host. Rather, it was the broken figure of one who radiated failure, a king who was running into exile.

And that meant that those who remained in his service would find life rather too exciting for their taste. The immediate problems were to get back inside and ensure that Meg and Perkin were safe, then to see what, with Baldwin, might be done to secure their escape from the Tower, and from London itself. Perhaps it would be possible to ride from the city and make their way to Devon by degrees. He didn't like to think of his daughter in Exeter, all alone but for her husband and father.

But problems of this nature were more easily dealt with one at a time. The first was how to return to the castle, and this was soon resolved. While they stood on the wharf, staring out at the grey river, Simon saw a rowing boat making its way towards them. It drew level, and as the man grasped a rope and lashed it to an iron ring in the stonework, Simon accosted him. 'Would you take us a little way down the river? I'll pay for it.'

'You three? Where you want to go?'

'Let us in, and we'll point it out,' Simon said. 'We're not from around here.'

'I can hear that,' the rower said suspiciously, but his face lit up at the sight of the coins in Simon's hand, and any reservations he might have felt seemed to dissipate. Soon they had all clambered aboard, and the little craft was moving out into the middle of the waters to miss a ship coming into the quay.

Watching, Simon saw a number of stevedores lining up. One in particular caught his eye. He nudged the oarsman and pointed. 'Those men. What are they doing?'

'They unload the ships that come in here.'

'They're all Londoners?'

'I don't know. Mostly, I suppose. There's always one or two

from outside, maybe, but most should be from London.'

'They were carrying goods into the Tower the other day. I saw one of them there.'

'They're stevedores,' the man said pointedly. 'That's what they do: carry things.'

'Yes,' Simon said. He could hear the contempt for this foolish foreigner in the man's voice, but ignored it. He was sure there was something about that particular man that spoke of danger. Even as he had the thought, the fellow seemed to notice him in turn, and he saw the man's eyes follow the boat down the river as though he had recognised Simon as well.

Recognised him as an enemy.

*Tuesday, Morrow of the Feast of St Michael**

Tower of London

It was a grim family who gathered for their morning meal, and although Margaret did all she could to lighten the mood, she knew in her heart that it was not possible.

The departure of the king, together with his Treasury, had been preying on her mind. It was some relief when, later, the vessel returned, with the king and his adviser still aboard, but Margaret had heard the comments of the people in the Tower.

'They all said he was running,' she said in a low voice to Simon as she served him with ale.

'What – from the realm?' Baldwin asked.

'They thought he was running because his wife would soon be here,' Margaret said.

'I did too,' Simon admitted,'but if he runs, he will lose all. He *has* to remain here. At least here in the fort he is safe enough. And gradually, if he is besieged, he will find that his loyal subjects will come to support him. They wouldn't let their anointed king be captured.'

---

* 30 September 1326

'You think so?' Baldwin murmured. 'Would you stay to defend Sir Hugh le Despenser if you were asked?'

'No!' Simon said, remembering the time months ago when the bishop had asked the same thing.

'And that is the problem for the king. He, I think, believes that the kingdom will rally about him, but he has his principal adviser speaking words of caution in his ear all the time, because Sir Hugh knows perfectly well that as soon as he is captured, whether the king is with him or not, he will be executed for the manifest crimes for which he is responsible. He cannot live. There is nowhere for him to flee to in exile, save perhaps the Holy Roman Empire or beyond. Certainly, if he was found in France, he would be killed on sight.'

'So you think Sir Hugh will persuade him to leave London?' Margaret asked.

Baldwin nodded. He shot her a glance, and she knew he was trying to keep her spirits up when he said, 'I think that Despenser will try to get him away, and that the city will go to the queen as soon as she deigns to show her face.'

'Will she have the king arrested?' Margaret said. It came out without her thinking, just a random thought, but as soon as she spoke, the hideous idea took hold of her.

It was unthinkable that a man anointed by God Himself should be thrown aside by mere men. There were times when a man set himself against God, but that was his own fault, of course. That a man might break God's commandments and take the king's throne, that was appalling. When the man involved had made his own oath of allegiance to the king, and now was committing adultery with the queen, the matter rose from the merely shocking to . . . Well, she didn't have words to express her feelings.

Baldwin was looking at her again. 'The main thing is, Margaret, I think you will be safe here with Perkin. If there were to be a siege, there is food enough in this fortress, but I don't think it will come to that. Despenser will want to get away, and he dare not fly without the king at his side, for the limited protection Edward can provide him. And once they are gone, the Tower will become a secure and safe place for us all.'

Margaret nodded, and she sat at her husband's side with a smile. But although she set bread and meats on her trencher, she found it impossible to eat. She had no appetite.

When the knock came on the door, Simon and Baldwin were sitting before the fire. The two of them watched as Hugh padded across the floor and pulled it wide.

'It's Sir Peregrine,' he announced with a scowl as he stood back to let the knight walk in.

'Simon, Sir Baldwin, I hope I see you well. Ah, Mistress Puttock, I trust you will not mind if I ask that I may make use of your men for a short while? Eh?'

In a few minutes, the men were all outside, Baldwin armed with a spare sword Sir Peregrine had brought for him, and then the coroner marched them across the green towards the drawbridge.

'Where do you want to take us?' Simon asked.

'We are to walk to the cathedral. There is to be an announcement at St Paul's Cross,' the knight said, and although he was perfectly polite, he spent the time looking about them, eyeing the walls of the fortress, glancing at the keep, up at the towers, and over to the river.

'Sir Peregrine? What is it that troubles you so?' Baldwin said.

'Is it that obvious?'

'You have the look of a man about to ascend the steps to the executioner's block,' Baldwin chided him mildly.

'I think you should ask this fellow, rather than me,' Sir Peregrine said.

At the first gate they found William Walle waiting. His face lit up as soon as he saw the three approaching, and he stepped forward. 'I am so glad you're coming too. I was really worried when it was only me.'

'What is happening?' Baldwin asked, and Simon could see that he was becoming alarmed. 'What are all these for?' He jerked a thumb at the men behind them. There were about twenty of them, all men-at-arms with mail and some plate, and all carrying polearms. 'They look like the garrison's men, but they aren't in the king's tabards. What is going on, William?'

'I thought that Sir Peregrine would have told you,' Walle said. 'No matter. There is to be a reading at St Paul's Cross.'

He explained as they marched off. The king had issued a papal bull of excommunication to be read at the cathedral. It stated that invaders of England would become excommunicate and forfeit their souls.

'That should settle the mood of the kingdom,' Walle said, and rubbed his gloved hands gleefully. 'You wait and see how the mob reacts to that!'

The mob had already begun to disperse as they trooped on to the bridge itself, then made their way up to La Tourstrate, and then along to Candelwryhttestrate, and from there to the cathedral.

This was fully deserving of its reputation for magnificence and beauty, Simon reckoned. A glorious, soaring building, set atop the Ludgate Hill, the first and most prominent hill in the city itself, it showed God's glory in all its splendour. However, the place had sour memories for him, because last year he had been here with Baldwin when the Bishop of Exeter was almost attacked by a small mob. At the time Simon and Baldwin had thought that it could be another manifestation of Despenser's ill-will, but it was as likely to be a mere mischance. The London populace were ever forward and troublesome.

Today at least they appeared less determined to disrupt. There was quite a crowd of men and women at the ancient folk moot.

It was a roughly shaped area of grassy land bounded to the south by the north-eastern wall of the cathedral, and to the north by the charnel chapel, and hemmed in by the massive belfry to the east. Simon and Baldwin went with the squire and Sir Peregrine to stand near the cathedral's wall, where they should have a good view of events.

They did not have long to wait. First, a number of men arrived, and from the fumes of alcohol, Simon could tell that they had been to the alehouses and taverns that sat along the roads. More, rougher-looking men appeared, some of them carters and hucksters, others the meanest of scavengers and tanners. They brought the smell of their business with them, and Simon was considering moving when he was grateful to see a party of apprentices turn up, younger, fitter and cleaner men all round.

Next to arrive were the bishops, five all told. They walked to the Cross, resplendent in their robes and mitres, their right hands aloft as they muttered prayers and made the sign of the cross towards the waiting audience. The Bishops of London and of Winchester, the Abbots of Waltham and Westminster, and behind them came Archbishop Reynolds, with a number of censer-swinging priests on either side; a thickset fellow with brawny arms and a threatening demeanour carried the cross on a tall pole. The way he stared at the public all around left Simon in no doubt that the fellow was keen to protect his cross, and Simon was sure he had been picked for his truculent attitude. Any man trying to steal it from him would receive a buffet about the head that would make him swiftly regret his inclination.

It was also plain that the archbishop anticipated some form of trouble. He irritably waved on the guards who followed his party, and the men reluctantly interposed themselves between the public and the religious, their polearms held upright, but all ready to bring them down and use them. That much Simon could see in their anxious faces and their alertness.

The archbishop began talking, but Simon scarcely heard a word. He was watching the men listening all around. Soon, a young priest darted forward holding a book, and stood as a living lectern as the archbishop peered at the writing. It was a fairly interminable reading, all in Latin, and there was a priest who bawled a translation. But to Simon's surprise, when the archbishop finished and his servant folded the book once more, disappearing as quickly as he had appeared, a bystander suddenly shouted out, 'When was that written, Archbishop?'

'What?' the archbishop said, and his uncertainty was instantly communicated.

'What's the date on the bull?'

'It is in force. The pope issued the bull to prevent wars in our land. Why, do you want to see war here?'

'That's not about this, is it? It's a bull about the Scottish, not the righteous queen of our country,' a man said loudly, and Simon, peering about, was surprised to see that it was an apprentice who spoke so rudely. He hadn't expected a youth studying his profession to be so insulting to an archbishop. Youngsters had so little respect nowadays . . .

'When was it dated?'

The cry was taken up, and now the scavengers were pressing forwards. There was a shout, and the guards before the priests lowered their staffs, but too late. The crowd was so close already that the staffs would only fall on heads and shoulders, and none of the men was willing to do that and begin the bloodshed. In preference, they all crossed their weapons and tried to keep the crowd back.

First it was an apple. A brown, rotten apple curled through the air, and landed a short distance behind the guards, some of the flesh spattering Reynolds's robes. He stared at the muck with distaste, then glared at the crowds. But before he could say anything, the apprentices started to throw old fruit and some bread, anything they had about them. Others were collecting small stones and aiming them at the guards. They rattled on their helmets, and one cried out, his hand going to his eye.

The bishops and abbots abruptly turned around and hurried across the grass to the door to the cathedral.

Simon watched as the guards also beat a quick retreat. Stones continued to fall, some larger ones crashing into the cross itself, or slamming into the walls of the cathedral, but none, by a miracle, hit any of the glass windows.

There was a slithering sound that he recognised, and when Simon turned, he saw that Baldwin had drawn his sword. Like a statue carved from moorstone, Baldwin stared at the apprentices, his sword-point resting on his boot's toe, his hand resting on the hilt.

Before Simon could ask why he had taken his sword out, he saw a couple of the apprentices glance around. One had a stone in his hand, which he hefted, a sneer curling his lip. Then he saw Baldwin, and Baldwin shook his head, slowly and deliberately, but with menace. The two looked away.

While he watched them, Simon caught sight of William Walle's face. He registered only horror. 'How could they do that?' he kept repeating, over and over again, as though it was a prayer that could eradicate the memory of that hideous scene.

Chapter Thirty-Nine

Tower of London

The Bishop of Exeter stormed back to the chamber in the Tower feeling a rage so all-enveloping, he was astonished he did not at once burst into flames.

'That damned fool!' he snarled, and kicked his door shut.

John de Padington eyed his master and gauged his mood; he had known him to get frustrated like this before. Bishop Walter was a clever man who was forced to work in conditions that not only taxed his mind, but then forced him to choose politics to explain his thoughts. Working to a worthwhile goal, only to see the achievable ambitions obstructed by others with more shallow desires for the kingdom, was hard to swallow.

'Bishop, I have some lobster for your lunch, and here is a very fine wine which you will enjoy.'

'Oh, I *will*, will I?'

'Undoubtedly. And if you sit now, and do not upset your humours any more than strictly necessary, it will aid your digestion too.'

The bishop eyed him, and then gave a small chuckle. 'Very well, John. You are right enough. Let me sit. Ah! That is better. Now, wine, you said? Good.' He took a long pull from the goblet and grunted his approval.

There was a knock at the door. 'If it's someone from that incompetent bastard Despenser, send him away before I wring his neck!'

John opened the door to find William Walle, Simon and Baldwin outside. He stood back to let them all inside.

'Dear God in Heaven, you lot look as though you've seen the

queen's host sailing up the Thames,' he said, only half in jest.

Simon nodded towards the squire, and William took a deep breath, before explaining what they had, in fact, seen at St Paul's Cross.

The bishop turned his face away. 'I told them it wouldn't work. I explained to the king and Despenser, but they wouldn't listen. They said I was an old fool who didn't understand how to sway the common man's mind. If there was a threat from the pope, that would bring the city folk around, they said – what – after so many years of Despenser's despoiling of the country? Almost all the peasants hate him; all the nobles do. If only Despenser could be sent away, many of the people would, I believe, rally to the king. But the king won't send him to exile or death, and therein lies the tragedy of our times.'

'What will the king do?' Baldwin asked.

'God knows. Two days ago he was in tears, beating his breast with despair because of the money.'

'What money?' Simon asked, confused.

'He sent money to Richard Perrers, Sheriff of Essex and Hertfordshire, to pay for a contingent of men to repel the queen. Perrers sent the money back, and has joined the queen. All are joining her. Despenser's bile and greed has sown the bitterest harvest any king could reap.'

Baldwin sighed. 'What of you, Bishop?'

'Me? I shall remain here while the king wishes for my advice,' Bishop Walter said with determination. He stood and stretched. 'Damn the soul of Mortimer! If it were not for him, even the excesses of Despenser could have been restrained, and in time he could have been removed from authority, but now, the only possible outcome is the destruction of the realm in years of war. And the king will suffer for it. Poor man! Poor man! He doesn't deserve this.'

He didn't. The bishop had been privileged to work with the king often in the last years, and he had always found him to be honourable, if temperamental. He also had a good brain, was thrifty, and understood organisation and administration. It was this one weakness of his – his affection for the fool Despenser – that had thrown his rule into turmoil.

Bishop Walter suddenly noticed that the others were standing and watching him. 'Well?'

'What do you want of us?' Simon said simply.

The bishop smiled. 'Simon, if you wish to leave me and go back to Devon, I will quite understand. This fight will be unpleasant. You are released from service to me, if that is your wish. You too, Sir Baldwin. You ought to return home at the very least. There is nothing for you to do here. The fellow who left me those vicious notes has gone. Perhaps he was knocked on the head by someone here in London, or maybe he has not managed to reach the city. In any case, there is more to worry about than him now.'

Simon nodded slowly. 'Perhaps. And perhaps he is very close even now, Bishop. I think I will have to remain here a little longer, just in case.'

In his mind's eye he saw again that face under the leather cap and cape of the stevedore. The fierce face of hatred.

Bishop's Gate, London

Richard de Folville, Roger Crok and Ralph la Zouche had ridden hard this day, all the way from Halstead, which was where they had stayed, the night of the Feast of St Michael. And now, today they had come down here to London, to bring messages and to view the lands for the queen.

So far, their journey had been quiet enough. The money Queen Isabella had given them had eased their paths no end. But she was comfortable with money just now. Wherever she went with her men, the townsfolk arrived and plied them with coin, because everyone wanted an end to the misery of the last years. So many remembered her as the kind, generous lady who had sympathised with the trials and sufferings of the common people, and they fell on their knees to her, treating her like a saint. And she, clad in black widow's weeds, acted her part: she was quiet and appreciative, grateful for their words of kindness and, as Richard Folville felt certain, entirely consumed with the lust for revenge on her husband and all his friends.

Folville could understand that lust all too well. It was natural, to wish to destroy all those who thwarted a man, and this queen was ruthless as fire, beautiful as a spring day, and dangerous as a viper. He would trust her no further than he could throw her.

At Bury St Edmunds she had discovered and taken the treasure left there by one of the king's justices, and distributed it among the mercenaries in her train. They were keen to remain with her, because so far they had not needed to fight, and were being regularly and richly rewarded for their marching. It was a merry band of men who accompanied the queen.

But she needed men to tell her what was happening in the land's most important city. They must ride to London and report to her. And she had chosen Crok, Folville, and la Zouche because they had shown their courage while protecting her son in Normandy. She said that she wanted to reward them by giving them the task of highest honour.

Riding under the Bishop's Gate, Folville glanced about at the others. *Highest honour*, his arse! The bitch didn't trust them to remain too close to her precious boy, that was more like it. Well, if she felt safer with a bunch of Hainault mercenaries instead of three Englishmen, that was her mistake. For his part, Folville knew that he had to look at the job in hand with great care. There was a possibility that he might be able to increase his profit. If it appeared certain that the king would win, and that the invasion was doomed, he would be able to give some information to show Edward that he was acting for him. There were stories that men were being offered pardons if they would serve their monarch now. He could do that – turn his coat and become a loyal subject to the king again. Perhaps help in the capture of Mortimer, or catch the king's son for him. That would be worth a goodly payment. After all, while many flocked to the queen, most among them had more than an eye on the boy at her side, Edward, Duke of Aquitaine, Earl of Chester, and the next King of England. Take away the boy, and many would begin to wonder whether they were right to place all their faith in the invasion.

Ralph was a possible ally in such an undertaking, but Folville still did not trust Crok. The latter didn't seem as driven by hunger for possessions as the others, nor was he so determined. Rather, he appeared happy to float along, waiting to see what would happen. The only time he got angry was when someone mentioned the Bishop of Exeter or Despenser, then he grew bitter and quiet.

Ralph la Zouche was the opposite. At the mention of Bishop Walter, he would immediately fly into a rage, blaming the bishop for his present dreadful position, and especially the death of his brother. So far as he was concerned, his exile was Stapledon's fault, and the bishop would have to pay for that – sometime soon.

Yes, if he could, Richard Folville would have to dispose of Crok, and then he would be able to use la Zouche – either to improve their position with the queen, or to leave her and go to the king.

It would all depend upon the next hours here in London.

Tower of London

Simon and Baldwin were quiet as they walked across the Tower green to Simon's chambers, and once they were inside, and Margaret had kissed Simon and gone to fetch them wine, Simon asked his wife to sit with them a while. Hugh had heard them arrive, and he now stood at the door with his staff in his hands. Rob and Jack appeared to have formed a loose alliance, and sat listening in the corner near the fire.

'Do you sleep with your staff now?' Baldwin chided Hugh.

'Reckon I do. 'Tis better than dying in my sleep,' Hugh said.

Baldwin nodded with some sadness. It was terrible to think that men could fear attack even here in the middle of the king's most impregnable fortress. 'Well, Simon?'

'I do not think I can leave here yet,' Simon said. 'There is one man I have seen who looks suspicious, and if something were to happen to the bishop now, I would be mortified.'

'Who is this man?'

Simon explained about the stevedore. To his relief, Baldwin did not treat his words with amusement.

'You are right to be concerned. A man could get work at the quayside with ease, and no one would think to check his name or details. Do you know who he may be?'

'I have no idea. I did wonder whether he might be that priest whom the bishop spoke of – the one who invaded his chamber.'

'Perhaps. But that name was almost certainly invention. We shall have to try to find him by some other means.'

'My fear is that the fellow might get into the castle and stay here.'

'It is hardly likely. There are too many within for a man like him to be able to walk about the castle without being seen.'

'Baldwin, he was walking about the cathedral – no, worse, he was in the Bishop's Palace – for weeks before he was discovered to be guilty of leaving those notes.'

'Yes, you are right,' Baldwin acknowledged. 'Perhaps we should delay any departure. But I prefer to think that such dangers are limited. While the bishop remains here inside the fortress, it will be harder for a man to reach him. We must bend our efforts to make sure he remains here.'

'Yes,' Simon said. He looked across at Margaret, who had sat quietly listening. 'Meg, what do you think?'

'I will stay if you wish to. My place is with you,' she said.

Simon nodded, but he had noticed the involuntary movement of her eyes towards their son's chamber. 'It does not suit me, I confess. I would rather be at home, or with Edith. But I have promised to help the bishop, and feel I have a responsibility. But that doesn't mean you have to remain, Baldwin. You ought to go home to Jeanne.'

'And I shall. But for now, the risk of bloodshed is all here. The queen may come here at any time, and the king is still locked up in the White Tower, so this is where the real danger lies. Jeanne will be safe. But our duty is to see to it that the bishop is safe, too.'

'Then we are agreed,' Simon said with a small sigh. 'We will remain a little longer.'

*Wednesday after the Feast of St Michael**

Tower of London

John de Padington was early to rise as usual. A man who would serve a bishop had to accommodate himself to the hours kept by his master – night as well as day. And early was the hour that the bishop tended to get up to visit his chaplain. He believed in the benefits of a clear mind.

It was all the same to John, for he counted time asleep as time wasted. There was work to be done, and he preferred to get on with it, rather than laze about like so many. And if there was time at the end of the day, he would enjoy the company of his friends and a jug of wine. That was the hour for rest and relaxation.

In the morning though, all was bustle for him because the whole day lay ahead of him, and he was sure that there would be plenty for him to do, as usual.

The morning looked pleasantly clear when he glanced through the window. Outside, the courtyard was bright, and if it were only a little less cluttered with men-at-arms, horses, racks of weapons, and the constant lines of men bringing goods into the fortress, he would have thought it a proud sight.

But now, with the ever-present threat of the queen's men reaching London, he was less content than usual. He knew that the future was uncertain.

Still, he had experienced the ups and downs of his master's career in the last years. From adviser to the king, to Lord High Treasurer, then returning to mere bishop, John had seen it all, and he had participated in Bishop Walter's rise and fall. He didn't care for the man's position though, except in the way that it affected the bishop himself. John had no thought for himself. He was happy just to serve the man he thought to be one of the kindest, best men in the country.

He smiled to himself as he set the table ready for when the

* 1 October 1326

bishop returned to the chamber, and went out to fetch food and drink. These he prepared in the buttery himself. He would not have anyone else touch the bishop's food, because there was too much risk of someone adding poison. Other meals would be taken elsewhere, such as the king's own hall. John could not do much to ensure that the bishop's food was safe there, but he would do all he could here in the man's own chambers.

The walk from the buttery was only short, but with a full tray it was a cautious journey. There were projecting obstacles at every point, from the chests on the floor to the bishop's own sword, which lay on top of another table near the entranceway.

Crossing the floor, he set out the meal ready for the bishop's arrival, and stood back, eyeing it all with a slight frown. There was nothing missing he could see, so he carefully poured a little of the wine into a cup and drained it, smacking his lips appreciatively. Yes, a good wine!

His work done for the present, he left the room to visit the privy.

Thus he was not present when the hooded and cloaked figure slipped from the doorway to the table.

He had followed the other stevedores into the fortress, all carrying their loads of fish and meats ready for the garrison. Their barrels rumbled like thunder over the cobbles, hundreds of them rolling simultaneously, and the stevedore thought his head must explode with the row, but he gritted his teeth and ignored it as best he might.

Last night, he had tried to clear his mind and consider the best way to attack the bishop, but always aware that the day for him to die was not quite yet arrived. However, he could still come here today and learn all he could about the bishop's movements.

He rolled the barrel along, one in a long line, looking about him as he went, and as he reached the Wakefield Tower, and had to roll it up the shallow incline to the green, he saw her.

She was walking briskly from a doorway just over to his right, and was forced to stop and wait for the line of men. Soon there was a gap and she darted through it to the opposite side.

For a moment, he nearly ran to her. Oh, the longing! It was such a powerful urge, he almost succumbed, no matter what the other stevedores would say, on seeing him behave like that. They would think he had lost his mind! No doubt they'd stare though, when Lady Isabella saw him and reciprocated . . .

If she would.

He suddenly recalled seeing her with that knight – the older man who had laughed and chatted with her so happily the other day. Perhaps she would be unwilling to acknowledge him. She wasn't in need of him any more, not if she had found a new lover. Women weren't as loyal as men, after all. If she had found a new home, she would be happy. That would be it.

Still, he stared at her fixedly, and as he made his way up the green to the larger storerooms at the northern wall, he almost changed his mind. She looked so small, so defenceless, he took pity on her. But in the process, he reminded himself what he was there to achieve: the death of the bishop. How would it be for her, if he showed himself to her in full view of all the men here, and later was caught for the execution of the bishop. Some of the responsibility for his action might then redound on her, to her great damage. No, he would leave her.

And then, just as he reached the door to the undercroft, he saw that man again – from his dress and bearing, surely a knight – who walked to her and spoke. The two of them looked so happy in each other's company, that it was hard to keep himself in check. Because just seeing her with that knight made him realise that there was a new risk to him.

If she had fallen in love with the man, she might decide that there was an easy way to ingratiate herself with him. The bitch could decide to betray him.

Christ alive! It took all his self-control to keep his head down and not rush over the grass to stab her to death there and then, her and her lover.

Chapter Forty

In his chamber, the Bishop of Exeter entered, and called for John. 'Dratted fellow. Never about when you need him,' he muttered, and began to pull his gloves from his hands.

Still, he was relaxed this fine morning. There was no news yet of the queen, and he had seen the king on his way back from the chapel. Edward had been chatting to his second son, John of Eltham, only ten years old and already witnessing the worst which the kingdom could suffer. The bishop had paused for a few words. The king had been almost his old self, chatty and amiable. Only a day or two before, he had been inconsolable in his grief, convinced that he would be caught and forced to exile Despenser, but today he seemed to believe that the queen would not want to harm him.

'Look at our boy here,' he said, affectionately patting his son on the shoulder. 'How could she hurt him or me?'

The two together, father and son, were as perfect a pair of males as could be imagined, with their long, flowing hair. The king kept his beard trimmed, but long, and the muscular set of his body was unaffected by his lifestyle. Meanwhile his boy was slender and elegant, with bright, intelligent eyes.

'I am sure your queen would wish nothing of the sort,' the bishop said.

'Ha! You hear that, John? Now, Bishop, you must know that our attempt to read the papal bull yesterday went awry. The damned crowd had some pedant in amongst them, who demanded to know when the bull was dated. Not that it matters a whit! What if it was written some days ago – weeks ago, or years? Eh? It's still correct, after all. If the pope made the invasion of our realm illegal some years ago, nothing has changed. Maybe we should have the bull read again, so that the crowds can understand its full force. I am sure Archbishop Reynolds would not mind doing that.'

'I fear he may well mind, sire,' the bishop said apologetically. 'He was pelted with rotten fruit as though he was in the pillory, and the guards could do nothing to protect him. They were attacked too. If you wish your bull to be read, you will need to look for another man. No!' he added hurriedly, holding up his hands. 'Were I to go out just now, they would pull my head from my body.'

'We are sure that they are not so filled with hate as you believe,' the king said, but to the bishop's relief the idea was chased out by another. 'When the queen arrives, we must have her greeted properly.'

'Your Majesty?'

'She is my wife, Bishop. We will not have her mistreated. She has been wayward, but we would have her position respected – and that of our oldest son. They must be welcomed when they arrive.'

'Your Highness,' Bishop Walter said. He considered the queen, imagining her arrival, the way that she would point to Despenser, to Edward himself, and order their arrest. Perhaps she would prefer to have Despenser strung up immediately though, and not bother to see him wait for trial. And what would she do to her husband, the king?

The king was in full flow now. 'She will arrive, perhaps within the week. Naturally we shall have to ensure that all is ready.'

'Your Highness, Mortimer is with her.'

'He is a traitor, and he will die. But my wife will be pleased to return and discover that we forgive her. And our son, of course. We could not see Edward punished. We doubt that it was his fault – I expect he was persuaded by Mortimer to behave so recklessly.'

The bishop had left him soon after, and it was this conversation which had so unsettled him on his way up to his chamber.

The king was deluding himself into the rosy vision of his wife arriving, apologising, giving up her lover, and Edward welcoming her back into his fold. He would probably think he could ask Sir Hugh le Despenser to arrange a party to celebrate.

It was insane! The queen loathed Despenser and wanted his head, just as she probably hated Bishop Walter. Certainly he had seen no residual affection for her husband when the bishop had travelled to France to request that she return. The response had been unequivocal: *non!*

As usual, his food was set out in an orderly manner, and he finished removing his gloves and set them to one side before closing his eyes and offering up a prayer of thanks for his food, before picking up his loaf of bread and breaking it.

Lifting the loaf made something move, and as he glanced down and saw it, the bishop leaped back, as though a giant spider had sprung forth. The goblet of wine was overturned, while the loaf fell to the floor even as he cried out.

And in the draught of his movement, the little parchment note skittered across the table as if it was impelled by its own malign influence.

It was obvious that the bishop was still suffering from the shock when Baldwin and Simon walked into the chamber.

William Walle was already there, his sword in his hand, standing near the door, while John de Padington stood a short distance in front of the bishop.

Baldwin looked down at the squire's sword with an eyebrow raised, and William shamefacedly lowered it.

'I am sorry, Sir Baldwin. I didn't know who it was. After this . . .'

'What exactly has happened?' Baldwin asked the bishop.

'I walked in to break my fast, and found a fresh note lying under my loaf,' the bishop said.

'Who put the loaf there?' Baldwin asked.

'I did, sir,' John de Padington said. 'But it was not there when

I put the loaf down. Someone must have entered the room after I left, and stuck the note beneath.'

'How long was the loaf there?' Simon asked, walking to the window and staring down into the green.

'Not long,' John said. 'I set out his breakfast, and only left the room for a few moments, and while I was gone I heard the bishop's cry, so I ran back . . .'

He saw the expression on Baldwin's face, and suddenly his nerve failed. 'No, Sir Baldwin, please, do not look at me in that way! I would have done nothing to hurt my master! It was nothing to do with me, I wouldn't have—'

'I don't suspect you, man! I am just considering.'

'Baldwin, over here,' Simon said urgently. 'William, you too. Look, that stevedore down there, the one with the reddish chemise and black hosen. See him?'

'Sweet Mother of Christ!' William Walle blurted out. 'It's him – the man who called himself Paul of Taunton!'

He could see her still, the bitch! Flaunting herself with her new lover, making herself appealing to the old goat like some seventeen-year-old bawd teasing a randy patron. He would put an end to her playing. There were dark corners even here in the Tower, and he could reach her no matter where she ran.

The undercroft was a cold place, like death itself. As he and the others rolled their barrels and hefted their heavy sacks of grain and flour into the areas pointed out by the officials, he found his mind turning more and more to revenge. It was so sweet a thought!

But the supreme ambition was to kill the bishop. Yes, first he must kill Stapledon, and then, later, he could decide what to do with the bitch Isabella. So long as she didn't betray him beforehand.

The barrel was in place. He gave it a practised roll with a twist, and it ended upright. With a leg either side, he hugged it, and forced it the last few feet, curling it in arcs over the stone floor. When it was in place he stood straight, feeling the muscles in his back slowly easing, and trailed out to the door with the others.

They had to wait there, in the gloom by the entrance, for the trail of barrels and men carrying sacks to decline, so that at last they could leave the place.

Blinking in the sunlight again, he glanced about, searching for her. She was still there with the knight, as though there was no shame in associating with another man of the king, and by implication, a friend of Stapledon and Despenser. The men who had killed . . .

There was a shout, and like all the others, he turned to see what was the cause. To his astonishment, he saw three men running at him. Two must have been knights, and the third was a powerful-looking man with a grim expression.

For a moment he wondered what they were doing, and he automatically looked over his shoulder to see who was sought, but then, before he could work it out logically, his legs had already overhauled his brain, and he was pounding away from them.

They were gaining on him fast. He ran to the left, almost collided with a wall, then was off again, down the hill towards the entranceway to the green.

There were shouts, and suddenly he was the target of every man out there in the green. There were three stevedores in front of him, one with long, spreading arms like a gorilla and a leer that showed he would enjoy bringing him down, but he wouldn't surrender that easily. Turning, he pelted breathlessly back up the hill again. There was a ladder up in front, and he ran at it at full tilt, catching hold and swarming up it almost without breaking his pace.

Above him, he saw a guard hurrying across the inner walkway of the wall, and behind him, two men were following. He only had one way to escape.

Reaching the top, he stood catching his breath, staring down at the men following him. There were rocks nearby, stored up here to hurl at attackers, and it would have been so satisfying to knock them loose with one or two, but the guards on the walls were close, too close, and one was fumbling with a crossbow. He had no time.

He stared about him a moment, and in that instant, he felt a sharp delight, as though this was the culmination of his life. He sprang up onto the battlements, with the men clambering up the ladder behind him, and then, as the guards on the walkway came close, he turned to leap into the moat, hoping to swim for the far bank.

But there was no moat. He had not realised that here the castle had a second set of walls, and to reach the moat, there was a stretch of grassy plain, and then a second curtain wall. The grassed gap between the two was an appalling drop away from him, presently filled with cattle and sheep, and as he stared down, a cow peered up at him ruminatively, chewing, as he felt the first of the fists grab his shoulder.

He was hauled back from that terrible drop, and when he tried to grip the wall to hold himself up, he was punched in the face, until his grip failed and he dropped back on to the walkway. A boot slammed into his flank, and he rolled over, pushing himself up again, but he was hit again, on the back of his head, and this time he felt his body grow enormously heavy, as though all his limbs had been filled with lead. There was a feeling of nausea rising to his throat, and he felt as though he was falling. In his mind, he saw the cow again, staring at him with that meditative expression as he tumbled down and down, until he landed softly on the grass, and knew no more.

The bishop heard their boots on the stairs, and he turned in his seat to stare at the door as it opened. 'Well?'

'My lord bishop,' William Walle said, and then his face broke into a broad smile. 'We have him!'

'Oh, thank God,' the bishop murmured, and he felt the relief wash through him. 'I feel a little dizzy,' he said, eyes wide.

It had been so alarming, when the first note had appeared. The second had made him angry, but the subsequent ones made him grow more and more concerned. Then again, there was the appearance of the preserved head. It had remained in his mind, proof of his own fragility, the ease of the assassin. His morale was quite eroded when that last message arrived at Canterbury, and this latest had shocked him more than he could properly express. There had been such a lengthy gap between them, and he had also felt the security of being here, at the heart of the king's authority in the country. It was as though the writ of the king overwhelmed any evil which could be aimed at him. The assassin's knife could not hurt him while he remained inside the Tower.

'Sir Baldwin, Squire William, Bailiff Simon – I owe you a debt which I doubt may be repaid. You have saved my life, and probably a more shaky thing – my sanity!'

'I am glad if we have succeeded in doing so,' Baldwin said. 'The culprit is presently languishing in your gaol, my lord bishop.'

'Has he explained himself? Has he told you why he wished to put me to this appalling test? He nearly drove me mad, after all.'

'He is not yet capable of answering our questions,' Baldwin said. 'He will be unable for some while, Bishop. He is quite mazed. However, I am sure that we will soon be able to get some answers for you.'

'Good. Very good.'

'Tell me though, Bishop – what did he write that alarmed you so much?' Baldwin asked.

Walter Stapledon picked up the parchment and passed it to him. 'He gives me the day of my death.'

Baldwin glanced at the small, crabbed writing. '*Only another fourteen days to your death*. Well, he is hardly poetic in his style,' he noted.

'Assassins are not noted for their style,' Bishop Walter said. 'I am glad you will have time to discuss his writings with him at leisure. I am sure it will be rewarding for you. And now, gentlemen all, if you do not mind, I have much work to get on with.'

He sighed happily as they left him. He had a pile of documents to read and check, and his clerks would shortly bring in more, but for all that, he had a feeling of ease and comfort such as he had not known these ten months past. It was wonderful that he could sit back without fear of another note.

Nor worry that he was about to be killed.

In the yard once more, Baldwin looked about him and breathed in deeply. 'So, Simon, I think that finally pays your duty to the bishop in full. You have no more to do here.'

Simon nodded. 'Meg will be pleased, and so will Hugh, after all his moaning and whining.'

'A curious matter,' Baldwin commented, as they marched across the grass. The stevedores had all gone now, but the grass was muddied and flattened where they had passed with their barrels and carts.

Simon gazed morosely at the ruts. 'Do you think that the Tower will be forced into a siege?'

'If the queen is in earnest, and the fact that she has come this far seems to suggest that she is, then, yes. I would expect so. What else may she do?'

'What does she actually want?' Simon wondered. 'Does she mean to kill the king and take the throne for herself?'

Baldwin sighed. 'I wish I knew. She is certainly intending that Despenser will be destroyed.'

There was a call, and both turned to see Sir Peregrine and Lady Isabella approaching. 'Sir Baldwin, Bailiff,' the knight said. 'Who was the man you captured? We saw you arrest him, but we wondered who it might be.'

'He was known as Paul of Taunton when he was in Exeter,' Baldwin said, 'but I doubt that is his real name. He was determined to kill the bishop – but for what reason we cannot tell.'

'Why would he want that?' Sir Peregrine asked with surprise.

'So many have disputes with the rich and powerful, it's a miracle more aren't murdered every day of the week,' Baldwin said lightly.

'But you are sure he was trying to kill the bishop?' Lady Isabella pressed. 'Why him?'

'Lady,' Simon explained, 'this man Paul was known in Exeter, and it was discovered that he dropped threatening, anonymous notes into the palace for Bishop Walter to find. Today there was another message left for the bishop – and the man was seen.'

'Seen leaving the message?' she asked.

'No. Seen here,' Simon said with a faint frown. 'He was here to upset the bishop again, clearly.'

She nodded.

Sir Peregrine was smiling, nonetheless. 'We have news, my friends, which I cannot keep from you any longer. Lady Isabella here has consented to become my wife.'

'That is wonderful news,' Baldwin said, and bowed to the lady. 'I give you my most heartfelt congratulations, Sir Peregrine.'

'I am glad of it, Sir Baldwin,' the knight replied happily.

Simon bowed in his turn. 'My lady, you have a good man there.'

'I know,' she said, but Simon noted that her manner was a little distracted. Strange, he thought, but it was hardly to be wondered at. She was worried about the situation in the city, no doubt.

'So the bishop is safe now,' Sir Peregrine said, as they all walked together towards Simon's rooms.

'Yes. I think it must be a huge relief to him,' Baldwin said. 'After all, the matter has been dragging on now for months.'

'Really?'

'Since he was in Exeter, yes. This madman followed him from Exeter to Portchester, to Canterbury, and now here, I presume. What his motivation could be, I do not know.'

A sudden blast of trumpets made Sir Peregrine groan to himself. 'Another drunken guard at the gate, I suppose. There appear to be too many who can gain access to the wine stores. Excuse me, Sir Baldwin, Bailiff. My dear, I shall see you later, I trust.'

'Of course,' Lady Isabella said, and watched as Sir Peregrine ran back the way they had come.

'So will you live with him in Exeter?' Baldwin asked.

'I suppose so. I had not thought of it,' she replied.

'No?'

She heard the question in his voice, and turned to face him. 'Sir Baldwin, there is so much danger in the realm just now, I have scarcely had a moment to consider where we may live. I am sure that Sir Peregrine's house will be adequate for us. There! And now, I must be off, too. Please excuse me.'

Baldwin and Simon bowed, and then watched as she hurried away from them.

'That woman,' Baldwin said, 'is not entirely happy about something.'

Chapter Forty-One

Once safe in her chamber, Lady Isabella Fitzwilliam remained leaning against the doorway, her heart racing like a horse at full gallop. It was enough to make her feel quite sick, and she had to sink to the floor, holding her head in her hands.

To have seen poor Ranulf, her stepson, captured like that . . . the sight of his face, distraught, staring over at her, as though pleading with her to rescue him, had torn at her heart, but she could only hope that he understood that she was here to finish the job they had begun. Poor Ranulf! The one time he had attempted something important, the poor fellow had been captured.

It was all her fault. She it was who had instilled in the boy a desire for revenge at any cost. She had been so enraged to learn that her dower was gone that she had reinforced his own fury and feelings of inadequacy, using them to make him persecute Stapledon. And now Ranulf was in gaol – a gaol from which he might never be released.

The bishop's murder was now her own responsibility. There was so much to be feared now. In a matter of days, the whole nation could be on fire, with war and death stalking the realm. Many would die. Boys and men, women and their children.

One more death would be nothing. The bishop deserved his end.

But she was scared. So scared. Tears were springing to her eyes even as she covered her face in her hands. She had never killed before, but now she must murder the bishop.

But first she would go and see Ranulf, if she possibly could.

*Thursday after the Feast of St Michael**

St Alban's Inn, Bradstrete, London

In the cold morning air before the fires were lit, Roger Crok walked to the door and peered out into the narrow street. It was filled with busy workers and traders moving up to the Austin Friars or down to the shops near the Cornhulle. The noises deafened, the smells assailed the nostrils . . . in different ways, London assaulted all the senses. It was both alarming and wonderfully stimulating. Brash and saucy as a whore from the Bishop of Winchester's brothels on the south of the river, but still elegant and attractive in more cultured ways.

Not that he was worried about tarts or culture just now. The danger that he and the other two ran by their presence here in the city was enough to occupy him.

He was not scared of the risks. It was stupid, he knew, but he was not worried by the thought that he could be captured and killed. Rather, he was excited by the whole experience of being here and having the chance to do something that might help the queen to bring down the king.

There was no doubt in his mind that that was her ambition: to have the king removed from the throne, and to rule in his place until her son could take over. Roger knew that she would succeed. He had a chivalric belief in that beautiful young woman's abilities.

Folville was close to him. He could feel the man's presence now, after living with him for so many months, and it was not a pleasant sensation.

'I need to talk to you,' Folville said.

As he followed Folville back into the bedchamber they had shared last night with five other men they had never met, Roger Crok reflected that he had never seen Richard de Folville smile properly. The man's mouth moved, but not his eyes. An old

* 2 October 1326

fellow had once told him that a man who smiled with his mouth alone was not a human being, he was a snake.

Well, Roger Crok needed no warning about trusting this fellow. He was not a friend. He walked into the bedchamber, thinking this, and saying, 'Well?'

As he did so, he felt the danger behind him, and threw himself sideways.

He would never know what feral awareness told him to avoid that blow, but as he tumbled onto a mattress, he heard the blade scythe through the air and slash the palliasse nearest. It was Ralph la Zouche, of course. Richard and he must have decided to rob him. He should have known the fools would try something like that. Grabbing at the palliasse, a thick one stuffed with straw, Roger launched himself at Ralph. He managed to thrust the bedding into Ralph's face, and the man swore as the straws pierced his skin, making him drop his sword to protect his eyes. Roger kicked viciously at his knee, and felt his boot connect, before scrambling for the door.

There was a crunch, and he glanced up to see Richard's sword firmly embedded in the frame.

Until that moment, he had only been trying to escape. But the sight of that steel so near to his head made him suddenly lose all reason. While Richard put both hands to the hilt to withdraw the sword, Roger turned about and aimed a fist at Richard's head. He was no fool, and ducked, but that only meant that Roger's left hand met his nose with a satisfying crunch. Richard flew backwards, with a fountain of blood from his nose spraying upwards and covering the palliasses with a fine red drizzle.

Ralph la Zouche was on his right, and Roger Crok bent, kicking sideways with his boot. The edge of his sole caught the knight's chin and lifted his head as it slid into his Adam's apple. With a choking cough and wheeze, Ralph fell again, scrabbling for his throat in his agony, but already Roger had drawn his own sword and was holding it ruthlessly pointing at Richard's breast. Richard was kneeling by the rough wall, holding his hand to his nose, staring disbelievingly at the blood cupped there.

'Why?' Roger asked.

'What is it to you? Just kill me and be done!'

'I don't intend to kill you quickly, fool. I will have you done slowly, at the gallows. You can dance to the tune of the hangman, you can. They have special trees for murderers here in London.'

'Then kill me slowly, Roger Crok. You send me to the justices though, and I'll see you dance at my side,' he sneered. 'You think you can make use of the law here? I'll—'

Roger brought his fist round in a sharp blow that knocked Richard de Folville off his knees as the sword's pommel hit him above the ear. Richard fell, snoring on to the floor, while Roger quickly went to his pack. He rolled up his few belongings in his blanket, picked up his satchel, and glanced about him before leaving.

He would finish his mission here, and then hurry to find the queen.

Tower of London

Ranulf lay on his back on the floor of the gloomy chamber. The rushes beneath him were ancient and already befouled, and she could not imagine how her stepson could sleep on that. She stared down at him from her place behind the bars. He was like a stevedore, with rough hosen, a plain chemise and leather cap, with a long trailing cape to cover his back. It was wrapped about him now, in a vain attempt to keep the cold at bay.

'Ranulf!' she whispered.

The gaoler, an ancient warrior with a belly like a barrel and a second chin that wobbled alarmingly, sucked at his teeth and gave a wheezing chuckle. 'You want to speak louder than that, my Lady.' He lifted his lamp and bawled, 'Hoi!'

Her stepson jerked awake, instantly alert like a cat.

'Please, gaoler, leave us a while,' she said, slipping a few coins into his hand. 'There's no need to mention this to anyone. I just want to see what makes a man behave in the way he did.'

'Oh yes, my lady,' he said with a leer.

She tried to smile, hating him for his foulness, and as soon as he was gone, leaving his horn lantern behind, she went to the metal bars. 'How are you, Ranulf? You poor dear, to be in here.'

He looked at her warily. 'I saw you. Yesterday, I saw you with that man. Who is he?'

'Sir Peregrine? He is a good man, but he's not our concern.'

'You looked very friendly.'

'Ranulf, I have to remain here. I was planning on killing the bishop myself, but to get close enough to him, that is difficult. Bishops do not entertain women in their chambers.'

'Unlike knights?' he said with a sneer.

'You think me a whore because I am trying to avenge your father?' she said with bitter reproof.

'It's hard to think anything good in here.'

'Remember that I am out here trying to finish the task,' she said.

'I will remember. I hope you do, Mother.'

She dropped her head. It had not occurred to her that he would be so bitter towards her.

'Mother,' he said again.

She could hear the softness in his tone, and she was instantly taken back to the time when they had been friends. When they first met, he had been suspicious of her as any bereaved child would be, to learn that his father had decided to take a new wife. A replacement mother. But they had grown to like each other, and when she had been so distressed by the death of his father, he had demonstrated this same gentleness. It was impossible for her to ignore it.

'Yes?' she said, and approached the bars again.

'Look at me,' he said, and letting the leather cloak fall away, he stood and walked to the bars himself so that she could see him.

There was a blackening bruise at his left eye, and his jaw was caked with blood. His neck was scratched and bleeding, his shoulder looked as though it was dislocated, he was holding it so tenderly, and his left leg was obviously hurting, from the way that he avoided putting his weight on it.

'This is what they have done to me, Mother. They killed my

father, they stole my inheritance, and now they've done this to me. I've lived like an animal these last months, working like a slave, doing anything that would bring me nearer to the bishop so I could avenge my father. And all this will come to nothing, unless you steel yourself and kill him in my place. Can you do that, Mother? *Can you*?'

Isabella nodded twice, emphatically. 'I will do it, my dear Ranulf. For you and for your father.'

Sir Peregrine left the king in the Tower, eating a good meat meal, and walked outside into the clean London air with a sense of disgust.

The king had ordered him to learn all he might from the man who had been leaving messages for the bishop, and had authorised him to use whatever means he thought necessary. In other words, *torture*.

Sir Peregrine had no doubt in his own mind that a man would give any answer the torturer wanted, would implicate anyone, denounce any faith, in order to make the pain stop. However, the fact that a man gave answers did not mean he would give the truth, and Sir Peregrine was quite sure that someone, who had lost fingers and toes, who had watched as his nails were ripped from their beds, who felt the scouring heat of the branding irons, or the crushing agony of breaking bones, would hardly know what the truth was any more.

He stared down at the door that led to the gaol with a feeling of depression that his own task was reduced to this: that he must create agony for another in order to satisfy the king. King Edward had a justifiable interest, after all. The bishop was his guest.

There was a shout and a cry from the gate. From here he could see nothing, but he called to a guard up on the wall, 'What is the commotion about?'

'A messenger, sir.'

'Any smoke from the east or north?' Peregrine enquired.

'No, sir.'

'Good.' So there would be no sudden arrival of a force ranting and ravaging all over Essex, seeking to burn the king from his Tower. 'Tell them to send him through,' he instructed.

The man had ridden hard, from what Sir Peregrine could see. He was pale, breathless, a skinny, black-haired man dressed in the king's blue parti-coloured clothing to denote his importance, but just now he didn't look very important. He looked scared.

Sir Peregrine studied him briefly, and then jerked his head. 'Come with me, lad.'

They turned and the knight marched him back to the chamber. Soon they were with the king, who yet sat at his meat. Sir Hugh le Despenser was behind the king's chair, and he stared at Sir Peregrine with a strange wildness in his eyes. The man was falling apart, the coroner surmised. Good. The sooner the bastard was dead, the better for all concerned.

'Wait!' the king said. He did the messenger the honour of glancing at him, but then sat with his meat skewered on a knife, waiting impatiently, staring at a trio who stood before him.

They were all rich men. Their robes were fur trimmed and lined, and the hats on their heads were similarly gorgeously fashioned. Sir Peregrine thought he recognised one, a large-bodied man in his fifties, with clear blue eyes and a grey beard, but startlingly black eyebrows. He glanced at Sir Peregrine as they entered, and Sir Peregrine was sure that he had seen him at the Guildhall in the last week.

The king pointed at him now. 'What do you say? Repeat it, my friend, so that I can fully understand.'

'Your Royal Highness, the City of London is most keen to support you. We support the king, the queen and the Earl of Chester, your son. Naturally we will fight to protect you, as you ask. However, the men of the city beg that they do not have to travel far to fight. We will do so, so long as we can leave after sunrise, and return before sunset on the day of battle.'

'So you will not form a host to protect me?' the king said with a mild smile and nod. Then he threw down his knife and stood, hands leaning on the table before him.' And *you expect me to accept this?* You think I should agree to such limits on my authority as to allow your menfolk to return to the city in the same day as they leave? Pray, how long will they deign to fight for me, then, if I march them to meet with my queen?'

'Sire, we only relay the news, I fear. It is not our decision alone.'

'You would see me hobbled? You would see me bound, so that I may not defend my realm? I swear, friend, I shall exact a terrible price on this city of yours when I have won back my kingdom! Be gone! Go! And know that you have today earned the hatred of your king!'

As the shouting continued, Sir Peregrine remained in the background. Looking at the messenger, he saw perspiration standing out on his brow. The king was sitting again, and now he stabbed a fresh piece of meat with his knife, and beckoned the fellow forward. Stumbling and nervous, the messenger began to speak.

Sir Peregrine had expected the usual form of message, perhaps words about the movements of the queen's mercenaries, a report of farms burned, or tales of nuns raped – the normal concomitants of war. But the messenger's gasped words sent a shock of ice into his marrow.

'Sire, Henry of Lancaster is marching to support the queen. He brings many men with him.'

The king sat for a long time with his knife held before him, his jaws moving rhythmically. To Sir Peregrine it looked as though the man had just been given his death sentence.

'You are sure that Henry does not march to support us?'

The messenger shook his head, and then fell to his knees. 'Forgive me, Your Highness! I would bring any other news than this if I could.'

King Edward II stood. 'We are not hungry,' he said quietly to no one in particular. Then he glanced at the messenger. 'Stand up, boy. This isn't your fault. It's the fault of those who hate me. By God's grace, they will be punished for their efforts against me. Yes, in God's name! This Henry of Lancaster shall pay, as will the *fine* burgesses of London. I shall not allow them to do this!'

As he spoke, his voice took on a new authority, and he slammed a fist into his cupped hand. 'Sir Hugh. You will have the household readied. Steward? Have all packed. We leave as soon as we may. We shall ride westwards, to the loyal lands of the West Country. If these rebels and malcontents think that they can come here and capture me, they are mistaken, and when I catch Henry of *bloody* Lancaster, he will wish he had never been born! I will make such an example of him, as will terrify any who attempt to overthrow their monarch. I will have him flayed alive for this! Now, leave me! All of you.'

Sir Peregrine hurried from the room, backing uncertainly from the chamber and marching down the stairs in a sombre mood, while others rushed past him to pass on the commands that would give life to the king's orders.

Outside now, he gazed about him. Looking up to the right, he could see the door that led to the gaol, and he felt a shiver of pure revulsion slither down his back at the thought of what he must do in there.

And then his face broke into a smile as he saw his Isabella walking out of the chamber, closing the door behind her.

The Templar, the Queen and Her Lover

Michael Jecks

1325: An atmosphere of dread and suspicion hangs over England.

The last years have been god-awful. A man was hard pushed just to survive with the realm stretched so taut with treachery and mistrust and the war with France.

When Isabella, Queen of England, is dispatched to Paris to negotiate peace with the French King, Sir Baldwin de Furnshill and his companion Simon Puttock travel with her to ensure her safety. But it seems no one can be trusted, not least those in the Queen's own retinue. Murder, betrayal, adultery and cold, calculating evil are just the beginning of Baldwin's tempestuous journey into the dark heart of the world's most powerful realm. Baldwin and Simon must fight to survive as the Queen struggles to stop a vicious war between her husband and her brother . . .

Acclaim for Michael Jecks' mysteries:

'The most wickedly plotted medieval mystery novels' *The Times*

'Atmospheric and cleverly plotted' *Observer*

978 0 7553 3284 7

headline

Chapter Forty-Two

Cornhulle, London

The roads were noisy as Richard de Folville pushed through, swearing and cursing as jostling traders made his head jerk and give him more pain. There was nowhere as frustrating as a city like this when seeking a single man. There were too many people.

When he got to the Walbrokstrate, the large thoroughfare that led south following the route of the river that divided the city in two, he continued along it, musing.

That prickle Crok! He had guessed somehow what Richard was up to. There was no malice in wanting him dead, it was purely that Crok was one of those men who would not act to betray someone, no matter what the logic, and Folville had grown to feel that the king was strong. The man would be a fool to sit here in London unless he knew he had the means to defend himself. So for Folville there was only one sensible path: he intended to go to the king and give news of the queen's movements. He could tell a good tale about how he had desired to serve his king and had come with the queen purely in order to betray her. And then he would be rewarded.

But Crok, that son of a whore, would never agree to such an action. No, he was far too fine to consider betraying her. He would stand on principle, as he might put it, and refuse. That was why Richard and Ralph had decided they must kill him. It was sheer commonsense.

His nose hurt. God, so did his head where Crok had hit him. It had felt like a hammer blow. He still felt queasy at the thought of it.

They'd discussed the bastard when they both came to. There

wasn't much they could do though. Sir Ralph had reckoned that they might as well get on with their plan and go to the Tower, but Richard was less keen on hurrying there with their faces in this state. He preferred to wait until his nose had stopped bleeding and he could wash the scabs from his upper lips, while Sir Ralph needed to rest. He was there now, back at the inn, sleeping. But Richard felt restless. He needed air, and longed for an opportunity to strike back at Crok.

He had visited the stables to see their mounts, but Crok's was gone. No surprise there. He would be off to the queen like a scalded cat. The coward! If it had been Folville, both his enemies would lie rolled in palliasses at the inn already, and he would be on his way. War was coming, and no one would pay attention to a couple of extra bodies. But Crok didn't have such ruthlessness. That was why he would have been no good.

Still, he would be able to deal with Crok when they had been to the king and told him all he needed to know. Then Folville could see to it that Crok was sought out, arrested, and killed. That would be a sweet revenge!

There was a great roaring sound, as of thousands of throats cheering, and it reached Folville even through his fog of rage. Idly, he followed the sound, down all the way to the next roadway, and found himself in a massive crowd of people.

'What is happening?' he demanded of his neighbour, a sandy-haired old peasant with breath that stank of ale.

'The king! The king's leaving!'

*Monday after the Feast of St Michael**

Peter and Paul Tavern, Paternoster Row, London

He had not experienced so many disappointments in such a short time in his life. Richard de Folville could barely speak without swearing and cursing Crok's soul, because in his mind, all the

* 6 October 1326

misfortunes which had piled up upon them in recent days had become one with the hatred of Crok. It was Crok who was responsible in some manner.

Folville had grown so desperate, he had prayed to God for help in finding Crok so that he might kill the bastard, but so far his search had proved fruitless. There was one thing of which he was certain, and that was that he would not go to the Tower to present himself now. There, so he had heard, was the source of much of his present grief – Bishop Walter of Exeter. The bishop had been commissioned, since the king's departure, as warden and keeper of London together with the mayor. Meanwhile the king's second son, John of Eltham, was to remain here in London, at the Tower.

What a ridiculous mess! In God's name, all he wanted was to be able to get away from this cursed city and make his way to the queen, because any idea of running to the king was long gone now. That had dissipated like mist in the sun when he saw the small party riding with the king to Acton four days ago. The number of men with him was pathetic, and although they carried silver with them, in a number of carts, from all the rumours, the people of London were glad to see the back of them all. There would be no honour guard from the city, and the idea of gathering a force to form a host in the king's name was ludicrous. Folville reckoned there was a scant hundred men in the entire city who would follow the king.

Yesterday he had tried to get away. He had an idea that it would grow more difficult to escape by the day, and he had gone to the stables to have his horse released, but the stableman had demanded three times the stabling owed! Three times! The bastard would have had his head cut off, but when Richard went for his sword, he found himself staring at three bows in the hands of the man's ostlers. He had taken his horse, and would have ridden off, but the gatekeepers wouldn't let him out. They were suspicious of all men who were not of the city, in case of spies, and he found himself under risk of arrest, if he was to try to escape. It was intolerable!

He still blamed Crok for the fact that he was here. If he'd had his way, he would have gone to the king quickly, given his news, and then disappeared with his reward. Now he couldn't even ride to the queen without running the risk of an arrow in his back as he left the city.

Draining his cup of wine, he walked out into the fresh air. Rain had fallen steadily through the night, and the roads were sodden. As soon as he set off up the street, he stepped in a puddle that proved deeper than he had expected. His boot slipped in halfway up his shin, and he cursed viciously as he brought his foot out, shaking it to release some of the water.

There was a man at an alley's corner who found his predicament amusing. Loud laughter echoed along the street, and others joined in to see this foreigner in such misery. There was nothing he might do with so many about, so Richard de Folville swallowed his pride and marched southwards. Before he had gone many yards, he heard the patter of feet behind him, and felt mud hit his back. Turning, he saw three ragamuffins pelt away, while more people showed their appreciation.

He left there in a ferocious rage, walking along an alley to get out of the way of Londoners, and after a short distance, found himself confronted by a small beggar-boy holding out his hands for money. Richard put his hand towards his purse, but in preference he yanked out his dagger and plunged it into the boy's breast, shoving his other hand over his mouth, watching as the life flared, burned, and was snuffed out in the lad's eyes. There was no sound. Richard picked up the body, and threw it in among some rubbish.

There was no one to see him. No one would care. The whole city was a festering sore, filled with maggots that sought to eat each other. No one could miss one brat.

Tower of London

'Sir Baldwin, I am glad to see you,' the Bishop of Exeter declared brusquely. 'Do you have a moment for me?'

They were in the green outside the Tower itself, and Simon had been walking with Baldwin, discussing the king's departure. 'Of course, my lord.'

'Sir Baldwin, you are to leave soon?'

'Yes. With the king gone, there seems little point in my remaining,' Baldwin said. 'I must return to my wife. She will be alarmed at the rumours of war.'

'But of course. And Simon?'

'I am at your disposal, Bishop. I would dearly like to return home, but the thought of riding west in the train of the king's host appeals not one whit. Especially not with my wife. It is too dangerous for a journey of that length. The realm is too disturbed.'

'I am glad to hear it, if only for purely selfish reasons,' the Bishop said. 'Now I have these new responsibilities in London, I would be glad of a man's help who was independent. I think that you would be a great source of comfort to the king and the queen, were you to agree to remain here in the Tower for a little, to help guard their son.'

'John?' Simon said. 'I would have thought he was as safe as a lad could be, here in the Tower.'

'Perhaps he is, but I would prefer to think that there was a man I knew here to see to his protection.'

'Well, I have no objection,' Simon said. 'The way home, as I said, is too dangerous.'

'Good. That, then, is decided. It is one less thing for me to worry about.'

'You should be careful in the city,' Baldwin noted. 'There are many who have taken a dislike to bishops just now.'

'Ha! I have been unpopular in London for the last five years,' the bishop said. 'I am only glad that now, at least, the most dangerous man is in the gaol.'

'He is to be tortured, I believe,' Baldwin said stiffly. He detested the very idea of its use.

'The king ordered it,' Bishop Walter said. 'But if you could persuade him to divulge any details without its use, I would personally be most glad. The man will be executed for trying to kill me, but there is no need to exact any more punishment than that, surely.'

'Has his torture not begun already?' Simon asked. 'I thought he was to be tested days ago.'

'Sir Peregrine has been too busy with me,' the bishop said. 'He has been involved in the disposition of the forces about the Tower, and is, I think, reluctant to interview the prisoner. Not many approve of torture.'

He shot a look at Baldwin. He knew of the knight's past as a Knight Templar, and Baldwin's view of the use of torture.

Later, Baldwin and Simon met with Sir Peregrine.

'Sir Peregrine, I hope you do not object to my raising the matter, but the torture of the lad in the gaol – are you to continue with that?' Baldwin asked.

'I am so commanded by the king.'

'You do so only with reservations?'

'I despise the very concept. If a man's guilty, let him be put on trial and, if guilty, hanged.'

'Then, would you object to my speaking with him?' Baldwin said. 'I would prefer to save him the pain of torture.'

'By all means.'

It took a short time to arrange, and then Simon and Baldwin were taken into the little gaol under the Tower.

Simon looked at the man in the gloom with interest. He had already lost the healthful appearance he had possessed as a stevedore, and now his eyes glittered with what looked like a feverish passion.

The fellow rose and walked to the bars of his cell, where he looked them both over, from their boots to their faces. 'You're the two who caught me.'

'We are,' Baldwin said. 'And now I hope we can save you from additional pain. You know you are to be put to the torture?'

'It's part of the torture, this waiting, isn't it? I've been expecting it for the last three days. Is it to start now?'

'Only if you wish it. What is your name?'

'Why?'

'We have heard it is Paul, but we know that's not true. You don't come from Taunton, do you?'

'I come from not far away. What is it to you?'

'I am Sir Baldwin de Furnshill. This is my companion, Bailiff Simon Puttock. What is your name?'

'You can call me Paul.'

Baldwin gave a fleeting frown. Such reluctance to give a true name was rare, in his experience. 'You know that you will not escape here? There is little hope for you, I regret. Whatever you fear about giving away your name truly is not worth worrying about, my fellow. Why not merely tell us?'

'Call me Paul.'

Baldwin nodded. 'In that case, Paul, tell me, why did you intend to kill the bishop?'

'Me?'

'You left him notes at different places. We know all this, man! Come, tell us why you wished him ill.'

'He is a thief, no better than a cutpurse. He colludes with Despenser to rob the innocent, no matter what their status. You can serve him if you wish, but he deserves death for his felonies!'

'You think yourself robbed by him, then?'

'I think he robs us all,' Ranulf said.

'Did he take your land? Money? What?'

'Leave me alone!'

'You will die here, but unless you help us now, you will die having endured great pain. There is no need for that,' Baldwin said infuriatedly.

'You think a man should be scared of death? That false bishop should be, after his crimes!'

Baldwin studied him very closely now. He always felt that a man's words could be measured, and sometimes it was more what a man did not say than what he did that mattered. 'You refuse to say where you come from, you refuse to say who you are, you refuse to do anything to explain your hatred of the bishop . . . Even though you have been sitting in this cell for days now, knowing that the result must be torture. What would motivate a man to keep so silent?'

'You may invent all the reasons you wish, Sir Knight.'

'The only reason I can imagine is that there is someone else who could continue to carry out your deed,' Baldwin said, watching him intently. 'Ah yes, that is it, isn't it?'

'I am saying nothing!' Ranulf said, but now Baldwin could see the sheen of sweat on his forehead.

Simon looked over at Baldwin. 'The date on the notes, Baldwin. The last note said fourteen days from last Wednesday. If he has an accomplice, and they intend to stick to the same plan, the Bishop will die on the Wednesday of next week.'

'What note?' Ranulf began, and then realised his error.

'Yes,' Baldwin said thoughtfully. 'Fellow, whoever you are, I am afraid that if you thought your accomplice would be able to succeed where you have failed, you are now mistaken. Whoever it is, they will fail just as you did.'

'Baldwin, didn't you hear that?' Simon interrupted. 'The man didn't know of the latest note!'

'Eh?'

'He didn't know there was a note last week! It wasn't him who left it!'

Petit Walles

If he had come here years ago with his father, this was precisely the sort of area Roger Crok would have been forced to avoid.

Nasty, odorous, filthy, it was a place where the dregs of the city would accumulate, downriver from all the better places where the rich lived. The only folk who were here were those with nowhere better to go. It had but one merit: Richard de Folville would never think to look for him here.

Roger had installed his mount in a stable over near the London Bridge, where he hoped it would remain safe, and had spent some days listening to the gossip of the streets, visiting alehouses and taverns all over the city, going to church and observing the temper of the crowds, and soon he had come to understand that the only desire in London was that the king should go – and be replaced by his elder son.

Four days ago, after Folville and la Zouche had tried to kill him, he had intended to hurry about his task and leave, but then he had heard of the rumours that the king was to depart, and had thought it would be better to stay and make sure that the story was true. But then, when the entourage had walked out from the castle, he had seen something which made him stop dead in the street.

'Mother,' he breathed, hardly daring to believe it was true.

She stood in the gloom of the gateway, a tall, courteous man at her side, who must have been a knight from the look of his great war-belt and weighty sword, but Roger scarcely noticed it. All he could see was his mother, pale and slender, watching the men marching from the gate, and in a moment, she was gone again.

It could have been a dream. A wonderful dream sent to remind him that his mother lived and loved him still. But Isabella Crok had looked so fair, so healthy and so real, he had no doubts in his own mind that this was no vision, but his mother.

From that day, he had come here to the Petit Walles, just outside the Tower itself, to look and see whether he might catch a glimpse of her again. It was as good a place as any, he told himself, to learn what he could about the Tower. He was not derelict in his duties. But she did not reappear, and today, he told himself, he must leave and see if he might find the queen. Yet he wanted to know if she was safe. And to learn who the man had been at her side.

Tower

The two burst in on the bishop as he sat eating his luncheon, and William Walle almost dropped the ewer in which the bishop was washing his hands.

'Bishop!' Baldwin blurted. 'My apologies for our unorthodox arrival, but we have news.'

'You have questioned him already?'

'We believe that he did not leave that note,' Simon said.

'But you found him. And it was he who left the other ones,' William said.

'Perhaps he did. But not this one,' Baldwin said. 'He had no idea about it, and no idea at all about there being two weeks to the attempt on your life. It was a complete surprise to him.'

'That I was to be assassinated?'

'No – that someone had sent you a note to tell you.'

'I think that the man is trying to force us into letting him loose,' the bishop said. His voice was not as steady as his words implied.

'Bishop, this is no laughing matter,' Baldwin said. 'I believe there is an accomplice of his in the Tower. It could only be someone who is inside the Tower, and that means it must surely be someone from your household whom you brought with you.'

'*What?*' the bishop demanded. 'How can you suggest such a thing!'

'One man did get inside your household, Bishop. I think a second must have as well,' Baldwin said. 'They could have infiltrated your household together, perhaps, or—'

'Sir Baldwin, this man in the gaol didn't manage to "infiltrate the household", as you put it. He was a clever man who pretended to be a member of the household. He would never have been able to come here with us, because his imposture would have soon become overly obvious. No, there can be no one in the household who would care to do such a thing. I am sure that my household is secure, the men all genuine in their care for me.'

'He will not give us his name, he will not tell us what evil you are supposed to have done him,' Baldwin said. 'To us, that implies that he is protecting another.'

'Who is he protecting? You tell me that, Sir Baldwin, and I will listen to you. But at present, all I hear is guesswork, and I have too much work to do. The city is collapsing into violence and ruin, and I am responsible. As it is, I am asked to join the Archbishop for a convocation at Lambeth in a week. I do not have time for all this!'

'On Monday next?' Simon asked.

'Yes.'

'Good. Because I would beg you, Bishop, please, to keep indoors and safe on the Wednesday of that week. Wednesday next, please don't go anywhere.'

'As the note said, eh?' the bishop said. He gave a small smile. 'Perhaps I can pretend to a headache on that day.'

'Good. And in the meantime, I think Sir Peregrine should begin his investigation into that man who calls himself Paul as soon as possible,' Simon finished. 'I know Baldwin detests torture, and I hate it myself, but that man is keeping something back, and it could be something that saves your life, Bishop. If he knows anything, it would be best that we learn it ourselves. Urgently.'

Chapter Forty-Three

It was not the command he wished to hear.

'Yes, Bishop. Of course I will do all I may to learn more. I will have the man put to the *peine fort et dure*.'

'I am sorry to hear it.' The bishop winced.

He was not the only man sorry to have to contemplate such a vile practice, Sir Peregrine told himself as he went down the stairs to the green and crossed the grass to the gaol. There, he ordered the gaoler to fetch three men to help, and had them go with him down to the cells.

'Come along,' Sir Peregrine said. It was a dreadful task, but the sooner they had the fool on the floor, hopefully the sooner they could release him and give his information to the bishop.

The cell was in darkness, of course. Peregrine could just make out the figure standing oddly like a shadow in the farther corner of the cell. 'You. Come here,' he called, but the man didn't respond.

Oh, to the devil with him! He was going to make it as hard as possible. 'I don't blame you,' Sir Peregrine muttered to himself, and then, louder, 'Open the door, gaoler.'

The steel door swung open on well-greased hinges, and Sir Peregrine marched in, walking to the figure, his steps slowing as he went. 'Sweet Mother of Christ!' he whispered.

His prisoner swung very slowly to face him, the eyes bulging in a head grown enormous, the features livid where the light from the lantern struck it.

'Oh, oh God,' he heard behind him.

'Hey, you puke there, you got to clear it up yourself,' the

gaoler complained as the splashes of vomit struck the floor, but Sir Peregrine paid no attention.

He remained fixed to the spot, staring up at the body with the stretched neck as it slowly turned, dangling from the ceiling.

*Second Wednesday after the Feast of St Michael**

Petit Walles

At last he saw her again. She was up there in the roadway that led down to the strange dog-leg entrance to the Tower, and Roger Crok felt his heart lift at the sight.

It was impossible to call out to her, for that would have brought him unwanted attention, but as she stepped out of the castle's gate and joined the throng of people, he was already level with her, and when she strode on in that determined fashion he recognised so well, he had to hurry his own pace to keep up with her.

She wasn't alone, of course. Since the disappearance of the king, the city had grown slightly less restive about the Tower, but it was still a very dangerous place, especially for a woman to walk alone. She had three men with her, a man who was tall and strong, although running to a paunch, who had a ruddy complexion like a committed cider drinker, then the tall knight he had seen with her in the gateway. The third was another man, one with a thin black beard that followed the line of his jaw, and he was sure that he had met this fellow before. Roger had to rack his brains to think where it was, and then he recognised him. It was the man he had spoken with in France.

He had no idea who these men were, and approached them with caution, eavesdropping on their conversation.

His mother spoke little. This was a talk about matters above her station, but it was clear that the others were happy to talk with her at their side.

* 8 October 1326

'He will have to come along here,' the bearded one was saying.
'Baldwin, I would not want him to ride along that road there.'
Baldwin shook his head. 'No, Sir Peregrine. This would be best. The houses are not so closely compacted.'
'It should suffice. What do you think, Simon?'
'I am sure that it would be fine for him. Where will he cross? At the bridge?'
'He won't swim,' said Sir Peregrine.
'I wondered whether it would be safer for him to take a boat across. At the bridge there are places a man could be pulled from his horse, or pushed out into the river.'
Roger Crok listened with some bafflement, wondering whom they discussed, but all the while his attention was fixed on his mother. She looked tired. Very tired. He wished only to speak with her for a short while, but the question was, how. And then he wondered if he could see her and make her realise. Hurrying on, he overtook the group, hoping that Sir Baldwin would not recognise him from Normandy. Once ahead of them, he stopped, and cast a careful eye behind him, meeting the gaze of Isabella.
She gasped, and for a moment he was torn between standing still and rushing back to her, fearful that she might faint. But his mother was made of strong stuff, and as soon as she caught her breath, she mustered her resources.
'Gentlemen, I feel rather weak. I had little food for my breakfast. You will kindly go on without me. I shall walk back to the castle from here.'
'Let me walk you back,' Sir Peregrine said at once.
Although she protested, he was most insistent, accompanying her back to the gates, and waiting until she was in the gateway, at which point she insisted that he return to the others.
Unknown to him, he was watched the whole time by Roger Crok.

They had both been walking for much of the morning when Ralph la Zouche suddenly stopped, grabbed Richard's arm, and pointed. 'That's the puppy! Look at the little shite, like butter wouldn't melt.'

Following his pointing finger, Richard gaped and nodded.

There, up ahead, Roger Crok was standing near the entrance to the Tower with a tall, elegant woman. She was earnestly speaking with him, and Crok was nodding enthusiastically, but then he shook his head in rapid alarm, and took her arm. Clearly she had suggested something that was little to his liking, and now she tried to take her arm away.

'Come with me,' Richard said.

Ralph was nothing loath, and the two walked quickly onwards, concealing themselves as best they could among the other folk walking about the streets.

They were in luck. The dispute between the two had caught the attention of one of the guards at the Tower, and he wandered towards the couple, even as the lad grabbed the lady's arm. She pulled away, and turned to placate the guards, letting them know that there was nothing for them to be alarmed about – she was only talking with the man, but then she stepped away from him, and appeared to be wishing him a tearful farewell.

Roger Crok stood at the bottom of the path with his head bent as the woman walked away. She did not turn once to look at him.

He did not notice his two pursuers until Richard whispered, 'Hello, Master Crok,' and clubbed him above the ear with a large stone he had picked up from the road.

Simon was used to investigating deaths, but not to anticipating them. This walk, from the Tower to the bridge, was taxing his intellect, he thought.

'I agree with Baldwin. Why not merely take a boat across the water, and be done? It will be safer than this long walk or ride.'

'You think so? The way matters are just now, I think the chances are that he would be seen, and men could ride to meet him at the other side,' Sir Peregrine said. 'It would be a terrible thing, were he to cross the river only to be killed within distance of the Archbishop's palace.'

'All this effort for a meeting of bishops,' Simon said.

Baldwin shook his head. 'It's not a mere meeting, Simon. It is to be hoped that this convocation may think of a means of averting bloodshed. That is what we must hope. The bishops of Winchester, Worcester, and Rochester and Bishop Walter, are all to join up there. With fortune they will hit on a scheme to avoid war.'

Sir Peregrine smiled sadly. 'They may try, but I can see no opportunity of avoiding it. I think we will have war.'

They had reached the bridge, and Simon stood a while, gazing about him glumly. 'Look at all these buildings. A man with a rock or two could drop them on the bishop's head as he passed here, and that would be that. Best make sure he wears his armour before leaving the Tower.'

Baldwin noted the buildings on the bridge. 'It is not only the buildings here, either. There are those buildings on the bridge, all giving excellent vantages to drop weapons on him. And if someone were to lift the drawbridge, it would be possible to hold him in one place and there to finish him off. I really dislike this idea.'

'I don't disagree, gentlemen,' Sir Peregrine said, as they retracted their steps, 'but he is determined to go. What would you have me do, lock him up like that other poor fellow?'

'He wasn't a poor fellow, he was trying to kill the bishop,' Simon said. 'He may not have left that last note, but I am sure he did the others.'

'A shame that he took his own life though,' Baldwin said.

Peregrine nodded. 'I blame myself. I should have seen that he could do that once I began to mention torture. I ought to have had him searched for straps and belts.'

The man called Paul had been able to kill himself by the simple expedient of taking his hood and cape, hooking the hood on a nail in the roof, then wrapping the trailing cloak about his throat. It made a firm noose. A bucket to stand on, which he kicked away, and his plan was complete.

'At least it means there is one assassin fewer for us to worry about,' Baldwin said.

They marched on, past suspicious citizens who glowered and spat as they passed, for the most part eyeing the buildings towering overhead, apart from Simon, who kept his attention on the faces of the people all around. He was not happy to be here, and would be so much happier were he at home. This city was not his natural habitat.

It was a relief to see the gates to the Tower again, down by the river, and his pace quickened.

Baldwin, however, slowed at the sight of two men kicking at a body lying between them. Two guards from the gate ran to the men. 'What is happening here?' one asked.

'This man is a traitor. His name is Crok, and he was in France until recently. He's a spy!'

The Tower

Waking was painful. His immediate thought was that Folville had stabbed him with a dagger in his head, because the pain was far too awful for it to have been a mere punch from a fist.

The second thought was that he needed to be sick, and he noisily gave into the urge.

He was in a large room – a hall, he realised. There was a roaring fire in the hearth, and when he cautiously looked around, he found himself meeting the gaze of a woman. She eyed him with a confident look, before calling out, 'Simon, he is awake!'

The man who walked in was the ruddy-faced one from the trio he had seen before. 'Where am I?' Roger asked weakly.

'In the Tower of London, and you can thank God you aren't in the gaol. There was a man killed himself in there only a few days ago, and we don't want you to do the same thing. A lady here pleaded on your behalf most fetchingly.'

'What do you want with me?' Roger said, gingerly feeling the lump on his head. It was larger than a goose's egg.

'The truth. We have been told that you are a traitor, that you were in Normandy with the Earl of Chester. Two men caught you and passed you to the guards at the gate. Is it true?'

'A pretty thought. So you wish me to tell you so that you can execute me on the king's behalf for treachery?'

'No. There will be bloodshed enough when the queen's mercenaries meet the king's host,' Simon sighed. 'However, I have to know, do you have any ill intention towards the Bishop of Exeter?'

'I hold him in no great esteem. He saw fit to have me thrown into gaol, and to have my mother dispossessed.'

'Who is your mother?'

'Lady Isabella Crok.'

Simon's head rose, and slowly a frown began to wash over his face. 'Isabella? Your father – did he die a while ago?'

'What do you mean?'

'Your mother – she lost her first husband, didn't she? And remarried, so now she is called Isabella Fitzwilliam, isn't she?'

Too late Roger saw that he had allowed his befuddled state to endanger his mother. 'No, my mother is—'

'I didn't realise!' Simon groaned. 'It was *she* who put the note into the bishop's room, Meg. It had nothing to do with that poor fellow who died. No wonder she pleaded for your life!'

'Which poor fellow?' Roger asked.

Simon gave a brief description of the stevedore, and saw the misery that washed into Roger's eyes.

'That sounds like Ranulf – my stepbrother. He was a good fellow, but headstrong. I am not surprised he killed himself, to try to save our family from any more shame.'

'Or to conceal his identity so that you or his mother could kill the bishop where he had failed?' Simon demanded.

'I should have found that enormously difficult. Until recently I was in Normandy. And your companion Sir Baldwin can confirm it,' Roger said. 'He saw me there in the summer. I have had no opportunity to plot any murder. And nor has my mother. She is innocent.'

'I shall leave that to other people to decide,' Simon said.

He rubbed at his temples. This was a terrible situation. If it was true that this fellow was indeed Isabella's son, it would be difficult to conceal the fact. 'Meg, could you send Hugh to fetch Sir Baldwin, and in the meantime, pour me a little wine, my love? My head throbs like a sapling attacked by a woodpecker!'

It took little time for Baldwin to join him, but to Simon's surprise, Sir Peregrine was with him.

'I thought it best that Sir Peregrine join us, Simon,' Baldwin said. 'This matter is too much for us alone.'

'Is it true?' Sir Peregrine asked. 'Is she guilty?'

Simon pulled a face. 'I have heard no one say it. This fellow is her son from her first marriage, but she was widowed.'

'My father fell from his horse,' Roger added helpfully.

'Later she remarried, this time to a man called Henry Fitzwilliam. And he, like she, already had a son, named Ranulf Fitzwilliam. I am afraid you have met him, Sir Peregrine. He was the lad who hanged himself.'

'That was her stepson?' Sir Peregrine breathed. 'Christ's cods! I should have realised. One day I saw her coming out from the gaol, but it did not occur to me that she was there out of anything other than simple curiosity. So many women like to see felons. It gives them a little frisson of excitement. I thought no more of it. I must be a—'

'Good and honourable man who is loath to see the worst in people,' Baldwin said firmly. 'Now, Sir Peregrine, do you love the woman?'

'I had promised to wed her.'

'Then do so. And do so quickly. Take her away from here, so that she cannot try to kill the bishop, and then, with luck, the whole matter will blow over.'

'And what if she desires to kill him later?' Sir Peregrine rasped.

'Sir, my mother could not kill a chicken. The idea of her stabbing a bishop is preposterous!' Roger said. 'I say this in all truth: she may have wished to avenge my stepfather, but she would not be able to put it into action. She has not the heart of a murderer.'

'I hope you are right,' Baldwin said. 'But how can you assure us?'

'I don't know. All I can tell you is my own firm belief, sir.'

'True enough. That itself is an honourable response, Sir Roger.'

'There is one other thing though. My mother's dispute is based upon the opportunistic theft of her dower. The bishop had her second husband gaoled for treachery, and poor Henry died in gaol, just like his son here. But afterwards, he took our inheritance, alleging that I was also a contrariant like Henry, and that my father was too. That is the sheerest nonsense. I was not, and neither was my father. But if you could help my mother to regain what she feels is hers, you will give her more reason to forgive than to try to avenge what has been done to her.' He winced as another shot of pain stabbed his head.

Sir Peregrine abruptly turned about, as though he was going to leave the room.

Baldwin felt a tearing pain in his breast at the thought of what must be going through Sir Peregrine's mind. He had fallen in love with women, but each time the focus of his affection had died – one of them in childbirth. This time, he had thought he was at last destined to be happy, only to suspect now that his woman was determined to kill Bishop Walter. It was unbearable to consider that all she had said, all she had done to this date, could have been intended purely as a means of getting herself close to the bishop to kill him. It was easy to imagine that Sir Peregrine was running through every meeting he had enjoyed with her, every conversation, to filter out the little snippets that indicated her desire to murder, rather than to enjoy his companionship. Sir Peregrine's face showed that he was enduring the most exquisite self-torture.

Baldwin took a deep breath. 'I think, Sir Peregrine, that this is a matter that we can keep to ourselves within this room.'

'You think I should trust her?' Sir Peregrine's voice was strangled. 'You think I could leave her to continue with this vile plan?'

'Her son declares that he thinks her incapable. Do you think she could kill? In truth?' Baldwin pressed him.

'How could I say? All she has ever said to me may be false, even that she . . . that she feels an affection for me. How can I tell?'

'You may have your doubts, Sir Peregrine,' Baldwin said, 'but the fact is, she has so far done nothing of which you could convict her. Writing a note? Pah! What of it? She has *not* drawn steel in his presence, has she?'

'Because the date which she predicted for the Bishop's death has not yet arrived.'

The date. Baldwin had forgotten that. 'The notes threatening the Bishop all gave him a short time to live, but the last gave him until one week from today. Why would that date have any significance?'

'I have no idea,' Roger Crok said, shaking his head and wincing as the pain shafted through his skull. 'Ach! It's close to the anniversary of my father's death.'

'The first note was sometime ago,' Simon mused. 'Why should she leave so long between the first message and the actual threatened death?'

'How long?'

Baldwin glanced at Simon. 'When was it? Before Candlemas?'

'I think so.'

'Forty weeks or more, then.'

Roger frowned as he considered. 'That long? I would have thought that . . . It is a coincidence, surely. My stepfather was held in gaol for thirty-nine weeks before he succumbed to the vile conditions in which he was held. Could that be it?'

Sir Peregrine said, 'I can ask the woman.'

Baldwin took his arm and pressed it. 'Sir Peregrine. This may be the last opportunity you have to be happy, old friend. Do not throw it away lightly.'

'Lightly? You think I will do anything in a burst of light-heartedness?'

'No, nor should you. Sir Peregrine, the woman has suffered enough. You, perhaps, can bring her to commonsense. Take her away from here for a few weeks. Take her home, possibly. Marry her, leave here, and you will, with fortune, win yourself a good, loving and kind woman. For if you remove her from this area, the bishop will be safe from her anyway. And later, perhaps this son of hers can bring her to reason with your help. Marry her, take her away, and have an enjoyable life, Sir Peregrine.'

'You think I can trust her?' Sir Peregrine repeated.

'I think so. Especially if you swear to win back her lands for her. Tell her that, and you will find her appreciative, I am sure.'

'A woman who could plot to kill a bishop . . .'

'Many have made dreams in the dark of the night,' Baldwin said, 'and her plotting so far is only a wild dream. If you marry her, you will save her from her living nightmare. Marry her, and you will give her a new reason to want to live.'

'I don't know . . .'

Baldwin ignored him, looking instead at Margaret and Simon. 'Do we all agree?'

Simon looked away. He had no desire to see a pleasant woman like Isabella executed for attempting murder, but to leave her free was also against his policy of adherence to the law.

Baldwin prompted him. 'Simon, if you have an objection, you must raise it now. Do you think she would go through with such a scheme on her own?'

'It is hard to imagine.'

'So, if she is kept away from the bishop, that will help matters. If she also sees a means of recovering what she has lost as well, that will no doubt comfort her too. I think this makes sense.'

Simon nodded. 'Very well. But Sir Peregrine must keep her close by him all day next Wednesday. If she does try to make an attempt on Bishop Walter's life, I will have no choice but to seek her out, and kill her.'

Roger Crok smiled. 'Gentlemen, I am deeply honoured that you are being so generous to my mother. Especially after you managed to break my head in so magnificent a manner.'

'That was not us,' Simon said. 'The guards at the gate said that there were two men who crept up on you and presented you to them.'

Roger's ease fled in an instant. 'Damn them! Folville and la Zouche!'

Chapter Forty-Four

*Second Monday after the Feast of St Michael**

Tower of London

Simon and Baldwin saw to their own horses as the bishop's guard prepared themselves.

It was a raw morning. The wind was howling up the Thames, promising snow and ice before too long, and hoar frost limed the grass even here in the Tower's yard.

Tugging on the cinch strap, Baldwin looked at his stallion's eye. Waiting a moment, he jabbed his thumb up into the mount's belly, and yanked on the leather again, tightening it two more notches. 'Old devil,' he muttered as he threaded the leather strap through its restrainer. 'Why do I have to do that every day?'

Simon was already in the saddle as Baldwin finished, checking the straps of the reins and harness. 'I hope we've done the right thing, Baldwin.'

'I am sure that we have,' he said with assurance. He set a foot in the stirrup and swung himself up, gazing down speculatively. It felt secure enough. 'I think we have saved Sir Peregrine from making a terrible error, while also protecting a woman who is in every way a wonderful mate for him.'

'What of the son?'

Baldwin shrugged. 'I would think that he could be released soon.'

'Hugh will be glad,' Simon said. He had set Hugh and Rob to

* 13 October 1326

guard their prisoner, and although Roger Crok was probably peevish at being held against his will, Hugh had made his own feelings abundantly clear on the matter. He wanted to be out of the hall and off to the tavern at the corner of the castle's yard, not stuck in here with Crok.

After some discussion, Simon and Baldwin had agreed that Sir Peregrine would escort Isabella, Roger Crok's mother, back to Devon, and that Roger himself would be held, on the promise of his not attempting to escape, at Simon's residence. There seemed little need to worry about his attempting to run away, for with the lump swelling his head, he was incapable of fast riding or making off on his feet, and clearly incapable of attempting an attack on the bishop. He could barely rise without the colour draining from his face. The blow that had knocked him down at the castle's entrance was a cruel one.

With both Isabella Fitzwilliam and Roger out of the way, Simon and Baldwin were feeling a great deal more comfortable. The threat from Isabella and the two men had been effectively eradicated, and there were no other sons of hers to fear.

However, it was one thing to remove a threat, and another to remove *all* threats.

'I don't like this,' Simon muttered again.

Baldwin grunted. They were riding with the guard to take the bishop to the Archbishop's Palace at Lambeth, where there was to be a great convocation of bishops, with the intention of discussing how to bring about peace and some semblance of stability once more. The madness and mob-rule had to stop.

'The city is close to riot,' Simon said.

The mood of the populace was clear enough as they rode out over the moat and left the Tower behind. Simon was uncomfortable in a steel breastplate and armour over his legs and thighs. It pinched at his flanks, and compressed his paunch, but he was glad that Baldwin had prevailed upon him to wear something. All around was quiet with the false peace of a summer's day before a storm. The men and women who could be seen were all glowering and disrespectful as the men trotted past Bishopesgate and up towards the great bridge. The bishop himself was clad all in steel – he had needed no encouragement to dress himself in protective clothing.

There were fires in the road at three places. The people had behaved as Londoners always would, building great mounds of rubbish and setting them alight. There were a few children warming themselves at the second of them, but at the others there was no crowd, which was itself a relief. Simon was beginning to hope that they might make their way to the London Bridge without injury, just as the first attack was launched.

A man bellowed, 'For the queen!' and hurled a lump of rock at them. It whirled past Simon's face and hit the man-at-arms on his left, the fellow giving a loud curse that was audible over the ringing sound of rock on steel, and then there was a general hissing of steel as all the men in the guard drew their weapons. In the brief silence afterwards, Simon heard the bishop's voice telling a clerk to find out who had been hit. He would be given a penance later for his blasphemy.

That rock was the signal for all hell to break loose. A scrambling mass of men threw themselves at the guard from the alleys, shouting and swearing, faces distorted with rage and hatred and fear, hands gripping bills and daggers and long knives, butchers in their leather aprons wielding cleavers, a mason with a great hammer, and a smith with a gleaming blade that looked as though it was fresh from the forge.

Simon found his horse rearing, and was hard pressed merely to keep his seat, but he bellowed, kicked, spurred and cajoled until the beast came under some sort of control, and by then he was in the middle of the press. Men tried to stab him, and he realised with a shock of horror that they meant to drag him from his horse and kill him. He had to swing his sword about, flailing ineffectually, just to clear a path. Others weren't so fortunate: he saw one guard hauled from his horse, to disappear beneath a mass of bodies – and then there was a scream and a gout of blood, and a cheer of animal success.

'Baldwin! Baldwin!' he shouted, and saw his old friend at last.

He was calm, to all appearances, and fitted to his saddle as firmly as a blade welded to a hilt. The horse was an extension of the knight, swivelling and kicking and biting, while Baldwin used his sword only when necessary. He caught sight of Simon and, recognising his friend's alarm, immediately glanced over his shoulder to see that the bishop was safe. Then he moved towards Simon.

There were three men between them. The butcher, a footpad with a thick cudgel, and a man who looked as though he might have been a priest, with thick hair about his skull, but a scant layer over his pate.

He was first to be pushed from Baldwin's way, even as the butcher swung his cleaver at Simon. He tried to knock the blow aside, but the massive two-handed cleaver came down upon his thigh and although it did not penetrate the metal, Simon could feel the steel buckle under the blow. He swore, and then felt the horse shiver. The blade had sprung from his armour and glanced off into the horse's back, and now the beast was shocked into movement, bucking and rearing to escape this hell. At least his wild hoofs made the attackers fall back, and soon Simon felt Baldwin at his side.

Simon was terrified that this great brute might suddenly collapse and die. He had seen it before with horses which were given even apparently small injuries: they could suddenly take fright at the pain and collapse. The thought of falling here, with so many men who would be pleased to cut his throat for him, was terrifying.

Fortunately, Baldwin's presence seemed to steady the beast for a moment, just as the bishop and the other men sprang forward and on, past their attackers. Simon set his head after them and clapped his spurs to the beast's flanks. The animal hesitated only a moment, and then was off, with Simon clinging on and urging it to greater speed. On and on they went, fast as the wind, until they had reached the bridge itself, and there they scarcely slowed their pace, but took the corner at a canter, and then rode on through the crowds lining the bridge without taking any care of the people thronging the place.

Lambeth Palace

They reached the great palace of the archbishop a short time later.

Simon rode in under the great gates with his heart still thudding painfully in his breast like the thunder of pounding hoofs. He dropped to the ground thankfully, his hand over his chest, but the metal plate would give him no comfort. It felt as though his heart must explode with the shock.

'Simon? Are you all right?' Baldwin asked solicitously.

'I think so. I don't have any wounds,' Simon said, and immediately felt the urge to weep. It was infuriating. He had survived an unannounced attack, and had every right to feel proud and glad to escape uninjured, and instead he felt an overwhelming lassitude and confusion.

'You need a cup of strong wine,' Baldwin said. 'Come with me, old friend.'

'Wait,' Simon said, and checked his horse. The glancing blow from the cleaver had by good fortune only nicked the animal, most of the energy being dissipated in the leather of the saddle, but there was a small scratch, and Simon asked a nearby ostler to put some tar on it to stop it growing infected.

Baldwin led Simon into a large undercroft near the gateway, in which a number of other men were gathered and talking in low, anxious voices. Some were guards who had come here today, but others were plainly travellers, servants and messengers. All turned to peer at them as they walked inside and crossed the flagged floor to the bar.

'Not the most cheerful welcome,' Baldwin noted.

Simon could not disagree. They took their jug of wine and cups out into the great yard and sat on a tree trunk waiting to be sawn into planks, sipping their wine.

'Why did they attack us like that?' Simon said after a while. He could feel the warmth of the wine making its way along his bones and muscles, soothing and relaxing them.

'The Londoners don't like bishops any more,' was Baldwin's assessment. 'They hate Walter in particular, and with the queen on her way, they reckon that it is time to assert their rights again.'

'So it's just that they wanted to kill Walter?' Simon said.

William Walle was in the yard and he joined them, taking Simon's cup and draining it. 'A fairly exciting morning, gentlemen. Who would have thought that the London mob could exert itself to attack a bishop so effectively?'

'Baldwin is sure that the good bishop was the target of their especial hatred,' Simon said. 'I find it hard to believe, though.'

'Why?' asked William. 'Because you and I know him for what he truly is, a decent, generous, good man? But think of all the hordes in London who only see him as the man who was, until recently, in charge of all the taxes. It has been said often enough that no one loves a taxman. Even his own mother, I believe,' he added with a grin.

'So you think that's what the attack was about?' Simon said sceptically.

'We saw the mob attack him last year,' Baldwin said thoughtfully. 'He was assaulted outside St Paul's, remember.'

'Yes,' Simon said, 'but that was different. Today a man was killed. I saw him.'

'Yes,' William said, 'and I think that the mob would have killed Bishop Walter if they could have reached him. It is fortunate that we had enough men with us to prevail.'

'We may not have next time,' Baldwin said.

'At least the other threat has been removed,' Simon said. 'It is one thing to worry about a mob, and another to fear a single, dedicated assassin.'

'Yes,' Baldwin said. 'Although I would like to be reassured of something . . . Tell me, good squire: the men I found in among the lists of the bishop's enemies – there were only the two, I think, weren't there? There was the Crok family, whom we have now discovered is no threat, and the family of Biset, is that correct? And one Londoner, a fellow called Hamo?'

'Yes. That's right, but how do you know Crok and—'

'You need not worry about them,' Baldwin said firmly. 'And I cannot divulge a secret which is not my own. It was not they who made me concerned. A friend has mentioned two more dangerous men who are in London, and who struck him down: a fellow called Richard de Folville and another called Ralph la Zouche. Do you know of them?'

William's face hardened. 'Know those two? In God's name, I wish I didn't! Folville is a detestable felon. His family has been an enemy to the law and justice these ten years past. The la Zouches are no better. The only good news I have heard recently is that Ivo la Zouche has died in France. It was these two families which attacked poor Belers and slew him. You remember that murder?'

Baldwin had known Belers slightly. He did not like the man, but he was a king's official, and to be slaughtered by the side of the road was a disgraceful matter. 'I have heard that they are in London,' he said quietly. 'Would they be enemies of the bishop?'

'Yes,' William said firmly.

It was a relief to hear that the bishop was to remain at the palace for the afternoon.

Simon had almost bellowed when he was told that the plan of Archbishop Reynolds was that the bishops should ride to St Paul's to meet and pray, planning to launch a new peace initiative by sending some bishops to meet with the king and the queen and begin negotiations.

'Does he never leave his own fortress here?' Simon expostulated. 'The streets are full of wandering killers! There was an assault on us this morning, in Christ's name!'

His were not the only words of protest. Several of the Bishop of Exeter's men-at-arms were heard to raise their voices angrily at the thought of fighting into the city, while clerks and even two friars lifted their own in their determination to prevent such a foolish task. 'It'll only lead to the deaths of innocents!' they declared, and began to preach to all who would listen how it was quite wrong to tempt the people of the city into committing the crime of attacking a group of bishops. The guilt for that would lie with the bishops themselves.

In the end, to the huge relief of all, the archbishop had bowed to the inevitable. It was a hundred and fifty years or more since the murder of Becket, and no one wanted to see another bishop killed.

Instead, Simon and Baldwin had ridden back to the Tower with William Walle, and on their way they discussed the morning's attack. Baldwin tentatively raised the matter of the two felons.

'Why should they want to attack the bishop?'

'The Folvilles and la Zouches have been enemies of Bishop Walter for many years. They blame him for their losses, just as they have also blamed the Despenser family. Any hardship they endure, they have to put at the feet of others whom they distrust.'

'Why Bishop Walter though?' Baldwin pressed.

William pulled a face. 'I have heard my uncle mention before now that he took some lands from the Folvilles. I think that there is no love lost between him and them.'

'Is it extreme enough for a Folville to wish to kill the bishop?'

'I would say that the dislike between them is strong enough for the bishop to want to kill them as well!' William said. 'My uncle was fond of Belers.'

Baldwin thought back to the man who had kicked the prone body of Roger Crok five days before. 'I could recognise him again. What about you, Simon?'

'I would, yes. But what are the chances of him still being here? Surely he would have ridden away by now.'

'Perhaps – and yet the city is ready for war. Escaping would be easy, but dangerous at the same time. Perhaps he is still here. And if someone could recognise him, that would at least make the threat of him attacking the bishop less likely.'

'Yes,' Simon said. He considered. 'So you think we ought to try to leave the bishop as bait and ride with him, then?'

William Walle began to shake his head with an anxious frown. 'No, you mustn't do that! What if you are in the bishop's guard and see those two? You could ride off after them and leave his protection sorely weakened!'

'William, you will be there with him, won't you?' Baldwin said soothingly. 'And not alone. There will be plenty of men with you. Leave it to us, my friend.'

*Third Wednesday after the Feast of St Michael**

Enfield

The day was cool, and Baldwin, sitting on his horse, could feel the chill air on his face. A kiss of ice, he thought idly, as the horse moved beneath him.

Bishop Walter had insisted upon joining the archbishop two days before in a second meeting at St Mary's, in Southwark. The little village was unused to the sudden arrival of so many bishops and men-at-arms, but at least there were no more armed assaults on the men, and to Simon and Baldwin's relief, the bishop had not encountered any further violence.

While waiting for him, Simon and Baldwin had begun to put into place a plan for guarding the bishop. Although there was no longer any reason to think that the warning notes would bring forward an attack on him, there was still concern about the man Folville and his companion, la Zouche. The pair of them had disappeared since their beating of Crok, and no matter how many people were offered bribes, nobody seemed to know anything of the two. Simon had grown convinced that they had indeed left the city, but Baldwin was less convinced, and he continued to worry at the problem, wondering where such men might hide themselves, where they might go, what they might do.

After that, the last two days had become hectic. Following the meeting at St Mary's, Bishop Walter had returned yesterday to Lambeth, where the bishops tried to decide who could be sent to the queen, but there was a singular lack of agreement. Eventually, Bishop Walter declared that the matter had been discussed enough and left, and with his guards rode up through the city. Instead of going to the Tower again however, he took the old drovers' road north, and spent the night at his manor here at Enfield, much to Simon's irritation; he wanted to return to his wife.

* 15 October 1326

Still, the rest away from the city had clearly done the bishop much good. He was much happier today, and now he came out from the doorway to view his guards with a more relaxed manner. His eyes were clearer, Simon thought, as though the sleep and his praying in the little private chapel had eased his soul.

He chatted to the men, walking amongst them, touching a man's knee, holding a mount's reins, while he spoke calmly and quietly, like a warrior leading his men into battle. And clad all in armour, that was precisely the impression he exuded, while behind him John de Padington and William Walle stood and grinned to hear his confidence. They both appeared to be congratulating themselves on having protected the bishop from the dreadful fears of those appalling notes.

It was early in the morning still when he finally went to the mounting block and the whole cavalcade could begin to make their way out through his enormous gatehouse and off to the road which led to London.

The weather may have appeared warmer in the yard, but now, trotting along the roads, Simon felt the need to pull his cloak tighter about him. The armour was hideously freezing, and the faint breeze that met his face felt as though it was flaying his flesh from his cheeks.

Still, London lay ahead, only some three leagues or so. It would be good, he thought, to get back there. After all the effort he had gone to, Simon felt quite sure that Folville and la Zouche could present little, if any, danger. The bishop must be safe.

Chapter Forty-Five

Frydaystrate, behind St Matthew's, London

Richard de Folville shivered in the cold morning air. This whole exercise was turning into a farce.

They had tried to leave London as soon as they had clubbed Crok to the ground, but the stable had been locked and barred, and when they threw a rock through the man's window, he had told them to clear off. He would not open today, he said. There was too much violence.

The next day, they had laid in wait for the fellow, and managed to catch him and drag him back to the stableyard, but then they were forced to change their own minds. The place was in the midst of a crowd of furious, baying citizens, and even la Zouche himself was nervous about entering with all those people in the way. They had the look of a mob which could turn on any stranger to their parish, and Folville had experienced enough danger in the last year already. He made the decision that they would have to remain here in London for another day or so.

That one day had become three, then four, and now it was a whole week! He could have killed that cretin Crok for keeping them back those first few days. God alone knew where the queen was now. She would probably not even remember them, and if she did, it would be only to punish their tardiness.

There was a shout, then more, and a steady rumbling noise that he couldn't understand at first, and then he realised it was the sound of many feet hurrying along a roadway. He walked up to Westchepe, and looked along it in the direction of St Paul's.

Heading towards him was the largest mob of men and women he had ever seen. It was a sight to strike horror into the boldest heart, and he stared dumbly as they approached, some waving weapons, others shouting obscenities, and he shrank back into the street away from them as they came closer, before sweeping on past him, in a torrent of humanity, towards the east.

La Zouche was behind him when he turned. 'What in Christ's name are they all doing?' he asked, visibly shocked.

There was a man in the road in front of them. 'The queen's left a letter on the doors of St Paul's,' he said. 'She's asking for the support of the city, and we're all going to the Guildhall to demand that the city agrees!'

This was a curious event, certainly, but if it went as the mob appeared to wish, it would help their escape from London. As soon as the queen came closer, the fears of spies must dissipate. Richard Folville made a quick decision. Any action was better than sitting here and doing nothing all day.

'Come with me. We'll go and watch this,' he said.

Cripplegate, London

As they drew nearer to the city, Simon knew that something terrible was happening. Smoke was rising from several great fires, and if the people of London were burning fires in the streets, that meant the mob was close by.

'You've seen them?' he said quietly to Baldwin, gesturing at the bonfires.

Baldwin scratched at his neck where his armour was rubbing. 'This looks bad,' he agreed. 'But let us hope that we may make our entry in peace.'

In that at least, his hopes appeared to be met. They rode in through the Cripplegate and down Wodestrate, past the large flint-built church of St Alphage where it was set in the wall, and on past St Alban. Already there was a curious stillness about all the men-at-arms, Simon noticed. Before reaching London, they had been a raucous, rumbustious group, but now, as they trotted along the broad streets, they seemed to gather together for security, their eyes all about, looking for the citizens who would normally be here. There was a feeling of danger, of threat, that was so strong, it could almost be smelled. And in return, Simon thought that they were adding their own subtle odour of fear to the mix of smoke, piss and filth.

They continued to Westchepe, where they halted. There was a terrible roaring and shouting from the west, nearer the cathedral, and for a while Simon feared that the bishop might suggest that they should go and investigate, but to his relief, he had a better idea.

'We will go to my house at Old Dean's Lane,' the bishop told them all.

Simon glanced at Baldwin, who nodded. But Simon could see that the knowledge was written on his grim visage. The city was about to explode.

Guildhall

The mob was already turning ugly by the time that Folville approached the Guildhall, and he chose the safer option of keeping back with la Zouche.

'I don't like this,' Ralph said, and Richard had to agree. 'Come,' he said, and the two fought their way free. At last they were on Westchepe, and with relief, Richard spotted a tavern that looked as though it was open.

Just then, there was a mighty shout from along the road, up towards the great conduit, and there they saw a man being dragged towards them, hemmed in by a large crowd of men and women, all baying like hounds.

'Who is that?' la Zouche asked nervously.

'I don't know,' Richard Folville said, and as he spoke, there was another roar from the mob. Someone had cut the head from the unfortunate victim, and now a man was holding it high by the hair, shaking it and sprinkling people with the man's blood. 'Sweet Jesu,' he muttered. 'This is no place for us, Ralph.'

'No,' la Zouche agreed, but before the two could make good their escape, they were thrust from the path of another crowd. This time there were men among them whom Richard recognised. There was the Abbot of Westminster and the Dean of

St Paul's – and even as Richard watched, they were forced to kneel in the road and beg for the protection of the city, while also stoutly stating that they were all devoted servants of the queen.

Taking their cue from the crowds, Richard prodded Ralph, and both began to bellow their support for the queen. After all, as Richard told himself, it was why they were there.

Holborn, London

If he could, Simon would have refused to stop here when the force reached the first of the roadblocks. There was a huge bonfire nearby, and the men could all see the heads of young and old alike beyond. The flames glinted from their steel caps, from the polished and sharpened swords and axes.

It was enough to drive the bishop to a sharp rage. 'What is all this?' he bellowed, standing up in his stirrups. 'I am riding to my house and you fools have blocked my path! I will pass!'

There was no response at first, and then a man shouted, 'Your home's out the other side of the city. Not that there'll be much left.'

'What is that supposed to mean?' the bishop demanded.

'The mob's gone to your house, bishop. They were seeking you, but since you're not there, they'll probably just burn it down!'

'Dear God in heaven,' the bishop groaned. 'All my books, and my register . . . Quick, we must go to my house.'

Simon grunted unhappily. 'We should carry on to his house in Old Dean's Lane, Baldwin. If the mob's up there at Temple Bar, that's the last place we ought to go.'

'Come with me, Simon,' Baldwin said, and spurred his horse on to catch up with the bishop. 'Bishop? Bishop Walter?'

'What, Sir Baldwin?'

'We really believe that you should not be heading this way. My lord, this city is close to riot: you can hear it and see it all about you. You should come with us to the Tower.'

'I will not run away from a mob of London churls when they attack my house!' the man said obstinately.

Simon could see his face. There was no fear in his eyes, only a cold determination and anger. 'But Bishop Walter, if you go to Temple Bar, it is likely you'll be killed.'

'Look at the men with me,' the bishop scoffed. 'Do they look terrified? No. And nor should you be, Simon. The threats of the notes is all over and done with. I am a bishop, in God's service. I don't think that the London mob will do anything to harm me. Englishmen don't tend to kill bishops very often!'

Baldwin and Simon exchanged a glance. There was nothing they could do to stop the bishop if he was set on this course. 'There are plenty of guards,' Simon said.

'I hope there are enough,' Baldwin said. He was not enthusiastic. But he had remained in London to help guard the bishop, and he wouldn't turn away now. 'Ach, come on, Simon! Let us stay with him, for good or ill. You never know – there may be something good to come of it all.'

And so it suddenly seemed.

As they rode back the way they had come, up Westchepe, Simon caught sight of a face that looked familiar. 'Baldwin – look there!'

Folville saw them at the same time. 'Shit! Ralph, we're being hunted. Come!'

Spinning on his heel, Richard bolted away from Westchepe and along Bredstrete, followed by Ralph, their boots rattling on the flagged way, while behind them they heard shouting, and then the stolid clatter of hoofs.

Folville did not know this part of the city, but he was gambling on the fact that their pursuers might not know it either, and he led Ralph la Zouche at a ferocious pace, down over West Fish Market, and then snapping right, along another little parish church. There was the sound of a horse skidding as it took the stones at the corner too quickly, but then the horsemen were after him again, and he must run still harder, while his blood roared and hissed in his ears, and his lungs felt that they must burst. It was awful. But then he saw an opening in a wall, and he bolted inside, feeling rather than seeing Sir Ralph stumble in behind him.

Motioning, he sent Sir Ralph to crouch at one side of the entrance, while he took the other, and both waited, motionless, panting, their swords out and ready.

The horses came, slowed, and stopped.

'We saw you enter, sirs. I call on you both, Sir Ralph la Zouche, and Richard de Folville, to come out. I am Keeper of the King's Peace, and I wish to talk with you both.'

'You want to talk? Give me your name, sir, and I'll think about it. I don't like to obey commands from any knight on horseback, no matter how honourable he may consider himself.'

'I am Sir Baldwin de Furnshill, Keeper of the King's Peace, and lately guard to the soul of the Bishop of Exeter.'

'And I am rector to the parish church of Teigh. What do you want from me?'

He suddenly felt a sharp prick at the base of his spine. It pressed forward slowly, and he was forced to take a pace, then another, hardly daring to try to wheel and stab the man who had crept up behind him, because he had so little time to consider the dangers.

Ralph saw his attacker, and lurched forward to help him. As he did so, a sword shot out from the gate, and la Zouche tripped over the flat of the blade, falling heavily to the ground.

'So, it would seem you have us!' Richard said sneeringly as Simon took his wrists and bound them strongly with a long thong.

'You will have to answer to the bishop for your actions,' Baldwin said. 'He is the guardian of the city just now, and I think he will be keen to speak with you. For my part, I am only glad that the last threat has been taken from him.'

He was kneeling on Sir Ralph's back as he spoke, swiftly binding the knight's wrists too, and then he and Simon lashed their thongs to longer ropes, and while Simon gathered up the men's swords, Baldwin led the two to the horses, which had been tethered outside the gateway. Soon they were trotting northwards towards St Paul's, the men walking at their side.

* * *

William Walle saw Baldwin and Simon suddenly pelt off southwards, and he wanted to tell the bishop, to suggest that they should at least wait a little for them, but the whole mood of the area was against him. There were men peering out from doorways and windows, and William was sure that he could see the gleam of oiled metal weapons when he looked more closely.

This was a strangely quietened city. It was odd, as though in the midst of this enormous city he had found a stillness and peace. He had never before seen these lanes so empty. Now there was only himself and the men about the bishop – no one else. It gave William a sense of calmness that was quite unlike anything he had known before.

And of fear.

Yes. It was there, deep in his breast, the certainty that there was something entirely wrong, as though the devil had come here to London and taken away all the people. It was too silent. The horses' hoofs echoed in the emptiness, and now William could feel his heart beginning to thud more painfully as the realisation began to seep into his soul that this was not normal. They were being lured on.

'Bishop!'

The cavalcade stopped, and William rode on urgently. 'This must be some sort of trap, Uncle. When have you ever seen the streets so deserted?'

'What would you have us do?' his uncle replied. He smiled. 'Don't worry about the mob, William. It's my books in the house that worry me!'

He gave the signal to ride, and they trotted on, but then William saw the men in front wavering. One turned and looked back at him, a small frown of concern on his face. 'Squire?'

That was when he heard it. Behind them came a low, visceral sound, like a thousand wolves seeing a herd of deer after a long famine. It was hideous, but not so bad as when William turned to look.

There, a scant hundred yards away, stood a great mob of

people. They filled the entire street from side to side, a feral mass of citizens – some, he saw with horror, spattered with blood from other victims. 'Ride! Ride!' he shouted, and spurred his own beast.

But it was too late. They had ridden beyond St Michael le Querne already, so the escape down Eldesfistrate was already denied them, and before them a second huge crush materialised as if from thin air. Men waving sickles, knives and polearms, with hideous grinning faces on seeing the horror and terror in the eyes of the men about the bishop.

'Bishop! Ride for the cathedral! Claim sanctuary!' he screamed, hoping that his voice would carry, and rode forward to try to protect him.

John de Padington was at his side now, and the old man gave him a wink. 'Don't worry, Will. He'll be all right. The old bugger always falls on his feet!' he said, and then coughed. And as William felt the splash of warmth on his face, he suddenly realised that John had been shot by a crossbow. The quarrel had hit his skull, and the blood and brains were spattered all over William's face.

'*No*!' he cried, but already John's senseless body was toppling backwards from his horse. Held by the stirrups, he rode forward, his horse witless with fear.

William gave a hoarse scream of defiance and drew his sword. He lifted it high, and would have ridden forward, but the press of riders about him was too thick, and then they were all engulfed by the mob, and he watched without comprehension as first one, then another, man disappeared, their bodies pulled from their horses, and while their arms flailed, their legs kicked, they were carried away. It was like watching ants consume a bee. The bee could sting and kill a hundred, a thousand, and still be borne off and absorbed.

There was a blow in his side, and he felt his arse lift from the saddle as a spear entered his breast. He did not fall. The spear was tugged free, and he tried to swing his sword at the man, but his strength and coordination were gone.

Through the confusion of men and weapons, he saw his uncle for the last time. The bishop had reached the north door of the cathedral, and there he was pulled to the ground. Now men were dragging his uncle up towards the great cross in the road by St Michael le Querne; he saw them manhandle him, strip him of his armour then beat him, forcing him to his knees, one shoving his head down so that the back of his neck was exposed, while another thumped him on the head twice, three times, with the handle of a knife . . . and then he saw the other man with the bread-knife sawing at his uncle's neck until there was a huge fountain of blood which smothered the nearest people, and then the man was holding up his uncle's head, dancing and laughing, while the crowd cheered and shrieked their glee like demented demons even as the bile rose, thick and acid, in his throat.

And he gave a groan that seemed to come from his feet and shivered throughout his body. And then he felt the moan growing within him, and it became a roar at the injustice, the disgrace, and he spurred his mount forward, lifting his sword over his head to ride in amongst the crowd and kill as many as he could, uncaring about his own safety, only determined to take as many with him as possible.

He was scarcely aware of the two swords that stabbed up under his breastplate, into his belly and chest, nor of the detonation of agony that lasted only a moment, and then he was toppling gently into a spinning world of flashes of light, which faded quickly to blackness.

Chapter Forty-Six

'*No!*' Simon cried, and would have ridden forward as William slowly toppled, lifeless.

Baldwin was staring at the man who had the bishop's head. He had thrust it onto a pole, and now the obscene symbol danced over the heads of the crowds, bobbing and weaving.

'Simon, we must go,' he said.

'We can't just leave Walter to them!' he said, distraught. 'He was our friend!'

'And he wouldn't want us to throw away our lives needlessly,' Baldwin said. He looked down at the two men, then nodded to Folville. 'Stand still.'

He pressed the blade of Folville's sword against the thong and saw it fall away. 'Take your sword, sir. You will need it in among this place. London is given over to madness and murder. Do you come with us to the Tower, and you will be safe.'

'You will arrest us?'

Baldwin looked at him bleakly. 'No. I am offering you your life. If you stay here, you will die. Release your companion and follow us, if you would live.'

He looked at his friend. 'Simon, there is nothing we can do for him. He is dead.'

'He was only a good man seeking to serve!'

'I know. But the mob will not hear reason. Not today. So come away, Simon. We must save ourselves. Your wife will be distraught, my friend. Come. Let us go to her.'

Simon nodded at last, and they set off at a fast trot, with Sir Ralph and Richard running lightly alongside. It was a stroke of good fortune that the Tower was so close. They made their way along narrow streets suddenly devoid of all people. All appeared to be hiding, or already at Westchepe, joining in the celebrations at the murders.

They clattered up the drawbridge into the Tower's courtyard, and there Simon dropped from his horse and stood like a man who had fallen into a nightmare.

Baldwin slowly dismounted. Overhead, ravens cawed and soared on the air, and a blackbird sat on the wall nearby and sang loudly. The air was cold. So cold.

Margaret appeared in the doorway to the hall and walked towards them, smiling. 'Simon, Baldwin – I am so glad to see you both. I had thought something was wrong last night when you didn't come back. Where's the bishop?'

Until that moment he had been fine, but as soon as she spoke those words, Simon began to weep.

*Third Thursday following the Feast of St Michael**

Tower of London

The last night had been appalling.

From the highest point of the Keep, Baldwin had been able to follow the worst of the fighting and terror in the city. The Bishop of London had fled, as had the archbishop (by stealing another bishop's horses), and the mob roved all over the city. They not only rampaged through the Bishop of Exeter's house at Temple Bar, they also pillaged the house of the Bardi, the King's bankers, and the manor of Finsbury, and St Paul's and the priory of Holy Trinity. In each there was money and treasure housed for safekeeping, and the mob stole whatever it could. All through the night, watchmen dare not go about their duties. They would have been slaughtered by the groups of laughing, singing men who roved the streets wielding swords or knives.

They heard what had happened to the bishop's body during the morning.

---

* 16 October 1326

Bishop Walter's head had been parcelled up and sent to the queen, who was then at Gloucester. His body was thrown to the dogs, and the mob made it clear that no one was to try to liberate it. The good canons of St Paul's ignored that, and they rescued it at Vespers, taking the remains into the cathedral; but there were malicious rumours that the bishop had died while excommunicate, so in the morning it was removed and given to St Clement Danes, the church just outside Temple Bar where his favourite London house was. However, the rector who enjoyed the living there, and who owed his livelihood to the bishop, would not have the corpse within. He was scared of the mob. It was an old woman, poor and frail, who did not know Bishop Walter, but who still showed him kindness. She found some old fabric with which to cover up the mutilated body and persuaded others nearby to take it to a cemetery.

They took it to the graveyard at Holy Innocents, which was derelict now, and unused. There, Bishop Walter II's body was dropped unceremoniously into a pit, and left to rot.

'Still watching?' Simon asked, as he joined Baldwin on the battlements.

'There is plenty to see,' Baldwin said.

There had been talk already of the gathering of men at Cornhulle. They had been clearly visible from several points, trudging up the roads. It was a quirk of London that it was built upon the two hills, Ludgate and Cornhulle, the two separated by the Walbrook River, so that from the Tower, there was a good view of much of the first hill.

'It doesn't bode well for us,' Simon said.

'No, it doesn't,' Baldwin agreed.

'I'm sorry, Baldwin. You should have gone home to Jeanne and the children. It was pointless for you to remain here with us.'

'Yes, but the trouble was, the journey would have been too uncertain just as the queen was moving to encircle the city. I am only sad that the bishop is dead.'

'Yes,' Simon sighed. It was still hard to believe that the good Bishop of Exeter was gone. 'I don't know that I shall ever get over seeing him yesterday. What a way to die!'

'Worry less about him. He is gone and cannot suffer any more,' Baldwin said with some sharpness. 'It is ourselves we must consider now.'

'I know. And yet the irony of it! To have striven so hard to protect him, from the death threats, from Crok, from Folville – from all the perils we saw – only to see him slaughtered like a pig by the mob. Where is the justice in that?'

'There is never justice in death – not when the law ceases to prevail,' Baldwin said. 'All you can do is try to bring the law back to the land. I hope we may succeed in that before it is too late.'

Late in the morning, a party of men appeared at the Tower's main gate, eyeing the place with ill-concealed greed. All knew that the crown jewels were stored here, deep within the Tower.

Baldwin and Simon went to hear the conversation.

'You are to come with the keys to the Tower, and you are to give them up to the commonality of the city. You must bring the king's son, John of Eltham, with you.'

All this was bawled from the far side of the moat, and it was the keeper of the Castle, John Weston, who agreed to the terms. He looked at the men in the courtyard behind him with a face that was pale and emotionless. Simon could see he believed he was marching to his death.

Still, his voice was calm enough. 'Any of you who think it'd be safer to be gone from here – leave now, and ride hard. There will be some in London who would seek to capture you and kill you. Don't let them. Ride fast, ride long, and may God give you a good conclusion. Fare well!'

Only half an hour later, Baldwin was at the gate again with his friend. 'Godspeed, Simon. I hope you are safe.'

'I hope I will be,' Simon said. The two clenched their hands together, both reluctant to be the first to let go the grip. 'Will you ride straight for home?'

'I will, but only to ensure that Jeanne is safe. Then I ride to the king.'

'You will be riding into danger, Baldwin,' Simon said. 'Why not remain at home?'

Baldwin looked away to the west. His sharp features were touched by a sadness bordering on despair that Simon had not seen for many years. 'Because I owe service to my king,' he said bitterly. 'Even though I detest the king's friends, who have brought him to this pass, still I owe him all the help I may give him.'

'I will not. I will ride home, and pray that I find the farm still whole, and that my daughter is safe. I hope for nothing more.'

'Well, when you go, ride fast, as Weston said. Do not delay, Simon. Ride like the wind!'

Simon watched his friend mount his horse with a strange feeling of desolation. Then he watched Baldwin waiting for Jack to mount his little pony, and then the two of them rode along the drawbridge, their horses' hoofs echoing. At the far barbican, where the new entrance took a dog-leg to the north, Baldwin paused and waved once, his teeth flashing in the sun, before diving under the outer gateway. Then he was gone.

'So that is that,' Margaret said.

Simon nodded. 'I think we should prepare too.'

'Hugh has almost everything ready. He and Rob are with the horses, I think.'

'Good,' Simon said.

Walking with her to the stables, he found himself reflecting on the last year. So much danger, the constant threat of invasion, and now all had come to pass. And Bishop Walter was dead – murdered here, in this cruel city. And for all Simon and the others' efforts, when it had counted, the bishop was not guarded with enough men. The notes and the leather purse had, in fact, succeeded. By distracting Simon from the real risk of the mob, they had helped kill the bishop, on the very day foretold.

'Wait one moment,' he said as they passed the Tower, and he walked into the bishop's rooms.

Little had changed. With Walle and John de Padington dead, no one had seen fit to enter and clear away his belongings.

It lay on the table. Simon went and took it up, pulling the drawstring loose and peering inside at the notes. The sight made a small shiver of revulsion run through him, and he tugged it shut again.

St Alban's

The tavern was one of the best in the town, Paul de Cockington had been told, and as soon as he entered, he could tell it was true.

He was exhausted. The sailing to Normandy and back had been terrifying, what with his fear of the water, and his more pronounced horror of blades. He had been convinced that he would be killed when they got to Rouen, and it was surely only the miracle of the murder of that man Pestel that had saved them all. Neither the duke nor Sir Baldwin wanted to be found near the corpse. A murder victim was always difficult to explain.

After they landed at last, it had been touch and go as to whether he would be snatched away by some eager knight who sought more men. It had taken a very swift visit to a barber to ensure that his hair was cropped into a tonsure again so that he might walk away, and he had taken flight as soon as he could.

There was still danger, of course. He might have been discovered by the queen's army. He had heard about that as soon as they landed. But once again, he had been fortunate. He had found a little abbey, and the abbot had been generous and kindly, and very hospitable. There, in the seclusion of the cloister, he had been sure of his safety, and for the first time since leaving Exeter, he felt truly at peace.

Still, yesterday he had decided he should try his luck again. He had his little chapel, after all, and it looked ever more appealing as the days passed. Never again would he put himself in such danger, he swore. No, he wouldn't look at a woman like that de Gydie again, gorgeous though she was, with her slim little hips and enormous . . . But no. From now on, he was a celibate.

In the tavern, he sat at a bench with some others, who looked at him with suspicion, but moved along to give him space. He would rest here today, he decided, and continue on his way tomorrow. With fortune, he would make it to Exeter in only a week or so.

The serving wench came and took his order, and he could not help but appraise her backside as she swayed with the athletic precision of a dancer between the benches and stools set all about. Dark hair, and that air of willingness that always took his fancy. Not that it would ever again, of course.

She was back soon with a large earthenware jug of wine. She passed him a cup, then bent to pour. And in that moment, Paul once again had a vision of heaven, as her tunic fell open and he could see the delicious breasts within.

He was gaping. As she stood upright again, he snapped his mouth shut and gave her a smile. She returned it – with a small wink, he thought, as though she was showing she knew what he had seen, and he was welcome to it . . .

Perhaps there was no need to hurry to Exeter, after all, he considered, watching her taut body as she walked away again.

Furnshill

Jeanne heard the hoofs and went to fetch her dagger. Edgar marched to the door, reporting, 'One rider – it's him again.'

She set the dagger back on its hook on the wall and wiped her hands on her apron. It was good that Peter had been coming here so often. There was a hope in her breast that he and Edith would be able to mend the fracture and live together again, although she was not sure that she herself would be willing to live with her own father-in-law, had he been so inconsiderate to her. Still, it was Edith's choice, not her own.

'Master Peter, you are most welcome,' she said, greeting him warmly.

'Lady Jeanne, I am very glad to be here,' he said, his eyes going to the room behind her. 'How is my wife?'

'She is well,' Jeanne said, and felt satisfaction that he had at least asked after Edith rather than his own son.

'I would like to speak with her, if I may.'

'I will fetch her,' Jeanne said. Edith was out in the little garden

Jeanne had created, and it took only a few moments to bring her back inside.

'Please, Lady Jeanne, don't go,' Peter said. 'You should hear this too, because you have been so kind to us all.'

'Very well.'

'Edith, I am here to ask you to have me back again,' Peter said. 'I know that the last months have been very difficult for you, and I promise I will do everything I can to make things easier in future. Will you have me again?'

Edith looked at Jeanne, but Jeanne could not interfere in the affairs of another married couple. This had to be Edith's own decision.

'Peter, I would like to live with you again, but I cannot give up my parents and their friends. Where would I be now, without the kindness and generosity of Lady Jeanne here?'

'I agree. And I will not force you to do that.'

'I will agree, then. But it is hard for me to live with your parents.'

'Then it is fortunate that I don't ask that!'

'You don't . . . ?'

'We shall return to our own house. I cannot live under my father's rules either, and need my own household. Will you return with me to the old house?'

'Very happily!' Edith said, and now she did run into his arms as Jeanne dabbed at her eyes and sniffed, and left them alone.

London

As they passed over the London Bridge, riding down into Surrey, Simon halted at the city drawbridge. He took out the purse and weighed it in his hand, and then hurled it as far as he could downstream, watching it as it bobbed on the water, and then disappeared out of sight.

It felt as though he had cast out a demon.

Author's Note

This has been a sad book to write. It's very difficult to lose characters of whom I have become fond, and Bishop Walter II of Exeter is certainly one of those.

I have used him extensively in my books from a very early stage, and feel as though I have grown to know him quite well over the years. He was a strange mix of the medieval educated man: intelligent, noted for his diligent efforts in the Treasury, determined to improve the quality of his preachers and priests, an enthusiastic supporter of education, proud guardian of the cathedral at Exeter who strove tirelessly to see the rebuilding works pushed on, and . . . sadly, also avaricious to an appalling degree, vindictive (see how he treated the queen), opportunistic – and violent, as he showed in the matter of the body of Sir Henry Ralegh (see Little & Easterling, *The Franciscans and Dominicans of Exeter*, 1927, pages 40–43).

Sir Henry died while at a confrater with the Dominicans in Exeter, and expressed a desire to be buried in their priory. Accordingly, the Dominicans arranged his burial in 1301, but this infringed on the monopoly on burials owned by the cathedral, so Stapledon and another canon, John de Uphaven (later to become sub-Dean of the cathedral), went to the friars to enforce their rights. Later the friars alleged that the canons had committed acts of violence while taking the body on its bier. 'He led a lawless rabble to attack the Dominican Convent . . . breaking into the cloister and church, wounding some of the brethren, and, after doing damage in the holy place, carried off goods to the value of £20' (*A History of the Diocese of Exeter* by Reverend RJE Boggis, Exeter, 1922).

Once the profits of the burial had been acquired by the

cathedral (burials involved gifts to the church and significant profits), the canons brought the body back. The friars refused to let it in, and the canons left Sir Henry's remains at their gate, 'whereof the said corps lay so longe unburyed that it stanke and the Canons dryven to bury the same yn St Peter's churche'.

But the bishop I will remember is the man who created the school at Ashburton and the college at Oxford (then known as Stapledon College, now called Exeter College), who was probably one of the most diligent bishops Devon and Cornwall have seen, who tramped all over the counties reviewing the quality of his priests, monitoring the canons and monks, noting with shock the disgraceful state of the nunneries in his lands, and doing all he might to improve them.

This book has been compiled with a view to exploring the appalling state of the realm at this time of huge national disturbance, and for that reason I have taken diabolical liberties with many men and women who lived in this period. However, the cases I have given against the bishop were all genuine – and Isabella Crok's life was as unfortunate as depicted, with two husbands dying and her son Roger being forced to flee.

The Rector of Teigh, Richard de Folville, is no invention. He was as disgraceful as I have indicated, being involved in several killings and many robberies. He and his brothers tended to kidnap and steal, often offering their victims the choice between handing over everything or fighting. They linked up with the Coterel family, another thieving band of nobles who, in their day, were notorious. Regularly outlawed, they kept winning pardons on the basis of helping the king in his wars with the Scots and Lancastrians.

Richard de Folville finally ended his criminal career in late 1340, or maybe early 1341, when he was bottled up in his church in Rutland, and after killing one pursuer and wounding several more, was dragged out and beheaded by Baldwin's equivalent, Sir Robert de Colville, Keeper of the King's Peace.

I have tried to get the history right in this story, because I think that invention is pointless when it comes to actual events which are as exciting as these. However, the record can be difficult.

Just as some books ago I discovered that no one seemed to know when the French King Charles IV actually married (and by that I don't mean there was confusion over the day or month, but over both – and the year as well), in the research for this novel I learned that although historians have traipsed all over this period, there is still dispute about the ships which King Edward II sent to Normandy, why he sent them, what happened when they returned – and so on.

The general facts are as I've portrayed them, with a small English fleet sailing to Normandy. I have speculated about a meeting with the Duke of Aquitaine, as proposed by Natalie Fryde in *The Tyranny and Fall of King Edward II 1321–1326* (Cambridge University Press, 1979; now available online), because it fits in with the history – but who knows? As Fryde says in her book, there was a specific pardon given to Sir John Felton 'for hostilely entering the land of Normandy and committing depredations and burnings when we were in those parts', which is intriguing, but I can find no other reference to it.

I have been accused by critics (I keep reminding myself of Sibelius's words: 'No statue has ever been put up to a critic') of using too much modern language, especially modern idiom in my books. Well, yes. I do. I use metaphors which are accurate for the period, I make sure I avoid words which are too twenty-first century, but I have no doubt the critic involved was anxious when she read of a 'posse' or of swearing involving comments about genitalia or offal – but these are all authentic.

It is a ridiculous argument to get into. If I were to be authentic to the language spoken in Exeter at the time, it would not even be pure Middle-English, which is hard enough to understand, but would also have a fair mix of Norman-French, Celtic, Saxon, plenty of Latin and a dollop of Arabic.

Then again, if I were to be ruthlessly authentic, I would also have to throw away my computer, and write the novels entirely by hand. Without a fountain pen. And then it would have to be reproduced by copyists, not printed by a publisher.

Somehow, I do not think that such activities would increase my sales.

And so, I will continue to use the correct terms and the correct language, and then modernise them – or, if you prefer, *translate* them – for a modern audience. Which is, after all, my job!

I have used many different books to make sense of this period. To all the authors and historians whose works I have vilely pillaged, I offer my grateful thanks. As usual, any errors are entirely mine.

Michael Jecks
North Dartmoor
April 2009

The King of Thieves

Michael Jecks

1325: Sir Baldwin de Furnshill and his friend Simon Puttock are in France guarding King Edward's son on his perilous journey to meet the French King, Charles IV.

But they are unaware that King Edward's wife Isabella has grown so disaffected that she has begun to plot her revenge. What at first appeared a simple diplomatic mission is in danger of becoming lethally dangerous. Meanwhile, two murders in Paris are causing alarm. Is there a connection between the killings and the shadowy 'King' of thieves?

Before long, Simon and Baldwin discover that the future of the English crown is at risk, but to protect it they will be putting their own lives in jeopardy.

In their most perilous mission yet, the pair's loyalty is tested to its limits as they encounter a deadly assassination plot that will alter the course of history . . .

Acclaim for Michael Jecks' mysteries:

'The most wickedly plotted medieval mystery novels' *The Times*

'Atmospheric and cleverly plotted' *Observer*

978 0 7553 4975 3

headline

The Prophecy of Death

Michael Jecks

1325: England is in turmoil. King Edward II is weak, his bloody reign staggering towards disaster. He has rejected his wife, Queen Isabella, and yet he still relies on her; she has been sent to France to negotiate peace with her brother, the French king, Charles IV.

King Edward knows his reign rests upon a knife edge, but his belief in the Prophecy of St Thomas's Holy Oil gives him hope; it is said that a king who is anointed with the oil will be a lion amongst men. He *must* have it.

Meanwhile, Sir Baldwin de Furnshill, Keeper of the King's Peace, and his friend, Bailiff Simon Puttock, return from France with an urgent message for King Edward. But the pair find themselves at the centre of a deadly court intrigue involving the most ruthless men in the country. In court politics, nothing is as it first appears . . .

Acclaim for Michael Jecks' mysteries:

'The most wickedly plotted medieval mystery novels' *The Times*

'Atmospheric and cleverly plotted' *Observer*

978 0 7553 4977 7

headline